"I CAN'T D[O]
HE SAID.

He leaned so close the frosty white of his breath met her face. "I can't stand one more minute of my life thinking that any day now some other man will scoop you up and have the life with you that I want. I want to wake up with you in the morning. I want to hand you your bathrobe when you get out of the shower. I want to find your favorite place to be kissed and I want to exploit it. Whether we sleep together or not, we can never go back to being just friends."

She wrapped her arms around herself as he came to stand in front of her once again. She wanted the same things he wanted. But desire wasn't the problem—they had enough of that. The problem was everything else between them that desire put at stake. "I'm asking you to forget this. I'm *begging* you. Don't do this right now."

"And I'm telling you I can't forget. I need to know what we are," he said, the words caught between clenched teeth.

"But why do we have to name it?"

"Because. I'm in love with you. I've always been in love with you. And I'm done living a lie."

Please turn this page for reviews for Lisa Dale . . .

MORE PRAISE FOR
SIMPLE WISHES

It Happened One Night

LISA DALE

FOREVER

NEW YORK   BOSTON

This book is a work of fiction. Names, characters, places, and incidents are the product of the author's imagination or are used fictitiously. Any resemblance to actual events, locales, or persons, living or dead, is coincidental.

Book design by Giorgetta Bell McRee
Cover design by Claire Brown

Forever
Hachette Book Group
237 Park Avenue
New York, NY 10017
Visit our website at www.HachetteBookGroup.com.

Forever is an imprint of Grand Central Publishing. The Forever name and logo is a trademark of Hachette Book Group, Inc.

Printed in the United States of America

First Printing: November 2009

10 9 8 7 6 5 4 3 2 1

ATTENTION CORPORATIONS AND ORGANIZATIONS:
Most HACHETTE BOOK GROUP books are available at quantity discounts with bulk purchase for educational, business, or sales promotional use. For information, please call or write:

Special Markets Department, Hachette Book Group
237 Park Avenue, New York, NY 10017
Telephone: 1-800-222-6747 Fax: 1-800-477-5925

For Pop and Gram, with love and thanks

It Happened One Night

Prologue

Lana Biel had always believed that the most significant experiences of life would most likely occur somewhere equally significant—like mountaintops, cathedrals, or under majestic skies. But instead, her whole future hung in the balance *here*—a place that until now had no significance whatsoever—the tiny cinderblock bathroom of the Wildflower Barn.

"Are you okay in there?" Eli asked through the door.

She stared with desperate focus at her Birkenstocks. She counted the number of forget-me-nots painted on the mirror's edge, and she thought of all the countless women who had done this before her. In ancient times, she'd learned, a woman who suspected she was pregnant would have urinated on fistfuls of barley or wheat, and then she would have watched to see if the seeds grew faster than normal. Lana had once found this idea to be beautiful—that pregnancy and plants could be so entwined. But it was hard to get in touch with her inner earth mother when *her* pregnancy test was a sterile plastic stick and directions ten pages long.

She leaned her forehead on the wall. "Has it been three minutes?"

"Four."

"I'm afraid to look."

"Either way," Eli said. "We'll get through it."

"I can't drag you into this," she said so softly she thought he wouldn't hear.

"I'm right here with you. I want to be. I wouldn't let you go through this alone."

She touched the center of the door; glad he was just on the other side. The test was little more than a formality at this point. And yet, she still clung to some small but entirely unfounded hope that the result would be negative. Her future hinged on nothing but the presence or absence of a pretty pink line. A big red STOP sign would have been more apt.

"Lana." She heard Eli's voice through the door. "Come on. It's time."

She sighed and wiggled her toes, stalling. She thought: *A million women have done this before—this worrying. A* trillion *women.* Some woman just like her was probably doing it right now. But did every woman feel like she was the first? And entirely alone?

Her friend Charlotte once told her that in the Middle Ages an anxious woman could learn if she was pregnant by paying a prophet to squint into a bowl of her pee. In the last century, a woman's doctor would inject a rabbit with her urine's hormones, then check the animal's ovaries for change. Today Lana had squatted over a small stick.

Why is it always about the pee? she thought.

Ages of nervous women alone in bathrooms, stalling the inevitable.

The moment had come; she raised her head and looked.

Two Months Earlier . . .

———— *May* ————

Dandelion: Taking its name from the French *dent de lion* (tooth of the lion), the dandelion is a survivor that can withstand even the worst treatment from fickle springtime weather. Folklore says that if a maiden attempted to blow the seeds off the dandelion, the number of seeds that remained foretold the number of children she would have.

May 9

Lana stood in the low field that sloped gently behind the Wildflower Barn, her face turned up toward the incredible, storm-mangled sky. There was work to be done in the barn—a new shipment of seeds to catalog, price, and display—but Lana couldn't bear the thought of staying cooped up inside. The first thunderstorm of the spring had swept across the outskirts of Burlington, and it left in its wake a sky that was wholly spectacular— thick purple clouds torn apart and edged in gold.

When she heard Karin's footsteps treading softly behind her, she smiled to herself, glad for her sister's company. "There might be a rainbow," she said, twirling the white head of a dandelion in her fingers.

"I hope you're not planning on blowing those seeds near my newly tilled field," Karin said.

Lana let her arm drop to her side. "Of course not." The flower slipped from her fingers to the ground.

"You left these in the stockroom." She handed Lana a thin stack of glossy colorful brochures. Lana recognized them—a tender white orchid, a misty cloud forest, a gauzy waterfall, and a smiling guide. Last week she'd been daydreaming over the photographs on a slow day at work, and she must have left them where Karin could see.

She should have been more careful.

For their entire lives, she and her sister had been a team. Despite their differences, hardship had forced them to move together like a single unit, soldiers who fought back-to-back. But when Lana was just a first-year student in college ten years ago, she'd realized that living in their mother's hometown near Burlington, Vermont, had been Karin's dream—not hers. Before Lana settled down for good, she wanted to travel. To have an adventure. Costa Rica had always held a mysterious allure.

The problem was, she loved her sister far too much to leave anytime soon. She and Karin were each other's only family. Karin was rooted in Vermont, her heels dug in. And so Lana had made a promise to herself: Once Karin had a family of her own, *then* she could see the world. In the meantime, brochures and library books had to suffice.

Lana opened a pamphlet; one page showed a white boat on open water, its sail translucent in the apricot sun. The opposite page offered the orange-pink burst of a blooming hibiscus, its long magenta stamen unfurled like an alien tongue. She closed it and sighed. "Don't look so worried, Kari. I'm not going anywhere just yet. I was only looking."

"I hope you're not sticking around because of me."

"Not at all," Lana said lightly. And she hoped Karin believed her. She stayed in Vermont out of love, and she had no interest in making her sister feel bad.

Overhead, the clouds were twisting and roiling in blue, violet, and gold. Lana was convinced there would be a rainbow—a good sign. *Come on*, she thought. *Come on.*

"When's Eli getting back?" Karin asked.

"His flight comes in tomorrow afternoon at 3:12. You know this is the longest we've gone without seeing each other in ten years?"

"I know," Karin said, as if holding back a laugh. "You've said."

"Oh, did I? Sorry." Lana tapped her fingers against the side of her leg, twitching with pent-up energy. For the last eight months, her best friend had been traveling to various conferences, conventions, and universities—though the bulk of his time had been spent in Australia, where he was working on a large field study. Sometimes they'd been able to talk, but often they'd been forced to go for weeks using e-mail alone.

"And look at you," Karin went on. "You're a mess. Where are the shoes we'd decided you'd wear to dinner?"

Lana looked down at her clunky brown sandals. "I like these better."

"But where are the heels?"

"On the floor in my closet. Where they belong."

Karin shook her head.

"What? My sandals are more comfortable," Lana said. There was no sense in going into the truth: She didn't like to get overly dressed up when she had a date. It made her feel uncomfortable, as if she were masquerading in some way when she put on heels and mascara. She knew she looked a little quirky and not entirely put-together, but she liked that about herself. She wanted to be seen for who she was—translucent blonde eyelashes and all.

Karin sighed loudly, gazing at the churning sky, and Lana waited for the inevitable nagging to start. *Why bother wearing such a pretty white sundress if you're going to ruin it with ugly shoes?* Or, *How is he supposed to take you seriously if you don't take yourself that way?* But apparently Karin had bigger things on her mind than fussing over Lana's love life. She grew quiet, withdrawing into herself.

Lana wished there was something she could do. Karin had been so unhappy for the last year. Everything that Karin wanted from life was the opposite of what Lana wanted. They were so different it was hard to believe they were from the same womb. Karin was short with their mother's Abenaki coloring—a red-brown tinge to her hair, a warm glow to her skin, a strength in her wide shoulders and limbs. But Lana had taken after their father's side of the family; she was tall and willowy—almost always the tallest woman in the room—with Nordic blond hair and the slightly prominent family nose. A person looking at a photograph of them together would be likely to identify them not as sisters, but strangers.

"Well, I have work to do. I'm going back in." Karin trudged up the wet hill toward the Barn, and Lana turned to watch her go.

Suddenly a glimmer of color caught Lana's eye, and there, high over the mountains, was a rainbow, the brightest Lana had ever seen. It rocketed skyward before arcing gently and falling back down toward the earth. *Heavens*, she thought. No wonder God was so often depicted in clouds. "Look! Karin! Look!"

Karin stopped, turned.

"See it? Over those trees? Over there?"

"Yeah. Sure. It's really great."

Lana stopped pointing. Eli had told her about rainbows once—that a trick of optics meant that technically no two people saw the same exact rainbow at the same time. Karin turned her back and started once again to walk away.

Sisters or strangers. She took a deep breath. Today was her twenty-ninth birthday. She had a date tonight. And Eli was coming home tomorrow. She felt so much *promise* in the moment, as if she were fast on the heels of a breathtaking future, that it blazed before her, distant but in plain sight.

She ran her fingers over the image of a white orchid in her hand, imagining the fleshy texture of a petal under her thumb. Then she glanced once more at the rainbow, its brilliance spreading and diluting like watercolors in a rainstorm, and she followed her sister back inside the Barn.

The woman smelled of tiger lilies, sweet but musky. He curled around her, pressed his face into the hollow of her shoulder. Sheets slid along sheets. Skin along skin. Her hair floated like moonlight through his fingers, and he kissed her: throat, sternum, navel, and down.

Of course Eli knew he was dreaming.

He was dozing lightly, awake enough to know he was asleep. This woman—he *knew* her. How many times had he dreamed of the turn of her wrist, the cinch of her waist, the sweet, hot secrets of her body? When he woke from her, he never sighed and stretched and told himself *God, what a great dream.* Instead, she'd always left him twisted up and sweating and a little disoriented, as if he'd gone to sleep on one side of the room but woke up on the other.

A faint click in the darkness pricked his consciousness.

He turned his face into the couch pillow, not ready to wake. The woman, she was making little sounds in the back of her throat, driving him mad.

The door opened and shut—*slammed*—and his eyes blinked open. Gray flickering light from the television pooled in the dark room. His body felt tight and gnarled. Where was he? *Oh, right.* Lana's living room. Her birthday. He was waiting for her to come home.

He could feel that his cheeks were crimson, that the hair at the nape of his neck was damp with sweat, and he hoped his overheated body would go back to normal by the time Lana got around to turning on the light. He took a deep breath, gathering his thoughts and strength.

Over the last eight months, he'd imagined a hundred different ways that he could tell her his life-changing news. Sometimes he would hold her hand and say, "I have something to tell you." Sometimes he would confront her, take her by the shoulders and say, "Enough is enough." Sometimes he would tell her without saying anything at all—just by reaching out to her with his gaze, by touching her face, by calling on the language that men and women had been using to say *I love you* since before civilization invented words.

But now, struck by how normal—how unromantic and entirely typical—it was for him to be dozing off on her couch, he felt suddenly nervous. In eight months away from her, the longing that he'd thought was merely homesickness had turned out to be nothing less astonishing than love—knotted up, terrifying, low-down, miraculous *love*.

And now the emotion choked him. He didn't want to complicate their friendship and he didn't want to risk being humiliated if she rejected him—again. But there was no choice. He loved her. He had to tell her. All of his hope for the future dangled from the fragile possibility that perhaps, deep down, she loved him too.

He took a deep breath, trying to shake the dream of her body from his waking mind. He waited for her to turn on the light. Which would happen any second now . . .

Any second . . .

He waited. But no light came.

Only breathing. Then more. The metallic thump of car keys hitting the floor. A dropped purse. A zipper. And that—Eli knew that sound too—a faint whimper, choked by a kiss.

He squeezed his eyes shut. Lana had come home. But not alone.

Not alone.

He heard a low chuckle, a man's. He dropped his head back down on the pillow, too stunned to think. The man gave a low carnal growl. And rage made Eli's head throb and spin, a wire pulling tighter and tighter between his temples.

At last, after they'd stayed in the living room so long that he worried they wouldn't leave, he heard Lana's bedroom door swing closed. The sound was a nail driven into his heart. He had a quick vision of himself kicking down the door and ordering the man to get out. But he had no interest in histrionics that might make him look like an ass. He was already enough of a fool—to regress into misplaced love.

Slowly, quietly, he got to his feet, groping in the semi-darkness for his jeans, sliding them over his hips and buttoning the fly, and then searching cautiously for his messenger bag. He didn't bother putting on his shoes; his feet would make less noise without them. His only saving grace was that no one would see him like this, sneaking out of his best friend's house. That was an embarrassment he could easily live without.

He was searching for the button on the remote that would turn off the television when he heard a door open and footsteps growing near.

"Lana," he said softly. Even before he could see her, he knew the sound of her bare feet in the hallway and the whisper of her fingertips as she dragged them along the wall.

She jumped when she saw him. In the flickering light from the television, he saw her spine go steel-straight, and he heard the sharp intake of her breath. "It's me," he said quickly, holding out his hands. "It's Eli."

She pressed her palm to her chest. "Eli! What are you doing here?"

"What am I . . . ?" He was taken aback by the need to

make an excuse to see her. "I got back to town early. I thought you'd be pleased."

"Of *course* I'm pleased. I'm thrilled! The timing's a little . . . uh . . ." Her voice trailed off. He could feel her looking at him. His heart was breaking, and he was glad she couldn't see him in the dark. "How was the trip?"

"Good," he said casually. "Yesterday I went to a kegger at the Museum of Natural History. Some undergrad showed Neil deGrasse Tyson her butt."

"And people say astrophysicists are stuffy," she said, laughing.

Warmth and gladness rushed over him. "It's good to see you," he said. He saw the moment she relaxed, the subtle loosening of her shoulders, her hand falling from its place over her heart. In the shadows the white of her sundress glowed luminescent against the light from the television. Her hair, shoulder-length and cut bluntly at the bottom, shone platinum like the moon.

"It's good to see you too." She glanced toward the flickering light from her old, boxy television. "I wondered how I could have left the TV on all night. Glad to know I'm not losing my mind."

"I fell asleep on the couch. I came to . . . to give you a present."

"What is it?" she whispered, her eyes glittery with delight. She looked like she might hug him. But of course she would not.

"Hold on." He went to his bag and rummaged around until he found her gift. It was a small box wrapped in recycled brown paper and tied with a polka-dot shoelace. Simple, earthy, and a little silly. Just like Lana.

His hand brushed hers as she took the box, a contact

so brief and slight it was barely contact at all, but she snatched her arm back as if she'd been burned. He acted like he didn't notice.

"Open it," Eli said.

She did. The shoelace wound around her index finger as she untied the bow, and the brown paper opened like a fortune cookie. A small purple box was inside, its hinges creaking as she lifted the lid and saw a large pendant hung from a black leather thong. It caught the bluish light of the television and gleamed.

"Oh, my . . . Is it . . . ?"

Eli took out the pendant and laid it on his palm. The gnarly black stone seemed liquid in the shadows, otherworldly and vaguely powerful. "It's from the Sikhote-Alin' Mountains. A fall in Russia, 1947. It reminded me of you."

"You got this on the trip when you stayed with those old KGB guys?"

"Yeah. The ones with the pet goat . . ."

She snatched the pendant back from him. She hung it around her neck and covered it with her hand. "I love it. It's perfect. Thank you."

For a moment Eli could only look into her eyes, rapt. She was beautiful, any man could see that. But it was more than beauty that held him so tightly he couldn't look away. It was *her*. Lana. The sheer rightness of standing here with her after so long. He wanted to draw her to him and hold her. To tell her how glad he was to see her again. How he'd spent the past three days in a kind of giddy haze because he knew he'd be home soon. How he'd realized something that made his heart want to leap and cower at the same time.

But there was no way to tell her. Not in words.

He knew he was staring. He saw her face change, tenderness slipping into a quiet disbelief, as if she'd heard what he was thinking and didn't know what to make of it. They were standing so close that he could smell her floral perfume, and beneath that, the scent of her warm skin. She ran her hands up the sides of her naked arms as if to fight a chill, and the soft brushing sound was amplified to excruciating loudness in his mind.

"Lana . . ." Eli could only stare, grappling with the urge to kiss her. He wanted his hands on her face, in her hair. He leaned toward her, a fraction of an inch. If they'd been standing across the room from each other, the exact same gesture would have meant nothing. But this close, where smell and sound were so heightened, his small, almost imperceptible movement caused shock to flash across her face, as if he'd told her he wanted to make love on the floor.

She laughed a little nervously, stepped back, and frowned.

"Lana?" A man's voice cut through the moment, breaking the connection between them, and Lana's gaze darted down the darkened hallway, panic showing on her face. Quickly, she reached out and flipped on the overhead light, blinding both of them. By the time Lana's date came into the room, Eli had grabbed his bag and was heading toward the door.

"What's going on?" the man said.

Eli paused, caught. Anger and humiliation gripped his gut.

Lana cleared her throat. "Ron, this is Eli. Eli, Ron. Eli just stopped by to give me my birthday present."

"Right, I've heard a lot about you," Ron said, smiling. His white dress shirt hung open like the flaps of a tent, and his hair fell to his shoulders in dusty brown corkscrews. He was tall and thick, and he had a strong nose with a bump at the bridge. On the surface his smile appeared genuine. But Eli could see what Lana could not—the subtle, private menace that passed between men in moments like this, when a beautiful woman stood exactly between them. "You're the meteor hunter. Crazy hobby you've got."

"Actually, it's *meteorites*. And it's a job, not a hobby."

"But I thought you were a teacher," Ron said.

"That too." Eli adjusted the weight of the bag on his shoulder. "And what do you do?"

"Mountain biker. Professional."

"Ah," Eli said. "I should probably go."

Lana crossed the room to stand before him. Her eyes were clear blue—almost aqua—and he didn't miss the message within them, meant only for him: *I'm sorry.*

He blew her off. The last thing he needed was her pity. From the look on her face, she hadn't felt that spark, that buzzing of attraction that was more than simple lust. What an idiot he was. "All right. Well, I'm outta here," he said cheerfully, pulling at the door handle. "You two kids behave yourselves."

"Won't do anything you wouldn't do," Ron said.

Eli didn't smile. *Poor guy*, he thought to himself. *Poor, stupid guy.* He gave it two months—three tops—before Lana got bored.

"Happy birthday, Lana."

She glanced down, suddenly shy. Then he closed the door, closed them in and away, and looked up at the stars, which were the same stars they'd always been, the same stars he'd been studying for his entire adult life. Only tonight they seemed much, much farther away.

Twenty minutes after she'd closed up the Barn for the night, Karin Palson reached her house in the quiet outer suburbs of Burlington. She opened the front door of her split-level and walked up the carpeted stairs to the living room. The small television was dark on its stand and the lampshades were filled with shadows. Apparently her husband was working late at the insurance office again. The plastic shopping bag in her hand, containing just one small book, felt heavy enough to pull her arm from its socket.

She sat down on the couch, not taking off her denim jacket, not removing her purse from her shoulder, not turning on a light. She dropped the bag beside her. The house was as empty and dark as her heart.

Karin had never been the type to put any stock in folk-lore. The idea that her menstrual cycles followed the pattern of the moon was a lovely idea, but as far as she could tell, it was bunk. When a woman from her book club said she'd conceived a son by having her husband wear socks while they did it doggie-style, Karin just laughed. And when Lana proclaimed that the reason Karin couldn't get pregnant was because she "wanted it too badly," she thought her sister was well-intentioned, but utterly wrong.

And yet for all her distrust of old wives' tales and rumors, she kept listening. She listened to her doctors, other women, books, and the Internet. She was familiar with every technique and method of family planning:

the calendar-rhythm method, the standard days method, the sympto-thermal method, the Billings ovulation method. So many methodical methods. Enough to drive a woman insane. She hoped that if she just kept listening, listening hard to everything, not missing a single bit of information, then she would find the answer she was looking for.

Unfortunately, while she was lying under the furious white lights in the exam room and trying not to shiver, her doctor told her the bad news. She wasn't necessarily infertile, but she wasn't necessarily fertile either.

In other words, he had no idea what was wrong. Technically everything checked out fine. From the way he'd stuttered and frowned, Karin could tell he'd felt pressured to come up with a pinpoint diagnosis, a reason for their broken hearts. There was a chance, he'd explained, that Karin and her husband were two perfectly healthy and fertile people, as unique individuals. But together their bodies might not be a compatible match.

This was the answer Karin had been dreading. Science had put a man on the moon, had developed "food" that had no calories, and had discovered a vaccine for cervical cancer. But in the most primal and important process of human life, they just didn't know enough to tell her what exactly was wrong or how to fix it.

So other than God—who was keeping mum on the subject—who could help?

She took the book out of the shopping bag and held it in two hands. Though she could barely see the cover in the darkness, it had been burned onto her retinas: It showed a woman meditating, surrounded by floating orbs of blue-green light. It was little more than a glorified pamphlet, and in her misery and desperation, she'd read much of it by the light of a streetlamp in the bookstore parking lot. The author believed that if a couple was having trouble conceiving, it was possible to talk to the spirit of an unborn child—to reason with it and coax it into life.

The book also said that some babies wouldn't come into a home that wasn't in harmony. Karin had banged her fist on the dashboard so hard that she'd almost made a dent. Wasn't her house in harmony? How could she and Gene be more in harmony than they already were? Hadn't they shown that they were ready?

Now, sitting alone in the living room with the book, she wished she hadn't bought it. She and her husband tried hard to be good Christians. They weren't perfect, but they went to church every Sunday, said grace before meals, and prayed at night. They'd managed to abstain from sex until two months before their wedding (the priest had chuckled when Karin confessed). And they'd never used condoms or birth control, only fertility awareness, which had been taught to them by a nun who called Gene's sperm "the swim team."

She and Gene both believed that if God wanted them to have a baby, they would have one the natural way. No hormones, no injections, no sperm banks, no surgeries, no adoption agencies. And *no* talking to spirit babies. She'd probably have to confess that too.

She heard the front door open. Quickly she bent and slipped both the book and the bag under the cushions of the sofa. At first Gene didn't see her. But she saw him, silhouetted in the light from the porch as he climbed the short flight of stairs to the living room. Though he was ten years older than her at forty-three, he still had a very strong look about him. She loved his thinning red-blond hair, his big shoulders and hefty build that she'd always believed were vestiges of Highland kings.

He saw her when he reached the top of the stairs. "The lights were all off. I was worried."

"I just got in."

He moved toward her through the shadows and sat beside her. He didn't turn on the light. "How did it go at the doctor's?"

"Not bad," she said.

"What was the verdict?"

"It's a hung jury. We need a retrial."

She heard Gene's sigh, saw his back—normally so straight and strong—slump into the slightest crescent.

"In some states, infertility is grounds for divorce," she said.

"That's not true. We'll go to another doctor. Get another opinion."

Karin tried to laugh, but it came out closer to a sob. "I'm tired of being poked and prodded and talked about as if my body were somehow *different* than me."

"I know," Gene said. He reached over to rub her back.

She leaned against him, put her head on his shoulder. Outside, even under the cover of darkness, the Vermont countryside was glorying in its own fertility: hepatica, bloodroot, trillium, columbine, and dandelions bloomed profusely, the mountains letting loose in emerald, olive, and mint. And here was Karin. Fertile as a lump of coal.

Still, she couldn't let this rule their lives. She hugged

Gene tight, breathing in the spicy smell of his deodorant. "Let's go out. Let's get burgers, go to a movie, and make out in the last row."

"Yeah?"

"Yes. Let's go on a date. Like two teenagers out on the town."

"Do I have to have you home by ten?" he asked.

"Only if you promise to keep me awake 'til eleven."

Gene laughed and helped her to her feet.

May 10

The next morning Lana stood in the Wildflower Barn and chatted with Mrs. Montaigne, one of the many regulars who made a point of stopping by during Lana's shift. The sun slanted hard and bright into the yellow room that had been built to house their shop. Other parts of the Barn were utilitarian and somber, used for storage and mixing seeds. But this room was Lana's favorite. She'd hung wind chimes and stained glass in the small, high windows to catch the light. Her coffee cup steamed on the counter in the cool air. And though she'd awoken this morning to find her bed empty, she refused to let Ron's lack of bedside manners ruin an otherwise good day.

"I just don't know," Mrs. Montaigne said, her Quebecois accent peeking through. "I've never liked these glaring colors. Orange, red, yellow . . . Do you have something less bright?"

"Of course," Lana said. "Follow me."

She led the way to their newest display of seeds and picked up a packet of their cool-tones mix. Mrs. Montaigne took it, her eyes brightening as she showed the packet to her granddaughter. "*Oui*. This is exactly what we came for. Isn't it, *ma fille*?"

Jackie peered shyly from behind her grandmother's floral skirt. She rarely talked, but Lana could see that she was always deeply interested, listening, trying to figure things out. Lana had always liked talking to children. Watching them puzzle through everyday life made her see the world a little differently, as if rediscovering it through their eyes. She looked forward to the day she could rediscover it through her own as well.

Mrs. Montaigne handed the packet to Jackie for a closer look, and Lana couldn't help but launch into detail about how optimum mixes balanced beauty with durability and diversity. But Karin had cautioned her not to give away too many secrets. They guarded their percentage allocations much like the makers of Pepsi and Coke guarded their recipes.

"Okay, okay, you've convinced me!" Mrs. Montaigne exclaimed, laughing. "To listen to you talk about flowers is like listening to this little one talk about cartoons. There's just no end!"

Jackie blushed shyly and Lana thought it would be fun to hear the little girl chatter for a while. But she remained silent as they walked to the counter to check out.

"I saw your boyfriend last night," Mrs. Montaigne said, giving a conspiratorial wink.

"Oh, did you? He took me out for my birthday. Did you know I turned twenty-nine? It was fantastic. Roses, candlelight, and he even sang me a song in the middle of the restaurant. Everyone was looking. It was the funniest thing."

"No, I don't think so." She frowned, lines etched deeply around her mouth. "I saw him in front of the college. He had a suitcase. Like he was coming back from a trip."

Lana laughed. "Oh, you mean *Eli*. He's not my boyfriend."

"Well, why ever not?"

Lana laughed again and couldn't help but wonder if Mrs. Montaigne had set her up. The question had been posed to her a hundred times—a thousand it seemed. And yet she'd never been able to articulate an answer that could make people understand. "Eli and I are just friends."

"But I see you flirting with him all the time."

"Laughing with him. I'm laughing. There's a difference."

"But I see the way he looks at you. You cannot tell me that isn't love."

"It is love. It's platonic love."

"If you say so, dear."

To change the subject, Lana bent down to talk to Jackie, asking what her doll's name was and if she wanted to pick a flower to take home. She loved talking to people—about flowers, about the store, about the Burlington area, about whatever was going on in her customers' lives. But Eli was off-limits—a pleasure so private she didn't like to share.

"Say good-bye to Miss Lana, Jackie," Mrs. Montaigne said, after she'd paid for her purchase.

Jackie took her fist out of her mouth and gave Lana a limp-fingered wave. Lana bent down to her level and smiled. "You know what I think? I think you've got a hug for me today, don't you, sweetheart?"

The girl grinned, instantly delighted—as if she'd been waiting for permission to throw her arms around Lana's neck. Then Lana straightened her knees, said good-bye to Mrs. Montaigne, and leaned on the counter, hard. She glanced at the clock, wondering what she and Eli would do tonight—if they would eat dinner at their favorite hole-in-the-wall Mexican place, if they would walk out by the lake.

At one point after he'd left last night, the meteorite necklace had become the only thing she was wearing on her body. Ron had gripped it in tight fingers and pulled just enough to make her worry it would snap.

"Is he a lover?" he'd demanded. "Was he ever?"

Lana had told the truth. Then she took the necklace off and tried to put her best friend out of her mind. Unfortunately, knowing that Eli was nearby but not being able to see him had made her distracted and anxious at entirely the wrong time. He was on her mind a lot these days, so much it was almost bothersome. The solution was simple: She just needed to see him. That was all.

She counted down the hours until her shift's end, floating moment to moment. And the second the store was closed, she dialed Eli's cell phone, eager to hear his voice. She worried her new necklace between two fingers until he finally picked up.

"What are you doing right now?" she asked. He was unusually quiet.

"Why?"

Why? Eli didn't ask *why*. A pang of worry made her grip the phone hard. "I just wanted to know if you felt like doing something with me."

"Oh." Again, another long, terrible pause. "I'm sorry. I can't."

"No?"

"I have plans."

She answered as quickly as she could, desperate to hide her disappointment. "Okay. No big deal. I'll catch up with you some other time."

When she put down the phone, her heart was beating frantically as if squeezed into too tight a space. She'd planned her whole week around Eli's homecoming. She even would have cut short her date last night had she known he was arriving early. She'd expected Eli would have done the same if their roles were reversed. But now she worried that something had changed, that maybe their friendship had weakened somehow in the months he'd been away.

She put on her jacket, picked up her purse, and told herself to cheer up. She was being ridiculous, completely overreacting. She would see Eli sooner or later. And when she did, they would pick up where they had left off. Things would return to normal. She just had to give it time.

June

Lady's slipper: This wild orchid requires unusual help to reproduce. The soil must be pH-perfect and must contain a unique microfungus that dissolves the seedlings' hard outer cells. It can take up to four years for a lady's slipper to fully recover from producing a single flower.

June 5

Someone in the science museum had turned the air conditioner to cryogenic. Eli was comfortable in his khakis and navy polo shirt, but his date, Kelly, had wrapped her little pink sweater so tight across her chest it stretched like shrink-wrap, and she was furiously rubbing her upper arms to stay warm. In every sense she had overdressed by being underdressed; her knees were exposed by her short black skirt, her small toes peeked out of high strappy heels, and her walnut-colored hair was twirled up in some kind of knot that exposed the goose bumps on her neck. Obviously she'd dressed for a different kind of date than a science museum—a date that didn't include roomfuls of children with light-up sneakers and jelly-smeared grins. But when Eli had picked her up and told her what he'd planned, she said she'd be happy to go. Now it was clear she'd said it just to be nice.

He tried to make the most of the afternoon by telling her interesting facts about the universe. The professor in him hoped to spark her interest.

"And this," he said, standing beside a colorful picture on the wall, "is an image from the Hubble. It's called the Keyhole Nebula." He looked at her, watching for her reaction as she looked at the swirls of red, blue, and green. Her face remained dull, as if she were a student sitting in an Intro to Astronomy class. He tried to connect with her another way. "What do you see?"

She frowned.

He tried again. "What does it look like to you?"

"It looks like . . ." She leaned closer, squinting. "Like a nebula."

He laughed. He and Lana had played this game a hundred times, like kids picking shapes out of clouds. But he and Lana weren't entirely *normal*, and so he gave Kelly a break. "Well, somebody saw this." He ran his finger over the image. "God's birdie."

"Why do they call it that?"

"Because it's a cloud shaped like God's middle finger."

"If you say so," she said.

Eli rubbed nervously at the back of his neck. Picking up women had always been easy enough. He had a good face—not rugged, but friendly, handsome, with a high forehead and a good solid jaw. The day after Lana's birthday—the most horrible night he'd had in years—he'd successfully scored Kelly's number at a downtown bar. But three dates later, the usual problems had begun.

For him, being romantic required too much showmanship—grandiose gestures, overwrought love poetry, power ballads, and heavy cologne. He preferred the "just be yourself" technique. But that was probably why he was single—and on the wrong side of Lana's "let's just be friends."

Kelly had wandered a few feet away from him, standing so that a six-foot-wide picture of Mars dwarfed her from head to toe. He caught up with her silently. She was rubbing her near-naked legs together, a pathetic attempt to keep warm.

He sighed. "Look. Do you want to get out of here?"

"Yes," she said. "I'd like that a lot."

Later, after a big steak dinner, they were standing at the back door of her apartment, far away from the stylish brick buildings of downtown. He could hear someone's television blasting commercials from a nearby living room, but otherwise the street was quiet and dark.

"I had a nice time," Kelly said.

The last two times they'd stood in this doorway, Eli had kissed her—not quite real kisses, but more of a courteous brushing of lips. Now the moment had come for him to either kiss her for real or put an end to it all.

He stalled. "I'm sorry about the museum."

"Don't be," she said. "I want to do things you enjoy."

Oh, man. She was going to invite him upstairs. Any second now. He cleared his throat, a little nervous. He'd been out of practice with women for a long time. But that was exactly why he was doing this, he reminded himself. Why he was dating. He couldn't expect it to feel perfectly comfortable right off the bat.

Kelly smiled, her lips shiny and parted, waiting for him.

Don't think of her, he warned himself. *Don't.*

For a long time, he'd believed the best way to have a relationship with Lana was as her friend. She'd rejected the idea that they could be more, and gradually he'd come to agree. Friendship meant he could hold on to everything he loved most about Lana, but he could shirk the responsibilities and commitments of being a lover. For a long time, he was happy that way.

At least, he thought he was.

There had been no single moment that made him realize he loved her. Wanted her. Over the years he'd told himself that occasional "blips" of attraction to her didn't mean he was *actually* attracted to her: Those moments were merely the natural and meaningless biological result of a man having a woman for a close friend. But over the last eight months, what had started as a whisper had become a four-part orchestra playing at full blast in his mind. And now he was here, on Kelly's front stoop, trying to get that terrible music to stop.

He looked down into Kelly's face. And he kissed her. Not gently. He put his hands in her hair and tipped her head to the side and did what he had to until Lana faded into the background of his mind. When he pulled away, Kelly had whole galaxies swirling in her eyes.

"Nobody's ever kissed me like that."

He said nothing.

"Do you want to come inside?"

"You want me to?"

"I want you to," she said.

He didn't mean to hesitate. But she saw.

"I'm not angling for something serious, if that's what you're thinking," she said, a smile on her lips. "No strings. Just . . . fun."

He stood still.

She unzipped his jacket an inch. "Well?"

So he didn't have to answer, he kissed her again. He wrapped his arms around her waist. He dragged her up close to him and felt her large, soft breasts pillowing low on his chest. Finally his body responded. Like he'd hoped it would.

She drew away. "Can I take that as a *yes*?"

He'd pulled off her cardigan before the door slammed shut behind them.

June 13

"Oh my gosh. You're *pregnant*, aren't you?" Karin asked.

It was evening, and she stood at the stove in Lana's house, stirring a simple soup of vegetarian broth and orzo that she hoped Lana could keep down. Lana lived near the south end of Burlington, where she rented a small Cape Cod–style house with white siding and navy trim. Everything about the house was small—the rooms, the windows, the yard, and the amount of furniture. But it was perfect for Lana since she didn't want a family of her own.

When Lana didn't answer, Karin turned around. Her sister was sitting with the flat of her cheek squished hard against the wooden tabletop. Her skin was ashen and dull. "Well?"

"I *don't* think I'm pregnant." She sighed.

"Are you sure?" Karin asked. She'd been teasing before. But the question that had been a joke just moments ago suddenly took on more serious possibilities. "You use condoms or something, right?"

"Why are we even talking about this?" Lana asked, lifting her head. "Yes, we used a condom. But even if we didn't, I got my period on . . . the day the mulch came. That was, like, three weeks ago or something."

Karin snickered. "You mean you got it *after* your visit with Ron."

"I just have some kind of stomach thing," she said, and she put her head back down. "Plus I didn't sleep that great."

Karin nodded. She didn't really think her sister was pregnant. The odds were far against it. No one knew that better than Karin. Under good conditions a couple had only a 25 percent chance of a successful pregnancy, give or take. Add in real-life factors like stress and timing, and the odds plummeted from there.

She stirred the soup one last time, then opened the old wooden cabinet where Lana kept the bowls. She supposed she was a little preoccupied with pregnancy these days. She and Gene had had sex twice in the last forty-eight hours. She would have slept with him tonight as well, but he'd left on business. Her house—so gloomy and quiet—was unbearable without him.

She ladled the soup out of the pot; the broth was so weak she could see the daisies painted on the bottom of the bowl. She crossed the little kitchen and set the bowl on the table with a *clunk*.

"I can't eat," Lana said.

"Try."

"Okay, *Mom*."

They shared a smile. Karin made herself a bowl of soup and sat down. "So tell me. Why aren't you sleeping?"

"I got a letter. Yesterday."

Karin cringed at the sound of her sister's voice. Lana stood, walked to her junk drawer, then dropped a yellowed and beat-up greeting card on the table when she sat. The front showed a picture of a watercolor lily; the background was striated purple and orange smears. Karin opened the cover.

Dear Lana. Happy Birthday. From Cal.

Karin frowned. With one finger, she slid the card as far away from her as the table edge allowed. *Calvert.* She and Lana hadn't seen their father since Lana had graduated from high school. As soon as she could manage, Karin had packed up with her baby sister and returned to their home state of Vermont—away from their father's Wisconsin boardinghouse. From that day to this, Karin had never looked back. And she'd assumed Calvert hadn't either. Until now.

"He's a little late," Karin said.

Lana shrugged—a gesture Karin was intimately familiar with, Lana's left shoulder always rising a touch higher than the right. "He must have forgotten the real date."

"Wouldn't surprise me," Karin said.

Lana shrugged again.

Karin searched her brain for an explanation, for the reason that Calvert would suddenly want to get in touch with them after so many years. "Maybe he's dying."

"You think?"

"If he was, would it matter?"

"I don't know. I guess not," Lana said.

Karin tapped a fingernail against the table. "It could just be that he wants money."

"Or maybe he was thinking of us."

"After he ruined our lives?"

Lana shook her head. "He didn't *ruin* our lives."

"He killed Mom!"

"Not really."

"Son of a— *Lana*! How can you defend him?" Karin said, and only after the words had flown from her mouth did she realize that she'd stood up, was looming over her wan-faced sister, and was talking a few decibels too high.

Long ago she used to have a temper. *Anger issues*, her high school teachers had said. Moving away from Calvert had helped her get her fury under control—that and an excellent therapist. Years had passed since she'd had the kind of flare-up that threatened to get the best of her now. She walked to the window, taking long, deep breaths. "Sorry. I'm sorry about that."

"It's okay. But I *wasn't* defending him," Lana said.

Karin nodded, but she wasn't so sure. While Karin had a tendency to fly off the handle, Lana bottled things up inside. In middle school she'd once been brutally bullied by a handful of mean girls. They sneered at her second-hand clothes, "accidentally" spilled milk on her in the cafeteria, aimed for her during dodgeball, and more than once made her leave class in tears.

After the girls finally moved on to torment someone else, Lana maintained that the girls were actually good,

kind human beings deep down. Some people thought
Lana said those kinds of things because she was angelic.
But Karin knew better. Kindness was Lana's way of re-
arranging reality so it became more bearable. It was always sunny in Lana-land.

Karin crossed the room, plucked the card from the
table, and threw it in the garbage can.

"You should have recycled," Lana said.

Karin ignored her. "Listen. I don't want you to get
upset about this. If for some reason we hear from him
again, I'll take care of it. For now let's just focus on getting some food in you, okay?"

Lana frowned into her bowl while Karin sat back
down. "It's not that."

"What's wrong?"

Lana stirred her soup but didn't eat or speak. She'd
always been reluctant about opening up to Karin. Karin
suspected the root of her silence went back to their childhood, when Karin was more like a mother than a sister in
Calvert's house. They'd hadn't quite figured out how to
find equal footing yet. But that didn't stop Karin from
trying.

"Is it Ron? Did you meet someone else?"

She shook her head.

"Did he?"

Again Lana shook her head.

"Then what's wrong?"

"I think I need to go lie down," Lana said.

Karin's heart sank. She didn't want to go home. Her
dark living room, the upstairs bedrooms that were meant
for children but instead stood full of storage bins and
unused exercise equipment—she couldn't bear it.

"Fine." She pushed out her chair and stood.

"Karin, wait. That's not what I mean. You don't have to leave."

"Look. I get it. It's fine."

"Just . . . please. Calm down for a second. If you want to hang out here, that's okay. I'm just really tired. I've never felt so tired. I should probably sleep."

Karin took a deep breath and counted to ten. She was angry. And as usual, Lana was the closest target in sight. She hadn't meant to be so curt. When she spoke, her voice was back under control. "It's okay. I'll go. I mean, you *should* sleep."

"I don't mind if you hang out."

"It's okay."

"Well. Thank you for making dinner."

"Don't thank me. Just finish it."

"I will."

"And if you start to feel feverish, give me a call."

"Okay. But I'm sure I'm fine."

Karin picked up her purse from the counter and looked around. There was nothing more to do. "Good night," she said. Then she grabbed her jacket, went outside to her minivan, and drove out of the city, heading as slowly as she could toward home.

Later, Lana woke from a nightmare for the second night in a row. She was lost in a fun house, crooked windows, slanty floors, and doors everywhere. So many doors. People rushed around her—men coming and going, their pupils dilated, their smiles as wide and floppy as clowns' mouths. When she woke she was sweating and afraid and smothered by her bedroom walls. She had to get out.

In her favorite pajamas—boxers and an old T-shirt of Eli's worn to near translucence—she padded barefoot downstairs, opened the screen door, and sat on the warm concrete of the front stoop. She dropped her house phone beside her. The neighbors' windows were dark. Cars were lined up front to back all along the curbs. The air smelled like asphalt and earth.

She ran her fingers through her hair and covered her face with her hands. It had been years since the dream had come back to her, so many years that she'd thought whatever cells in her brain had once stored the information must have died off and taken the memories with them. But that wasn't the case.

Unlike Karin—who could remember every detail of their years with Calvert—Lana remembered things in stops and starts. She suspected the fragments were better left scattered to the four corners than brought together. The pieces, she could handle. The whole, she could not.

She fingered a bit of chicory growing up around the front walk; its stalk was tough and strong, its short-lived petals cool against her skin. She tried to focus on the positive. She supposed if there was one thing to thank her father for, it was her love of flowers.

Calvert had made money by opening up his creaky old Victorian to cash-only boarders, mostly men. Lana never knew who would be standing behind the door of any given room. The house seemed to breathe transients: truckers, construction workers, addicts, recovering addicts, and the endless parade of girlfriends—women who smoked, drank, and swore with the same ribald fervor as the men. Calvert had made it clear from the get-go that his daughters weren't to ask too many questions. They were to lie low, to leave him and his tenants alone.

He'd never given them anything beautiful or indulgent, never owned anything that was brand-new. But once she'd seen him pause at the edge of the yard in front of a bright orange bush to pick a flower. And when he'd passed her where she sat on the front step, he'd dropped the flower beside her and said, "Here."

It wasn't poetry. But how Lana's heart leaped to see the jewelweed in her palm, its petals folded like the most complicated and elegant origami. And what breathlessness, to discover that the spatterings of purple at the edge of the lawn were actually the most heartbreakingly delicate heal-all, each pinprick of a flower like a universe of its own.

And now even as an adult who lived every day among flowers, she still felt humbled to think that a wildflower could coax the most iridescent purples or fierce magentas from the most inhospitable soils. She wanted her own life to be like that, to grow something worthy from hardship and strife.

Somewhere a mockingbird was singing in the darkness. The phone dangled heavy in her hand. She stood and sank her bare toes into the damp grass of the lawn, and above, the sky was peppered with stars.

Calling Eli was practically instinctive. He calmed her. He made things right. She put the phone to her ear and listened to the static breath between rings.

Ever since he'd returned from his trip, things had been different between them, so different that she worried she'd done something wrong. Instead of spending his every waking minute with her when he returned, she was lucky if she saw him a couple of times a week. And when she did see him, she was nervous around him, her whole body on edge.

When at last his voice came over the line she knew he'd been sleeping.

"I woke you," she said. "I'm sorry."

"Is everything okay?"

"I just haven't talked to you in a couple days. I wanted to say hi."

"Hold on."

Lana waited. There was some shuffling, the sound of Eli muttering to himself. She guessed he was fumbling for his glasses. Maybe he'd fallen asleep leaning over his books or watching a documentary. She could picture him, the way he looked when he woke up, his adorable grogginess, his rich brown hair spiked on one side, flat on the other. He had the most charming freckle just under the lower lid of his left eye, which he rubbed when he was tired.

At last he came back on the line. "So what's going on?"

"What's going on with you?"

His voice was low and raspy with sleep. "I dreamed that I was giving a lecture about the constellations, except I'd forgotten their names."

"Stargazing even in your dreams."

"Always." He paused. She felt the luxurious comfort of silence between them, thick as the hiss of static over the phone. "You can't sleep?"

"I went to bed too early."

"A nightmare?"

"No."

"Is it . . . did something happen with Ron?"

Lana took a deep breath of the cool, crisp air and lifted her face to the sky. "Nothing out of the ordinary."

Eli was quiet for a long, long time. She spun slowly in place in the cold grass, and the sky pivoted in a circle, twirling on the point of a single star.

When he spoke again his words were flat. "Are you in love with him?"

She thought about the question, but not for long. Passion was like a flower that bloomed for one night a year—exquisite, poignant, and tragically brief. She gave herself completely to passion when she was lucky enough to find it. But she didn't delude herself into thinking it would last. Not like her mother had. Only a week after meeting Lana's father, Ellen had been so head over heels in love that she'd had a shepherd's staff tattooed on her shoulder blade—as if she was endlessly sure that the name Calvert not only meant "shepherd," but meant it specifically in relation to *her*.

How wrong she'd been.

"No," she said. "I don't love him." She wasn't sure, but she thought she sensed relief on the other end of the phone. "Does that surprise you?"

"No. But I won't say I'm not glad."

Lana stopped spinning, trying not to read too much into his words. The last thing she needed was to invent subtext where there was none. This was Eli she was talking to. What-you-see-is-what-you-get Eli. What she loved about his friendship was that it was predictable—even routine. She always knew where she stood with him.

She heard a noise in the background on his end of the phone.

"Just a minute," he said.

But he wasn't talking to her.

Suddenly Lana realized: Eli wasn't alone. He was with a woman. He was sleeping with her. A knot of irrational fear gripped her stomach. She couldn't have predicted *this*. Things had moved along more quickly than she would have thought, much more quickly than with any of the others. What if this time, he'd found the One? And Lana couldn't even remember her name.

"Sorry about that," he said, talking to her once again.

"I should let you go," she said. She wanted him to contradict her, but he did not.

All at once, she was tired. Tired down to her bones. She could sleep right here, standing on her feet in the front yard, the sound of Eli's voice weaving and looping through her consciousness like ribbons drawn through water.

Kelly. The woman's name was Kelly.

"Good night," she said, and she hung up the phone. She carried it upstairs, put it on her nightstand, and willed herself to find safer, gentler dreams.

June 20

Eli put his heel against the edge of the shovel and leaned to puncture the hard-packed dirt. The Kansas sky was a brilliant blue and the temperature of the afternoon had cooperated with him, mild and fair. He could see for miles. In the distance to the south, the Wintermutes' little white farmhouse sat motionless as a ship on the ocean's horizon. He remembered an article he'd read once, about the efforts of some colleagues to determine if Kansas was actually flatter than a pancake. Even without the financing, Eli could have reached the same conclusion: Yes, it certainly was.

He wiped the sweat from his forehead with the back of his canvas glove and kept digging. A few minutes ago his wheeled metal detector—Excalibur—had given a loud, aggravated whine. Whatever was down there, it was solid.

This was Eli's favorite part. The anticipation. The hope.

He'd thought, ages ago, that he'd wanted to be a scientist. He'd pictured himself looking distinguished in a long white coat and carrying a clipboard. Unfortunately when he was done with his very expensive geology degree, he realized that he just didn't have the heart to work in a lab. And so he decided to teach. And when the grant money was good, he headed for the fields to hunt for buried treasure. After his first big find, he was hooked.

He leaned on the handle of the shovel, tired. The fields were quiet as an afternoon nap. In the distance, a hawk spiraled slowly against the empty sky.

Lana would love this, he thought. One of these days he hoped she would be able to leave the Barn long enough to go on an expedition with him. After all, she'd been there for that moment in his life when he'd decided to study the skies.

In their first year of college, they used to sneak out of their dorms in the middle of the night. Lana hadn't been very good at sleeping—she still wasn't—and so from time to time, they fled their stuffy, cellblock-style dorm rooms to walk the dark low-lying golf courses just beyond the athletic fields.

They were both such nerds—just slightly outside what was considered normal. Eli had been fifteen pounds underweight, worn his hair so his bangs flopped over one eye, and had terrible allergies that made his nose constantly run. Lana, on the other hand, had been beautiful in broomstick skirts and flowery blouses. She might have passed for popular, except that she hung out with people like him.

That night, they were lying in the grass looking up at the stars, talking and not talking as the mood suited them. Then, all at once, a blaze of light ripped through the clear sky. It wasn't lightning; there wasn't a cloud to be seen. But the streaking fire was as shocking as the sun, as if daylight had been smeared across the darkest opacity of night.

Lana had screamed. Later, she confessed that she'd thought it was a bomb. But Eli had known what it was— that soundless, startling brilliance. He'd never particularly cared about fireballs—large meteors that blazed in the earth's atmosphere—because reading about them on paper had never made them feel real. But then when he finally did see one, it was not only the sky that was illuminated; it was him.

He'd been amazed, dazzled, invigorated. And more, when he looked at Lana, he was amazed, dazzled, and invigorated by her as well. He felt as if someone had put a match to his spirit and turned him into flame.

He leaped to his feet, wanting to cheer for the sky, for

Lana, for himself. When she stood up beside him, he didn't think about it: He just kissed her.

They made love on the grass, with the sun coming up over the Green Mountains and dew falling gently from the sky. It was over fast—a fire burning fierce and bright, combusting. They hadn't even taken off all their clothes. But Eli remembered every moment of it. The smell of the earth in her hair. The scrape of her teeth. The feel of her skin on his tongue. It was the most surreal, most unspeakably intense connection with another person that he'd ever had.

Unfortunately he'd thought it was only the *first* time they would make love.

He finished his water and threw the bottle on the ground to pick up later. When he attacked the earth again, it was with renewed fervor. If this dig didn't pan out soon, he'd have no choice but to quit.

At last he felt his shovel stop with a *clunk*. He climbed into the hole and began to dig with a trowel. He was excited now, his blood pumping, his brain abuzz with the certainty of a big find. He would take Kelly to dinner at Burlington's most expensive restaurant. He would order their best bottle of wine . . .

He reached into the earth when it was loosened and pulled up—

A hoe.

A stupid garden tool.

He sat back on the edge of the hole he'd made and laughed.

He had to face facts: He'd never been a particularly lucky guy. Not in this and not in love. Searching for the right woman and hunting meteorites were the same in a way. There were superficial signals—the whine of a metal detector, or the sudden promise of sex in a woman's smile—that said to a man, *What you want might be right under here.*

Sometimes, you hit the jackpot.

And sometimes, you got a woman who was perfectly nice, pretty, and conversational, but who, in the end, was little more than a diversion—not a fireball that turns night into day, and certainly not the wish of someone's heart, hidden in Kansas farmland, deep underground.

June 21

The attic of Calvert's house was only half-finished, painted cobweb yellow. The plaster-and-lath walls showed through where the drywall hadn't been cut to size. There was one window—high as a belfry it seemed—that let a long beam of sunlight in during the evenings so that the little room turned pinkish-yellow and shimmered with floating dust. Karin's and Lana's beds were matching twins pushed up against the walls on opposite sides of the room, and the ceiling sloped so steeply they had to hunch their shoulders to get into bed. Though other bedrooms in the house were often vacant, Calvert had given the girls no choice but to live together in the attic until well past the age that was comfortable. He made more money off his real bedrooms that way.

"Excuse me?" A tall woman with big blonde hair smacked her fingers on the counter at the Wildflower Barn, jerking Karin from her thoughts.

"Can I help you?" Karin asked.

"That young woman in the clothing section just told me you don't carry pickle seeds."

Karin looked carefully at the woman's face for a moment to see if she was joking. She wasn't. And when she glanced toward Meggie, the latest seasonal employee to help her out at the Wildflower Barn, the girl had a wide smirk on her face. Obviously, she'd thought the question was funny enough to send the woman Karin's way.

"We have them," Karin said. "Actually by a stroke of luck I have a small packet back here. Let me just . . ." She bent down and retrieved the packet of cucumber seeds that had been left by another customer on the front counter. "Here you go."

The woman took the packet and stared at the picture on the front. "No. I'm sorry. I'm looking for *pickle* seeds."

Karin said nothing.

"Thanks anyway," the woman said. Then she left, leaving Karin totally tongue-tied and Meggie laughing out loud.

Karin shook her head and took the next customer. She would have to talk to Meggie later. But there wasn't time now. Children were playing tag among the blown-glass pinwheels, parents were scouring the store for gifts, touristy memorabilia, and more. The Barn was a madhouse.

But this was to be expected. It was tourist season. It was the longest day of the year.

It was also Father's Day.

Karin started to ring up her next customer and forced herself not to think of Calvert or the life she once lived in his run-down boardinghouse. She wasn't in some stuffy and menacing attic. She was in the *Barn*. This was her place, with its cheerful lemon-yellow walls painted with sunflowers, wild roses, speedwells, and forget-me-nots. A line of customers wove its way through the aisles, mothers clutching their children's small hands.

"That'll be $19.50," Karin said, putting a woman's items into a bag—an Audubon guide, a card printed on recycled paper, and novelty-item fava bean "seeds" for growing Vermont moose. All standard tourist fare.

The phone at her side rang.

"What's happening up there?" Lana asked, her voice coming from the line they'd installed at the back of the Barn.

"It's insanity. And Meggie's on the warpath."

"Don't worry. I made sangria for later."

"I hope you made a lot." Karin laughed. Later they would get together on Karin's back deck to watch the sun set among the cattails of the marsh behind her house. It was what they did every year on Father's Day.

Karin supposed she shouldn't let the holiday get to her. Calvert had never abused them—she knew enough to be grateful for that. But he'd never quite known what to do with them either. The boardinghouse was full of rough-around-the-edges, blue-collar men—and two motherless little girls. Calvert's idea of parenting was giving them a room to sleep in and telling them they could help themselves to whatever was in the fridge. Karin washed and folded myriad sheets and blankets, cooked big dinners for the boarders and served them with paper plates and plastic forks, and when she wasn't keeping house she did the best she could to keep her sister out of harm's way.

That had always been the scariest part of life in what was little more than a run-down hostel. Lana was a rail-thin, pretty-eyed blonde who loved to talk, talk, talk, and once in a while a boarder would take an interest in her that Karin didn't like. Karin had learned to monitor her sister's every move, whether Lana was taking a bath, doing homework, or picking the clovers one by one out of the lawn. At night Karin climbed from her bed three times before feeling satisfied that the door to the attic was well and truly locked.

"Oh, no."

The sound of Lana's voice brought her back to the present once again. "What's wrong?"

"Karin, I'm shutting down my register for a minute."

"But I've got such a huge line here . . ."

"I *have* to go!"

Karin hung up the phone and started on the next order. Only one thought could get her through this day: a vision of having a little boy all her own to take Father's Day shopping. Gene was going to be an excellent father. She couldn't wait to give him children. She could think of nothing more rewarding than laying a newborn baby in her husband's arms. She wondered if it would be preemptive to start planning Father's Day presents now.

In the bathroom Lana gripped the smooth, cold white sides of the toilet bowl. There was nothing left in her stomach. For a moment she thought she might faint: She was dizzy and seeing black, sparkling stars. She flushed the toilet and scooted back along the tile to sit against the wall.

She couldn't remember the last time she was this sick. The oddest thing was that it wasn't a twenty-four- or forty-eight-hour virus. She wondered if it might be food poisoning.

Or . . . could it be . . . ?

No. She'd had her period. It had been a light period—an extremely light period—but still, it was a period.

Wasn't it?

She forced herself to concentrate. She'd never been very good at paying attention to the signs of her body. She never knew she was getting a cold until it was full on. And she didn't really notice hunger until she was ravenous. But now her body was screaming for her attention. She just didn't know why.

She stood up slowly and used her hand to bring big gulps of cold water from the faucet to her mouth. She surveyed her reflection in the mirror. Her hair was pulled straight back in a smooth ponytail, and she grabbed a bit of toilet paper and wiped at the beads of sweat near her hairline. Normally she barely noticed her periods. They came and went with minimal cramping or bloating. But now, coupled with the puking, it was hard to ignore the possibility that she was—

Oh, but she wasn't. There was the period last month, and this month, she wasn't due to get it until . . .

She'd missed a period.

No. She missed two—if she counted the one that was very light. The one that was more like spotting than bleeding. Why hadn't she paid more attention?

She felt the ground tip; her ankles turned to jelly.

This wasn't possible. A baby. What would she do with a baby? She didn't want a child. She didn't have hard feelings toward them, but a child of her own was unthinkable.

Impossible. She wasn't *meant* to have children. She couldn't be a mom.

She put a hand on her chest, where her heart was frantic as a bird beating its wings against a cage. She couldn't seem to get enough air. There must be some mistake, she thought. But if there wasn't, how on earth was she going to tell Karin?

She felt the world slipping out of place around her. She'd always held firm to the idea that the universe was more gentle than cruel. But now she felt only that she'd been duped, violated, and maliciously used.

So much for her generous universe. A vision of Costa Rica flashed in her head—a narrow path through thick woods, hiking boots, waxy-leaved trees, and a verdant green valley—steaming, catching fire, and then turning to ash.

"Lana?" Karin banged hard on the door, annoyed that her sister had been in the bathroom for so long. "Are you okay?"

"Fine," she said, cheerful as ever.

"Can I open the door?"

Lana did it for her.

"Oh, Lanie, you look terrible," Karin said. Lana's lips had turned white and the capillaries under her eyes had darkened into a purple-gray.

"I'm okay," she said, not meeting Karin's eyes.

"Are you really?" Karin asked, desperate. She wanted Lana to be okay. She needed her to be okay. She'd just got terrible news, and she couldn't bear it alone.

"I'm fine," Lana said.

"Good. Because we have a problem." She tugged her sister toward the door, but Lana stayed put.

"What's going on?"

Karin dropped Lana's hand. "I just got a call from the jail," she said, not sure how to begin.

"The jail? Who do we know in jail?"

"Two guesses."

She watched her sister's face go a shade paler.

Karin nodded. "He wants us to come get him."

Lana closed the lid of the toilet seat and sat down. She rubbed both her palms on the tops of her knees, a nervous kneading, her hands clutching and going slack. Karin waited for her to ask one of the dozens of questions that were at this moment racing around her own brain, but Lana remained silent, asking nothing. She just rocked a little on the edge of the toilet seat, totally immersed in her thoughts.

"He got pulled over for not coming to a complete stop," Karin said, unable to read her sister's blank face. "But they hauled him to the station for driving without a license—or registration—I can't remember which."

"What do we do?" Lana said. Her voice was faint, barely a whisper.

"Nothing," said Karin.

A customer in the store shouted. "HELLO? Is *anyone* even *working* here?"

Karin ignored the voice. She loved the Wildflower Barn, but she wouldn't dream of putting her work before her family. Especially not now. Her sister was trembling. Karin could only imagine the memories that were sluicing right now through Lana's veins.

"We can't just leave him," Lana said. "He needs help."

"Are you kidding?" Karin folded her arms. "Watch me."

"You stay." When she looked up from her perch on the edge of the toilet, there was a focus, a determination in her eyes that hadn't been there before. "I'll get Calvert."

"But we'll lose business," Karin said. Her sister had completely taken her aback. She'd expected Lana to whimper and cower, not dive headfirst into the fray.

"People are understanding," Lana said, her voice soft. "We'll put up a sign that says there's a family emergency."

"People are not understanding. And we *don't* have a family emergency because Calvert is *not* our family."

"We have to do the right thing. Whatever the right thing is, that's what has to be done."

"And what are you going to do with him once you've got him?"

Lana put her head in her hands. "Oh, God, I don't know. I don't know what I'm going to do. But I have to do something."

Karin shook her head. "I just don't get you sometimes."

"Karin, oh—I don't know how to say it. Something's gone wrong . . ."

"Fine. We'll close down the whole store and get him if that's what you want."

"It's okay. You can just stay here with Meggie."

"I'll come with y—"

"No! I want you to—I mean, someone has to stay."

Karin felt the first hot currents of anger taking shape,

burning inside her. Lana was irrational; she never made
sense. Karin hadn't told Lana about Calvert being in jail
because she'd wanted to go get him; she told her because
she wanted sympathy. Someone to understand.

Lana stood up. She held tight to the lip of the sink as
if she didn't trust herself. "Eli's plane got in a few hours
ago. I'll see if he can come with me."

"HELLO?" another customer called out.

"Just *wait* a minute!" Karin shouted over her shoulder.
She turned back to Lana, panic making her stomach
twinge. "Just think about this rationally for a second,
okay? Who knows what he's here for? I don't trust him,
and I don't want you to go anywhere near him. Lana,
listen to me. Please?"

"But someone has to get him."

Karin squeezed Lana's wrist, part desperation, part
command. "Please. Don't do this."

Lana wiggled her arm to free it.

"Fine. Go then." Karin turned her back.

"Karin . . ."

"Just go if you're going to go!" Her heart beat hard.
The room full of bustling, angry people fell silent.

Lana nodded once, her face utterly blank and passion-
less, then left.

Eli put his car in park and unbuckled his seat belt.
Lana sat beside him. She'd called him twenty minutes
ago, and now they were at the police station, on the
strangest errand Eli had ever imagined. He could count
the number of times he'd heard her say her father's name.
And now here they were, picking him up just like they
would have done for any old friend.

Eli glanced toward the woman beside him. The car was tinged lightly with the smell of her, something floral he couldn't place. She seemed so small and feeble—younger in a way, as if some of the spirit had been drained from her body. She'd said only a few necessary words to him when he'd picked her up. Then she'd looked out the window, turned away from him, and grown silent. In the glass he could see the translucent reflection of her face, ghostly white like the moon at midday.

He wished she would let him touch her. Not because he wanted something from her—though part of him did—but more because he wanted to give. He could put his arms around her, lay her head on his shoulder, and stay that way until their breathing was in sync. And yet, the distance between where he sat and where she sat seemed as expansive as years measured in light.

"Are you sure about this?" he asked.

"No," she said.

"We can go back. You can change your mind."

She turned toward him now, her eyes glassy and distant. "We're already here. We might as well."

"But why?"

She closed her eyes for the briefest of moments. "Because. When someone needs help, we have to help them. There's nothing more to it than that."

Eli narrowed his eyes at her, not quite trusting her words. There was something different about her, something he couldn't put his finger on. But as usual, he had no choice but to take her at her word.

"Is that him?" he asked, though the question was pointless. He would have been able to pick out Lana's father from a police lineup, even though he'd never seen the man before in his life. He was leaning against a wide-leafed oak, a black bag at his feet. He was as tall and leggy as Lana, but more gangly than svelte. Even from a distance Eli could see that he shared her fair coloring.

"Yes," Lana said. "I think that's him."

He looked at her for one last moment; if he saw the slightest bit of hesitation in her eyes, he would have put the car in drive and ensured that Calvert would be nothing but the memory of a man leaning against a tree in his mind for all time. But Lana didn't waver. Instead her face was blank, as if all emotion had been drawn out of it, and whatever animated her was less human than machine.

"Stay here," he said. "I'll be right back."

He got out of his little car, slammed the door, then headed straight for Calvert. Lana might be afraid of this man, but Eli wasn't. And before Eli let him in the same car as her, there had to be some ground rules.

As he approached, Calvert met his gaze, a cautious question in his almost freakishly blue eyes. Eli stopped walking a few feet away and crossed his arms.

"You her husband?" Calvert asked.

"What are you doing here?"

"Lost my house." He stuck out his chin in a way that suggested the admission had cost him something. "The State took the property for redevelopment. Paid me as little as they could and still have it be legal. I got nowhere to go."

"Well, you can't stay here. She doesn't want to see you."

"I don't expect she does."

Eli was quiet for a moment. What little he knew about this man had come from Karin. She'd explained that

Calvert had married their mother, Ellen, because of an unplanned pregnancy when they were both quite young. He took off shortly after Lana was born. Then, when Karin was ten and Lana just six years old, Ellen had died in a car accident one day on her way to the lawyer's. Apparently some kind of child support–related letter from Calvert had set her off, and to this day Karin held Calvert to blame.

For a day or so, Karin and Lana had been wards of the State. Then, for the next twelve years, they lived in their father's boardinghouse inside the endless revolving door of his tenants, buddies, and girlfriends. Eli couldn't help but wonder about the connection between the come-and-go population of Lana's young life and her penchant for come-and-go boyfriends now. But aside from that vague connection, he knew little about Calvert and her past. All he knew was that the only way Calvert was going to bother her again was over his dead body.

"Here's how this is gonna work," he said. "You're gonna get in the car, say hello, and after that not a peep. We'll drop you off somewhere you can stay, but then we don't want to hear from you again. Have I made myself clear?"

Calvert kicked his bag with the toe of his work boot. "Why's she helping me?"

"She always tries to do the right thing and be a good person. Even when she doesn't want to. But just because *she's* nice doesn't mean *I* am. And I'm not gonna let you take advantage of her on my watch."

"I already done enough of that," Calvert said.

"We have an understanding?"

"I won't bother her."

Eli nodded. Then he headed back toward the car and left it up to Calvert to follow.

Lana closed the door to her house, closed herself in. Through the translucent white curtain of the window beside the door, she watched Eli walking in long strides down the uneven concrete walkway toward his parked car. She wondered where he was going. Home? Or someplace else? Someplace with Kelly?

He'd offered to stay with her. She wanted him to stay. But there was no sense in postponing the inevitable. At some point she would have to be alone with herself. With the truth. With the baby that had staked a claim on her body and now demanded a reckoning.

She pushed the curtain aside, watching him hitch up his dark jeans and then bend his knees to look at something on the hubcap of his old green car.

She'd always assumed that if she were to get pregnant she would know the moment it happened. There would be some spark, some quick shift in her sense of herself that would alert her that she was no longer alone in her own body. But the revelation hadn't been a moment of mystical female intuition; it was just a dull and unfeeling fact.

Of course it was only fitting that the day she'd realized she must be pregnant would be the day Calvert resurfaced. And yet for a moment when she was sitting on the closed toilet seat under the harsh bare bulb in the bathroom of the Wildflower Barn, Calvert's appearance had felt no more significant than if she'd got the hiccups after having just learned she had nine months to live.

The pregnancy was what mattered, the thing happening to her body that she could not stop. In a way it was lucky for Calvert that he'd called when he did: The fact that she was so consumed with her missed periods meant that coming face-to-face with him again seemed a bit removed and unreal. She wondered: If his call hadn't come right at that second—right at the instant when she herself so desperately needed help—would she have gone to him? Probably not. She'd felt such an overwhelming sense of claustrophobia she would have taken any excuse to escape from the moment. The world had gone upside down, and she'd needed to do something—anything at all—to right it.

Not even her memory of Calvert was safe from being distorted by the heaviness of realizing that she was pregnant. She'd remembered him as being larger-than-life, like some brooding tyrant who could order men dead with only the flash of his eyes. And yet at the police station today, his face was long and gaunt. His hair—once blonde like hers—was mostly gone on top, and his bald crown was pocked with liver spots. His shoulders were thin and bony, and the collar of his shirt had yellowed. She couldn't find the connection between the shrunken, feeble Calvert who had shown up in Burlington and the terrible, mythic Calvert of her youth.

Eli had been a godsend through the whole ordeal. He'd taken care of everything, and he did most of the talking. Except to say hello, Calvert hadn't spoken directly to Lana at all, as if he was afraid to push his luck. She'd sat in the front seat of the car while Eli dropped her father on the doorstep of a run-down former hotel. He hadn't asked her any questions or tried to make small talk—and she loved that about him, that he knew her so well.

She wondered, What would he think when she told

him what she'd inadvertently done? What would Karin think? She knew they would support her, no matter what, and part of her wanted to call Eli back inside right now and confess. But at the moment, she was far too ashamed and stunned to speak.

The enormity of the situation was only just beginning to sink in. She knew she was being reckless when she decided to sleep with Ron. But she hadn't realized just how *big* the risk was, how far and wide the consequences reached.

Some of her neighbors and customers would look down on her—another unwed mother with no respect for the sanctity of family. Eli might be affected too—they'd always taken great pains to never talk with each other about their sex lives, or romance, or anything too intimately female or male. But all that was about to change. Lana worried that her best friend would feel alienated when her belly grew big. It would be like flaunting her sex life—and her irresponsibility—in his face.

Karin and Gene too would be affected by the shock waves—poor Karin, who had wanted her own baby so badly and for so long. How on earth would Lana tell her? She might as well confess that she'd stolen for herself the experience that Karin had wanted all along.

Ron would be affected too, though she had no idea how she was going to get in touch with him to tell him what had happened. She didn't have his number or his e-mail address, and she didn't know where he lived. With the exception of her birthday, their dates had never been preplanned. She'd liked the spontaneity of being with him, of not knowing when he would drop by. He was a nonconformist, a wanderer—and he probably wouldn't want to parent anyone's child, not even his own.

Then there was the baby to consider—it deserved a good and loving home to grow up in. But Lana wasn't sure she could give a good life to a child, even if she wanted to. She simply wasn't cut out for the job.

She banged her fist against the door. She loved her life as it stood right now. She loved the Wildflower Barn and she loved working with her sister. She loved not having a mortgage, or a car payment, or even a dog. She loved that her life was fundamentally good, and she also loved that she stood on the brink of something even better, something out of a fantasy. As a young girl, she'd watched men coming and going—servants of the open road—but she'd never let herself become bitter over the fact that her lot in life was to stay home. Eli was a traveler. Ron too. And Lana had pinned all her hopes on the idea that she could level the playing field—that despite her obligations she was as much entitled to freedom of movement as all her male counterparts. But now . . . now she was pregnant. Her uterus was dictating her future, doomed her to it in a way.

She leaned her forehead against the window. Of course, there was a way to end all this doubt, fear, and self-hatred: The prospect of abortion flitted through her mind. But could she go through with it?

She'd always been a free spirit—an adolescent who had petitioned town hall to permit skateboarding in public parks, a teenager who had loved the Grateful Dead, and a college student who had regularly protested political injustice. It hadn't been a stretch to conclude that women were better off deciding for themselves whether abortion was right or wrong.

But in her heart, her personal instinct had always been to protect life in all its forms—whether that meant using organic fertilizers over synthetics, or choosing soy products over meat. Abortion was a choice, but it wasn't a choice for her. If she gave in to the temptation of abortion, she would lose a fundamental part of her identity—and she would never be able to live with herself again.

Through the window she watched Eli jerk open the heavy green door of his VW Bug. In the few moments that had passed since he'd crossed from her door to his car, she felt like she'd aged a thousand years. Yesterday, she'd seen the timeline of her life stretching out before her, bright and clear. Now, she still felt as if she was on the verge of a new beginning—but of what future, she could no longer say.

June 24

As Karin pulled into the parking lot of the Wildflower Barn, she saw that Lana hadn't brought the wicker chairs outside for the second day in a row. Lana was always forgetting things, missing appointments, and showing up late. Karin often joked with customers that Lana was predictably unpredictable.

But she resolved not to say anything about her annoyance over the chairs. She suspected she was a bit more irritable than normal. Knowing that Calvert was around was like being told someone had planted a land mine in town, but no one knew where. To make matters worse, last week Gene had compared making love with her to taking out the garbage or doing the dishes. Not a good sign.

She parked the car at the far end of the parking lot, leaving the best spaces for her customers, then walked toward the store. Yesterday Karin had fretted over choosing the right words to apologize about her behavior the other day, about yelling when Calvert had called from jail. But Lana had interrupted her even before Karin got the words out, dismissing the apology so fast that Karin knew she would have been forgiven even if she hadn't apologized at all.

As she pushed open the front door she saw that Lana and Charlotte were talking near the gardening DVDs, their heads bent low, their voices hushed. Even from across the room, Karin could tell that their conversation was both intense and intensely private.

"Hi, Lana. Hey, Char." Karin smiled.

"I brought this for you," Charlotte said. She picked up a small wicker basket with a purple bow tied around the handle. Karin took it with both hands.

"I had nothing to do with this," Lana said, laughing.

Karin grinned and flicked her sister's arm with the backs of her fingers. "So this is what you two were whispering about."

"Go on. Look through," Charlotte said. Today she wore a violet skirt and a gauzy cotton shirt. She was almost fifty, with a round face and lively green eyes. Lana had met her at a yoga retreat ages ago, and the two had become quick friends. "There's pumpkin seeds," Charlotte said, pointing. "An egg candle. Some incense. And a few other odds and ends."

"What for?"

"For fertility," Charlotte said, her smile beaming. She reached into the basket and pulled out a small clay medallion. There was a crudely drawn woman on the front, her breasts rendered as two half-circles with dots for nipples. Wiry serpents twisted in her hands. "It's a Minoan snake goddess. You don't have to wear it if you don't want to. I just thought . . ."

Karin felt her eyes begin to tear up. Part of her thought that if Charlotte told her the key to getting pregnant was eating nothing but cupcakes and learning to walk on her hands, she would do it.

"Thank you," she said sincerely. She didn't believe in Charlotte's gifts, but she appreciated the sentiment behind them. She gave Charlotte a big, heartfelt hug. "That was really very sweet."

"This must be hard for you. Especially with Calvert coming back."

"I'm trying not to think about it so much," Karin said.

Charlotte put a hand on her shoulder. "That's probably a good thing." She glanced at Lana, her expression softening. "I have to go. Lana? I'll see you?"

"Right," said Lana. "We'll talk later on."

When Charlotte was gone Karin couldn't help but feel a little off, as if she was being kept out of the loop somehow. On good days Gene called her "overly sensitive"; on bad days she was merely "paranoid." But Karin believed that even if her suspicions were right only one time in ten, that was still a high enough percentage to make her trust her gut.

She tried to hear Gene's voice in her head, telling her

to not be jealous, to not grip Lana so tightly to her heart. Every day Karin lived with the knowledge that Lana would leave Vermont if the opportunity ever arose—not that Lana ever mentioned it. Lana was like a kite that sailed in whatever direction the wind happened to be blowing; only Karin kept her from drifting away.

"I drove past the Madison," Karin said, hoping Lana would want to talk. "I can't tell if he's still staying there or not."

Lana didn't answer. She was staring at a daisy that she rolled between her fingers. She was somewhere else.

"Did you hear me?" Karin asked.

"Right," Lana said. "Yes."

"Don't you think it's kind of ironic that the man who made us so miserable with his endless procession of boarders is now nothing but a boarder himself?"

"What goes around comes around."

"What do you think he wants?"

"I have no idea."

Karin tried a few more times to get Lana to talk about Calvert, but Lana had clammed up. Her answers were always appropriate but never really intimate. Finally Karin said she was going to go sort the storeroom items, pleased to find a reason to sneak away. She threw herself fully into the task, and an hour later she looked up from the new canvas carryall bags to see Lana standing in the doorway to the storage area, her purse on her shoulder.

"Leaving?"

"I'm sorry. I have to go out."

"Oh." Karin bit her tongue. She had a very, very strong sense that she was not allowed to ask where. "Can I help you do something?"

Lana raised her arms over her head, pulling her straight blonde hair into a ponytail. "I just have to run some errands before everything closes."

"Okay. Well, good luck."

Lana nodded and left.

Karin stood up from the box that she'd been leaning over, something ugly and suspicious roiling around in her guts. *Of course* Lana was going to run errands. So why didn't she feel better knowing that?

It wasn't until she was back to the register at the front of the Barn that she realized: What if Lana wasn't going to run errands? What if she was going to see someone?

Like *Calvert*.

Karin's stomach tightened. She didn't want to believe it. And yet there was no other logical explanation. Lana had been so distracted lately, so different from her usual, cheerful self. It was as if some part of her had been sectioned off, tucked away, and was even more unavailable than usual.

The pieces fell together. Lana had been surprisingly insistent that she pick Calvert up from jail. And now she was whispering with Charlotte and leaving the Barn in the middle of the day. What if her loyalties were shifting? What if Karin—who had practically raised her sister after Ellen died—was being relegated to a lesser role now that Calvert was around?

She pulled a bundle of beige bags out of a box and let them flop over her forearm.

Maybe she was overreacting. That was probably it. And yet knowing that she was overreacting didn't lessen her fear. Whether it was irrational or not, Karin couldn't shake the idea that her sister was hiding something. She hoped that the truth would come out. Fast. Because until she saw an alternative, she wouldn't be able to shake the suspicion that Calvert had come to Burlington to drive a wedge between her and her sister, though why he would want to, she couldn't say.

Along the eastern shore of Lake Champlain, the sun was turning the atmosphere translucent, the stars emerging through the gossamer sky. Eli and Lana sat together among the pines on the high red rocks alongside the lake. Lana's bare feet hung over the rock's edge, her shoulders slumped prettily as she leaned back on her palms. Below them the waves sloshed against the cliff. The sound it made, sucking wetly on the rocks, was like a pulse—the irregular and wild heartbeat of night.

He and Lana sat in rare silence. Usually Lana liked to talk. About anything and everything. The first time Eli had come up here with her, Lana had told him a story her mother had told her—a fable that explained the origin of Lake Champlain, which had been called Odepsék before the French settled the area. Another time she had talked about the historic shipwrecks that were hidden under the surface of the water, preserved perfectly by the motionless cold at the lake's deep bottom. She'd always delighted in sharing the things that made her happy. But there were no charming stories from her tonight.

He felt that after all these years of being her friend, he should know more precisely what was going on in her mind. A new distance lingered between them lately, a distance that he knew he'd caused. He'd been trying desperately to make his feelings for her recede back into whatever place they'd come from—Kelly had proven to be a good distraction from time to time—but the longing that he'd felt for her while he was away was still as strong now as it had been then. Even though he'd been home for weeks, he still had the odd feeling that he *missed* her somehow.

He stole a look at her while she gazed out toward the dark water. She'd always been beautiful. Something about her high cheekbones gave her face an openness, an eagerness that made people interested in her even before she said hello. Children threw their arms around her knees just moments after meeting her and dogs rolled belly-up before her, begging to be petted. She might tell a total stranger the most intimate details of a trip to the dentist, or offer up a play-by-play description of a first date. But she rarely offered information that was more than superficial fact. Part of her outgoing, carpe diem attitude was protective: Her good manners and cheerful spirit were actually like a barrier that she'd drawn around herself.

If he wanted answers, he had to tread lightly. To tell her, in not so many words, that he would listen if she wanted to talk. "I might go for a bike ride this weekend," he said.

"Oh?"

"I don't know yet. I was hoping to do something a little different. I thought Ron might know a trail to recommend."

Lana said nothing.

"Maybe you could ask him for me?" He held his breath. He hoped, in the silence that followed, that Lana would say, "Ron and I aren't seeing each other anymore."

But instead she said, "I could ask him. If he stops by. But I never really know when that will be." A moment passed. When Lana spoke again there was a hard, sharp edge to her voice. "Why do you think Karin wants a baby so badly?"

Eli plucked up a bit of grass growing from a crack in the rock and then tossed it away. He could have answered her question. Like Karin, he too worried he was running out of time. But instead he said, "You tell me."

She got to her feet and brushed off the folds of her blue cotton sundress. "A baby just . . . ties you down. Keeps you from doing things. Things you want to do."

"You don't think Karin might be worried that if she doesn't have a baby, Gene will leave her?"

"He'd never leave her. And she'd never leave him. Neither one of them will ever leave each other, or the Barn, or Vermont, or anything else."

Eli watched her carefully, the muscle tightening beneath the delicate skin of her neck, the quickened rise and fall of her chest. The time for subtleties was over. He asked her, point-blank, "What's on your mind?"

She stood at the edge of the cliff and gazed into the darkness. During the day high school boys liked to moon the tourists on passing ferries. They also liked to jump and dive into the deep, cold waters below. Lana hung her toes off the rock, and Eli bit back a warning: *Be careful, please.*

There was no way he could have been prepared for what happened next even if she'd spontaneously launched herself off the cliff.

"I'm pregnant," she said.

His heart dropped, hit the bottom of his chest like an

anchor hitting sand. "Are you sure?" he asked. "Because maybe it's just . . . false symptoms. Did you take a test?"

"Not yet. I'll do it tomorrow after work . . . if you want to be there."

"Of course I'll be there. It might all turn out to be nothing."

"Maybe." She turned to face him, her eyes glinting madly in the moonlight. "But all signs point to yes."

"That's why you've been sick."

She nodded.

He got up and stood beside her. He tried to keep the panic out of his voice. "Does Ron know?"

"How could he? I haven't seen him," Lana said, laughing with a kind of hysteria now. "I don't even know Ron's last name. Isn't that funny? I don't know where he lives. I don't know anything about him. And I don't think he's going to look me up again anytime soon."

"How do you know?"

"He hasn't been by in a while. That's all."

Eli was not an angry man. But now he couldn't remember a time in his life that he'd felt so furious. His fingernails dug crescents into his skin. "We'll find him."

"He doesn't want me to find him."

Neither do I, he thought. In the most secret corner of his mind, he worried not only for Lana, but for himself. What if she got married? He would lose her forever.

"I can't have a baby," she said.

"Why not?"

"Because I have . . . I *had* . . . plans."

"Costa Rica?"

"I can't live in a jungle if I'm changing diapers and breast-feeding," she said.

"Would you . . . I mean, would you consider . . . ?"

"Abortion?" She shook her head. "I don't think that will work for me. I mean, I've been a vegetarian for half my life. I can't even eat a hamburger without feeling like I committed a mortal sin."

Eli nodded.

"Adoption is probably the answer." She looked at him, her gaze seeking his, looking for confirmation of how she felt. "I want to do something with my life. To not be pinned down. I'm not cut out for motherhood, so I see no choice but adoption."

She still had her arms crossed over her chest, her fingers curled around her shoulders. He wanted nothing more than to unfold those crossed arms and embrace her and rock her and tell her wordlessly that he loved her, that she had him—no matter what.

But that wasn't going to happen.

"I know what you're thinking," she said. "And yes, we did use a condom."

"I wasn't thinking that," Eli said.

"You know I don't take anything," she continued, toying with a wooden bead of the bracelet on her thin wrist. "I'm not on the pill. Something just . . . went wrong."

"What exactly happened?"

"I don't know. There must have been some kind of a tear."

He ran a hand through his hair and didn't care if it looked a mess. He tried to ignore the anger, but it was there, a pinching, twisting pain. "I just don't get it, Lana. Why were you with him?"

"He's an interesting person."

"They're all *interesting* people. Every single time."

"Please," she said, her voice pleading. "I don't want to talk about this anymore."

He drew in a deep breath. The air was scented by the lake and something sweetly powdery on Lana's skin. His heart was pounding and his mind reeled. He stepped toward her, to put a hand on her shoulder, to give what comfort he could. But the moment his hand was close enough that he could feel the warmth rising from her bare arm, she slipped away.

She kicked off her sandals with a fury that sent them flying toward the trees.

"What are you doing?"

"What do you think?" With her back turned toward him, she pulled her dress over her head. She wasn't wearing a bra; she rarely did. He saw the long bony curve of her backbone, the flexible strength of her shoulder blades, the trim column of her waist and hips.

All at once he was struck by the strangeness of the evening, of his relationship with her. She could take off all her clothes and stand entirely naked before him, and he still felt as if there were a hundred layers between them, as if the air itself obscured them one from the other.

She didn't hesitate. She ran off the edge of the cliff into the dark, where she hung suspended for a brief moment like a slant of moonlight before she fell into the blackness, into the water far below.

Eli sat down on a rock at the top of the cliff and waited. He'd swallowed his own desires so deeply and efficiently that he'd once believed them to be gone.

And he'd suffered rejection—humiliation even—when he'd offered everything in his heart to her all those years ago, and she'd turned him down. He'd allowed himself to be relegated to the sidelines, and he told himself he could be content. But the plain fact was, he wasn't.

He heard Lana swimming in the water at the bottom of the cliffs. The rocks weren't impossible to climb, but they were treacherous even during the day. He could picture her down there in the darkness, her skin pebbling in the cool air, her hair ropy and clumped about her shoulders like some Grecian naiad as she began to hunt among the rocks for the best route.

He stood to peer over the edge, wondering if this time she would let him help her climb back up.

July

Queen Anne's lace (also known as wild carrot): Some say the white flower was named because the purple center represents when Queen Anne pricked her finger while making lace. Some say that purple mole is the queen and the "lace" is her collar. Some say Queen Anne challenged her ladies to see who could make lace as lovely as the wild carrot; the queen won.

Queen Anne's lace has reportedly been used as an abortifacient.

July 4

Lana stood with her hands on the railing overlooking the lake from the vista of Battery Park. On the grass far behind her, Karin, Gene, Eli, and Kelly were sitting together on a picnic blanket. The twilight sky was a deep, wide azure, and the horizon had been tinged a yellow so soft a baby might grab a corner and use it like a blanket.

She could remember the exact moment she first thought she didn't want children. Karin was downstairs preparing a meal for the boarders, and Lana was sitting cross-legged in the locked attic, a consignment-store baby doll in her arms. The doll had a smooth bald head like a newborn and a soft cotton body that was stained yellow in spots. She had been cooing and cuddling the baby in a way that made love bubble up in her heart, when she heard her father come into the house. His footsteps were as heavy as an executioner's. She paused a moment to listen. Then she returned to the doll on her lap, searching out that feeling of love once again.

But it was too late. The feeling was gone. Unrecoverable. Eventually, she put the doll back in a milk crate in the corner and didn't take it out again.

Of course back then she'd been only vaguely aware of the connection between the sound of her father's return and the doll. And certainly the change hadn't been instantaneous—probably, it had been building up for some time, and that moment in the attic was the last straw. But whatever the chronology was, from that moment on she knew she would never want a baby of her own. She wanted an adventure—to come and go as she pleased just like the boarders did. The stories all those men told her had fired her imagination. She had no patience for just sitting home.

A handful of skinny, elementary-school kids ran past her, cackling and playing tag. Children were everywhere, flailing and wiggling and squealing. Parents pushed strollers, chased down wayward toddlers, and wiped dirt from their children's hands. Some of the families looked happy, but some did not.

Lana dropped her head in her hands.

"What are you doing over here by yourself?" Karin asked.

"Huh?" Lana looked up, startled. "Oh. I'm just enjoying the view."

"You've got to come back. No offense, but I can't stand Eli's new girlfriend. I mean, good for him for *finally* getting in the game. But she's driving me nuts!"

"Oh, come on. They're not that bad," Lana said, laughing and looking toward the couple. All evening long, Kelly had clung to Eli's arm when they walked, kissed him at every possible opportunity, put her hand in his back pocket, and played with his hair. Lana turned in time to see Kelly sit back against Eli's chest—and an emotion she couldn't quite define made her chest go tight.

At one point in the very beginning of her friendship with Eli, she'd been attracted to him. Even now she remembered the first moment she heard his voice, so warm and fervent, when he'd raised his hand in biology class to question something their teacher had said. She'd noticed him, not in a passing way but on a deep, meaningful level. And she realized she was drawn to him. They meant something to each other.

With other men—boys who plied her with cheap beer and who only pretended to understand her fascination with flowers—she sometimes gave in easily, because it meant so little deep down. But Eli was different. He too was fascinated by everything, always asking questions, always reading. He understood her then and he still did now. They had slipped once, taking their relationship beyond friendship, and it had almost ruined everything. She certainly wasn't going to make that mistake again.

But now, as she forced herself to watch Kelly running her fingers through his hair, possessiveness spiked hot and fierce in her heart—not appropriate feelings for a casual friend. She dismissed them and turned away.

"Well, Eli must have a reason to like her. We just have to figure out what it is."

"When I left, she was trying to make him lick the Doritos powder off her fingers."

"Okay, *that's* pretty bad."

"I think she feels threatened by you. I'm good at reading people. I think she suspects you and Eli are a thing."

"But we're not," she said.

For a moment they listened to the seagulls, to the children yelling behind them, to the college students playing Ultimate Frisbee on the lawn. The tension in the air was palpable. The whole town was wound up, waiting for the fireworks to start.

"Lana? Do you want to talk about Calvert?"

Lana rolled her eyes playfully. "Do I ever?"

"No. But now might be a good time. Given that he's back in town."

"He might have left."

"You mean you don't know?" Karin asked, something sly in her question.

"How would I know?"

Karin grabbed the thick metal railing in front of her, her knuckles going white. Lana saw that she wasn't even attempting eye contact. She was staring at the lush peaks of the Adirondacks with intense focus. Something was definitely wrong.

"I just want to know the truth," Karin said, steel in her voice.

"Karin, I . . ."

"I want to hear you tell me, so I don't have to be mad when I find out later on."

Lana stiffened, her poise failing. She should have

known Karin would put everything together. No one was more of an expert on reading the signs of pregnancy than Karin.

"I'm sorry," Lana said. "I thought you'd be upset."

"I *am* upset. I feel like you've thrown me under the bus. How could you do this to me?"

Lana was quiet, ashamed.

Karin sighed. "I just feel so . . . betrayed. If you wanted a relationship with Calvert again, why wouldn't you just tell me? I don't understand."

All at once, the fog in Lana's mind lifted. "Wait. You think I . . . I haven't had anything to do with him since that day at the jail. Why would I?"

"He came here to see *you*, not me. He sent that card to you. And you've been acting so weird. Leaving work early. Having secret conversations that stop usually right when I'm in hearing range. You must be talking to Calvert."

Lana shook her head. "I'm not."

The fire in Karin's eyes didn't die immediately, but instead flickered, then faded, then grew dark. "You're not?"

Lana touched her sister's shoulder. "Why would I want to see him? And more, why would I see him without you?"

"I don't know. I just thought . . ."

"You thought I was trying to keep him to myself?"

Karin grimaced. "I'm ridiculous."

"Not at all," Lana said gently, letting her hand fall from Karin's shoulder. "I understand."

"So why were you so ready to go running to his rescue when he called from jail?"

Lana looked studiously at her hands. "I just wanted to do the right thing for someone who needed help. But I don't want to see him again. Not really." Lana let her voice trail off. She could have said more. It still hurt to think of how little he'd cared for them. But talking to Karin about their childhood always made her feel so claustrophobic. Probably because Karin shared the same memories she did, and so there was no outside perspective to let any light in.

Karin put her hand on her forehead and closed her eyes. "So if it's not Calvert, then what were you apologizing for?"

Lana kept her face motionless. "I got confused."

"Maybe you can pull that over on somebody else, but I've known you for your whole life."

Lana turned her back on the lake, suddenly disgusted by it—by the sky, by the birds, by the spectators throwing their crushed beer cans into the water and chanting for the fireworks to start. She leaned her lower back against the thick round railing and looked up into the branches of the honey locusts overhead. Should she tell Karin that she was pregnant? She didn't want to—no more than a person would want to tear her own sister's heart from her chest.

Karin watched Lana's face as if she could read the thoughts in Lana's mind. "It's Ron, isn't it? You and Ron broke up and you didn't tell me."

Lana realized what this was. An out. She *had* to take it. "He hasn't called me in a long time."

"What happened?"

"My birthday was the last night I saw him."

"You mean, after he met Eli?"

"I hadn't thought of it that way."

"Jealousy. Simple as that."

"No," Lana shot back. But the gears were turning in her mind, the logic closing in. Could it be that Ron had given up on her because he'd met Eli? Did he, like so many of her other attempted boyfriends, write her off as a dead end?

"You're upset. You feel like you blew it," Karin supplied.

Lana heard the first firework explode and crackle over the lake, and the crowd let up a surprised cheer. She saw Karin's face change from pink to green to blue.

Maybe Karin was right. Maybe she'd scared Ron off when she confessed that she and Eli had once been lovers. She wasn't brokenhearted to think that Ron had lost interest in her. But perhaps her lack of heartbreak was simply because she was overwhelmed by a more urgent, crushing reason for regretting her confession. She pressed a hand to her belly, hard.

"I hope you don't mind me saying this," Karin said. "But I think the problem with your relationships is that you're too close to Eli."

"How does he factor into it?"

"A man doesn't like to share the woman he loves."

Lana's heart gave a shattering *bang*, bursting with the intensity of gunpowder. Warmth spread from her chest to her fingertips to the tips of her toes. "Eli? Eli is in love with me?"

Karin laughed. Her brown eyes glinted weirdly green under a firework. "What? No, I didn't mean *Eli*. Wow. You should have seen the look on your face. No, I meant the other guys. Men in general. They don't like to share."

"But he's just a friend," Lana managed. Gradually her

breathing returned to normal. The world slipped back into place. *What on earth was that?* she thought. "Eli doesn't want me that way."

"I know that. And you know that. But the men you date? *They* don't know that. I actually think it might be good for you to put a little space between you and Eli. I mean, look at him, Lana. *Really* look."

Lana looked toward the picnic blanket, where Gene was leaning back on his elbows and where Eli was sitting with Kelly, wrapped up with her in a handmade quilt. They both had their faces turned upward. The image made her eyes burn. Quickly, she turned toward the fireworks, lifting her face to the wild sky.

Over the course of her long friendship with Eli, moments had arrived that required her to be merciless. To look square at the facts. Right now, she saw a relationship that was changing, a best friend who was moving on. Eli had been acting so distant, and the more he pushed her away, the closer she longed to be. She *yearned* for him—not a word she would use lightly. She didn't think it was a sexual yearning, but it was a strong, deep, unignorable yearning, nevertheless. She felt Karin rubbing her back, not gently to soothe her, but hard as if urging her on.

"Whether we like the woman or not, Eli has a chance to be happy," Karin said, her voice quiet yet firm. "But he can't focus on his relationship with Kelly if you're in the picture. And Kelly won't be able to relax around him if you're always at his side."

"You're right," Lana said. "You're right."

"And as for you . . . well, maybe if you weren't so close to Eli, it would have worked out with Ron."

Lana nodded. Tears turned the fireworks into red

smears. She wiped them away with her hands. "What should I do?"

"You've got to give Eli room. When you and Eli are together, it's like you live in this little world that only the two of you have access to. If you'd let a little distance come between you, you'd both be happier."

Lana closed her eyes and gulped down a deep breath. The air tasted sweet with sulfur and smoke. Above, the fireworks raged, but the lake was placid, reflective beneath the restless lights.

Eli was the most kindhearted and deserving man she knew. It would be selfish to endanger his relationship with Kelly just because she was having a minor lapse in common sense. She longed for him, wanted something from him that she couldn't quite name, but whatever the feeling was, it would pass. It had before, it would again. In the meantime she needed to lie low. For both their sakes.

"Feel better?" Karin asked.

"Yes," Lana said. Above her, the fireworks burst into flames.

July 5

The next day, Lana sat on the front stoop of the Wild-flower Barn, waiting. In the distance, church bells chimed six o'clock, their tones muted and sleepy-sounding. A brown bunny perched on its back legs at the perimeter of the property and sniffed the air.

Once again, Lana had locked herself out of her car and

Karin was on the way to bail her out. Because she didn't have a cell phone, she'd had to walk a half a mile to a pay phone to call Karin. Then she'd headed back to the Barn with nothing to do but kill time. Now she was alone with thoughts she'd tried all day to ignore. For almost a decade she'd avoided thinking about the day that she and Eli had made love, but now the memories crowded her at every turn—so much bigger in her mind today than when they'd first happened.

Even now, she grew warm thinking of the way her whole body had come alive when suddenly he was kissing her, all instinct and joy. Their lovemaking had been amateurish, rushed, and fumbling. Yet Lana had never had a more intense connection with another person in her life. For one split second, everything she'd come to regard as dependable and predictable had burst into chaos. Eli had lain with her under the wide dark sky and brought her a kind of pleasure that drove a wedge between friendship and lust. It had scared her. That wild passion. That uncontrollable desire. It was no more sustainable than the flash of a meteor in the sky.

When she looked into the future she saw two paths: one filled with independence, traveling, and adventures; the other here in Vermont—a quiet, satisfying, but uneventful kind of life. A life that would involve getting married and starting a family. A life she didn't want.

Limiting their relationship to friendship had seemed the only compromise. But after she'd slept with him, she no longer trusted herself to set boundaries and keep them where he was concerned. If he pursued her, she would not be able to resist. And so she had to find a way to ensure that he would *not* pursue her, so that she alone wouldn't have to bear the responsibility of staying friends. Both of them had to be committed to never crossing the line. That, or they would fail.

So the night after they made love, she'd invited Chip, her study partner, to her room. The television was on but muted. The bedsheets had been drawn back. Again and again, she'd glanced at the clock, bit her nails, and flirted aggressively, laughing far too loud.

When at last Eli opened the door, he was softly silhouetted in industrial yellow light from the hallway. Her legs had been draped across Chip's lap.

"What are you doing here?" she'd said.

At first he'd been too stunned to react. She detangled herself from Chip, needlessly tugged down her shirt and smoothed her hair, and walked toward him. His brown eyes, normally so warm and gentle, grew steely and hard. She'd never hated herself more in her whole life. But she needed to do more than just end his feelings for her. She needed to destroy them. She saw no other way.

She started to make a fake excuse, to feign surprise. But he held up his hand. "This is sorta funny," he'd said, though there wasn't a trace of laughter in his voice. "I came to tell you I made a mistake. But I guess you already knew."

Then he left, leaving her speechless, hurt, and stunned. And when the door slammed shut behind him, the room went back to shadows once again.

Now, she watched Karin's minivan pull into the driveway. Lana stood, pulled her purse on her shoulder, and said a prayer of thanks.

She didn't know where these nagging thoughts were coming from all of a sudden. Maybe it was because Eli was seeing someone else. Whatever the reason, this had to stop. Karin had been right. She needed to stay away.

Karin opened the door of her van and tossed Lana's spare set of car keys.

"Sorry," Lana said.

Karin shrugged. "You really need to get a cell phone one of these days."

"Are you doing something with Gene tonight?"

Karin shook her head. "No, but I'm going over to the firehouse for a tricky tray. Why? Do you want to come?"

Lana smiled with relief. "I'd love to," she said.

July 6

Karin rubbed the last of the coconut moisturizer into her hands as she came through the bedroom door. The television and bedside lamp illuminated the otherwise dark room. Her husband was lying in bed, his glasses low on his nose as he read a newsmagazine. His pajamas—classic pin-striped blue—were buttoned wrong.

Last week, she'd told Gene her suspicion that Lana was secretly seeing their father, and it had turned into a fight. Tonight they were quarreling about Gene's parents in Montpelier (she'd refrained from calling it *Mont Peculiar*, though in light of her in-laws, the name fit). The fight had ended with Karin shouting and Gene walking out of the house. They *never* fought like that.

She pulled down the covers and climbed into bed. Gene didn't so much as glance her way. "Anything interesting in the world?" she asked, peeking over his shoulder.

"No." He closed the magazine, took off his reading glasses, and reached to shut off the light. She turned off the television with the remote. Her eyes adjusted to the shadows as Gene tugged and tucked his blankets into place.

The darkness gave her courage. "Honey?"

He didn't answer. He hadn't talked to her in hours.

"Look, I'm sorry. If you want to go to your mother's for the weekend, then fine, we'll go to your mother's. Lana will have to work and get over it. Okay?"

Still, nothing.

"Gene, please," she said, reaching under the covers to find he'd turned his back to her. "This isn't us. Please?"

He sighed. "I'm just tired of you arguing with me all the time."

She buried her face in her pillow for a moment. Gene was going through as much as she was. She owed it to him to get herself under control. "I'm sorry. I'll try harder."

"It's okay," he said. "I'm not a barrel of laughs either these days. I shouldn't have promised my mother we'd go see her without asking you first."

"That's okay."

She heard him snuggle down deeper into his covers, getting ready to fall asleep. She knew he didn't really want anything more to do with her tonight. But . . .

"Gene?"

He rolled over a little too fast. "*What?*" He rubbed at his face; she heard the sound of his fingers itching stubble in the dark.

"Honey, don't you think we should . . . you know? Just in case?"

For long minutes he said nothing.

"Honey?"

"Just go to sleep," he said.

July 11

In the evening, Lana sat at the kitchen table in her house, her queasy stomach just beginning to settle down as she flipped through the pages of a landscaping catalog. Across from her, Karin was venting while they worked, huffing like a steam engine with her face turning purple-red. *How were she and Gene supposed to get pregnant if she couldn't even remember the last time they'd had sex? Karin had said. And what was she supposed to think of her own attractiveness when he acted like sex was a chore?*

In the meantime Lana's whole body ached down to her bones, as if her guilt over being pregnant had manifested itself as physical pain. The room was a thousand degrees too hot.

She had to tell Karin the truth. But Karin didn't always take bad news very well. Her reactions were strong and visceral. In high school she and Karin had both tried out for the field hockey team. Lana made the cut, Karin did not. And even though Lana tried to explain—to apologize even—Karin had been so mad that she'd all but stopped speaking to her. Lana didn't get the feeling that she was being malicious; rather, she thought Karin was learning to stomach the lot she was dealt in the best way she knew how. Three days later, Lana quit the team.

Of course Karin was much better now than she used to be. But telling Karin that she was pregnant was a much bigger deal than telling her she'd made the field hockey team—and she dreaded it for Karin's sake and her own.

The other hindrance to telling Karin she was pregnant was that she'd yet to *feel* pregnant. For all the changes that were happening to her body, she had no sense that she was going to have a child. How could she own up to a truth that she'd yet to accept as true?

Well, whether she felt pregnant or not was irrelevant. If she didn't tell the secret, it was only a matter of time before the secret told itself. "Karin . . ."

"What?"

Lana kept her eyes on the catalogs, gathering courage.

"And did I tell you that he thinks I'm obsessing about Calvert?"

Lana shook her head.

"Obsessing!" Karin said, half laughing. "The man shows up after how many years, he may or may not be lurking around any corner, and Gene thinks I'm *obsessing*."

Lana nodded and rubbed at her temples with both hands. She felt as if her brain didn't have the capacity to hold the hugeness of her worry about the baby and the mire of her anxiety about Calvert's return. Her nerve was failing. Maybe now wasn't the right time.

The pregnancy had made her incapable of making decisions, of taking action. She was certain that she wanted to give the baby up for adoption, but she wasn't the only person involved in the decision. She'd yet to decide how hard she should work to get in touch with Ron. The man had abandoned her—she wasn't so naive as to think that he would be pleased to learn about his child. Also, some part of her felt guilty about getting pregnant, as if she'd got pregnant alone—and so she alone deserved whatever hardship the pregnancy entailed.

The other part of her wanted to stomp her feet, point her finger, and scream, "You did this!" And yet, she knew she and Ron were equally to blame.

Last night she'd dreamed that her feet were sprouting roots, and that if she didn't keep running, the roots would take hold in the earth and she would never move again. She remembered an old myth from her college Flowers and Fiction class, about how Apollo was chasing a woman because he wanted to have sex with her—rape her—and one of the other gods had taken pity on the girl and turned her into a tree. And yet Lana had always wondered who had actually been punished in the story: Apollo, who was left with the freedom to roam the earth and slake his lust with other women? Or the girl, fastened to that one spot of dirt for all time?

If only . . . if only she could talk to someone about how she was feeling. The one time in her life she wanted to open up about something important . . . and Karin was a basket case, and Eli . . . Eli was off-limits. She couldn't go to him. She couldn't give in to that need. He deserved a chance at happiness. And that meant she had to stay out of the way.

But still, she wondered if he'd realized that she'd stopped calling. If he thought of her.

No—that was stupid to consider. Lana had forfeited

her claim on his heart many years ago. She had no right to expect anything from him now.

The doorbell rang. She and Karin looked up from their catalogs like mirror images.

"Ron?" Karin speculated.

Lana's heart bottomed out. "I don't think so. I'll be right back."

She rubbed the back of her neck as she walked through the living room, past the couch with its beaded throw pillows, past the shelves with little figurines from all over the world. If it was Ron, she would deal with him head-on. She could handle his reaction, whatever it might be. She gathered up her courage and opened the door.

"Hi," Eli said.

The breath went out of her. Eli. She gripped the doorknob tight, but it was no substitute for what she wanted to do. Tonight he wore trim khaki pants and a green-striped polo shirt. His hair was between cuts, and he'd done something to make it sort of spiky and messy. Through his glasses, his eyes were the same dark-rimmed brown that so often haunted her dreams.

"Hi," she said, not trusting herself to say more.

"Lana."

She heard a door slam and saw that Kelly had gotten out of the car that was idling near the curb. She was wearing fat heels and a fluffy black skirt. She came around to the passenger side, waved, and leaned against the window. Lana got the message: They were being watched.

"Where have you been?" he asked.

She tried to smile. "Around."

"I left you two messages."

"I've been busy."

"Doing what?"

"Just . . . stuff."

He shook his head, a sardonic smile tugging the corner of his mouth. "That's what I thought you'd say. Anyway, I can't talk to you now. But I wanted to tell you something. You're not going to like it."

She didn't move. "Okay?"

"I saw Calvert here this afternoon when I drove by. He was on the porch ringing the doorbell. I guess you weren't home."

Lana began to tremble. "Are you sure? Couldn't it have been someone else?"

"Lana. Come on. It was him."

She leaned hard against the doorjamb. Calvert had been here. On her property. At her house. The place where she was supposed to feel safe. She turned and pressed her forehead into the wood of the doorframe, as if that were any substitute for leaning all the heaviness inside her against a man she could not touch.

"I came by," Eli said, his voice caustic, "because I wanted to tell you in person. I know stuff like that upsets you."

She nodded, not quite sure how to respond. She wanted to invite him in. But Kelly was at the foot of the front yard, glaring. Lana *had* to keep her distance. She'd brought this on herself.

"Is there anything else?" she asked, as lightly as she could.

He looked at her for a long, long moment. There was something new in his gaze, something angrier and more heated than she'd ever seen before. And she felt a strange and unexpected echo of it in herself, a dark ember coming to life deep within.

"No," he said. "There's nothing else."

Then he crossed the yard in what seemed a matter of seconds, and Kelly was there waiting for him, to raise herself up on tiptoe, to touch his face with her hands, and to receive his kiss with a kind of operatic intensity that would have been funny if it didn't hurt so bad to see. Lana didn't watch the kiss's ending, whether it was a slow unraveling or a breathless full stop. She closed the door. But what she didn't see was already burned into her imagination, trailing her as she made her way back to the kitchen to share with her sister their mutual bad news.

July 12

By the next morning, Karin had made a decision. She wasn't going to let a fear of bumping into Calvert drive her or Lana to paranoia. She couldn't have him lurking around her sister's house. And she was tired of feeling like she was becoming a smaller and smaller person, one who worried only about her ovaries, her father, and her sister, but did little else. She used to have a life. She used to have fun. Maybe Gene was right to suggest she was obsessing. It was time to take a more proactive approach.

Karin had put Meggie in charge of the store for the morning. Then she picked up Lana from her house so they could run errands together. They were only a block away before Karin divulged their alternate destination.

Lana turned pale at the news. "Take me back."

"There's no going back," Karin said. "That's why we have to do this. That's why we have to get him out of here."

Karin looked at her sister, her long neck gently bent and her eyelids drooping so low Karin thought they might be closed. Karin wished there were some way to spare her sister this ordeal. She'd been just a child when Ellen died, so young and hopeful. She'd believed they would get to Wisconsin, fresh from their mother's funeral, and be welcomed into Calvert's home and his heart. It hadn't taken more than two seconds for Karin to realize that Calvert didn't want them. And for the most part, she gave up on him quickly, focusing all her energies on being there for her sister.

But Lana hadn't been able to cut Calvert immediately out of her heart. The more Calvert ignored her, the more Lana struggled for his attention. "Daddy, do you think I'm pretty? Do you want to hear me sing? Am I your favorite youngest daughter?" Lana flirted and preened and pranced before her father, and Karin's heart broke.

Eventually Lana began to understand that her efforts were useless. Calvert barely acknowledged her, except to tell her to go outside, to go to her room, to just go away. As a result Lana had transferred all her bright-eyed affection to the boarders—the itinerant and lonely-eyed men who let her amuse them for a few days or weeks before they moved on. Once she got into the rhythms of their comings and goings, once she learned to accept that they would go, she stopped being let down when they did.

Karin sighed, hating herself momentarily for dragging Lana along with her. What if she'd acted more out of her own need for Lana's support than out of her wish to get their lives back to normal? She wanted to keep Lana out of it, she really did. But sitting at home and cowering while Calvert prowled the streets was out of the question. Neither one of them could rest until they knew what he wanted.

"I don't see why we can't just leave him alone," Lana said. "He'll go away if we ignore him long enough."

"Do you want him to just show up at your house again when you least expect it?"

"No. But I don't want to do this."

"Neither do I," Karin said gently.

Lana looked at her for a long minute. "Okay," she said at last. "You're right. I'll do what I can."

Karin parked the minivan in front of the Madison and got out. As they walked down the weedy and crooked path to the front door, Karin had to slow her pace to keep Lana by her side. It felt too much like the old days, when they'd walked home together from school. The walks were nice, a time of possibility and a glimpse of freedom, but at the end of their walk, the wide, flat face of the boardinghouse was always the same: not pleased to see them—just resigned that they were there.

The gray paint on the door was chipped and peeling. Karin knocked, but no reply came.

"Let's just go," Lana said.

"Wait." She banged her fist hard against the wooden slats. Paint crackled and fell. Finally the door swung open, and Calvert was there, slouching and rubbing his eye.

"Hello, girls."

He was wearing faded jeans that were just a little too baggy and a T-shirt that read "Glendale, 1985." It shocked

Karin to see him again. Lana had mentioned that he looked tired. But the circles under his eyes suggested the kind of exhaustion that no amount of sleep could fix.

"Well, come on in."

The common area of the boardinghouse was dusty and dark, with low ceilings and a big, boxy television on a card table in the corner. Cup circles the exact white of bird poop were splattered across the scratched-up wood of the coffee table. Calvert gestured for them to sit on the faded and dusty red couch cushions, but they remained on their feet.

"Nice to see you both," he said. "I was hoping you'd come find me."

Karin squared her shoulders. "We want to know why you're here."

"Why I'm here . . ." His voice was like truck tires on gravel. He sat down slowly in a worn brown armchair. "It's been a long time."

Karin crossed her arms. "Tell us why you came here."

"I told you, my house got taken away," Calvert said, looking at Lana. "I got nowhere else to go."

Karin redirected his attention back to her. "When will you leave?"

"We're all leaving one day or another."

"That's not what I mean."

"When am I leaving Vermont? Don't know. Depends."

"On what?"

"On how long it takes me to figure out why I came here in the first place."

Karin looked at Lana now, willing her sister to speak. Calvert always had a way of backing Karin into a corner,

making her doubt herself. Part of the trouble with him
was that he'd always been exceptionally smart. Not that
he was formally educated—he hadn't graduated from
high school. But there was a glint in his eyes that hinted
he was always two steps ahead of the game.

"We want you to leave," Karin said.

"We? As in, *both* of you?"

Karin looked at her sister. In the dim light, she seemed
almost otherworldly, haunted.

"If you have no reason to stay," Lana said, "then why
should you?"

He sucked briefly at his front teeth. "I thought maybe
I'd like to see you."

Karin snorted. "We're not giving you any money."

"I don't want money."

"And we're not going to just turn into your *adoring*
daughters, or something."

"That's fine. I ain't asking."

Karin sighed. "This is a waste of time. Lana, let's
go."

Lana followed her dutifully toward the front door, and
Karin could almost taste the fresh air on her tongue. This
errand had been pointless. She wanted out, now.

"Wait." Lana stopped in her tracks. The force of the
word shot through the musty darkness, and she turned to
face their father. "Are you sick?"

Karin rolled her eyes.

Calvert hesitated as if weighing what to say. "Nah. I'm
not sick."

Lana nodded. Then she glided past Karin and out the
front door, passing through the dusty old building like a
ghost of herself. She had never been much help in the

trenches where their father was concerned. Karin turned back toward him again. "One more thing."

He put his hands in his pockets and seemed to shrink ever so slightly, as if he'd already conceded that Karin would have the last word.

"Yeah?"

The sorrow in his voice almost made her hesitate. But she didn't buy the act. "Stay away from me and stay away from Lana. You got it? I don't want to hear you've been hanging around her house again. If I see you, I swear I'll call the cops."

She slammed the door behind her when she left.

July 18

Kelly's cheeks were tinged russet by an afternoon on the water. She stood before Eli in a baseball hat, bathing suit, and life jacket. When she hugged him, she smelled of the lake, the faint sweetness of seaweed and the coolness of water. Normally Eli associated these particular smells with Lana.

"We won!" she exclaimed, giving him a high five. "Did you see me out there? I was like a machine!"

"I had no doubt."

She smiled. Behind her the hard slate blue of the lake was muted by an overcast sky. The Adirondacks were hazy and dull, but the mood on the beach was upbeat. Blue and white tents had been set up near the water, and teams of women in pink, purple, and yellow were congratulating one another and laughing. In the water, forty-foot-long canoes were lined up and bobbing gently. On the front of each was the head of a dragon. The sides were painted with scales.

Eli had heard of the Dragon Boat Festival on Lake Champlain—everyone in Burlington had. But he'd never been to watch before. Kelly had invited him to come and cheer for her and the other participants as they raised money for a breast cancer charity. Eli had put on his sandals and grabbed his binoculars, but in truth, even though he was present, he wasn't fully *there*.

After he'd given Lana the message about Calvert, he'd stopped trying to talk to her. Maybe he'd hoped that she would notice his absence and come after him. Maybe he wanted to make her as miserable as she'd made him. Whatever his conscious or subconscious ambitions, nothing had happened. Lana had stopped calling him and he'd stopping calling her. He still didn't know exactly why.

Only once before had he ever felt so distant from her. After they'd made love in the field that night, he'd walked her back to her dorm. He couldn't stop touching her, holding her hand, wrapping his arm around her waist, pulling her close to press his nose to her hair. Sometimes he wished he could go back to that moment ages ago and put his foot down. *All or nothing,* he would say. And if she said nothing, at least he wouldn't be caught in this terrible limbo that became more painful by the day.

Since he couldn't go back, all he could do was live in the moment and try to stop thinking so hard about his best friend.

Kelly smacked his arm. "So does it bother you that I'm a dragon boat champion and can kick your butt?"

He laughed. "Kick my butt? Right." He picked her up and carried her kicking and laughing to the edge of the lake.

"Don't you dare!"

He waded into the water in his khaki shorts, threatening to toss her. She kicked her feet in the air and squealed. Her wiggling was no match for him and he laughed.

Then, out of the corner of his eye, he saw Lana. She was standing in the crowd on the shore, her bare feet sticking out from under a long lavender dress.

Lana.

He set Kelly back on her feet—perhaps a little too quickly. He'd started to say *Lana!* when the woman's blonde hair caught the wind. He was going crazy. Absolutely nuts. He bent to pull his wet cotton shorts from his thighs.

"It's not her," Kelly said. "What's going on here? What are you not telling me?"

He straightened, and as he did, the truth tumbled out. "Lana's pregnant," he said. And the moment the words slipped from his lips, he realized how much better he felt to have said them aloud.

"Why didn't you tell me sooner?" she asked, her voice tight.

"I don't know. She only told me about three weeks ago."

"Three weeks!" Her face dropped as if he'd slapped her; he couldn't imagine why. And then she was trudging past him, white flares of water frothing at her knees as she marched toward the shore. It took a moment before he understood what had happened, and he hurried to catch up.

"It's not mine!" he said. "Kelly, stop."

"Just leave me alone!"

Eli caught her arm, but she shook him off. He hurried to stand in front of her, and she stopped. "Did you hear me? It's not mine."

"Wait. What?"

"I'm not the father. It's some guy Lana met. Some mountain biker. She doesn't even know his last name. *That's* why I'm worried. That's why when I thought I saw her on the beach—"

"The baby's not yours?"

"No."

"Oh, Eli." She hugged him close, buried her face in his chest. She squeezed him so tightly he couldn't breathe. This wasn't the reaction he'd expected.

The sun was starting to set now, the first warm effusion of yellow light rising over the tops of the Adirondacks. The seagulls were wheeling in the air, scavenging bits of hot dog and fries from the race. People were walking, soggy and happy, to their cars to go home.

"I don't know why you and Lana aren't a couple," Kelly said, her forehead resting on his sternum. "But whatever the reason, I'm glad."

Eli didn't know what to say. The conversation had already gotten a little too deep. It was entirely his fault, but he didn't want to encourage anything more. "Why is that?"

She looked up at him, her eyes bright, but she said nothing.

"Let's go get dried off," he said.

• • •

July 20

Lana looked out the window of the Wildflower Barn,
watching the summer tourists fumble with their digital
cameras to snap pictures of the black-eyed Susans, Queen
Anne's lace, and dame's rocket that grew behind the
building. Every time the bell above the door chimed, she
looked up, expecting Eli. But always it was the tourists,
visitors who came to Vermont for the state's guileless
beauty and wholesome amusements. This time the family
pushing into the Barn boasted a half dozen chattering
children and two women who laughed and said, "Oh, isn't
this place adorable," like they were either sisters or best
friends.

Lana tucked her disappointment about Eli as far down
inside her as she could. All week she'd been hoping he
would come find her. Even if they didn't talk, even if she
didn't have enough time to unburden her heart with him,
she craved the comfort of seeing his cheerful smile, his
bright cycs. But since the days continued to pass without
him, all she could do was give to her customers the smile
she would have reserved for him. "Hello. You folks here
for the wildflower walk?"

The older woman, who wore a wide-brimmed straw
hat and big sunglasses, looked around while she talked.
"This place is so great. I'm so glad we found it."

Lana grimaced at the sound of a half dozen little
sneakers squeaking on the floor. The children were running through the store, among the displays of lawn art
and wind chimes. Lana held her breath. The younger

woman frowned sternly and went chasing and yelling after the kids.

"Yes, we're here for the walk . . . er, maybe the run," the woman with the hat said. "How much?"

Lana peered around her, to where a little boy was spinning a stained-glass pinwheel faster and faster by batting it with the palm of his hand. "There's no charge for the walk. The paths are open to the public."

The woman called over her shoulder. "You can go out! Angie? Take them out." She rolled her eyes and smiled when she turned back to Lana. "Do you have any children?"

Lana started to say no. But then she remembered. And for a second she felt as if she were answering not for herself, but for someone else. "Not just yet."

The woman nodded. Her smile was warm and her irises were dewy white and green, like the jack-in-the-pulpits that grew behind the barn in the spring. "Well, you're young. You have some time."

"It seems like an awful lot of work," Lana said, nervous.

"Oh, it is." The woman laughed. "Tons of work. But tons of joy too. You'll see, once you have your own."

Lana was struck silent for a moment. Not long ago this would have been the part of the conversation where she said lightly and certainly, "Oh, I don't want kids. I want to live in Costa Rica." And then the woman would have answered the same way all the veteran mothers would answer: "You might change your mind."

This time, however, the script was unwritten and entirely new.

"I don't know," Lana said. "Your kids seem perfectly

sweet, but there's so much sacrifice you have to make for them, isn't there? So much to give up?"

The older woman peered at her thoughtfully a moment. "Sure, I've given things up. I always wanted to be a lawyer, you know? Go to law school. Work long hours and get designer shoes."

"I'm guessing you're not a lawyer?" Lana said, embarrassed now by how urgently she clung to each word the woman spoke.

"Dreams are tricky things. They ebb and flow. They change as we change, you know? It's not . . . it's not a matter of right dreams and wrong dreams. I mean, sure, choosing one sacrifices another. But it's not about what you give up. It's about what you get."

Lana fought the odd urge to reach out and grasp the woman's hand, just for a moment. There were a hundred questions she wanted to ask. A thousand. But propriety got the best of her; customers should never be burdened by the storekeeper's personal life.

"Well, like I said," Lana replied. "It's not really something I'm thinking about right now."

The woman watched her, and Lana felt as if those clear green eyes could see straight down to the truth. "Sometimes it's hard to know what you want. But that's okay. Things have a way of working themselves out."

One of the children who had come in with her poked his head inside the door. "Ma? Ma? Are you coming?"

The woman gave one last smile to Lana, her scrutiny replaced with what Lana thought might have been embarrassment. "I didn't mean to lecture you," the woman said. "Sorry. Maternal instinct, I suppose. Enjoy the rest of your day!"

"You too," said Lana. Then, too quiet for the woman to hear, she added, "Thanks."

The stoplight turned red and Karin banged her fist on the steering wheel. "Oh, fudge!" When she finally got home—the ride from church had never taken so long before—she opened the front door, said hello to her husband in the living room, and tried to act normal as she set down her purse and tote.

Unfortunately she'd never been very good at keeping her feelings inside. She jerked at the laces of her sneakers, unable to get them off fast enough. "Gene! My period is late!"

Gene put down his bowl of cereal and stood up from the couch. He'd already changed out of his work clothes and was wearing his favorite maroon sweatpants and a T-shirt that made his chest look burly and wide.

"Whoa, Kare. Slow down."

"What if this is it? What if it really happened this time?"

He didn't return her smile. "Let's not set ourselves up for disappointment. Take it slow. Let's eat dinner together first."

"You want to . . . to wait?"

"Just so we can be calmer when we do it."

Karin laughed. "You think I'll be calmer if I wait *longer*? No way. We have to do this *now*." She brushed past him, heading for the bathroom and knowing he was following. Just before she reached for the knob, it occurred to her that maybe he was as nervous as she was, if not more. She paused for a moment, to take his hand and rub its warmth against her cheek. "Will you wait outside the door?"

"Kare . . ." There was concern in his voice.

"Don't worry," she assured him, then she shut the bathroom door.

She'd taken pregnancy tests so many times she could do it in her sleep—and it was a good thing too, because her hands were trembling. She watched the clock on the wall, waited the appropriate time, down to the exact second, and then she looked.

NOT PREGNANT.

Her joy took a huge, stomach-flipping nosedive, but then swelled slightly again. *Maybe it's too soon to tell*, she thought. She reread the box; it predicted accurate results from the first day of a missed period. She'd just started to convince herself that she needed to do a retest when she realized that the line between optimism and denial could be shamefully thin.

"Well?" said Gene through the door.

She opened it. Then she shook her head.

"Oh, Kare," he said. He hugged her, but she didn't quite hug him back.

"Next month," he said. "You'll see."

"I'm sure of it," she said.

July 21

Early in the morning, Lana hiked the 5.2-mile trail to the top of Mount Abram. She sat on a lichen-speckled rock and looked out. In the distance the blue luster of Lake Champlain glittered in the soft morning light. A wispy line of thin clouds lay on a bed of air just above the peaks of the Adirondacks, contrasting rock and cloud.

Climbing up the mountain, past the ashes and maples and pines and scrubby bushes, usually made her head clear, as if the thinner the air got, the easier it became to think. But not this time. No matter how she tried, she couldn't shake the feeling that she'd been walking around in a fog.

The problem was that she *still* didn't feel pregnant. She was twelve weeks along, and her body was changing— there was no denying the way her nipples had darkened, the way her belly was no longer a taut vertical plane, the way her appetite raged. She'd googled pictures of other women's bellies to see how she compared, and if there hadn't been such a surprising disparity from one woman to the next, she wouldn't have known that she was quite small for being so far along. Her belly was noticeable, but easily hidden.

She stretched her arms over her head, trying to loosen the tension in her back. She wondered: What had her father thought when Ellen told him she was pregnant? Was he glad? Did he have one single moment of genuine joy about fatherhood?

She took in a deep breath, exhaled. She needed to try to find Ron. That much was clear. She owed it to him. And to the child. The baby deserved a father. And if Ron wanted to do that job, who was Lana to stand in the way?

If only she could talk about how she felt with someone. But Karin was involved in her own pregnancy issues, and Eli . . . Eli was gone. How many times a day did she catch herself thinking, *I need to remember to tell this to Eli,* only to realize that she wouldn't be telling him anything at all?

She was off-balance and empty without him. And yet she *had* to stay away.

He deserved a chance to be happy. He deserved the chance to get clear of her, to break away from the mess she was making of her life. But she needed him. More now than ever before. She needed him to reassure her that everything was going to be okay with this baby, with Karin, with Calvert. She couldn't do this on her own.

She wondered where he was and tried to imagine him—to picture what he was doing—but she couldn't. Wherever he was, she hoped he was happy. Only that would make her longing for him worthwhile.

July 22

On Wednesday afternoon Lana was on her knees outside the Wildflower Barn, tugging tiny weeds from hard soil around the post of a split-rail fence and sweating in the bright sun. She wore old, grass-stained overalls and a purple bandanna to cover her hair. Charlotte, who was on her lunch break and too dressed up for weeding, was sitting on a Victorian wrought-iron patio chair, thumbing through a Sierra Club magazine.

They'd just come back from the doctor's. Of course Lana knew how it must have looked, two women who could complete each other's sentences going to the obstetrician. At one point the nurse had referred to Charlotte as Lana's partner, and Lana hadn't corrected her. She felt better having Charlotte there by her side, and she would take whatever kind of partner she could get. The doctor had listened to the heartbeat for what seemed a very long time; though her belly was small, the baby inside it was developing fine.

"So when are you going to tell Karin?" Charlotte asked.

Lana sat back on her heels. "I tried once already."

"If you don't tell her, she's going to figure it out. I can't believe she hasn't already."

Lana nodded. "I think she's depressed. It's like a vicious cycle. But I'm just the little sister. What do I know?"

"About having babies? Apparently more than you'd think."

Lana rolled her eyes and went back to weeding. A shadow fell across the earth before her, and when she looked up and held her hand up to block the sun, Kelly was there, wearing a short denim skirt, a hot pink tank, and sunglasses so big they covered most of her face.

"Hi, Kelly," Lana said, smiling and getting to her feet. Hope swelled within her. She looked toward the parking lot, expecting to see Eli coming toward her across the grass. But no. She felt his absence like a cold soaking rain, but she smiled on. "Do you know my friend Charlotte? Char, this is Kelly, Eli's friend."

"Girlfriend," Kelly corrected her, taking Charlotte's hand.

Lana felt the word like a punch to her gut. "Of course. Sorry. *Girlfriend*. So what brings you this way?"

"I need a bag of those little white stones—what's it called? Limestone."

"No problem. I can certainly help you with that!"

"No!" Kelly said quickly, her fingers resting light as a butterfly on Lana's shoulder. "I need a twenty-pound bag. Isn't there some young set of muscles around here to help?"

"Well, there's Meggie . . ." Lana saw a look flicker over Kelly's face, a narrowing of her eyes, the hint of a smirk. Or maybe Lana imagined it. She pulled at the fingers of her glove and tossed it to the ground. "But I don't mind getting it for you. They're just right over he—"

"Really," Kelly interrupted. "I know you're not supposed to lift anything too heavy. I can find someone else."

Lana stopped taking off her glove, her gaze darting to Charlotte. Her friend was scowling with the rage of a hundred wild bulls.

"How are you feeling?" Kelly asked. There was no mistaking the righteousness in her smile now. "Is everything going okay?"

Lana finished pulling off her glove and tossed it on the grass with its mate. Anger and hurt stretched her apart, a slowly splitting seam. This was betrayal, pure and simple. Eli, *her* Eli, had thrown her to the wolves. "You know?"

"Yes. But don't worry. I know it's not *Eli's* baby. He said he doesn't find you attractive. Obviously."

Lana smiled to cover her discomfort, but it was entirely fake. She hoped her hurt didn't show on her face. Of course Eli wasn't attracted to her anymore. And yet the fact seemed oddly painful when it was said out loud.

"I think you should go," Charlotte said.

"But my limestone . . ."

"Forget it," Charlotte said.

"I really don't see what the problem is."

"I do," Charlotte replied. "And it has terrible taste in sunglasses."

Kelly smiled, showing her teeth. "Good-bye, Lana. I'll let Eli know you said hi." There was a little bounce in her step as she walked away.

Charlotte spoke once Kelly was out of earshot. "Are you okay? What hurts?"

Lana was puzzled for a moment, then realized that sometime during the conversation, she'd put a hand on her belly, her palm pressed against the hard, comforting warmth. It was a gesture of protection as well as comfort, one that caught her off-guard because of the odd question of who was comforting whom. "I'm fine." She dropped her hand and sat down on the bench.

He doesn't find you attractive. The words stung.

Charlotte crouched to look her in the eye. "You need to talk to him. This isn't healthy for either one of you."

"Eli and I will get through this."

"I mean you and the baby."

Lana closed her eyes for a brief moment, gathering strength, and when she opened them, Karin was charging toward them from across the yard. She was covering ground in long, fast strides, her brown-red hair bouncing around her shoulders and blowing back.

"What happened?" she demanded.

"Eli's girlfriend happened," Charlotte said, rising to stand.

"What did she do?"

Lana panicked. She could feel Charlotte's gaze on her, her friend's silent communication that she should tell

Karin *now*. But if Lana confessed right this second, she would have to explain the whole story, about how Eli knew, about how he'd told Kelly, about how Charlotte knew as well—and then the only thing Karin would be able to think of was why everyone was told but her. The bad news would be hard enough to take without the added injury of being the last one to know.

"Turns out Kelly is nastier than I thought," Lana said. "She came over here to flaunt her thing with Eli. I guess she just wanted me to know that . . . that he picked her over me."

Karin nodded and put her hands on her hips, as if she'd expected this. "Have you been seeing him?"

"No."

"Good. Don't. You need to give them some space."

Charlotte put an arm around Karin's shoulders. "Maybe what we should do is give *Lana* some space."

"I give her plenty of space. Don't I, Lana? Is something going on?" Charlotte tried to steer Karin back toward the Barn, but she shook off Charlotte's arm. "Lana, tell me what's happening. Are you . . . are you in love with Eli?"

"No!" Her heart was thudding hard in her chest and her palms were damp. "Of course I'm not in love with . . . with him. Why would you think that?"

"Why else would you get so upset about his stupid girlfriend?"

Lana couldn't take it anymore. Karin obviously thought she was jealous. But she wasn't jealous of Kelly. She was just . . . just . . .

She was jealous of Kelly.

She was out-of-her-mind, tear-her-own-skin-off *jealous* of Kelly.

That had been the truth all along. But even if she was jealous, she wasn't *in love* with Eli. She couldn't be. She was attracted to him occasionally—it was bound to happen, really, since they were so close. And maybe being away from him had sort of . . . augmented that annoying little bit of attraction. But she wasn't in love with him. It was insane to even be considering love when Eli went around telling people she wasn't attractive, *and* he'd gone behind her back and told the biggest secret of her life.

Karin hesitated. "Are you sure?"

She nodded. She could see that Karin knew she was missing something, and she wished her sister could hear her thoughts: *Please just trust me. I'll tell you very soon. I promise.*

Karin nodded, then allowed Charlotte to take her arm and walk her back inside.

Lana took a deep, cleansing breath. She wasn't in love with Eli; what she felt was just a passing longing. She knew it, but she felt the need to reassure herself of her feelings somehow.

There were reasons people didn't let themselves even think of having mushy feelings about their best friends. If friendship—that most durable, trustworthy, and lasting kind of relationship—could make a person hurt as badly as Lana did right now, then she couldn't imagine actually letting herself fall in love with Eli. Losing a friend she was also in love with would be the devastating burn of lost passion coupled with the hollow, unendurable chill of losing a part of herself.

She couldn't be in love with Eli. But she was hurt. And

lonely. There was only one thing to do: confront him. If he confessed what he'd done, she would forgive him. And if not . . .

If not, maybe it was time to sever her life from his once and for all, and end the torture of this long, slow pulling apart.

That evening, after Karin had sent her sister home and closed up the store by herself, she stopped at the grocery store to pick up bread and milk—and a Payday, Lana's favorite candy bar. She walked toward the back of the harshly lit store and pulled open the glass door of the refrigerators.

She did feel a little bad for what had happened this afternoon. She hated when she felt kept out of things, and she supposed she'd asked if Lana was in love with Eli more out of desperation than any belief that it could be true. She hadn't known the question would upset her sister as much as it did.

She noticed the price of milk had gone up by a few cents yet again. She shook her head and reached in for a half gallon. When she had shut the glass door and turned around, she heard someone say her name.

"Evening, Karin."

The door banged closed.

Calvert. She felt as if she'd been knocked down by an enormous wave. Dry one moment, dripping the next. He was standing in the aisle, blocking her way to the register. The milk was freezing cold in her hand. "Did you follow me?" she asked before she realized that was impossible, since he didn't have a car.

He turned a can of soup around so its label faced front

on a shelf. "Don't suppose you're heading over in the direction of the Madison after you check out? Give an old man a lift?"

She nearly laughed out loud. His audacity was almost impressive. Then she walked completely around the aisle he blocked to get to the register on the other side of the store. By the time she made it back to the parking lot, she was shaking.

She wanted to believe he was a nonentity in her life. That he didn't matter. But that wasn't true. From the day she arrived at his home, Karin had always secretly wanted them to be a family—Calvert, Lana, and her. On a practical level she'd managed to cut herself off from him. But while she'd disciplined herself to stop *expecting* his love, she never could stop herself from hoping for it.

As a teenager she'd tried to turn Calvert's busy house into a place where a family, a real family, could live. She cooked meals and forced Lana to eat with her at the kitchen table, where they were very visible and where Calvert could join them if he saw fit (he never did). When winter came it was Karin who made sure Lana was bundled up nice and warm for school, Karin who bought, set up, and decorated the Christmas tree in Calvert's living room. Karin had never attempted to invite Calvert to school functions—plays, chorus concerts, softball games—but she sometimes put flyers on the fridge about upcoming events, just so he knew they were happening. The only side effect was that what Calvert knew, the boarders knew too. And it pained Karin to watch them one by one respond to Lana's overtures of friendship— only to see them leave every time.

She got into the car, locked the door, and backed out

of her parking space as quickly as she could. There was
no question that Calvert's appearance was affecting Lana
for the worse. Lana was gaining weight—not a lot, but
enough to notice. It was mostly visible in her face, but
Karin knew that if her sister ever wore anything but sundresses and overalls, she would probably be able to see it
in her hips and thighs too.

Karin headed toward home. She wondered if Calvert's
presence was contributing to her physical stress level too.
The doctors told her she needed to stay relaxed and
healthy if she was going to get pregnant the natural way.
And Calvert was definitely not making her feel relaxed
and healthy. If she wanted to have a baby, she would have
to end all this stress, to get rid of him. What she needed
was a plan.

July 23

Lana found Eli at UVM, where he was teaching a com-
munity education class on meteorites to a small group of
adult students. She snuck quietly into the back of the
room, sliding into a metal folding chair and pulling her
oversized purse onto her lap. Eli caught her eye. Instantly
his body language changed. He stuttered, lost his train of
thought, and went on. He used his hands too much when
he talked, and he kept turning around to point to the
whiteboard for no apparent reason.

She wondered when he'd gotten to be so uncomfortable around her. This was entirely new and didn't make
her feel particularly calm. She had the unavoidable sense
that nothing was going to be the same between them

again, that what she'd done by avoiding him and what he'd done by betraying her had set into motion an irreversible change.

Finally the lecture concluded. And after Eli answered a few polite questions from students who approached him after class, he made his way toward her. He was wearing a pale blue dress shirt. His glasses caught the light as he approached, and she felt her heart beat hard in her chest. Something about him seemed different—the moderate thickness of his arms, the tilt of his chin. Every female cell in her body sparked as he walked toward her. If she didn't know better, she might say it was attraction. Was it possible, she wondered, for attraction to come in forms that weren't sexual? That maybe the longings of two separated friends could be mistaken for an unexpected jolt of sex?

She took a deep breath. Who was she kidding? She was getting more and more confused about what she wanted from Eli by the day. There was no other name for this feeling but attraction, *sexual* attraction—a drawing together of two bodies as he came closer to her. She had to put an end to this feeling, fast. When had she become so spineless that she could no longer stand up to herself?

"Lana." He approached cautiously, hanging back. "Good to see you. What are you doing here? Do you want to get coffee or something?"

"No." She pulled her bag tighter against her body. She felt as if she couldn't breathe, but she stayed strong. "I think we need to talk."

To his credit, he looked genuinely puzzled for a moment. He kept an eye on the last two students who were leaving the classroom—a stall tactic, Lana thought—and when they were gone he closed the door behind them. The big classroom became suddenly very small.

He stood before her, his face serious and focused as he crossed his arms. "I haven't seen you in a while."

"I wasn't sure you noticed," she said, and then regretted the words immediately because bitterness wasn't at all like her. And because she'd given away too much.

"You were avoiding me on purpose?"

She shook her head. "And I didn't come here to talk about me."

He shifted on his feet, just slightly, so the rubber of his shoes creaked. "Then what did you come to talk about?"

"Kelly. She paid me a visit," Lana said.

"Oh?" He pulled in a deep breath, so his crossed arms seemed to widen with the swell of his chest. She tried not to look.

"I know what you told her. I just don't know why."

"What do you mean, you know what I . . ." He dropped his arms, looked away, and ran a hand through his hair. "*Shit.*"

She nodded, vindicated but mad. "Why would you do that? Why would you say that to her? I haven't even told my own sister that I'm pregnant, and you go and tell a total stranger. What am I supposed to make of that?"

Eli pushed his hands into his pockets, and she could tell he was fighting to control his voice when he spoke. His words were breathy and low. "You. *You're* asking me?"

"Yes, I am."

"You of all people. A woman who's just admitted

she's avoiding me. My best friend who hasn't bothered returning my calls."

"I was giving you space."

"You were cowering."

"Why on earth would I cower?" she asked, even though he'd stepped closer to her, and she found herself grappling with the need to step away.

"I don't think you like it when I date other women," he said.

"Please." She moved away from him, acting as if she needed to put her purse down on a chair. "Why would I care what you do with other women?"

"I don't know," he challenged, pulling his hands from his pants pockets. "Why would you? You always have. But I'm done putting my love life on hold for you."

"What are you talking about?" she said, gripping the hard back of the wooden chair beside her. "I have nothing to do with who you date."

He laughed, bitter. "Until recently, my entire sex life was on hold because of you. And I think you're annoyed and jealous that I'm spending more time with Kelly than you."

"But how is it *my* fault?"

"Remember Joanne what's-her-name? From textile arts class?"

"What about her?"

"Remember what you did when I told you she and I were dating?"

She tried to remember but couldn't.

"You brought a date over to my dorm room the Friday that she and I had our first date. You said that your roommate was having a party and you needed a place to be alone with the guy. In *my* room. When *I* had a date of my own!"

"I didn't think it was that big a deal," she said, buying time as the memories slowly returned. "I figured you guys were going out anyway. And that was ages ago. Why are you bringing it up now?"

"To prove that you don't like it when I date other women."

"You're just being ridiculous."

"And what about the woman from the tennis team?"

"What about her?"

"Lana, when I started dating her, it was like all of a sudden, you were everywhere! Everywhere I turned you wanted to hang out with me. And you know damn well that I've never been able to tell you no. I couldn't have seen her even if I wanted to. She just got phased out. And then when she was gone, you turned right back into your old self again. You get weird when I date other women. Every time, it's the same."

"I think you're imagining this," she said, breathless.

He gripped her arm, looking firmly into her eyes. "No. I'm not."

Her heart was pounding terribly hard, and though gut instinct made her want to deny that she'd ever gotten in his way romantically, some part of her worried that it was true. She suspected herself. She didn't like it when he dated other women. But she'd never in a million years dream of sabotaging his love life on purpose . . . Would she? What if she'd been deliberately keeping him off the market without quite knowing she was doing it? She could feel the rightness of his accusation—and it terrified her. What did it mean? There was a heat and vehemence in his words that she'd never heard before. She *had* to get the conversation under control.

She stood there a moment, holding his gaze, unwilling to back down. His hand was hot on her bare arm. The strap of her sundress fell and landed on his knuckles. She forced herself to hold his stare. "If that's true, that I get in your way with women, then why didn't you say something sooner?"

She felt his grip on her arm loosen, and somehow that gentleness was even more disconcerting. "Because I liked it."

She said nothing, stunned.

"I liked it when you got in between me and other women. It meant you cared about me. I think that's why I didn't really notice it, until now."

She pulled away. But the truth was there, crowding her at all sides, unavoidable. All the pieces of the past came together, logic pointing out emotions that she'd thought were long gone. She trembled slightly with astonishment and surprise. And she realized: She wanted him. Physically. All to herself. The thought that another woman was in his bed . . . She couldn't bear it. She'd wanted some part of his love life to *belong to her* even if she didn't acknowledge it, like a toy that she owned but refused to take out of the box.

She felt herself blushing hotly, a low internal hum resonating through her whole body. The solidarity of their friendship had succeeded mostly because they didn't talk about these kinds of things. Dating was private. Sex, taboo. And now that Eli was bringing it all into the open, there was no more protocol, and she had no idea how to restore the rules he was breaking. She cleared her throat. "Well, you don't have to worry about my getting in the way with Kelly. You've made it abundantly clear that she's the one you . . . you care for."

He took a step back. "I . . . I'm sorry. Lana, I really am. The words . . . they just slipped out."

She was quiet.

"Please understand. Your pregnancy . . . it's been eating me up inside," he said, his voice distant and reserved. "There was no one I could talk to."

"You couldn't talk to me?"

"No."

She swallowed hard. "Why not? We're friends. You can tell me anything."

"All right." He took a deep breath; she heard the air whisper across his lips as he exhaled. When he spoke, his words were soft and slow. "I don't like that you're having another man's baby. I don't like that you slept with him, or anyone. And I don't like the idea that some other man now has a connection with you that I never will."

"I understand." She lifted her eyes to his, summoning everything brave within her. "I feel the same way about Kelly. A little bit." He leaned toward her and she saw his gaze drop to her mouth. Her heart sped up, so she talked. Fast. "But that's why I wanted to give you a chance with her. I want to see you happy and in love. So I stayed away."

His eyes narrowed darkly. "Do you know what she told me? She said that it's like you and I are dating, except that we don't have sex."

Goose bumps ran up her back. The word *sex* hung in

the air between them, and she knew he was thinking about it—that they both were. That night in the field.

"We don't have sex," she managed. "So it shouldn't be a problem."

"It *shouldn't*," he said.

She held her breath, astonished by what she saw in his eyes. It was need, pure and simple. Physical, sexual need. And it made her sweat and jolt in places she should not. She couldn't believe it. After all these years. Some small part of him still wanted her—she hadn't thought it possible after what she'd done.

She didn't have time to think it over. For now, all she knew was that she needed to get away from that heat, that edge. She needed to put them back on firmer, more familiar ground. And she would decide what to do about this . . . chemistry . . . later on.

She put her hands in the deep square pockets of her dress. "I knew when I met you all those years ago that being your friend wasn't going to be easy. That we'd probably step on each other's toes and get in each other's way."

"Why?"

"Because I'm a woman. And you, well, obviously you're a man." She kept her expression blank, her voice cool. He frowned, his eyes searching, almost as if he was waiting for her to say more. "Can we call this a truce?" she asked. She put out a hand for him to shake and hoped she wasn't trembling. It had been years since she'd deliberately touched him, even in the smallest way. She hoped this would be taken as a gesture of goodwill.

He looked down at her outstretched hand for a long minute, his lip curled in disbelief—as if to say, "That's all you got?" Her resolve wavered; she almost drew back. But then, he seized her hand, her whole hand—not with one of his, but with both.

Her skin burned; heat bloomed like a flower in the center of her chest. This was not a handshake; this was his thumb, sliding over her fingers, his two big hands wrapped around one of hers. "We're okay?" he asked.

She met his eye, her heart pounding wildly. "Nothing's changed."

His mouth curved downward, but his concentration didn't break.

Then she pretended she needed to dig lip balm out of her purse, and she let him go.

Eli sat on a swinging love seat in the glassed-in porch at his house. Lana was beside him. The night was warm, hazy, and quiet, and the air that came through the window screens was humid and fragrant. Porch lights twinkled in the water on the other side of the lake. Around them, moonflowers sighed open, the nubile, nocturnal cousins of morning glories. Night-blooming jasmine warmed to the dark sky, and flowering tobacco caught the errant moonlight and amplified it, turning that cold silver glow into a succulent luster.

Lana had put the moon garden together for him as a birthday present last year and she still maintained it. She'd carried pot after pot of beautiful plants to his back porch, turning it into a paradise. It had been the perfect gift for an astronomer and lover of the night skies. He came out here often, to watch the lake and to think—often about the woman who was sitting beside him now. The way her hair shimmered in the darkness, glowing as platinum as the night flowers around her, made him think she was very much like a flower herself. There was a kind of quiet strength to her. Beauty that was stronger than it looked.

Something had changed today. Not in the last hours that they'd spent talking and catching up like any two old friends. But at the school during that first raw collision, the closest thing to a fight they'd had in years. What he'd seen in her eyes had been nothing less than attraction. She'd hidden it well, for the most part, but he saw.

All this time he believed she'd shied away from him because she was appalled. He'd imagined that every time he bumped against her in a narrow hallway, and every time she cringed if he so much as brushed her hand, she was reminded of the unfortunate mistake she'd made with him that night in the field. He wasn't sure if she *consciously* knew what she'd done by shying away from him. He'd doubted that she purposefully tried to hide her true reactions. Instead, she'd used her feelings to her advantage—twisted them around in a way that would cause him to misinterpret her consistent and unchanging reactions. She'd been misleading him—and herself.

She *wanted* him. It made him want to shout to the rooftops, like a wrongfully accused prisoner cleared of misconduct at long last. And it made him want to say to her, *I know what you're hiding*—not say it by speaking the words, but by dragging his mouth behind her ear, by slipping a finger inside her lips, by pausing on the brink of taking her and daring her to say no.

The question was, What should he actually do with his newfound power? Part of him wanted to test it out, to see if she would let him go as far as he wanted to go, do what he wanted to do. That night in the field, they'd been so young. They'd rushed and fumbled and groped and sprinted to the finish. And now, when he was alone in the dark, Eli remembered that haste with a regret that bordered on mourning. They should have spent years getting to know to each other's bodies. That bliss they'd found in college should have been the low point, not the high.

He knew he should leave it alone, for her sake. She certainly had a lot on her mind. But he was desperate to know the truth of how she felt. Even if it was only a salve for his ego, and nothing more.

"What are you thinking?" he asked.

She looked at him and smiled. The breath she took was so deep her shoulders lifted and fell. He thought of running his fingers over her collarbones, their marble curves. And for once, he didn't banish the thought from his mind.

"I'm just thinking that I'm glad we're here. That it helps," she said.

He knew he shouldn't, but he let his gaze trail down the front of her sundress, over the gentle swell of her breasts, the firmness of her rib cage, and then the slight mound of her belly. She shifted and the white cotton of her sundress whispered against her skin.

"I don't understand it," she said. "But when I'm with you, it's like my head clears."

He had to look away. When he'd first started studying the sky, he naively put his eye up to a telescope and marveled for long minutes at the moon's stark landscape. It felt like his whole eye, his whole head, had been filled up by the bigness of the moon. And when at last he pulled away from the lens he realized that he couldn't see, that he'd gone momentarily blind in one eye because of all that huge and overwhelming light. That was how he felt now—she was more than he could stand.

"What is it that you want?" he asked. The harshness of his voice surprised him. And it must have caught her by surprise as well. She turned her head, and because of where they sat shoulder to shoulder, swinging gently on the love seat, her lips were suddenly, excruciatingly close to his. He couldn't help it; he turned toward her. "Lana. Tell me what you want. What you really want."

He saw the quickening rise and fall of her chest and felt the same intensity rising in him. He looked down, took her hand from her lap and curled it into his. And she let him. Amazingly, she let him. "Lana . . ." He wanted more. The desire he'd thought he'd seen in her eyes earlier was still there. He hadn't been mistaken. He pressed her fingers hard in his, his whole body tightening in anticipation. He felt they were so close to something. To stark truth. "You can say it. It's okay."

"Help," she said. "I want help."

"Tell me what to do."

"I need . . ." She drew her hand away. "I need you to help me find Ron."

The man's name splashed down on him like ice water. He stood, affronted, knowing full well that he had no reason to feel that way. How many times would he need to be rejected before he could bring himself to quit?

He drew in a deep breath. "But why?"

"Because he is this baby's father. Whether I like it or not. And he needs to know."

He shook his head. He didn't like any part of a plan

that had to do with Ron. The guy was a jerk. He was the kind of man who would push his way to the front row at a concert, then get too drunk to enjoy the music. He didn't deserve a woman like Lana, whose grace lay in the subtleties of her personality—the paradoxes and complexities that could not be understood by an occasional lover, but only by an intimate friend.

She went on. "I tried to find him myself, but I can't. I end up chasing down leads that are dead ends when I search online. I can't find any mountain bikers named Ron in Colorado—I think that's where he's from. And I'm too embarrassed to ask anyone in town if they've seen him. I mean, a couple more weeks, and everyone's going to know what I got myself into . . ."

"You don't have to tell him. He doesn't need to know."

"No?"

"He could go the rest of his life not knowing or caring. Whatever happens, you would be totally in control."

She mulled it over; he could see her worrying the corner of her bottom lip. When she stopped there was a shell-pink shine on her mouth that nearly killed him.

"Morally, I do have to tell him. I mean, imagine if it was you."

"Lana, if that was my child you were carrying—" He had to stop himself. If she was having his baby, this would be a lot different. There would be no question of a wedding. No question that they would keep the child. And as for Eli, he would spend the rest of his life making absolutely sure she saw how much they belonged together—even after her doubt was gone.

But that was an alternate universe. A fantasy. Lana might be attracted to him, but she didn't want a relationship with him. Never had, never would. She had dictated that they would only ever be friends—attraction or not. Every time she'd introduced him to a new boyfriend she'd made that clear. And even now, when he thought he saw a spark of attraction in her eyes, she'd asked him to help her find another man.

She sat up a little straighter, her blue eyes turned silver in the moonlight. "What did you say?"

"Don't you think that if Ron wanted anything to do with you, he would have been back by now?"

She slumped back hard against her chair. "You must think I'm an idiot."

He sat down on the bench beside her but did not put a hand on her shoulder, did not touch her back. He wished more than ever that he could undo everything that had happened between them—everything that had come before—and start over, so that he could be the kind of man who was allowed to touch her. With his hands, with his lips. And she would be the kind of woman who wouldn't reject him when he did.

He tried to comfort her. "You just had bad luck."

"This is more than bad luck. This is Bad Decision Making 101. A whole lifetime of it."

Part of him didn't disagree.

She stood up. "And look at this." She smoothed her sundress down over her belly, a pronounced bump at the level of his eye. "Can you see it?"

"Yes. But I know your body better than most." He wasn't sure, but he thought she might have blushed, just the faintest tinge of pink on a pale flower. "What is it about Ron that you like so much? Why *him*?"

She was quiet a moment. "Do you know what he said to me once? He wanted to know how I could say I loved wildflowers, when Karin and I try so hard to control them and make them . . . less than wild."

Eli was quiet. He hadn't thought Ron capable of such thoughts. He'd obviously been wrong. "So you have a connection with him. Is that what you're saying?"

"I don't really know him." She let the dress go. "But he deserves to know about the baby. Even if I don't think he'll like to see me pregnant."

"He's a fool." He watched her closely, wishing that just for once he could really know what she was thinking. He loved her, but she . . . she was only attracted to him and nothing more. The man she wanted was the man who didn't know her and didn't deserve her. The man she wanted was Ron.

Lana seemed to sense that he was staring; he could tell from the way she didn't turn her head toward him when she spoke. "Will you help me or not?"

"I don't like this."

"But I need to do the right thing. And I have no one to turn to but you."

Eli sighed. This was the last straw; he knew it. He could not go on like this. She was killing him. His heart couldn't stand to see Ron claim the future that he wanted for his own. This was it. They were coming to the end.

He wouldn't be able to live with himself if she asked for his help and he turned her down. But he could make himself a promise: Once she and Ron were well on their way toward happily ever after, he wasn't going to stick around to see it. He couldn't stand to be humiliated one more time. "Yes. I'll help you," he said, his voice flat.

"Thank you," she said, looking down at him from where she stood. Her voice was kind, as if *he* were the one who needed consoling. Privately, in the silence of his mind, he was already making plans.

August

Toadflax: A common and easily recognized wildflower, toadflax has been tagged with at least thirty folk names, including: butter-and-eggs, brideweed, larkspur, pedlar's basket, gallwort, impudent lawyer, Jacob's ladder, wild flax, devil's-flax, devil's flower, patten and clogs, churnstaff, and more. Call it what you will, toadflax by any other name is toadflax.

August 5

Eli leaned back in his chair on the deck of the old steamship, waiting for Kelly to get out of work. The evening wind blew cool through his hair, and the trees beyond the deck were bending and swaying, flashing the silvery undersides of their leaves. There was a thunderstorm, somewhere. He couldn't see it or hear it yet, but he could feel it—the slight, barely perceptible electricity in the air.

"Whew!" Kelly dropped down into the deck chair next to him. "I thought that birthday party would never end. I mean, the kids always get rowdy, but *those* kids . . . monsters!"

Eli didn't smile. He looked out over the portside railing toward the old lighthouse, sitting like a tired sailor on a cluster of massive, jagged rocks. If he closed his eyes, he could almost believe they were sailing on the water of the open lake. But they weren't.

The steamship *Ticonderoga* sat not in water, but on a grassy, waterless basin at the Shelburne Museum. It had been dragged there from Lake Champlain at the behest of an eccentric heiress who had collected old structures like other women collected dolls. The lighthouse beside the ship was a charming and whimsical companion to the decades-old steamer, making the hillside feel strangely like the waters of Lake Champlain.

He didn't turn his head until Kelly pinched the skin on his arm. "Do you want to help me clean up? Or just wait around?"

He looked at the sky, at the ominous dark haze slipping in on the horizon. "I came here to talk."

She smiled. "Can we talk while I'm working?"

"Sure," he said. "Why not?"

They walked inside, where wood paneling, low white ceilings, and green carpets spoke of a different time—talkies and jazz and handwritten letters back home. Kelly began picking up cake-coated paper plates and throwing them into a large black garbage bag. They were the only two people in the room. There was no reason to put off the inevitable for a moment longer.

"Lana told me you went to see her," Eli said. She moved smoothly, picking up plates and cups, pushing in chairs. He went on. "She told me everything. That you didn't want her to lift a bag."

Kelly reached for a ball of wrapping paper. "I didn't want her to get hurt."

"I told you no one knew about Lana's pregnancy."

She stuffed the garbage bag with a forceful jab. "I didn't realize it was such a big deal."

"That's it?"

"It's not like I told her anything she didn't already know."

"But you did." He put his hands flat on the table and leaned toward her. "You told her that I trusted you with her secret."

She dropped the garbage bag on a chair. "What's going on here?"

"I was hoping you'd tell me."

"If you didn't want me to know that she's pregnant, you shouldn't have told me."

"I told you because I thought you could keep a secret."

"And I *did* keep it. Why are you so touchy about this? Lana should expect that we're going to tell each other things. It's not my fault she's uncomfortable with that."

Eli crossed his arms. This wasn't what he'd expected. He'd thought Kelly would have been ashamed or at least contrite. But she wasn't. And it was a huge turnoff. He'd thought that if he just kept trying to feel something for her, then eventually he *would* feel it. Now he knew that wasn't so.

"Eli?"

He looked at Kelly, her brown eyes and small nose. She was waiting for him to say something, as if she knew what would come next. Maybe he could have made it work with Kelly if he hadn't seen the flash of desire that flickered—just for a second—in Lana's eyes. But no man could have the kind of thoughts he was having and keep up the pretense of dating someone else.

"This isn't going to work," he said as gently as he could. "I'm not going to say sorry or that I wished things had turned out differently. I think this was bound to happen at some point. I'm just going to go."

"Eli . . ."

He turned on his heel and headed to the exit. Outside, the thunder was rumbling loudly, lightning coming from all directions at once. The leaves were shaking insanely on their branches and the wind gusted hard and fast. He walked toward the foredeck, where a gangway led down to the grassy hillside that surrounded the great, beautiful ship.

"Wait! Eli! Please, just *wait*!" Kelly called out behind him. She ran halfway down the gangway to grab him by the arm. The wind pushed her clothes against her skin.

"What do you want?"

"You're right," she said, raising her voice to compete with the sound of the thunder. "I'm sorry. I admit it. I wanted . . . I wanted Lana to know that you told me. There it is."

Eli ignored the first few drops of rain that flecked his glasses. "We should stop seeing each other."

She grabbed his wrist. "But why? I thought we were having fun! Why don't you want to get serious with me?"

A thousand reasons, he thought.

"Is this because of Lana?"

The thunder rumbled. He said nothing.

"Do you think she wants you? I mean, really? Her best friend?"

Eli frowned.

"I know what you're thinking," Kelly said, a touch of desperation in her voice. "One minute you wonder if maybe she could be attracted to you, and the next she's off with some other man. I'm warning you, Eli. You'll embarrass yourself if you go after her. You need someone more steady than her. Someone who isn't going to flake out."

Eli kept his face blank. She was right. Lana broke hearts. She'd broken his. He couldn't bear to go through that again.

"Don't break up with me just yet," Kelly begged. "Let's just . . . let's not do anything until I come back from vacation. Things could look very different in a week."

The rain began to fall so hard that he had to shout to be heard. He felt it flattening his hair and soaking his clothes. He suddenly understood how little he knew her—that her reasons for wanting to keep him may or may not have had anything to do with him at all. "I'm sorry. This has already gone on too long."

Thunder boomed. He walked down the gangway toward the grass.

Maybe it was the romance of the old steamship, maybe it was the excitement of the storm, but for a split second, Eli had a vision of watching himself from another angle—and it was as if the old ship wasn't a landlocked, impractical relic of some other time, but a bustling, working vessel of ages past, just come into port on a rainy day.

How long had he been lying to himself? It was amazing what the mind was capable of believing sometimes.

August 6

Karin sat in her parked minivan for a moment to collect herself and quiet her nerves.

For the last ten minutes, she'd watched the Vermont landscape passing beyond the windows of her car. She saw its pastures full of classic Holsteins, its small houses worn down by hard winters, its sprinklings of cheerful yellow trefoil and pink crown vetch crowding in at the roadsides. Her mother had made her life here, her mother's people had made a life here, and now Karin was forging her way, preparing to raise a family of her own. That was why she'd snuck off to the police station today—to protect what was hers.

She opened the door of her minivan and headed inside.

The front office was small but quiet. She told a woman with dark, gel-flattened hair that she was here to speak with Officer Gervais. The woman picked up a phone, dialed an extension, and a few moments later Andy was shaking her hand. His smile was wide and genuine.

"Karin, what a surprise. Everything okay?"

"I was hoping I could talk to you for a minute. Privately, if you have time."

Andy glanced back toward the receptionist—a look Karin couldn't quite read—then crossed his arms and frowned. "Let's take a walk."

He held the door, and Karin adjusted her purse on her shoulder as she stepped outside. She'd known Andy for years. He was older, with a graying military-style buzz cut and a heavyset face. She'd chatted with him and his wife countless times at countless church functions. But she'd never had much interaction with him outside coffee hour, and she'd never spoken to him alone.

They sat together on a bench in front of the station. The traffic rumbled past and a collection of cigarette butts littered the ground. They made small talk for a moment before the conversation changed.

"So what can I do you for?" Andy asked.

"I need advice."

"Well, usually the wife's in the advice department. But as long as you don't mind second rate, I'll do what I can."

"Do you mind if we keep this between us?"

"Does it involve a bank robbery?"

"I didn't rob a bank," she said, laughing. She set her purse down at her side. She wasn't sure how to approach the situation, how best to get what she wanted. It had taken some time to come up with this plan, and then it had taken a little bit more time to find the courage to go through with it. She picked at the cuticles of her fingernails. "My father's come back to town."

He reacted: the slightest downturn at the corner of his mouth. "Sure. I remember Calvert. How could I forget? Used to terrorize the girls who worked over at Penny's."

"Well, he's back."

"How long's he been here?"

"Just a couple weeks."

"Hmm. He hasn't caused any real problems yet."

"*Yet* is the key word." Karin felt a flutter of excitement in her chest. Just a few more well-placed hints should inspire Andy to come up with the right idea. "You know where he's staying?"

"Should I?"

"The Madison."

Andy twisted his torso toward her. He put his hand on the back of the bench, so his arm was almost around her. She didn't like it, but she couldn't move without being rude.

"He wouldn't hurt you, would he? He hasn't threatened you?"

Karin let her eyelids lower—her best impression of a damsel-in-distress. "No. But he wasn't in town more than two minutes before they had him here at the station."

"I hadn't heard that."

"And I'm worried about Lana," Karin went on. "She's always been fragile, you understand. But having Calvert around is too much for her. She's been acting so weird. I don't know what to do."

Andy put his hand on her knee. She told herself he meant to be comforting. "Listen, if you think Cal's going to cause trouble, I believe you. But I can't just go and boot him out of town, if that's what you're asking."

"Of course not! I would never ask you to do that!"

Andy stared at his own hand on her knee. She felt her neck flush with discomfort, but she didn't move. "What I can do," he went on, "is keep an eye on him—"

"That would be great—"

"Let me finish. What I can do is keep an eye on him in a very visible way, if you know what I'm saying. I can have one of my guys hang around the Madison, maybe even make some inquiries with Mr. Delucca about his new tenant. You and I both know he doesn't want any attention from the police. I'll bet my Glock that Calvert will be outta there the moment his next rent check is due."

Karin repressed a smile. "Do you think it would work?"

"Might. But in the meantime . . ." He inched closer. "If there's anything else I can do for you, if you need someone to talk to or you just want to get out of the house, you know where to find me."

Karin gathered her purse. Was Andy making a move on her? It didn't seem possible. She couldn't remember the last time she'd been hit on. She detangled herself from Andy's arm and stood up.

"Thanks so much, Andy. You're a really great friend. And your wife's a lucky woman."

He stood. She hadn't realized how tall he was. She felt a slight tingling at the base of her neck, as if she was doing something wrong.

"It's been a long time since my wife thought she was lucky," he said, a tinge of sadness in his voice. "In any case, I'm just glad to help."

Her heart softened toward him. When she looked into his eyes, she saw a loneliness there that surprised her, a loneliness that she recognized in herself.

"Keep me posted," she said. "I mean, stay in touch."

"You bet," he said. "Karin."

August 8

Eli sat with his friend Moe at the café of the lakeside aquarium. Fries, hot dogs, and soft drinks in paper cups were arranged on plastic brown trays before them. Children ran circles around tables, their squeals bouncing off the high ceilings.

"Here's something." Moe leaned over his laptop and refreshed the slowly loading page. "A list of the races he's competed in."

"Not exactly Lance Armstrong," Eli said.

Moe was a ticket sales assistant at the museum, but his résumé was diverse. Like Eli, he was a meteorite hunter and he made regular trips to the Mojave Desert, where meteorites could be seen somewhat easily against the cracked earth of a dried-up lake. Over the years he'd had a number of jobs to fund his amateur expeditions—auto mechanic, aquatics store assistant manager, junkyard night watchman, summertime security guard at a ski slope, and, at one point, he was an assistant private eye.

"How did you find him?" Eli asked.

Moe gave a self-deprecating smile. "Well, the hardest part was figuring out his last name. But I used what we know about him—the bike racing stuff—to figure it out. The trouble was, I had all kinds of false starts because there was no professional racer named Ron that I saw who lived out west."

"What do you mean?"

"Maybe this guy still thinks he's a mountain biker, but he hasn't raced seriously in years. See that? His competitions just drop off. Did he get hurt or something?"

"Not that I know of. Can we find out where he's living now?"

"Already done, my friend. I called in a favor from the old agency I used to work for in Reno. The owner owed me one."

"What'd you get?"

Moe pulled up a program, typed in an address, and Eli watched as the screen showed an image of a globe as if from a satellite. The view zoomed in on America, then Vermont, then, when Eli thought it couldn't possibly get any more precise, it zoomed in on a small house with a large yard and a long driveway.

"Voilà!" With a magician's exuberance, Moe turned the laptop to fully face Eli. "Our quarry's house."

Eli frowned. "In Vermont?"

"Near Rutland."

"You've got to be kidding me."

Moe handed him an envelope, no doubt filled with Ron's basic information. "The house belongs to Jean-René Ashley, Ron's brother. They're from Canada."

Heat crept up Eli's neck. "He lives with his brother?"

"They run an Internet bike supply store out of the house."

Eli leaned back in his seat and forced himself to breathe out.

"Are you okay, man? You look like you're going to kill someone."

"I'm fine."

"Who is this guy, anyway?"

Eli stood. "Someone who's got big problems. What do I owe you?"

"I'm thinking of getting a crew together next year, do a little digging in Greenland."

"I'm in," Eli said. "Thanks again."

"Just be careful."

"*I'm* not the one who should be careful," he said. Then he pushed through the glass doors of the museum into the blazing sun.

• • •

Lana took a deep breath, as deep as her lungs could hold. The store was momentarily empty—the tourists having gone off to their various destinations for lunch or afternoon naps—and Karin was standing beside her, leaning over the drafting board that she used to help customers plan their gardens. Her hair fell around her face in short red-brown waves and her posture spoke of deep concentration. Of the two of them, Karin had always been the more gifted at design, and she could turn the unruliest acres into careful works of art.

Lana put a hand to her belly and let her breath go. Six weeks had passed since she'd confirmed she was pregnant. Six weeks, and she couldn't bear one more moment of secrecy. This wasn't going to be easy, but she had to tell Karin what had happened. It would hurt them both, but it had to be done.

"It looks like we've finally got a second of peace," Lana said lightly, looking around the empty store.

"Good. I've been meaning to talk to you," Karin said.

"Oh?" Lana was taken aback; Karin had spoken her line.

"I did something for us, for both of us. I got in touch with a friend—a cop—who's going to help me get Calvert out of town."

Lana didn't speak for a moment, taking the information in. Thinking about Calvert required her brain to switch gears since he was the last thing on her mind. "You don't just want to ignore him?"

"This is better," Karin said. "Do you think it was wrong?"

"No," Lana said. "I mean, if you think that's what we need to do . . ."

Karin nodded and Lana saw there were tears in her eyes. "Oh, good. I've been so, so stressed out, I can't tell if I'm going crazy or not. I mean, Calvert is stressing me out. And Gene isn't acting like himself. And we're barely even trying to have a baby anymore . . . I just wasn't sure if I was doing the right thing. I'm at the end of my rope, you know? I don't think I can take any more."

Lana sighed and put her hands on her hips, feeling the way her body had changed. Her secret was no longer on the tip of her tongue; it was choking her. And it would have to keep choking her for another day. "No, I don't think I could either."

Karin looked up. "But don't worry. I've got the Calvert situation under control. Just you wait. He'll be out of our hair in no time and then everything will be okay."

"I hope so," Lana said.

Karin's smile was full of reassurance. Then she leaned down over her designs of cardinal flowers and lupine, trying to bring some order to her world with her work.

Ron's house was a shabby, white-sided ranch set atop a steep hill. The porch was held up by visible cinder blocks and the aluminum awning over the side window sagged in the middle. A rusted, dull blue muscle car sat with its top down in the driveway, as if someone was making a halfhearted attempt at restoring it. From the looks of the round splotches of yellow grass in the lawn, at least one resident of the house was a dog.

A red pickup drove past, sending white dust into the air, and Eli gripped the wheel. He'd never been the confrontational type. The first and only fight he'd ever had ended with one of the playground supervisors ushering him off to the nurse's office with a bloody nose and tear-streaked face. After that, he'd learned to hold on to a measure of his dignity by either agreeing with or ignoring bullies.

But now he was furious. And even though he suspected that he had much less experience with fighting than Ron, he was prepared to take action if it came to that. The difference between those fights in middle school and the rage that roiled in him now was that in school, the arguing had been about him. But this was about Lana, a cause worth fighting for.

The driveway leading to Ron's house was steep, and Eli took it on long strides that made his jeans tighten against his thighs. To keep from losing courage, he focused on the most infuriating things he could think of: Ron touching Lana's hair, lying next to her. He bruised his knuckles banging on the front door. He knew he could have just told Lana where Ron was living. But he wanted to see the guy for himself.

"Yeah?" Ron was wearing a white tank top and blue nylon shorts. The top half of his hair was pulled back in some kind of elastic or clip. "Can I help you?"

The guy had no idea who Eli was. "Ron. We've met."

Recognition came over Ron's face, but he wasn't entirely friendly. "The meteorite dude. Right. What can I do for you?"

A movement in the room behind Ron caught Eli's attention, and a woman's voice followed. "Ron?"

"Be right there, babe." Ron stepped into the yard and pulled the door closed behind him. He took a long drag on his cigarette and flicked the ashes into a silver, dirt-speckled pail by the door.

Eli crossed his arms. "We've got a little problem."

"What's that?"

"It's time you paid Lana a visit."

Ron laughed. "Excuse me?"

"You heard me."

"Yes, I heard you. But you're going to have to get me up to speed here, man. Lana and I have been over for a while now."

"That's just it," Eli said between clenched teeth. "It's not over."

Ron shifted on his feet. "I'm not an idiot. It was over with us even before it started. I'd think you'd know that."

Eli scowled. "What are you talking about?"

Ron laughed. "Nothing. You know what? Nothing. Look, I'm just going to go back inside and forget I saw you. Good luck, man."

Ron started to go back inside, but Eli grabbed his arm, hard. "Tell whoever is in there that you're leaving, because you're coming with me. Now."

Ron frowned. "I don't want any part of your negative cncrgy."

"Cut the crap," Eli spat.

Ron's nostrils flared. "Listen, my thing with Lana ran its course. It's over. She's all yours. I know damn well that you and Lana have some kind of tangled-up karma. And I don't want any part of it."

"You have to talk to her."

"What's your deal, anyway? You like her so much, want to be her little lapdog? Why don't you date her?

She'd probably let you, if you had even half a testicle in your whole body."

Eli's fists went tight. "I'm telling you, you're coming with me."

Ron stepped close, got in Eli's face. Eli stuck out his chin.

"I'm not going anywhere," Ron said.

Eli glared, frustration boiling over. He wanted to do something mean. He picked up the garbage can full of cigarette butts, and then walked to Ron's rusted blue convertible.

"What are you—"

A mix of rainwater and nasty cigarette butts ran down the seats, ash soaking into the yellow foam where the seat covers were torn. Eli threw the bucket into the woods and dusted off his hands. It didn't come close to the trouble Ron had caused, but it was something. He felt better already.

Ron threw his cigarette. "You're a *dead man*!"

Eli ducked under the first blow. He went for an uppercut but missed, and Ron's fist slammed into his stomach—once, twice. He couldn't breathe. His head swam and he put his hands on his knees, doubled in pain. The ground before him wobbled as he tried to breathe.

Come on, he told himself. *Come on.*

Ron laughed. And when Eli looked up, he was walking away. Laughing and walking away.

Eli ran with a speed he hadn't known he possessed. He meant to push him into the wall of the house, to grab his hair and slam his forehead into the white wooden siding like he'd seen in so many movies. But Ron moved at the last moment, threw Eli off-balance, and the next thing he knew, the wide blue sky filled his vision, the dark shape of Ron's head blocking the sun.

"Did you come here with a death wish, you little shit?" Ron yelled. "I don't know what your angle is, but you went after the wrong guy."

In a millionth of a second, a hundred scenes flashed before Eli's eyes—each of some old humiliation or failure. His teacher pointing at him in front of the whole class and telling everyone he had to cheat because he wasn't smart enough to pass on his own. Lana practically laughing in his face after they'd made love. Lana knocked up with some other man's baby. And now—Ron kicked his rib cage, knocking the breath out of him—and now this.

Rock fucking bottom.

"Get up." Ron bent over him. "Get the f—"

"Ron!" A woman's voice came from the direction of the house. "Do you want me to call the cops?"

Ron grabbed Eli's collar and pulled until Eli's shoulders came off the grass. "Pick yourself up and get out of here."

Eli said nothing. Ron let go.

Slowly Eli got to his feet. "This isn't over."

"Oh, I think it is," Ron said.

Eli stared at him hard for a moment before he limped toward his car. In the driver's seat, he glanced at his face in the mirror and saw that he'd avoided a busted lip or black eye. But pain exploded when he breathed, maybe a cracked rib. He put his face down on the steering wheel and squeezed his eyelids closed.

He took the deepest breath he could, and when it hurt so bad that it made him dizzy, he began to laugh. Just a chuckle at first. Then an out-of-control hooting and cackling that verged on hysterical. He threw his head back against the seat and brayed. It hurt, but he couldn't stop. Trying to hold it in made it hurt worse. His eyes teared up. He beat his hand on the steering wheel, only to discover his hand hurt too. That made him laugh more.

He thought: *Nowhere to go but up.*

He put the car in drive and kicked up as much dust as possible as he drove away.

Lana was alone in the store, sitting on the old stool beside the counter and flipping through the pages of a childbirth book that Charlotte had given her. She knew she should scour the pages, sow each point of information like seeds into her brain. And yet she could do little more than glance at the pictures and skim the words. The language of pregnancy simmered and bubbled around in her head like a Latin Mass: anovulation, corpus luteum, endometrium, lunaception, oocyte, ovum, os, *amen.*

She didn't want to be a parent—she planned to start doing preliminary research on adoption very soon—but for now, the first order of business was to deal with the actual facts of pregnancy and childbirth. Her body was demanding more and more of her attention every day, and she had little choice but to give it.

She looked at a line drawing of a fully dilated cervix. It seemed so impossible it was almost funny: an inconceivable conception. Not just labor, but what came after too.

Eventually it was time to close, and so she spent a half hour counting the register, running reports, and cleaning. She was just about to close the Barn door behind her when she realized she'd left her book out on the counter. She tucked it away and didn't miss the irony: She was now hiding her baby book where her Costa Rica brochures used to be.

Outside, the sun was setting. She paused a moment on the concrete slab in front of the Barn's side door. The trees and power lines were stark silhouettes against a pale sky. And there, at the top of the hill on the far side of the parking lot, was a dark figure, the hard-edged shadow of a man.

She was just pulling in a breath, ready to yell, "We're closed," when, to her surprise, she saw the man's arm lift, thin as a bare tree branch, and he gave her a little half-hearted wave.

Calvert.

What was he doing? She didn't move. And after a moment she saw his hand fall dejectedly before he turned around and left. Lana gripped her bag closer to her side.

He'd been watching her. Waiting for her to get off work. And yet, instead of approaching her, he'd turned tail and ran. She shook her head and fumbled in her purse for her keys, eager to get inside her car and lock the door.

Eli and Moe lounged in beach chairs on Moe's boat dock, tucked away in a cattail-spotted cove far south of the city. Eli was sloshy drunk, no more stable than the water under the boards beneath them. Of the twelve bottles of Long Trail that they'd started with, Eli had drunk six; Moe, one.

"And you know what else?" Eli said. "The guy had some other woman with him! Prob'ly seeing her the whole time."

"Trash," Moe said, shaking his head. "Total trash."

Eli stood up from his lawn chair and wobbled on his feet.

"Easy, man." Moe laughed.

"I should have been quicker, you know. Got in at least one good punch. Broken his nose."

"Tough break."

Eli shook his head, and the whole world teetered. He leaned down and clasped both of Moe's shoulders. "No, Moe. No. Don't you get it? It was the best thing that could have happened."

"I don't follow."

He stood and looked out over the water. A fish broke the dark surface and made a splash. How could he say what he was feeling? Ever since the day Lana had first rejected him, he'd been acting like a complete coward. He'd decided he would follow her lead, would be satisfied with what she wanted and put his own desires out of his mind. Better than having his heart broken again. Better than being humiliated.

But now—all bets were off. He'd taken a good look at himself, at his worst and most pathetic self, and he saw what he was capable of, all the pain that he could make himself withstand. He'd glimpsed a strength within himself that he hadn't known he had. He knew now that he'd gone to Ron's not to help Lana, but to pick a fight. It had been selfish and inappropriate—he would need to apologize to Lana—but emotionally, it was exactly what he'd needed to do. All these years he'd been so afraid of *not* getting what he deserved that he didn't even *try* to get it. He just wished it hadn't taken getting his ass kicked to find out.

He held his beer bottle up in a toast. "I love her. Did you know that?"

"Well, we all always wondered . . ."

"I *want* her, Moe. I want her in all kinds of different ways. I've been pussyfooting around worrying about whether Lana is comfortable, how Lana feels, doing what Lana wants. But it's time for Eli to get what he wants."

"Talking about yourself in third person is not a good sign."

"Did you hear me?" Eli held on to the back of his chair, desperately trying to make Moe understand. "I'm going after her. Even if I end up losing her, I owe it to myself to try. When I was on the ground getting the shit kicked out of me, I thought, *Dude, it's worth it. She's worth it. Whatever it takes.*"

Moe saluted him with his beer. "Well, then, it's about time."

Eli looked into the mouth of his bottle. "Problem is, even if I can get her into bed, I don't know if I can get her to stay there."

"What do you mean?"

"She might flake out again. She probably will."

Moe reached down to set his bottle on the boards. "But you just said it yourself. You've spent too much time worrying about what she wants and not enough time worrying about what you want. Time's up, man. It's now or never. You got to jump headfirst."

"Yes! I've just got to jump—" Eli stepped closer to the edge of the dock and somehow his chair ended up in the water, sinking slowly down.

"Whoa there. No jumping anywhere right now."

"Right. Sorry."

"Never did like that chair."

Eli watched a few bubbles rise up as the chair disappeared under the surface. He was a different man now than he'd been this morning. And yet nothing had changed. Just his own understanding of himself.

Even in his drunken muddle, it was all very clear.

August 10

On Monday morning, the store was quiet. A soft rain was falling, soaking students on their way to summer classes, old men waiting at bus stops, and the die-hard runners who sprinted daily along the shores of Lake Champlain. Lana sat alone at the counter of the Wildflower Barn, listening to the rain dance and tap on the roof. Water from a gutter outside fell and splashed thickly on the concrete before washing down into the sewers. It was going to be a slow morning.

She looked up at the sound of tires on the gravel parking lot and saw Eli's beat-up VW pulling in. She stood, pulling her dress down to cover the bump of her belly. She was grateful it was summer because she'd grown out of every pair of her pants. Her pregnancy had hit the fifteen-week mark, and this morning was the first time in quite a while that she didn't have the urge to throw up. Her body had become accustomed to being pregnant, even if her brain had not.

She watched through the window as he got out of his car, aware of a niggling nervousness in the back of her mind. The last time she'd talked to him, he'd accused her of jealousy, of ruining his sex life. He'd stripped away all the rules that had kept those dangerous subjects at bay. What she'd seen on his face that day had been nothing shy of full-on, unquenchable, plain-as-day lust. And she worried: Had it been a fluke attraction? A lapse in judgment? Or something more?

She took a deep breath to quiet her nerves. She had to admit that lately she'd been feeling that same fire, that heat. But so what if she felt a passing attraction toward him? It was nothing she couldn't handle. And it would pass—as all attraction eventually passed. For all she knew, Eli might walk into the store and things would go right back to normal. There was no reason to be worried. She and Eli were solid. To stay solid, she just had to set boundaries—that was all.

Confident, she rose and walked toward the door as he pushed through it. He wore black flip-flops and khaki shorts. His T-shirt was flecked with rain, pinpricks of navy on pale blue. His eyeglasses were speckled too, and he looked at her through the lenses, focused happily on her face.

"You look beautiful," he said.

Lana laughed, surprised but flattered. Since when did Eli notice she was beautiful? Her hair was in its customary ponytail, and a few strands had fallen out around her face and on the back of her neck. She was sure she didn't look beautiful. But she loved his compliment just the same. "How are you?"

"Never been better," he said, and even though they were nearly the same height, Lana had the sudden, inexplicable sense that Eli had become *bigger* somehow. Even if his physical size was the same, his presence was larger. How was it possible that he'd become so disconcertingly sexy? Especially since nothing visible about him had changed?

She waited for him to say something. But he only looked at her, smiling with a slight dreaminess, as if he'd just come in from the rainstorm because he'd stepped off a cloud.

All of a sudden the melancholy she'd been struggling with all morning turned into a bright and warm tenderness that spread in her chest like sunshine. Here was Eli, *her* Eli. There was no reason to be afraid that he would try to change things. She trusted him. They were merely having an "off" moment in their relationship. If she were a different woman, she might have rested her head on his shoulder, just to lean on him, to feel his beating heart.

She teased him. "You're all wet."

He chuckled, a low rumble like thunder.

Carefully, so she didn't touch his skin, she reached up and slid his glasses from his nose. His eyes were a warm brown. If he was surprised by the action, he didn't show it. He simply stood still, watching her, not breaking eye contact. She suddenly felt sheepish to be holding his glasses. "I'll dry these for you," she said.

She turned away from him quickly, glad he couldn't see her face as she wiped his lenses with a soft tissue. She handed him back his glasses once they were dry.

"Thanks," he said. "How you feeling?"

"Not bad. At least, physically."

"And *other* than physically?"

"I'm okay."

They walked to the counter. Shaky, Lana went around behind it to sit on a stool, and Eli leaned a hip on the

Formica. She was glad for the solid three feet of counter-top between them.

"I have to tell Karin," Lana admitted.

"Yes. Soon."

She blushed; it was obvious to both of them that her body was changing. But she was still comparatively small, and unless a person knew to look for the swelling of her belly, it was not readily apparent under her endless supply of billowy sundresses. Still, Karin needed to know.

"I . . . uh . . . I found Ron," Eli said.

She swallowed hard. She hadn't expected this so soon. She thought she'd have more time before she had to face him. "And?"

"I don't think he'll be coming to see you. I'm sorry. I tried."

She looked at him for a long moment, knowing she was missing something but unable to figure out what. "What do you mean, you tried?"

"I went to see him. To bring him to you."

"You did what?"

"I'm sorry. It was wrong."

She shook her head. "That doesn't seem like you."

"It's not."

"Oh, Eli." She sighed. Eli's brow was furrowed in the middle and his gold-brown eyes hid nothing. He was upset. She couldn't read him anymore quite like she used to, but she had the feeling that he was working through something big, something that may or may not have to do with her. She just wanted things to feel normal again, so when he looked into her eyes, she wouldn't feel so swallowed up by him. "I know you were just trying to help. Did you tell him about the . . . you know." She gestured toward her belly.

"No. It wasn't my place."

"That's okay. I didn't think he'd want to talk to me anyway. I'll go see him myself, one of these days."

"I'll go with you."

"Maybe." She changed the subject. "But in the meantime, how's Kelly?"

"Don't know. Haven't seen her." An unreadable look passed over his face, and her heartbeat spiked.

"Is . . . Is everything okay?"

"We broke up. It's more than okay."

She blinked, taken aback by his quick confession. Her stomach fluttered with surprise—her mind racing with possible reasons for their split. She paused when she landed on one she liked. "I can probably guess why."

"Why?"

"Because of what she did. I mean, when she came here to talk to me about the baby. That really wasn't very nice."

"Maybe," he said.

She cleared her throat. "If it's not that, then . . . what is it? It's not because of me?"

He was quiet.

"Right?" she insisted. "It's not because I got in your way again? Is it?"

"No," he said. "It's not that."

She clasped her fingers, twisting them hard. She wondered if he knew how difficult this was for her, pretending it didn't affect her that he and Kelly had broken up. It shouldn't matter to her whether or not Eli was single.

She hoped that if she kept telling herself it didn't matter, it would start to feel true.

"Let's not talk about this," he said. "Kelly is old news. Out with the old. What are you doing this weekend?"

She hedged, taken aback by his abruptness yet again. When had talking to Eli become so stilted and strange? "I . . . I might be busy."

"With what?"

She laughed to hide her nervousness. "I have to check my calendar."

He came around to the same side of the counter that she was on, as if he needed to get closer to get a better view. His nearness made her oddly uneasy. She edged away.

"What are you thinking about?" he asked.

"The pregnancy," she said quickly, though at the moment the only thing bothering her was the warmth rising from his skin, the curve of his bottom lip, and how much she wanted to run her fingers through his rain-damp hair.

"Is that *all* you're thinking about right now?"

"What else would I be thinking of?"

"You tell me."

She couldn't stand it. His gaze was so confident, so *knowing*, she feared he was looking right into her soul—like he could see the way his closeness affected her in the deepest part of her core. She needed a cold, hard dose of reality to cool her too-warm skin. "I don't want to be a parent," she blurted.

"No?"

"Do you think I'm lying?"

His gaze didn't waver, but it became gentler, inquisitive. "You've always said you didn't want a family. But then when little kids come into the store you're the first person to show them the toy section. And I've never seen you turn down an offer to hold a newborn."

"I like kids," Lana said. "But that's different than wanting to be a mom."

"Are you sure? Is it that you don't *want* to be a parent? Or you don't think you're capable of it?"

"Don't think I'm capable . . . ?" she repeated the words, trying them out. She hadn't considered the link between wanting a family and believing herself capable of having one. Eli was suggesting that she'd gone out of her way to eradicate her own desire to have a family. By clinging to the idea that she wasn't fit for motherhood, she'd shirked the question of whether she *wanted* to be a mother or not. Maybe she'd pinched off some of her emotions so she could hold fast to others—the part of herself that wanted to travel the world.

She felt him move closer, and then she saw the tips of his flip-flops were inches from the stool where she sat. He reached for her hand and pulled her to her feet. "Lana . . ."

She looked up, her gaze colliding with the fathomless warm brown of his irises. He didn't say a word, but slowly, deliberately stepped closer, swallowed what distance was between them. A flame twinkled deep in her body. "What are you . . . ?"

"Shh," he said. Then he wrapped his arms around her, gathering her to the firm press of his chest. She giggled a little, nervous. His hands ran slowly up the length of her back. Her breasts were flush against him, the fabric of her shirt drawn tight across her nipples. She didn't wear a bra, and she prayed that the cotton of their shirts would be enough to keep him from feeling her instant reaction.

"Thanks," she said, and she patted his back a little to imply that the hug was done.

But he only pressed tighter, and she felt the deep inhale of his breath, the brush of cool air being swept across her skin. His fingers found the strip of naked skin above her collar, his thumb running over the bump where her back met her neck, filling her with heat and longing. She gripped his belt loop, willing her hands to stay still, to not tug his shirt and seek the smoothness of his bare back. His whole hand was in her hair, pulling enough to pinch, and it set off a warning inside her, a hot red flare. She should end this now. This was not an embrace of friendship. The desire she'd seen in Eli's eyes hadn't been a fluke after all. Their whole bodies were lined up, shoulders to shoulders, belly to belly, hips to hips.

She pulled back, but he didn't let her move away completely. He was staring at her intensely, his two hands firmly on her waist. His eyes, normally so open and friendly, were guarded and dark. She'd never felt more conscious of her lower lip in her entire life.

Finally he let her go. His hands fell reluctantly to his sides. She missed him already, her skin crying out for that closeness again. She couldn't look at him; she knew her cheeks were flushed. *This* was the reason he'd broken up with Kelly: she *knew*. This was a chemistry that could not be neutralized or undone. But if she gave in to the desires of her body, her heart would forfeit *its* desire; to keep the best friend she'd ever known.

"I'm going away soon."

"Yes, I know," she said, a frisson of worry snaking through her gut. She was used to his coming and going, but each time he left she felt the same illogical fear that he might not return. In the past, she'd consoled herself by reminding herself of her own future full of independent travels. But she wasn't sure that future existed anymore.

"Are you busy on Saturday?"

Lana got the organic citrus cleaner from under the counter and started to wipe down the countertop—not that it needed cleaning. She just needed something to do with her hands.

"Why do you ask?"

"I thought we might do something before I leave."

She scrubbed in big circles with false concentration. "I don't know yet."

"Why not? Do you have better plans?"

"No," she said, feeling oddly competitive. "Do *you*?"

"No," he said.

She waited for him to say more. He didn't.

She began to work the fingerprints off the edge of the counter. "What'd you have in mind?"

"The planetarium has a new show. It's a tour of the universe set to the music of David Bowie."

Lana knew what the planetarium entailed: children kicking the back of her seat, greasy armrests, stomach-flipping graphics of nebulas, galaxies, and black holes. She loved it. But with her skin still tingling where his fingers had threaded into her hair, she was afraid to tell him yes. "Can we just play it by ear?"

"I guess so." He smiled, but she knew him well enough to see there was a tinge of frustration behind it.

She simply couldn't figure out her best friend these days.

Perhaps she never would.

August 19

Karin pulled into the dusty parking lot of the hot-dog place and wondered if Andy had good news or bad. He'd called her a few hours ago and asked to meet her here, far from the Wildflower Barn, so far that she'd gotten a leg cramp on the way over. Now she sat nervously in her parked car, listening to the stock market report on the radio. The sun glared on her windshield, making her skin feel sticky and flushed.

Fifteen minutes later, she was ready to give up when she saw Andy pull in, get out of his car, and walk toward her. Though older than her husband, he carried himself as if he was stacked with muscle, his elbows slightly bent beneath the sleeves of his T-shirt. He went around to the passenger door, and she didn't want to insult him so she popped the lock.

"Hey." He climbed into the car, smiling. "Good to see you."

"Good to see you too."

He sat and leaned toward her, and for a moment she didn't understand what he was doing. *Oh, right.* He wanted to kiss her cheek, but he couldn't quite reach across the seats. She had no choice but to lean in his direction and accept the greeting. His cologne was strong.

"How's things?" he asked.

She glanced out the window toward the lip of gravel

where the parking lot fed into the oil-stone road. In the twenty-five minutes that she'd been waiting, not one other car but his had pulled in. The lights in the ancient hot-dog joint shone dimly, but no one was banging down the door for a table. In fact, the place might have been entirely empty. The hairs at the nape of her neck stood on end.

Andy was a cop, she reminded herself. He was sworn to protect and serve. She was fine.

She gave him her best smile. "Have you got any news? Did Calvert leave town?"

Andy laughed and shook his head. "You seem a little nervous. What's wrong?"

"Nothing. I just figured—I thought the reason you called me . . ."

"I have my guys working on it, don't worry. We've got a car outside the Madison twenty-four seven. It's just a matter of time."

Karin nodded.

"But there's something else I thought you'd want to know."

"What?"

"That he's been hanging around your sister's house. And dropping by the Barn every now and again—though he never makes a move to go in."

"Lana told me she saw him." Karin leaned her head back against the headrest. "Can we do something? File some kind of harassment charges or get a restraining order?"

"You could. But I don't think you'll need to. I don't get the feeling that he's out to do anything harmful. It's more like he's just . . . lonely. Give my guys more time to smoke him out."

Karin nodded and sighed. Maybe Andy was right. As much as she hated her father, some small part of her was beginning to understand his misery. If Calvert felt even a modicum of the heartbreak she felt over her children—those she could not have—then maybe she did feel a little sorry for him.

"Are you okay?" Andy asked.

"Just thinking."

"Anything you want to talk about?"

She looked at the man sitting next to her, this man who—despite all he'd done for her—was practically a stranger. There was heartwarming sincerity in his eyes.

She and Gene had stopped talking about anything important these days—no more discussion about the baby, about Calvert, about their future. She couldn't talk to Lana either—Lana, who preferred to share with Charlotte and Eli, not her.

But here was Andy. An unbiased listener. A fellow churchgoer. A person who was unentangled in the problems of her life.

"Actually, yes," she said. "I wouldn't mind someone to talk to."

"Let's go inside."

Karin hesitated, turning to look at the dilapidated restaurant, attempting once again to see if anyone was inside. She *did* want to talk with Andy, but she wished there was some way she could do it without being alone with him.

He opened the car door an inch. "The place may not look like much. But the hot dogs are killer. And anyway, no one will see."

"Why would I care if anyone saw?" Karin said quickly.

Andy laughed nervously. "Well, you shouldn't. I mean, *I* don't care."

She swallowed. All she wanted to do was talk. She was doing nothing wrong. "We'll have to split the check."

"No, really, let me—"

"That or no deal."

"You are stubborn." He laughed, then pushed the door open wide. The smile he gave her before he climbed out could have melted glass. "Your wish is my command," he said.

August 20

Lana sat in the store alone, eating a sandwich of tomato and fresh mozzarella, and drinking occasionally from a single-serving carton of whole milk. It had been a moderately busy afternoon, but now the flow of tourists and locals had waned. The light slanted through the window in golden, razor-sharp beams, and outside the poppies in the wildflower meadow flared orange and red. The only car in the parking lot was hers. She had a feeling that people were more interested in grilling and swimming than planting flowers this late in the season.

She was still hungry when she finished her sandwich—she was always hungry, it seemed—but instead of eating more, she busied herself wiping up the faint layer of dust that constantly emanated from the parking lot and coated every item in the store. When she was done, she flipped through a catalog showing pages upon pages of wreaths and holly, pondering orders for the upcoming season. She thought: *By spring, I'll be somebody's mom.*

The little silver bell over the front door rang. And when she looked up, already launching into customer-service mode, what she saw made the words slip off her tongue.

Ron.

He wasn't smiling. He wore slightly frayed jeans and a leather jacket. His hair curled toward his shoulders, longer than before.

She dusted off her hands and smiled as she walked toward him. "Ron. You're here."

"Here I am."

She mustered up some enthusiasm. "How are you? What have you been up to?"

"Not as much as you, apparently." He crossed his arms. He was as handsome now as when they'd met—the only two people in Burlington buying crepes in a snowstorm. He wore a striped dress shirt tucked into his jeans, and Lana couldn't help but wonder if he'd dressed up.

She wanted him to say something, to ask how the store was doing, how she was doing. But he remained silent, his face like stone.

She forced herself to take a deep breath. "Do you want to sit down?"

He lifted his chin. "I don't think this should take that long."

"Eli told you I was looking for you?" she asked, though of course she knew he had.

"You *sent* him to me, yes."

She shook her head but didn't correct him.

"I wasn't going to come," he said. "I tried not to."

"Then why did you?"

"Because I don't want your boyfriend to pick another fight."

She blinked, stunned. Eli hadn't mentioned a fight. In all the years she'd known him, he'd never got in a fight.

Ron went on. "If you're going to say what I think you're going to say, let's just get it over and done."

"All right." She pinched the bridge of her nose, fighting a headache. "I'm pregnant."

She saw from the look on his face that he wasn't surprised. "Are you sure?"

"Yes."

"But how are you sure? How do you know it's mine?"

"Well . . . I mean . . . I haven't been with anyone but you."

He laughed. "That's a little hard to swallow, if you get my drift."

Lana wanted to sit down, to step away from the situation and think. He was right to doubt her. Their relationship had been nothing more than a quick fling, and he had no reason to think she was seeing only him. In fact, she wondered now if he had someone in his life as well. She'd never asked.

She stepped toward him. She knew exactly what he was going through right now—the fear, the disbelief. She was prepared to let his insults roll off her back. "I know this is scary. And I'm sorry it happened. I really am. I didn't want this either."

"Let's be clear on one thing," he said quickly. "I don't have any money. Nada. None."

Her head throbbed. "Why would I care if you had any money?"

"All that stuff I told you about having a condo in Denver and a house on Lake Tahoe? I lied. Yep. I don't even race anymore. I got hurt a few years back and now I'm just a has-been. A nobody. Completely washed up. I run a store out of a bedroom in my brother's house. You can take me to court for child support if you want to, but I'm flat busted broke."

The room tipped; she half expected her terra-cotta pots to slide off their shelves.

"Now who's surprised?" Ron said.

Lana stared at him. Everything he'd told her had been a lie. And she'd fallen for it. Or rather, she'd *let* herself fall for it. All the questions she should have asked, the details she should have demanded . . . she hadn't wanted to know. She'd kept him, like every man she'd ever dated, at arm's length.

"Why didn't you tell me the truth?" she said.

"Come on, Lana. It would have killed the fantasy for both of us."

"I still would have liked you if I knew you weren't racing. It's not your fault that you got hurt."

"Maybe," he said, looking away from her. The pain in his expression was real. "But let's be honest. Neither one of us wanted something serious. It worked better when you thought I lived out west."

She crossed her arms. "I didn't need you to *lie* to me; I knew what I was getting into."

"Are you sure?"

She pressed a hand to her belly. "Look. What I'm trying to say is that I'm not telling you this because I want your money. I just thought you deserved to know." He was quiet, and her heart went out to him. Getting hurt had obviously done a number on his self-esteem. She felt the urge to reassure him that everything would be okay. "I'm thinking of putting the baby up for adoption. But I wanted to clear it with you. I mean, technically it's yours too."

He snorted. "Oh, how kind."

"Would you rather I didn't tell you?"

"Honestly?"

She felt her fists clench tight, and she thought of her father, a man who'd had the task of parenting foisted on him long after he'd rejected the job. The anger that exploded came from a place so deep she hadn't known it was there. "How *dare* you!" she said, her voice rising. "You bring another human being into this world and you can't even bring yourself to acknowledge it?"

"You're the one who decided to keep it, not me."

"I didn't get this way by myself. But I'm the one who's been dealing with it—all of it. It's *my* body that this is happening to. Mine. While you've been walking around without a clue. Do you have any idea how hard it's been?"

Lana touched a hand to her throat, the muscles there tightening painfully. She heard the soft sound of a footfall on the concrete floor of the Barn, and she thought, *Please, don't be Eli.* She couldn't stand the idea that he would see her in the middle of this mess. But when she looked up, it wasn't Eli she saw, but her sister, with her stout shoulders squared and her chin stuck out as if she'd seen the battle and was ready to plunge in tooth and nail.

"I don't know what's going on," Karin said, her voice

almost a growl and her eyes boring into Ron. "But I suggest you get out right now."

Lana forced herself to relax. "Ron was just leaving."

He pointed a finger at Lana's face. "I'm done with this, Lana. And I'm done with you. Do whatever you want with it. As far as I'm concerned, that baby is *not* mine."

He barreled out of the Barn; she could feel the moment he was gone, as if the plants around her, with all their delicate green leaves and thin stems, trembled with reverberations of his anger. The silence in the Barn was thick.

Karin stood stone-still, her eyes wild with the instinct to fight, but her whole body seeming suddenly very small. "What *baby*?" she said.

"Kari. Oh, Kare. I'm so sorr—"

"Don't," Karin whispered. "Just don't." She stood for a moment as if trying to get her balance or her bearings. Then she turned around and left.

Karin drove ten miles over the speed limit on the cramped city streets. There were no cars in the parking lot when she got to her church. One small blessing: She was alone.

Inside was dim but airy, the cathedral ceilings letting in clear white light. She walked to the front of the church, crossed herself, then slid into the second pew from the front. She waited for a prayer to rise up in her heart, impulsive and genuine and unscripted, as her prayers usually were. But she felt nothing.

She put her head in her hands.

Lana. It made no sense. Her own sister, who didn't

have a maternal bone in her body. Who was still a child herself. How could *Lana* be pregnant?

A smarmy, coiled-up voice from inside her gave the answer: *Because God loves Lana more.* Everything was always so much easier for her. When Lana graduated from high school, Karin had spent countless hours searching for scholarships and scrounging pennies from her job at the grocery store so that at least one of them could get a college degree. Then, when Lana had graduated and they didn't know what to do, *Karin* was the one who came up with the idea of the Wildflower Barn, *Karin* had done all the legwork so they could have a means of supporting themselves, and *Karin* had found a way to make Lana's passion for flowers into a practical way of life.

She looked up at the cross above the altar.

For a moment, rage clouded her vision. Her teeth gnashed together so hard she thought they might crack. Her muscles clenched from head to toe.

Her screaming was silent: *How could you do this to me?*

Maybe she would go to the doctor again. She and Gene had promised themselves that they would have a baby by God's grace or not have one at all. But that was before Lana ended up with the baby that should have been Karin's.

She put her head on the lemony-smelling wood in front of her.

What was she saying? Lana hadn't gotten pregnant on purpose. She knew that. It wasn't rational to be this mad. But that single kernel of knowledge was nothing compared to the wild storm of her emotions.

Karin had forgiven her sister for a lot of things. Year after year. Time and again. And in all those instances, she'd never once considered what she was considering now: If she refused to forgive her sister for this one last act of injury, she would never, ever have to forgive her again.

September

Sunflowers: Sunflowers are loved as much for their many uses as for their beauty. The stalk of the sunflower is one of the strongest and yet lightest natural substances in the world. The sunflower is also a willful seedling: In the early twentieth century, naturalist John Burroughs reported having seen a sunflower pushing up through the pavement "like a man's fist."

September 1

The water sucked and sloshed against the slatted sides of the rowboat in the center of a wide lagoon. From where she lay on her back in the bottom of the hull, Lana could see nothing of the mountains and houses along the lake's shore. There was only sky, endless and vast as the universe beyond the blue.

Evenings like this, longing and loneliness never failed to rise up from the marrow of her bones. As a teenager she hadn't been able to place it. But as an adult she recognized what it was. She missed her mother; she wished for her soothing voice, her steadying hand. Ellen was the bridge between Lana and her sister, the first word between them and the last. Ellen would know what Lana should say to Karin, words that not only apologized but healed as well.

And maybe she would know what to say about Eli too, about the war waging between Lana's mind and heart. Eli had broken up with Kelly. He hadn't told her why, but she knew that something was different within him. Something had changed. The desire growing hotter by the day in his eyes spoke to her at the deepest level of her being.

She closed her eyes. The wind washed into the bottom of the boat and blew over her skin. There was a story her mother used to tell. Lana couldn't remember the specifics anymore. But it was about a beaver and a bear, and it ended with the bear feeling guilty that the beaver was sentenced to cutting down trees for all time because he'd kept silent when he should have spoken up.

There was a moral to the story, as there was a moral to so many of Ellen's stories. *When truth is known, it should be spoken.* How many times had Ellen said that to her daughters? And yet decades later, the lesson still hadn't sunk in.

Lana should have told Karin about the baby. Immediately. She should have insisted, even though she knew the truth would cause her sister pain.

And as for Eli, she was keeping secrets from him too. Perhaps she should talk to him. To get it out in the open. She could confess that she was attracted to him, but didn't want to change the balance of their friendship. There was logic in confessing her true feelings. She could appeal to the rational side of his brain, the side that would want to protect their friendship as much as she did.

Or she could just sleep with him.

Wasn't that what she wanted deep down? She could

offer him a bargain. They would go to bed together just to get it out of their systems, and then their relationship could go back to normal. For all she knew, it might be terrible if they tried to sleep together. Maybe fifty years from now, they could look back on their awkward efforts and laugh . . .

Who was she kidding?

Sex with Eli wouldn't be terrible. When he'd wrapped his arms around her the other day, her whole body came alive in ways that it never had with any other man but him. In all the years since they'd made love, she'd never felt as overtaken and devastated by passion as she'd been with him. If a man flirted with her, drew her out, then she could often convince her body to enjoy the act of making love. But with Eli, she hadn't seen it coming. One minute, they were strictly friends, and the next . . . the next . . .

They'd tried going down that road before, and it had almost ruined the most meaningful and lasting relationship she'd ever had. If she allowed herself to sleep with him once more and only once more, it wouldn't be a compromise. It would be devastation. *Friendship* was what worked for them. Friendship could unite two people on two very different paths. Lust . . . that was fleeting. Dangerous. One night could ruin ten years of their lives.

A heron flew overhead, its great wings dark against the filmy remnants of the sunset. She had to get back. And when she did, she had to start dealing with things. With Karin, she needed to bring her secrets out into the clear. Once and for all. And with Eli, she had to talk to him. Really talk to him.

He'd been away on a trip for over a week—sent by the university to procure more meteorite samples for their collection—but when he returned she needed to set down some rules. He wouldn't push the issue. He never did.

When truth is known, it should be spoken. She gave a long, deep pull on the oars, and then dragged the tips of her fingers on the surface of the water, watching the trail her fingers left behind.

September 3

Eli stood before his intro to astronomy class, and he could only hope that his chronically tired students wouldn't notice their professor's exhaustion. He'd been away on an expedition and had taken a red-eye back to Burlington last night in order to make his class—his first of the year, and the only course he was scheduled to teach for the fall. He always loved the first class because it set the stage for all the mysteries yet to come. Today he was introducing his students to dark matter, which made up more than 99 percent of the mass of the universe but constantly eluded scientists' grasp.

Unfortunately, today the lecture felt a little rote. Thoughts of Lana consumed him. Before he'd left, she'd bailed on the date they were supposed to have at the planetarium, and he'd sat home by himself, frustration tying him up in knots. He worried that she was staying away because she'd sensed the change in him. Maybe he should have hidden it better. Or maybe he should have sprung it on her all at once—just taken her face in his hands and kissed her without preamble—so that she couldn't talk herself out of her own feelings before she even had them.

Whatever method he chose, there was a very real risk

that he might ruin their relationship. But there was no way he would ever be happy with her if she kept him on the sidelines for the rest of his life. He had to do something. But the sophomores in his class probably knew more about seduction than he did. What they *didn't* know—couldn't know—was the force of a yearning that had been building for ten years, the triple-threat of friendship, love, and desire all rolled into one.

He realized that he'd been talking to his class, but that they hadn't been listening to what he was saying any more than he was. He decided to let them go early. Though no one uttered a word, he could feel their collective sigh of relief as they packed up their bags. Eli shared their sentiment, though he'd never let on.

As the class filed out, Meggie—the same Meggie whom he'd helped get a job at the Wildflower Barn in the spring—made a beeline for his desk as he packed up his things.

"Eli? I mean, Mr. Ward?"

He tapped the edge of the students' group papers against his desk. "What's up?"

"I don't get this whole dark matter thing."

"You're not the only one," he said, laughing.

She put her hands on her hips. "How do they know it exists if they can't see it? It makes no sense."

Eli nodded. He understood where Meggie was coming from. Learning about the universe could be frustrating. He put his bag back down on his desk and tried to recap, emphasizing that even though dark matter wasn't visible, the effects of it were.

She shook her head. "Well, I guess if scientists can't figure out what it is, I sure as hell won't solve the mystery in Astro I." She sighed and heaved her big backpack higher on her shoulders. "You haven't been by the Barn lately."

"I was away." He looked down at his desk so she couldn't read his face. "How's Lana?"

"Ron came to see her."

"Wait. What?"

Meggie smirked. "Secret's out. We all know Lana's knocked up. Karin knows too."

Eli fumbled his messenger bag onto his shoulder, his hands shaky. He hadn't thought that his efforts to persuade Ron were successful, given his bruised ribs. But maybe he'd been more persuasive than he thought. Or maybe Ron had a conscience after all. "What did he say?"

Meggie crossed her arms. "Shouldn't you be hearing this from Lana?"

Yes, he thought. "Listen, if you see her . . ."

"If?"

"Okay, *when* you see her, tell her . . ."

"What?"

That I'm in love with her. That I want her. That I always have. "Tell her I'll stop by soon."

"Today?"

"No."

"Why not?"

"I have a lot of follow-up work to do from the expedition. Funny thing about these grant-giving types. Everything's got to be documented three different ways."

She laughed.

"And . . . thanks for the heads-up about Ron."

"How many points do I get on my next paper?"

Eli crossed his arms.

"I'm *kidding*," she said. But he didn't think she was.

Eli finished packing up his things. They chatted for another minute or two about nothing special as they walked toward the parking lot, then parted ways.

He leaned for a moment against the hood of his car and looked at the clouds sailing big and white overhead. The gears of the universe were turning, the future coming inevitably closer, but it was never what anyone expected. Ron had beaten the crap out of him, and the result wasn't a defeat: It was a revelation. Karin had wanted a baby, but Lana was the one who would soon be a mom. There was no telling what the future held, and there was no way he could control it, but failure was guaranteed if he didn't try.

He unlocked the car door. He knew what he would have to do. Once, he and Lana had touched something together that was bigger than them both. They'd found a space that existed outside fear, worry, and self-doubt. Right or wrong, Eli wouldn't want to look back on his life some day and wonder, *What if?* He had to go back to that place again. And Lana would be going with him.

September 4

In the acres behind the Wildflower Barn, the dense woods were mottled with cool patches of shade and bright, warm light. Fall was moving in, and Karin had wrapped her nylon jacket around herself tightly as she walked along the hard-packed path that led through the grove. A handful of children followed behind her, some shuffling their feet, others tripping over themselves in excitement.

"Miss Karin? Miss Karin?" A blond-haired boy in a Lake Monsters hat swatted at her elbow. "Anne said 'penis flytrap.'"

"That's what it's called!" the girl shouted back, her big green eyes panicked as if she knew she was going to get in trouble—as if she'd been in trouble for saying *penis flytrap* before.

"I think you mean *venus* flytrap, honey. But we don't have them here."

"*I* have a penis flytrap," the boy said. "Lookit! It's the zipper on my jeans!"

Karin bit back the smile that threatened to give her away. She didn't want to encourage them—a bunch of eight-year-olds would be reporting to their parents that they'd seen penis flytraps at the Wildflower Barn.

"Come on, guys. I'll take you to see the pond."

She led them farther down the path, among the stalky brown remnants of the summer's flowers. She pointed out Stumpy the chipmunk and told them about Amos, a great brown moose that ambled across the property twice a year. Movement behind her caught her eye and she saw Meggie walking quickly to catch up with them. Her nose ring caught an errant beam of sun and threw it like a javelin toward Karin's eye. She wove her way through the pack to Karin's side.

"Is everything okay?" Karin asked.

"Lana's inside."

"And?"

"She wants me to take over for you."

"Tell her I'll be in when my tour of duty is over," Karin said.

"I really don't mind . . ."

"I said, I'll be in soon."

Meggie nodded and left.

Since the day she'd learned about Lana's baby, she'd been able to avoid all but the most clipped and mandatory conversations with her sister, and Lana hadn't tried to parlay a quick discussion about delivery fees or displays into a heart-to-heart. But eventually, Karin would have to face her. She supposed she'd given her the silent treatment long enough.

She forced herself to focus on the task at hand. "Come on, kids. Time for the petting garden."

They broke out in cheers and grumbles, and she led them down the path toward the small greenhouse on the property that held planted soft moss, bull thistle, teasel, lamb's ears—plants that begged to be "petted." She instructed them to touch but not pluck, and they darted among the wooden tables, squealing and laughing.

Their enthusiasm was vivid and contagious. How wonderful it would be to raise children here, so much better than the place where Karin and Lana had come of age. But of course, Lana's child would be picking flowers in these fields long before her own.

Lana looked toward the door when it opened, and Karin was there, unsmiling. She wore jeans that were faded at the knees and white sneakers that had turned brown-gray. Her hair was pulled back on top, leaving her kinky amber curls to hang to her shoulders. Even with her brow creased and glowering, she was a sight for sore eyes.

"Hi, Kari," Lana said softly.

Karin came to stand before her, but said nothing for a long minute. Her expression was so disapproving that Lana felt like a child waiting for her sentence to be pronounced. "All right. How far along are you?"

"I'm not sure exactly. About nineteen weeks?"

"You've known for four months? Four whole months?"

"No," Lana said, embarrassed. "More like two."

Karin regarded her belly with disgust. "You're tiny for four months. I'm guessing those overalls aren't maternity?"

Lana shook her head.

"But you *are* in maternity."

"I don't know. I haven't tried."

"But you don't fit into your old clothes anymore."

Lana said nothing. She braced herself for more questions, questions that Karin deserved to ask. She felt like she was before a jury, being tried for her crime.

"What's your due date?"

"January thirtieth."

"January thirtieth," she repeated.

Lana could almost hear what her sister was thinking: *On January thirtieth, you'll be a mother, and I won't.*

"It seems so far away," she said, her voice distant.

Lana sighed. She'd never found a good way to say I'm sorry. The words always seemed like a superficial substitute for some kind of real reparation, like trying to patch a broken arm with a Band-Aid. She needed some other way to show that she was sorry. Some other way to confess. "Do you remember how when we were kids you used to have that stuffed cat in the blue dress?"

"Miss Kitty," Karin said. "I lost her on the bus."

"No, you didn't. I accidentally spilled mustard all over her. I buried her behind the old tire swing and I cried the whole time."

"And you're telling me this now . . . ?"

"I figure since we're getting it all out in the open. Might as well."

Karin's sigh was rife with defeat. "You know you drive me crazy?"

"We're sisters."

"That's just it. I can't *not* forgive you. Even when I don't want to, I do."

Lana reached for her hand. "The last thing in the world I ever wanted was to hurt you."

"I know." Karin squeezed her fingers. "But I can't understand why you didn't tell me."

"Two reasons, I guess. I thought you'd be mad at me. But also, I knew you'd be hurt."

"Or was it that if you didn't tell me, you could pretend it wasn't happening?"

"Maybe it was a little of that."

Karin held out her hand. "Can I . . . ?"

Lana stared at her a moment, not comprehending.

"I mean, do you think I could, you know . . . ?" She gestured to Lana's belly.

"Oh. Oh, right." The baby. Karin wanted to touch her belly, to feel the oddly steely fortress of her bump. Lana didn't blame her; it was a curious thing, what a woman's body could do. "Okay. Why not?" She took a step closer, and very hesitantly, Karin pressed her palm against the slight swell above her belly button.

"Wow," Karin said.

Lana was quiet, transfixed by her sister's wonder. The respect—reverence—in her eyes seemed almost sacred. She watched as Karin bent down until she was nearly even with Lana's navel.

"Hi there, little one," she whispered.

Tears sprang instantly to Lana's eyes, as quickly as a gasped breath. She put her own hand on her belly, her muscles trembling. She felt the press of both Karin's hand and her own.

Hello, baby, she said in the quietest part of her mind. *Hello.*

"Have you felt it kick?" Karin dropped her hand and stood back up.

Lana shook her head, blinking back the tears in her eyes.

"You're nineteen weeks? And no kicking?"

"Is that bad?"

Karin frowned. "If there's no movement, we need to go to the doctor right away."

Lana looked away, embarrassed. "Well, sometimes I think I feel . . ."

"What?"

"Gas!" Lana blurted, embarrassed but glad to finally be able to talk about her pregnancy with Karin. "At least, I think it is. But then, there's no—you know. No actual gas."

Karin laughed, her eyes lit up now with the first real enthusiasm Lana had seen in ages. "That's the baby!"

She looked down and gave Lana's belly a gentle nudge

with the heel of her palm, and at once, Lana felt a slight pressure like a small firework popping inside her. It made her laugh.

And when Karin looked up from her belly, Lana's whole vision was filled with the warmth of her sister's brown eyes, so much like their mother's. Karin hugged her, lightly patting her back. "I'm happy for you, little sis. I really am."

Lana squeezed her sister tight, tears coming to her eyes for how right and good it felt to have Karin's company and friendship once again. And yet here Karin was, saying she was happy for her, while Lana was feeling only the tidal conflict of her emotions—the sudden shock of realization that the baby inside her was a life of its own, and the desperate fear that came with it. She held her sister tighter and squeezed her eyes closed. "I'm afraid."

"Don't worry," Karin said. She pulled away to look into Lana's eyes. "This baby is going to have a great life. We're a good strong family, you and I."

"I don't know if I'm going to keep it," Lana said.

"You mean . . ." A flicker of fury raced across Karin's face.

"I might give it up for adoption. I'm not sure yet."

She watched Karin's face fall. And she knew she'd caused yet another injury to her sister's heart. Karin must have glimpsed their family's future, a future with Lana's baby in it. And Lana had hinted she was going to spoil even that small happiness.

"I can't be a mom," Lana said, watching her sister's face to gauge her reaction, to see if Karin agreed.

Karin's face was unreadable. "No. I can't picture you as a mother."

A pang of disappointment shot through Lana's heart. She was hoping that Karin would have contradicted her, that she might say, "I think motherhood is something you can do." If Karin believed Lana could be a good mother, then Lana knew she could do it. But true to her nature, Karin didn't sugarcoat the truth: Lana *would* be a bad parent. Karin had all but said it aloud.

"It wouldn't be right to raise a child if I knew I was going to do a bad job," Lana continued, twisting the knife further. She didn't *want* a kid. So why did it hurt so much to admit what she already knew, that she wasn't mommy material? "I mean, it would be cruel, wouldn't it? To have me as a mom?"

"A child needs someone steady. Someone who can give it the life it deserves."

Lana nodded. A crack was opening in her heart. "Adoption seems like the only way."

Karin withdrew her hand. "Well, it's your decision."

"Thank you."

"But in the meantime, no more of this being in denial about the baby. It's coming whether you want it to or not. Trust me. It's all going to be okay."

Some of the worry drained out of her. *It's all going to be okay.* Karin was on her side once again. And Lana knew that they—the two of them—could get through whatever obstacles they faced, even if those obstacles were each other from time to time.

"Thank you," Lana said. There was still a lot to talk about. About Eli. And about his betrayal. And about Ron.

But for now, she simply took what comfort was before her. And she hugged her sister tight.

That evening Karin went back to church. She kneeled in the second row and bowed her head low over her hands. From now on she would try harder to be a better person. To put her family first and to cherish the ties of blood. To be more forgiving and generous. To stop stressing so much about the future and to trust it to God. Why hadn't she realized it before? The future stretched out before her like a sunlit path. She knew what she was meant to do.

September 5

The sky above City Hall Park was overcast and chilly, gray that was nearly violet. Despite the weather the farmers' market was crowded when Eli arrived. The smell of fresh produce sweetened the air. Apples, carrots, kale, turnips, and other early fall fare gleamed in the sun. People shouted and reached over one another's shoulders to hand money to busy vendors.

Eli headed to the back corner of the park, past the circular concrete fountain toward Lana and Karin's booth. He pulled his light brown jacket closer to his chin, his thoughts focused with knifelike precision on finding Lana.

There were customers at the Wildflower Barn booth when he arrived, a crowd of people watching Lana assemble impromptu flower arrangements while Karin rang up orders. He stood off to the side of the line and watched her. Her skin reflected pinkish in the glow from the canvas over their booth, and she was wearing a Wild-flower Barn T-shirt under a brown jacket. At her neck was a simple choker made of wooden beads, and her hair fell around her shoulders.

He watched her work. Unlike other flower arrangers, Lana had no patience for symmetry and uniformity. Her bouquets were always wild, unkempt, sprigs of thistle and willow branches sprawling in barely controlled chaos. How many times had Eli gone home with a fistful of flower stems in his hand from this market? And how many times had he thought to himself: *I love her* and tried to convince himself he meant it only as a friend?

He waited his turn to speak with Lana, watching her hand wrap long stalks in brown paper and hemp twine. The smile she gave him when he said hello might have looked entirely warm and genuine to anyone else, but he saw a subtle wariness in her eyes.

"We have to talk," he said.

She looked past his shoulder, where a line had formed. "What about?"

Karin stopped ringing up customers to stand at her sister's shoulder. A protector if Eli ever saw one. "She's busy. Come back later."

"I can't. I only have a minute. Lana, come with me?"

She said nothing. He moved around to the other side of the table. "Lana."

Her eyes met his, full and blue. She shook her head and Eli tried not to lose heart. Years of damage had built up. Years of denial that wouldn't be cleared up in five minutes. But he had to try.

"Please?" he asked.

He saw her eyes flicker toward the line of customers and then toward her sister. Karin shrugged her shoulders as if to say, "It's up to you."

"*One* minute," Lana said.

He took her hand and held tight as they walked around the table and through the crowd. Her fingers didn't tighten around his, but still he held on. He could feel the calluses on her fingertips and it made him ache to feel the rasp of them on his skin. He led her down the path through the park and only when they stopped in a shady spot away from the crowd did he let her hand go. The leaves overhead made the dry, whispering sound that meant autumn was near. He felt as if his senses had been adjusted, set to exquisite sensitivity. He felt the breeze that stirred with the sway of her hair. He heard the cotton of her jacket whisper against her skin. He was painfully aware of the natural parallel lines their bodies made when they stood face-to-face. How easy it would be to take one step forward, to close the distance between them and make two lines one.

"I'm mad at you," she said, slipping her hand out of his.

He nodded, oddly relieved that she'd admitted it so easily, that they could simply get it out in the open.

"You didn't tell me you got in a fight," she said.

"No," he said. "I figured I got what I deserved."

Her face flooded with concern. "Are you . . . are you okay?"

"Better every day," he said.

"Why would you do that? You never fight."

"I don't know. Some sort of caveman gene."

He thought he saw a slight smile pull at her lips.

"You missed me," he said.

"Maybe."

"You did."

She pushed lightly against his arm. "*You* missed *me*."

"Yes," he said, "I did." He held his breath, not wanting to break the moment of easy flirtation. A leaf, red as poppy petals, swung down from the top of a tree, fluttering before it veered sharply toward the ground. It was such a relief to see her smile. But there were serious issues at hand. "So tell me what Ron said."

Her grin faded. "He's out of the picture. It's my problem as far as he's concerned."

Eli nodded. He'd expected this. "Are you relieved?"

"Why would I be relieved?"

"Because you don't have to answer to anyone else now. Just yourself."

She sighed. "I guess you're right." She reached up to scratch her throat, and the movement made her jacket fall open just a little, and her belly was suddenly *there*, between them, arcing gently, no longer hidden by big dresses or overalls. She nervously put her jacket back into place. And when his gaze returned to her face, he could see that she was feeling self-conscious that he'd looked so blatantly at the evidence of her mistake.

"Do you . . . do you think it's terrible?" she asked, her voice full of vulnerability and hope.

He felt his fist tighten, thinking of the way her body was changing, and of how it had nothing to do with him. The child wasn't his; the primal, territorial male tucked away inside his DNA would not let him forget that fact. There was something instinctive in his blood that wanted the swelling of her body to be because of *him*, because of something he (and she) had done. And yet, through the pangs of jealousy came a complicated feeling of tenderness, love, and even devotion. He felt as if he'd been charged with taking care of Lana and her baby—that she needed him. And it felt good, to think he could do some good for her.

"I think it's amazing what your body is capable of. And what you're capable of," he said. "You're beautiful. And your baby will be beautiful too."

She smiled. "Thank you."

He spoke as gently as he could. "You're still thinking of adoption?"

"It's the only way."

He tried to keep his feelings from showing on his face. He'd heard her talk about adoption before, but not with so much sadness and resignation in her voice. "I don't believe that. Listen to me, Lana. I think you'd make a wonderful mom, the best, if you decided to raise the child as your own."

"I don't know," she said. "It's just that I can't stop thinking about Calvert. About how he didn't want us, but got stuck with us anyway. And seeing Ron reject this child . . . It just brings everything back all over again. I don't want growing up to be as hard for this baby as it was for me."

"But you can give it a good life."

She shook her head. "You have to be dependable to be a parent. And me? I'm a flight risk. Other than Karin, you're the only steady relationship I've ever had."

"But you *are* steady with me. So that proves it. You can raise the baby, if you want."

She hesitated. The wind sent a wave of brown leaves tumbling at their feet. "Are we?" she asked.

"Are we what?"

"Are we *steady*? I mean . . . you don't want anything to change?"

His heart beat painfully hard behind his ribs as silence stretched long between them. How to answer her? He was challenging the boundaries of their friendship, deliberately, more each day. And while he didn't plan on retreating, he did want her to know she was loved, safe, and that he wanted to be there for her and comfort her even while his demands increased.

He moved closer to her, leaned down. Her hand was close to his. He let his fingers brush hers. He thought if he could look down, he would see tiny blue sparks leaping between their hands. "Do you know why I broke up with Kelly?"

"No?"

"I think you do." His heart beat hard. He'd all but told her the truth—that he loved her. But would she hear it? And accept?

"I'm sorry it didn't work out," she said, but even though her voice was strong, he knew her well enough to read the discomposure in her eyes, the slight clip of her breath. *Good*, he thought. He wanted her senses on their most sensitive setting.

"Eli?"

"Mmm?"

"I'm glad we're friends."

He smiled, no longer fooled. Then he leaned down and kissed her cheek, so close to her mouth that the corner of his lips brushed hers. It nearly killed him to draw back. "You're a flight risk I'd take on any day."

Her eyes widened. "I . . . I have to get back."

He nodded. As she walked away, the light caught her hair, gleaming white gold. He watched her until she disappeared into the crowd, and then he hummed a little under his breath as he headed home.

September 16

On Wednesday of the next week, Lana was giving a seasonal talk at the local library about preparing home gardens for the winter. She usually enjoyed the friendly, intimate conversations about soil and weather. But today she felt a little distracted from what she was saying. Days later she could still feel the imprint of Eli's kiss—so light it was barely a kiss at all—but it stayed with her, a warm press on her skin.

To make matters worse, the secret that she was pregnant was now as prominent as her belly. Over the last few days, she'd "popped." Mrs. Montaigne had wanted to know which of her boyfriends had done it and which Lana planned to say did it. Fred Daly, who worked the front desk at the post office, gave her the business card for his church—he said they had a program for helping unwed moms. Jenn O'Toole said she could loan her a homemade cradle, and she asked to be invited to the shower.

The shocking fact was that of everyone who knew about the baby, only Karin had implied that she wasn't fit to be a mom. The whole town had assumed she was going to keep the child. And amazingly she found herself thinking, *What if I did?*

For her entire life she'd believed that she never wanted kids. And, like Karin, she didn't believe that people could totally and fundamentally change who they were. But she was beginning to see that it was easy to confuse a change in one's personality with discovering the truth of it. She wasn't *changing* into a person who suddenly wanted to have a child. She was merely discovering the possibility that maybe she'd been interested in children all along.

She wondered: What if she didn't rule out motherhood completely? She wasn't at all certain that she wanted to keep the baby, but she was starting to feel that perhaps she'd been too quick to rule it out. Worse women than her became mothers. Since the moment Karin had leaned down and said hello to the baby inside her, she'd become more and more attached to the infant each day. When she let her mind wander, she found herself wondering whether it was a boy or a girl, whether it would like flowers or meteorites or bike rides. She wondered if her baby would have the same wanderlust she had, and she prayed silently that it would.

She'd yet to settle on adoption one way or another, but she now knew that she wasn't leaning as far toward giving the baby up as she once was. She still felt pressured by the future, that maybe she couldn't truly be a parent. That she didn't know how to reconcile motherhood with her dreams. But even if she wasn't the world's best mother, maybe she wouldn't be the worst either. She needed more time to think it through—to decide what was right for her and the child within her.

Finally, her lecture concluded. Most of her students

were repeats from last year and the year before; she knew them by name. She packed up her cardboard posters, organized her handouts, and headed out the door.

Her father was standing in front of the library, waiting.

Her stomach went sour. "How did you know I was here?"

"Seen it in the paper. You look good. Better than last time."

She didn't say thank you. Apparently, Karin's plan to get Calvert out of town wasn't working.

"How's your sister?" he asked.

"Fine."

"And what about that boyfriend?"

Lana guessed he meant Ron. "I can't stay and talk . . ."

"Oh, I know. And I don't mean to bother you. It's just, see, I'm in kind of a tough spot right now."

Lana said nothing.

"You see that car over there?" He tilted his head in the direction of a sleek black sedan, but he didn't point or look directly. "For some reason or other, I got the cops following me. I didn't do nothing wrong—I don't know why they're hounding me. But the landlord wouldn't let me renew my rent, and now I got nowhere to go."

"Why are you asking me? Why not Karin?"

"Always seemed like you were a little easier on me than her."

She took a deep breath, shaking. Maybe she'd been better at hiding her feelings than Karin, but that didn't mean she liked Calvert any more than her sister did. "Do you remember that time Karin came to pick me up at the police station, and they wouldn't let me out because she wasn't my legal guardian?"

He nodded. "You and your friends put those photocopies of the mayor's face all over those trees they were gonna ax. Hell of a thing to get arrested for."

Lana fumed at his good-natured nostalgia. He remembered the incident as a charming anecdote of a wayward daughter. But *he* hadn't spent the night in jail. "The cops called you to come get me, but you were nowhere to be found," she said.

"I'm sorry."

"It wasn't that terrible. There was food, a nice cop, and a space heater. But do you know what Karin did that night? Do you even know?"

Cal shoved his hands into his front pockets.

"Karin never came home that night either. She sat in the car, in the parking lot of the police station all night in the freezing cold with a broken heater. She would have stayed in the cell with me if they'd let her."

"I didn't come here to talk about Karin."

"Tough!" Lana said, seething now. She couldn't remember the last time she'd been this angry. "You have to hear this. You were terrible to her. Do you even know? It took her years before she ever even thought about giving her heart to someone because of what you made her think love was. If she wasn't such a strong person, you could have ruined her life."

"Her life, Lana? *Just* hers?"

"You should never have had kids if you couldn't commit to them," she said. Tears came to her eyes now, real tears that she wouldn't be able to control. She had to turn away.

"We're going to have to talk," he said. "Let's head over to your place. Have some nonalcoholic beer."

She let her canvas bag fall away from her chest, so it hung by her side. "I'll never sleep under the same roof as you again," she said. Then she walked away.

She drove only half a block before she pulled over under the thick red plume of a Japanese maple. Her breath came in starts and stops.

She dialed Karin's phone number, but when the answering machine picked up, she had no idea what to say. She put together some words that she hoped were sentences. She wanted something more from the answering machine, something to make her feel better. But it offered nothing. She and Karin would talk later on.

For a moment, when she'd looked into Calvert's face, it wasn't the face of a shabby and useless old man—it was *her* face that she saw. Her eyes, her nose. She could see herself looking out from behind his pupils.

Karin had inherited Ellen's strength, her fortitude, drive, and gumption. But Lana had been cursed with her father's propensity to flee, to run. She didn't love that about herself, but over the years she'd come to accept it. Part of her understood him—understood his need to not be tied down. As an adult she'd tried to regard his neglect with forgiveness and kindness because she saw part of herself in him.

But now the thought of sharing DNA with her father made her want to scratch off her own skin. What on earth made her think that because she had fond feelings for her child now, she wouldn't one day resent it for crushing her dreams? What if she turned out to be the same kind of parent he'd been?

Her heart split open. She put her head on the steering wheel and cried. Her decision to give the baby up for adoption had been a knee-jerk reaction—a choice made in self-defense. But deep down, she realized she hadn't let herself think too much about the decision because she didn't *want* to put the baby up for adoption. And as time had gone by, she'd let her guard down, toying with the idea that she could keep the baby for her own.

But now that Calvert had appeared today—and asked to move in with her, no less!—she had no choice but to look truth in the eye. There was a very real possibility that she would not be a good mother. And so she had to do the right thing. No more would she flirt with the idea of keeping the baby. She had to put her child's future first. And that meant giving the child to someone who would be a better mother . . . to Karin.

Outside the car, the wind whipped against the low gray clouds, and a shower of leaves and paper cups went sailing across the road. Lana took a deep breath, then another. She could get through this. She had to. The baby did a slow and leisurely roll in her belly, but she didn't let herself think of it as *hers*.

September 17

For over a week Karin had been trying to figure out how to tell Gene the news—not that Lana was pregnant; she'd told him about that as soon as she could. She was looking for the perfect way to give him the *other* news, the more important news. It would take patience and care to catch him when he was in just the right mood, at just the right time. She hoped tonight would be the night.

They were sitting on the back deck of their little house, listening to the red-winged blackbirds crying shrilly in the marshes at the bottom of the hill. Gene was drinking a tall glass of iced tea, a bag of pretzels on the plastic table beside him. He was in a good mood. He'd just learned that a big client he'd previously worked with had requested him, specifically, again. His smile was big and his color was high.

To warm him up to the subject she had in mind, she talked about going shopping for maternity clothes with Lana. Over the last few days, she and Lana had been spending a lot of time together, doing research, shopping, talking about everything Lana would need to know to give birth. The subject of adoption didn't come up, though Karin was sure it would soon.

"You know," she said as calmly as she could, "Lana says she might put the baby up for adoption."

Gene looked surprised. "Why?"

Karin shrugged. "She doesn't want kids."

"I can't imagine anything harder for a woman than giving up her own child."

"If a woman doesn't want kids, she doesn't want kids," Karin said, irritated. She reached for a pretzel from the bag and snapped it between her teeth. "I think it's great that Lana's being real about this. I mean, she can barely take care of herself, let alone a baby. But the idea of giving the child to strangers . . . it just seems a little, I don't know, *wrong*."

Gene crossed his arms. "Karin . . ."

"I mean, that baby is going to be her flesh and blood. And *our* family. It just doesn't make sense to send it off to a stranger when . . . when . . ." She felt her throat constrict. "When there's so much need and love for a baby right here."

"We already discussed this," Gene said gently. "If God wanted us to have a baby, we'd have one. We want a baby that's our baby. Our own."

"But that was before we knew *Lana* got pregnant." She looked at her husband a moment, then made the decision to crawl into his lap. He opened his arms and she lay against him, settling her cheek on his chest. He smelled like laundry and sweet tea. "What if this is what God wants for us? What if the reason we haven't been able to have a baby is because we're supposed to help Lana? Doesn't it all make perfect sense?"

Gene rubbed her back. "Are you *sure* Lana doesn't want to keep the baby?"

"That's what she told me."

"Are you really sure? Has she gone to an adoption agency?"

"Well . . . not that I know of."

"Has she hired a lawyer?"

"She's going to—"

"Has she done any research? Any at all?"

"I don't know. But she told me she's *thinking* of adoption. And Gene—who would be better parents to Lana's baby than you and me?"

Gene breathed in deeply and cuddled her closer. "I need you to listen to me, okay, sweetheart? You have to promise me you won't ask Lana if we can adopt her baby."

Karin lifted her head to look at him. "Why not?"

"Because it's *Lana's* baby. And it has to be Lana's decision. We can't go putting ideas into her head or putting more pressure on her than there is already."

"But Gene—"

"It's Lana's pregnancy, honey. Not ours."

Karin rested the point of her chin on his chest. Why couldn't he see how much sense it made? She saw that she wouldn't get anywhere with this campaign tonight. She decided to let it go—for now. She laid her head back down. "You should at least think about it. Search your heart. See if it feels like caring for and loving Lana's baby would be the right thing."

"I don't know . . ."

"Just promise you'll think about it."

"Fine. But you have to promise me you won't bring it up with her."

"I won't," she said.

"Do you promise?"

She snorted. "I *promise*." She relaxed more deeply against his wide chest. She was never one to go back on her word. But if Lana didn't reach the obvious conclusion, Karin wasn't above a few well-placed hints.

She felt Gene sigh beneath her, and her body sank with his breath. "I love you."

"I love you too," he said.

September 23

Eli took Lana's arm as they left the foyer of the country club and followed the rest of the wedding guests into the huge, elegant hall. The bride and groom—old friends from college—were off somewhere getting pictures taken. During the service, they'd seemed so happy, so genuinely in love that their smiles bordered on triumphant. At the moment, Eli was feeling more than a little triumphant too.

He wore his best navy suit, which also happened to be his only navy suit, and a crisp white shirt. He looked good, he knew. But he was no match for the woman at his side. In a draping, cabernet-colored cocktail dress, Lana was more than beautiful. She was statuesque. Her hair was pulled up into a smooth, high bun, so her neck—her long, beautiful neck—was entirely exposed. A simple silver chain lay against her skin, glittering where her collarbones met. It was the sexiest thing he'd ever seen.

"Don't be nervous," he said. He leaned toward her and stole a breath of the perfume behind her ear. "You look gorgeous."

"I look like a whale."

"You look breathtaking. The sexiest woman in the room," he said. And he meant it. The way her dress was gathered, her figure was beautiful, lithe and long. But there was no hiding her belly anymore. When he looked at her, he felt an odd pang in his heart—a longing. Sex was part of it, he knew. But what he wanted couldn't be summed up so neatly. Her belly didn't appall him—it fascinated him as every part of her fascinated him. He couldn't take his eyes off her, not simply because she looked dazzling in her low-cut dress, but because he was held rapt by her changing reactions to him.

He moved his hand from her arm to her back. His palm connected with her naked skin. A flicker of surprise lit her face, but he pretended not to see. *Patience*, he told himself. They'd been "just friends" for so long that even if he moved with excruciating slowness, it would feel like moving fast to her.

"What's got into you?" she asked, laughing nervously.

He kept his mouth shut.

They walked together into the center of the main hall, with its marble floors and high white ceilings. Wedding guests were chatting and hunting for their seats among fresh flowers and satin-covered chairs. He linked her arm more securely with his and his forearm pressed against her ribs.

It had surprised him, actually—how receptive she was to casual touching after they'd starved themselves of it for so long. Certainly she'd seemed a little skittish and timid when he took her coat from her shoulders or brushed an eyelash from her cheek. But overall, he'd met with less resistance than he would have thought. She didn't glare, or swear at him, or tell him to knock it off. And for the life of him, he couldn't figure out how he'd held back for so long.

"I think this is our table," he said, pulling out a chair from the empty table and motioning for her to sit.

She took her seat, looking nervously around the room.

"You okay?" he asked.

He saw the muscles in her throat go tight. "Everyone's going to ask about the baby."

"No one's going to think anything except what a beautiful, intelligent, fascinating woman you are."

"Can I just tell them I did it myself? That it was a spontaneous conception?"

He sat down and brushed a tendril of hair back behind her ear, not because it needed placement, but because he relished the feel of it between his fingers. It killed him not to push all his fingers into her hair, to rumple that neat bun.

He drew away, exhaling.

Whether he succeeded with her or failed, there would be no going back to friendship ever again. He had to do everything right. This was his last chance.

One by one people sat down at their table, and with each arrival Lana felt a little more at ease. She knew a few of the guests who had joined them and she was pleased that the conversation flowed easily, without those fragile, awkward pauses that could sometimes taint an otherwise vigorous conversation among old friends. She leaned back in her seat and tried to relax, but having Eli so close wasn't making it easy.

The wedding ceremony had been beautiful. The couple had written their own vows, and they read them to each other with impassioned voices and visibly trembling hands. Tears had come to Lana's eyes. Here were two people confidently embarking on their future together. They spoke of the love and support they would give each other, and of the children they would one day raise. They seemed entirely unafraid of what was before them. If their future was a vast and unpredictable ocean, they were eagerly pushing away from the shore.

They were lucky that marriage was such an easy decision. Every day Lana saw one of her customer's eyes land with pleasure on her belly, then linger on her naked left hand. People would expect her to get married. They would feel sorry for her and for her baby if she didn't. But marriage had never held much appeal.

She'd been too young to see her parents' marriage fall apart, but she had walked through the kitchen at the boardinghouse time and again to see strange women eating breakfast at her father's table, trying to make small talk with the back of Karin's head. As far as Lana could tell, romances came in two sizes: people who got into restrictive and stifling marriages, and people who had flings. Perhaps that was why Lana's best relationship had always been with Eli, who broke that mold and fell into a category all his own.

There was no getting around the truth. Some old vestige of her desire for him was rearing up again. But she would learn to get it under control—she had to. She would suffer through anything to keep their relationship sturdy and the same. What they had *worked*. She took comfort in knowing that once the baby was born and found a family, she would be able to go to Costa Rica without the fear that things between her and Eli would change. She could have her own adventures, just like Eli was having his, and they would never make demands on each other or hold each other back. Even though some part of her fantasized that one day she might look into Eli's eyes and see that she was the only woman who had ever truly understood him or claimed his heart, she didn't believe passion would earn her that permanent position. But friendship might.

"What?" Eli asked, a twinkle in his eye.

"What do you mean, *what*?"

"You were staring at me."

Quickly, she turned her gaze away. "I was daydreaming."

"Don't let me stop you," he said. His smile was flirty and sly. "I like the idea of being in your dreams."

She took a sip of her water; the lemon was cool against her lips, a good distraction. Eli's sudden interest in her had to have come from somewhere. But where? Maybe breaking up with Kelly had done some damage to his ego, and now he needed a little harmless flirtation to restore his pride. Maybe all this was just rebounding.

Who was she kidding? This was more.

She ran her finger through the droplets of condensation on her glass. The baby kicked her bladder and she drew in a big breath. *Time for a bathroom run.* She excused herself and began to slide her chair back, suddenly desperate. It was dazzling, how quickly she could go from having an empty bladder to feeling suddenly and painfully full. She put her napkin down on her clean plate and stood.

"Oh my goodness, Lana!" Leroy, who had been "Mr. Federer" to her in college, threw his napkin down on his plate. His eyes had gone right to her belly when she stood. "Why didn't you tell us you were expecting?"

Lana watched as one by one the faces at the table turned toward her. Protectively, she put a hand over her belly button, which as of last week wasn't much of a belly button at all. The baby was growing more rapidly than it had before, bigger each day. She smiled nervously and shrugged.

"When are you due?" he exclaimed.

She told him. Eli got to his feet beside her as if he might shield her.

Leroy also stood to shake Eli's hand. "Nice work, Eli. We all used to wonder how long it would take you kids to get together."

Lana stuttered, trying to pick out just the right words.

He went on. "Better late than never, I say."

"Yes, well . . ." Lana blushed and crossed her arms before her. She was mortified . . . but poor Eli. He must have felt a hundred times worse. She had to set the record straight. "Actually, the truth is—"

"We're slow learners," Eli interrupted. "But thanks."

Then she felt his hand at the small of her back, guiding her away from the table and toward the exit. She felt every eye in the big hall glued to her belly, as if it were the leader of a parade and she merely a follower. She hurried, wobbling badly on the high heels that Karin had insisted she buy.

Finally they turned a corner, stopping beside a white-lit ficus in the secluded hallway that led to the ladies' room. And then they were alone. Blessedly alone. She leaned toward him and whispered in case anyone came near. "Why did you do that? How are we going to go back there and explain that it's not yours?"

"We're not," he said.

She looked up at him. He wore contacts tonight, his brown eyes gleaming warm but serious below his dark lashes. His face was calm, determined, and his gaze was focused solely on hers. Warmth uncoiled and spread within her. She tried to contain it, to tamp it down, but she could not.

He reached up and settled his hand into the crook of her neck, fascinated by something there, perhaps the contrast of his skin and hers. He was so confident, so sure that everything would work out. It made her want to simply put herself in his hands, in every sense. She would give herself to him entirely, and then everything—the baby, her father, her memories, the future, her body, her feelings about *him*—would stop being her decision and become his. She would let him pull her into the flames, into the fire that would incinerate them both.

"It will be okay," Eli said, his gaze gentle. "Trust me."

She couldn't stand to look at him, afraid he might read her feelings in her face. The man she'd spent the evening with had been a stranger to her. This was not Eli, the best friend who'd gone uncomplainingly with her to see chick flicks, who never "took her out" to dinner but was always glad to "join" her, who looked away from her when she met his eye. This new Eli was steelier, more confident and more demanding. And he wanted something. He wanted her.

She had to stop this. Right now. She would cut him off. She would hurt him. Just like she'd done before. She would be terrible and cruel and hateful and say, *No matter how much I wish it was true, telling people it's your baby won't make it yours . . .*

But when she opened her mouth to speak, the words died on her lips. "Eli . . ."

The pad of his thumb slid along her neck, heat slicing through her like a blade. She inhaled sharply. All at once, her whole body remembered him. Reason was useless. No amount of logic could undo how he'd made her feel that night on the fields. How he was making her feel right now.

"Lana . . ." His gaze dipped down to her mouth, then rose back to her eyes.

Yes, she thought. *Anything you want.*

He stepped back. "The bathroom is over there."

She nearly fell forward. She hadn't realized she'd leaned all her weight on the balls of her feet. Cool air rushed around her, fanning her hot skin. "Oh. Thanks."

"Are you okay?"

She laughed. "Am *I* okay?" But once she was inside the safety of the ladies' lounge, she had to clasp her hands to keep them from trembling.

He was pushing her. Deliberately. Purposefully. She hated it. She loved it. She was out of her mind. She leaned her hands against the black granite sink and looked herself square in the eye. "Nope," she said. "Not okay at all."

Karin turned off the lights of the Wildflower Barn and set the alarm. An entire four days had gone by since she and Gene had talked about adopting Lana's baby. And Karin congratulated herself for having had the strength not to bring it up. She walked to her car under thick autumn clouds and copper-tinted leaves. A footstep on the gravel parking lot made her jump out of her skin. And when she turned around, Calvert was there, lurking in that particular way of his. He wore old jeans and an old coat. He hadn't shaved. She guessed his duffel bag was everything he had in the world.

"Hello, Karin."

Her emotions churned. She wasn't entirely surprised to see him; Lana had told her that he'd paid her another visit earlier this month. She looked over his grungy clothes and tired posture, and on one hand she thought, *Good, he deserves to look that terrible*. But on the other hand, her heart reached out to him, felt bad for him, and saw only a person in need of help. Her plan had worked perfectly; Calvert was officially homeless. And yet now that she'd gotten what she wanted, vengeance turned to acid in her throat.

She opened the car door and threw her purse inside.

"Karin, I'm sorry. I don't know what to do. But I need . . . I need . . ."

"What?"

"I tried to handle it myself these last couple days," he said. "But I need *help*."

Her heart thumped in her chest. He needed help. He needed *her* help. He needed *her*.

She knew the man standing before her was her father, and yet for some reason she felt as if he was a complete stranger, like their pasts had been erased—or balanced out—and they were meeting as equals for the first time.

"I got nowhere to stay. They want me to leave town."

"So what do you want me to do?" she asked.

Calvert hung his head. "Don't know."

Karin sighed. This wasn't what she'd planned. She hadn't wanted him to be homeless. She'd thought he would just disappear. Vanish back to wherever he came from. But here he was, calling on her for help.

Oh, Lord, she prayed silently.

How could she refuse him? Things were different now than when he'd first shown up and from when she'd set the police after him. Now that Lana was pregnant, she could see the direction her own life was heading. There was a baby in her future. Her near future. And she knew she had to be grateful for that. She'd made a promise before God to be a better person. If she refused to help Calvert now, it would be going back on her word.

Calvert went on. "I got a job working construction by the lake. Making eight bucks an hour under the table. Just 'til I get back on my feet. And I'll be able to get a place soon. But I don't start work for another few days. And I didn't know what else to do, except to come see you."

"I don't know," Karin said. To his credit, she couldn't remember a time when he'd ever lied to her. But still, she didn't trust him. She pressed her lips together and looked over the man who used to be her father, his scruffy work boots, his jeans that had been washed so many times they were more gray than blue. The picture he presented said he'd done real penance and now he was begging at her proverbial door. She couldn't refuse him. Especially since part of his misery had been caused directly by her.

"Karin, I know I messed up with you girls. And I probably shouldn't have come back to town. But I thought . . . I thought I might be able to set things right. See if there was something I could do to make up for it all."

Karin was silent.

He laughed, a hollow sound. "But now I messed up again."

"Where have you been sleeping?" she asked.

"Here and there," he said. "The weather's been warm. It's not so bad."

She looked away from him, unable to imagine him sleeping on the ground. She hated to think he was unsafe. "How long do you need?"

"Well, I . . ."

"What if I just buy you a train ticket back to Wisconsin?"

"That's nice of you. But I only need a few days. Three, tops. See, I—"

"Fine." She leaned against the minivan, its paint still warm from the sun. "I can put you up in a motel for a little while."

"Thank you. Thank you so much."

She pointed at him and frowned. "And don't think that because I'm helping you it means anything's changed. I don't like you. I never will."

"I understand," he said.

She hesitated. This was crazy. She felt as if she was opening a door for him to come back into her life. *But maybe*, a small voice inside her said, *maybe this is what you've wanted all along.* "This is only temporary," she said.

Then she unlocked the door of the van and let him in.

September 25

Lana and Charlotte sat next to each other on matching chairs at the women's clinic. Two teenage girls also sat together in the corner, so committed to their ferocious texting that there was no way to misinterpret their intense typing as anything but nerves. Under an old TV set that showed Julia Roberts and Cameron Diaz, an older couple sat leafing through month-old magazines. Lana had the urge to ask them, *So what are you two in for?* She stared at the wall of pamphlets before her, and a dozen drawings of worried faces stared back.

Charlotte sat playing with one of her earrings, a tiny wrench hanging from a silver chair. "You haven't said a word about the wedding. How was it?"

"Fine," Lana said, though her head was still spinning from that night. She'd almost let Eli kiss her. Or worse, she'd almost kissed him. She didn't know what was more excruciating—knowing what had almost happened or knowing what didn't. "Eli has been acting . . . funny."

"What do you mean?"

"He . . . I don't know. He's different."

Charlotte frowned. "You're going to have to give me a bit more to go on than that."

Lana bit the inside of her lip, afraid of speaking the thing she didn't want to acknowledge in words. "He's been flirting with me!" she said fast.

"Flirting. You mean, *really* flirting?" Charlotte asked, pushing her gray-brown hair behind her shoulders. "Like, more than your usual flirting with each other?"

"I think he wanted to kiss me. I saw it in his eyes."

Charlotte laughed. "Tell me something I don't know. Lana, he's had a thing for you for years. I thought you knew."

Lana looked down. "In the beginning I thought he did. But then . . . then I was sure it went away. I guess I was wrong."

Charlotte's smile was a little sad. "He's in love with you. But I could see why you'd downplay it in your mind. I mean, it's easier that way."

"I don't know what to do. He's changing the rules."

"Is it a game you want to play?"

Lana took a deep, heavy breath. "Part of me does.

But . . . I don't think I could make it work with him romantically. I'd be too afraid of losing him."

"Why couldn't you make it work? You've been friends for so long. What exactly would change apart from the physical stuff?"

"I don't know." Lana rubbed her palm hard against the cushioned arm of her seat. "Maybe he would change. Maybe I would. And then what? I'd lose him if it didn't work out."

"There's always risk when you're talking about love."

"I don't want any risk," Lana said, anger rising from some deep, hidden well. "I want something steady. Something that I can depend on but that isn't going to chain me down."

"Isn't that exactly what Eli does for you?"

"Yes. Right now. As my friend."

"I'm really not convinced."

"It's like baking a cake," Lana said. "Why would I want to change the recipe if the cake is perfect just the way it is?"

Charlotte nodded, her eyes warm and understanding. "But what if you only think the cake is perfect because you've never had anything better? What if there's more?"

The nurse announced a name from the doorway, and the two teenagers looked up with twin "deer-in-the-headlights" expressions. Together they rose and followed her out of the room.

"I suppose you might be right," Lana said.

"And what have you decided about the baby?" Charlotte asked, lowering her voice.

"Adoption."

"But could you really do that?"

"Why not?" Lana looked down. "It would be more ethical to give it away than to keep it. I mean, look at me. Look at my life, my dreams. I'm not ready to give up on having an adventure. So I'm not cut out to be a mom."

"You can have an adventure *and* be a mom."

"No. I know what it's like to live in a house where people aren't dependable, where they just come and go. This baby needs a mother who's down-to-earth. Solid. Predictable. Someone less like me."

"You would have help," Charlotte said warmly.

"You mean Karin."

"And me. And Eli. The baby wouldn't want for family."

"No, I suppose not. But no matter how much help you guys would be able to give me, at the end of the day, I would still be its mom. It would all come down to me. Either I have to give up my dreams of traveling, or put them off for the next twenty years until the baby's grown. And even if I do keep it, I might screw it up."

"Why do you think you'll screw the kid up?"

"Because even if I love it right now, what if I end up resenting it in a few years for getting in the way of the life I want to live?"

Charlotte shook her head. "Lana, you're not *him*. You're not like Calvert. I don't think you should be worried that you are."

Lana lowered her voice. "The thing is, Karin is the one who was meant to be a mother. Not me. I feel like our fates got shuffled. I feel like it's pretty clear what I'm supposed to do."

"My God." Shock flashed across Charlotte's face. "You want to give the baby to Karin."

Lana sighed. "If she even wants it. But I'm not sure she does. If they were going to adopt a baby, they probably would have by now."

Charlotte frowned.

"It's not really that bad. It makes sense. I could still see the baby and be in its life, but I wouldn't risk screwing it up by being a bad parent."

"Does Karin know?"

"Not yet. But I think maybe she's been hinting. Nothing too obvious. The other day, she was talking about storing her exercise equipment and she said, 'Gene and I put the treadmill in the extra room that was supposed to be for the baby. Too bad you don't have any extra room at *your* house.'"

"That's mean," Charlotte said.

"Not exactly. It's just Karin's way."

"You shouldn't give Karin the baby just because Karin wants you to."

"But it's not totally about Karin. It's about me too. I told myself that when Karin had a family of her own, then I could go away for a while. So it makes sense: I give the baby to Karin, Karin gets the family and stability she always wanted, and then I'm free to live in Costa Rica for a while like I've always wanted."

Charlotte shook her head. "There's something missing from this plan."

"What?"

"Your feelings." Charlotte took her hand. "That baby is yours, Lana. It's part of you. And you've always had such a soft and caring heart. I just don't think you're going to have as easy a time handing over that baby as you think."

Lana swallowed the lump in her throat. She worried that Charlotte was right. It would be hard to give up the baby, but she had to. From the doorway, a nurse called her name, the summons as finite as a judge's gavel. "I think it's the only way," she said.

Eli pulled a handful of crumpled dollar bills from the pocket of his jeans and did his best to flatten them out before handing them to the cashier. He and the woman, a young redhead who might have been the same age as his students, had somehow fallen to chatting about crossing guards and busy intersections, but the conversation had been cut short by Eli's groping for bills. She started packing his groceries into his reusable bag while he fumbled and apologized. She was laughing when he handed her the money at last. He took his bags and drove home.

Generally, he was in a good mood these days. He felt as if he'd turned a corner, but that it was just the first of many corners and whatever waited around the next one was big. For the first time in his life, he felt totally and completely like himself.

The consequences of this transformation had been astounding. It suddenly seemed as if people liked him more, and he liked them too. He was interested in everything. He felt generous and good toward everyone. Women were especially responsive. He wasn't sure, but he thought they flirted with him more, or he caught them checking him out. Ordinarily he might not let himself believe it was happening. But why deny the truth? He was different now.

He carried the groceries into his house, humming under his breath. And when he started to unpack his food, he found a receipt that wasn't his, with the cashier's name and phone number written in swift blue ink. He laughed a little to himself but crumpled the receipt in his hand.

There was only one woman for him. The possibility of failure, of being forced to use his newfound confidence to forge a future without her, was real. But he would not cave. He was more optimistic than he'd felt in years; this was the same high he felt when he was on an expedition and he felt certain of finding something big. He was too close to give up now.

Lana had thrown on an old sweater made with inch-thick wool and a slouchy brown collar that piled up to her chin. If Eli had been surprised to see her at his door at nine o'clock in the evening, he didn't show it. She didn't miss the way he put his arm around her on the pretense of ushering her inside.

Eli's house had always been a safe haven for her. His taste in furniture was much more studied than hers. While she tended to favor exotic colors and mismatched chairs, his brown leather couch and russet walls showed a preference for economy and simplicity. And yet, for all his interest in design, he took no pains to keep his apartment overly neat. Books were strewn on the floor and papers obscured the coffee table. Various remote controls sat on armrests, and his sneakers were untied in the middle of the floor.

"What can I get you?" he asked.

"Nothing," she said. She sat down on the couch, her back not touching the cushions behind her.

"Are you sure?"

"Yes. Come sit with me."

His mouth turned down slightly at the corner. He sat on the couch beside her, closer than she would have liked.

She took a deep breath. The conversation they needed to have would not be easy. He seemed to be in a good mood and she hated to ruin it. But what choice did she have? Waiting would only make things worse.

She'd practiced her lines a hundred times at home and on the way over. *Eli, I just want you to know that I value you as a friend, a very close friend. I'll always feel that way.*

Yet now that she sat beside him, she trembled with nerves and realized she had no idea how she was going to launch into the conversation they needed to have. She hadn't schemed up any introductions, hadn't preplanned how to broach the topic aloud. Talking with Eli had always been so easy. But now, no words came.

"What is it?" he prompted.

She looked into his eyes, their brown so rich and luxurious and caring. The freckle that winked like a star just under his lower lashes. Tonight he wore a navy blue hoodie and slouchy jeans, and his chestnut brown hair stood up at the very back of his head as if he'd been sleeping. She could smell his laundry detergent and the sporty scent of his body wash. All at once, she wanted to bury her face in the warmth where the cotton of his sweatshirt met the smooth heat of his skin.

His eyes narrowed as if he knew what she was thinking, as if he registered the subtle shift in her gaze and was reading her mind. She panicked, trying to make herself look away. Yet the gravity was unbreakable. He shifted slightly, turning toward her a fraction of an inch. She caught the scent of mint on his breath. She saw his gaze drop to her mouth.

Eli, I just want you to know that I value you as a . . . The words were stuck in her throat, replaced by a longing that had burst inside her like a geyser, rising from someplace hidden and deep. *Please just kiss me*, she pleaded. *Please.*

And when he did not, she took his face in both hands and leaned in.

She felt the delay of his surprise, and for a split second she thought, *Oh, no, I misjudged him*. Maybe she'd been imagining the longing in his eyes. Maybe she'd attributed to him a need that was entirely her own.

But then his hands were in her hair, on her shoulders, everywhere, and his mouth was a demanding, greedy heat, fire bursting through an open door. She dug her fingers into his sweatshirt, rising up on one hip to slant her body closer. This was better than she remembered. So much better. He shifted on the couch, pressed her back into the soft cushions to align their bodies, and when his chest pressed flat against hers, she arched toward him, her whole body crying out for more. She was overwhelmed by him. He touched the beginning and end of every nerve in her body, those on the surface of her skin and deep inside. She'd meant only to dip a toe in water, to test the temperature. But now she was in over her head, drowning, sinking with him.

His hand curled around the back of her knee, and with a quick tug, her leg was bent and lifted, linking their bodies in age-old alignment. The intimacy of it shocked her, the firm pressure of his hips. She came up for air, struggling to clear her head. But she caught only a glimpse of that clarity before his mouth was on her neck, driving her crazy, dragging her back down once again.

Wait. She heard the word in her head long before she found the lucidity to say it aloud. "Eli. Wait."

A gruff noise came from the back of his throat.

"Please. *Wait.*"

He didn't lift his head immediately. He'd stopped moving, but she could feel the difficulty of his restraint, the pounding of his heart and his breath hot against her skin. When he finally looked up, his eyes were cloudy with want. He moved back slightly, and she pushed him off the rest of the way. She stood as quickly as she could, blood rushing to her head, and she went to the other side of the room. She couldn't bear to look at him, and so she stood at the window, peering through her own reflection at the dim lights in the street.

She needed to say something. He expected it and deserved it. But words seemed worthless and lame. When she spoke, her breath marked the window in a mottled, shifting white. "That wasn't what I meant to happen."

He said nothing.

Panic warred with the urge to explain herself, to undo what she'd done. She thought as quickly as her sluggish brain would allow. "Eli. I came here to tell you that I value you as a friend."

"I know you do." She turned around to face him and saw that he was sitting on the couch, leaning his forearms on his knees and looking at her intently. His hands were clasped tight. "I value you as a friend too."

She nodded, not quite sure they were on the same page. "I didn't mean to kiss you."

"But you did."

"I did." She leaned back against the windowsill, both hands holding on to the wooden edge. A thrill of something exciting and wonderful raced through her, burning up darkness and doubt. "I definitely *did*."

He stood, began walking slowly toward her.

She went on, forcing herself to remember the logic of why it was a bad idea to kiss her best friend. "I did kiss you. But I didn't mean to. Because, I mean, this isn't good timing." He took a few more slow steps toward her; she couldn't tell if he was listening to her or not. But she went on. "I don't know where these feelings are coming from. I need us—you—to be dependable right now." He stood before her, close. She knew she was babbling, but she couldn't stop. "Don't you see? It's such a strange time in my life. I need stability. I need friendship. I need—I need . . ."

"You need . . . ?"

She looked at his mouth, those lips that she knew could drive her mad. There was no more denying it. "I need you," she said.

He kissed her, but it wasn't the kiss she'd wanted. Only a teasing and soft kiss, one that left her gripping the front of his shirt and seeking more. She had to close her eyes a moment to calm down. "We have to talk about this," she said.

"Yes. We do." He stepped back, cool air rushing between them. "But not tonight. Neither of us is in a position to talk right now."

"Thank you," she said.

• • •

Outside, the night was blustery, the trees bending and creaking. She drew her coat more tightly around her and headed toward the car. She took a breath of fresh air, waiting for a feeling of liberation to soar through her, waiting to feel like herself again. But instead, she had only the paradoxical sense that she'd just managed to escape from a place she'd always wanted to be.

On the lonely and dark roads, she rolled down the windows of her car to let in the freezing air and she turned up the radio until the speakers buzzed with thumping bass notes. The fields that stretched toward the distant mountains were dark and spooky, more smoky gray than black in the light of the moon. Above, the sky was starless, lit by a swollen moon.

She drove as fast as the curves of the road would allow. There were reasons people didn't fall for their friends. She had to remember that. She'd been around long enough to know that when fantasy collided with reality, the result was usually a breakdown. The high expectations of fantasy and the baser truths of real life simply couldn't combine. That was part of the reason that she'd trained herself to compartmentalize her feelings about Eli, tucking away desire and bringing feelings of friendship out into the light of day.

But the place Eli occupied in her heart was too big, too expansive to be superficially labeled or contained. All this time she'd counted on him to be her reality, her welcome, her dependable day-to-day. But now he was telling her that he was something different: He was also her fantasy, a secret promise of pleasure, passion, and sex.

And she worried, How could he be both *and* be lasting? How could she make a life with him?

She had taken such care to build the structure of their relationship; she'd spent years honing her own feelings toward him, dulling them when they became too hot and sharp, encouraging herself to feel distant and mild. For ten years, friendship had seen them through Eli's many travels—the ups and downs created by his absence and presence. Friendship had protected Lana's dreams of traveling on her own—as long as she kept herself at arm's length from him, she would not be tempted to forfeit her dreams for his. Her rules had served them both well.

But as the miles disappeared under her tires and she told herself, again and again, to be logical—to be realistic and smart—some part of her remained with him, in his living room, in his arms, demanding everything he had to give, and seeing the evening through to a different, more satisfying end.

October

Evening primrose: As a flower pollinated by nocturnal insects, the evening primrose is made for night. Some have theorized that the petals are mildly phosphorescent. Others speculate that the flowers do not give off their own light, but instead store up sunlight during the day. Whatever the cause, the true nature of the evening primrose is most clearly seen when the sun is down.

October 1

After her shift had ended, Karin veered off the walkway to the motel where her father was staying, and she made a beeline straight for the front of the building. It was getting dark early now, the streetlights flickering on during what seemed like early afternoon. The trees were bright orange and red on the distant mountains, brilliant as flames against the cold slate sky.

When she rounded the corner of the motel, Calvert was waiting for her in the doorway of room 41, just where he'd said he'd be. His breath rose in thick white clumps. He wore a tired brown jacket with white wool at the collar, old jeans, and big tan boots. His hands were folded across his chest to keep warm.

"You hungry?" she asked.

He nodded, eyeing her as if he expected her to follow up with the words *Well, too bad*.

"Well, come on. Let's go."

He followed her to the van.

For the first leg of the ride to the restaurant, he didn't try to make small talk and Karin was glad. Being in the same space as him again took some getting used to. About a week had gone by since she'd agreed to help him, and as the days had passed Karin had been doing a lot of hard thinking. She was starting to look at Calvert's reappearance in a different way. She had before her the opportunity to talk to him, one adult to another, for the first time. Maybe she deserved an explanation for how he'd raised her. And maybe he deserved the chance to explain.

The houses passed by—the lake peering between trees on their right-hand side—and mile by mile, the distance between buildings shrank until the country gave way to the energy of the city, with its busy sidewalks and intersections strung with traffic lights. As she pulled into the parking garage, he held out a handful of bills; she gestured for him to put them in the center console so she could keep her eyes on the winding concrete ramps. "What's this?"

"The money I owe you for the three days at the motel."

She peered into the dimness of the low-ceilinged garage, concentrating perhaps a bit more than she needed to on finding a spot.

"And I wanted to thank you," he said.

"It wasn't a big deal to loan you the money."

"Yes, thanks for the money. But thanks for calling the dogs off too."

Karin rubbed her palms hard against the leather of the steering wheel, more than a little embarrassed. She slid the minivan into a free space and cut the engine. "How did you know it was me?"

"I would have done the same thing," he said.

She nodded, warring with the urge to apologize to him. It suddenly struck her how insane the whole thing seemed. She may have overreacted a bit.

"Don't say sorry," he said. "I wouldn't want me showing up in town either after all these years. You did the right thing."

"Let's just go eat," she said.

A few blocks later they were seated in two wooden chairs, looking over their menus in silence. The restaurant, which sat near the corner of Cherry Street and South Winooski, had bright beige walls, a long diner-style bar, and big picture windows that offered views of the busy street. When the waitress came to the table, Karin ordered buckwheat pancakes with local maple syrup, and Calvert got a tortilla filled with chorizo sausage, scrambled eggs, and Monterey Jack. He folded his menu and set it on the table, but Karin picked it up and handed it directly to the waitress before she left.

He crossed his hands in his lap. "So how long you been married?"

"Three years," Karin said.

"He a nice guy?"

"The best. He'll be a good father. Once we have kids."

Calvert took a sip of his water. "And when will that be?"

"Hard to say," Karin said, her throat tightening around the only words she could manage.

He didn't follow up. "And how's Lana doing with her . . . thing?"

"I guess she's fine. Healthy, if that's what you mean."

"Is that boyfriend going to take responsibility?"

Karin laughed. "You should know better than that."

Calvert grew silent.

"What?" asked Karin. "What is it?"

He picked up his napkin and tore the corner off. "You remember the day Lana graduated from high school?"

"Sure. We gave your ticket to the neighbors."

"Well, I went."

"You did not."

"I sat up on top of the hill, in the woods where the kids liked to go smoke pot after the football games, and I watched the whole thing."

"Did you do that for mine?" Karin asked.

"No. No, I didn't."

The sounds of clinking silverware and music bled into the silence between them. Karin stared absentmindedly at the waitresses hurrying around the crowded room, hardly able to process what she'd heard.

"I'm sorry," Calvert said.

Karin couldn't look at him. "I wanted so much for you to like me . . ."

"I did like you. It's just . . . Lana was always easier to

get along with because she didn't seem to care as much about anything."

"She cared," Karin said, angry. "She just never showed it."

"That may be. I ain't trying to make an excuse for myself. It's just—once Lana graduated I knew you girls would have no more reason to stick around. I knew you'd be gone the second you could go. So I sat up there on the hill above the football field and listened to all the terrible speechifying, and I thought to myself, *I should get square with them*. But you know as well as I that I'm nothing but a coward. And there was nothing I could have said or done to make it right back then."

"I'm not sure there's anything you can do now," Karin said. "Maybe your feelings have changed over the years, but mine and Lana's haven't. You could be made pope tomorrow and you'd still be the same old Calvert to us."

"I can't apologize for how I raised you because you two girls just about raised yourselves. But I can tell you that if I knew back then what I know now, I would have done things differently."

Karin watched him closely, resisting the urge to hold her arms out to him. She heard a deep, tremulous vulnerability in his words. And though the part of her that was still angry screamed in her ear not to believe him—not to fall for it—she rejected that negative voice. Calvert needed to reconcile with the past as much as she did. She thought of how hard the last few months had been—how difficult it was to grapple daily with her own anger. It would be a balm to both of them to forgive, even if they could not forget.

"I appreciate what you want to do," Karin said slowly. "So if you want, I can forgive you."

Calvert looked down at his plate, so quiet Karin thought he must be hiding tears.

"But I'm going to tell you this," she went on. "Forgiving you doesn't mean we can be one big happy family again. Do you know what I mean? There's too much between us. Too much history. That stuff . . . it doesn't just go away."

"I know that," Calvert said. "I don't expect to be invited to Christmas dinner. This was just something I had to do. I thought I might be able to help you girls, to make up for everything. And once I'm done here, I'll go."

Karin nodded. She wished her life could be like others' lives in books and movies, when prodigals could come back, reconcile, and everything would be happily-ever-after perfect in the end. But real happily-ever-afters were so much less flamboyant and more complicated than in movies. Sitting here talking to Calvert was closure. And she was glad for it; it satisfied her. But she wasn't about to ride off into the sunset with him by her side.

"We don't really need help," Karin said. "So I guess you have no reason to stay here anymore. I guess you can go back."

"But what about . . ." His voice trailed off. "Lana still won't talk to me. Would you talk to her for me? Would you tell her . . . tell her . . ."

"What?"

"I don't know. Maybe you could ask her to cut her old man a break."

Karin took a deep breath, remembering how she'd

made Lana confront Calvert with her instead of doing it on her own. "I don't know if I can do that. That's between you and her. And I think I've already asked too much of her when it comes to you."

Calvert worried the hem of his sleeve.

"But I'll think about it," she said.

The waitress came to the table, setting their plates down one at a time. "Pancakes for you, tortilla for you . . . Can I get you anything else?"

Karin looked at her plate, heaped with mounds of food. Even without taking a bite, she already felt full. "Thanks," she said. "I think we're fine for now."

Gene was waiting for her in the kitchen when she got home from the Barn that evening. The room smelled like buttered toast and scrambled eggs. Breakfast for dinner had always been his specialty, and yet she wasn't thrilled at the idea of eating two breakfasts today.

"Hey," he said, not turning around. "You're home late."

"And you're home early."

"I called your cell."

She put her purse down on the table and took off her coat. She'd turned off her cell phone at the table with Calvert. She must have forgotten to turn it back on. She took off her coat and hung it on a peg by the door. So much had happened to her today. So much she wanted to share with her husband. It was hard to know where to start.

"Do you want an egg?" he asked.

She sat down at the table, watching the folds across the

back of his sweatshirt shifting as he moved the spatula around.

"I ate," she said. "I had dinner."

"With who?"

"With Calvert."

For a moment he didn't move. He only stood there, motionless, as if waiting for something else to happen. "Why?"

"Because I needed to," she said.

Quickly he turned around, the spatula raised in the air. "But you've spent every day since the moment I met you telling me how much you hate him, how hard it was growing up in the boardinghouse. I don't get this."

She studied the wrinkle between his eyes, the furrow in his forehead. "Why do you sound annoyed?"

He turned away from her again, scraping the bottom of the frying pan. "I just think it's weird that you want to see him all of a sudden."

"It's not, though," she said. "I'm telling you, I feel . . . better."

"Well, good for you," he said.

"Gene . . . what . . . where is this coming from?"

"The man is a scumbag. Karin, when I met you, you wouldn't sleep if a door wasn't locked. You wouldn't take a shower unless someone else was home with you. And now you're telling me that you're having father-daughter night?"

"I'm learning to not be so angry," she said, unsettled by the growing sense of how close they were to having another fight. This wasn't what she'd expected; she'd thought he would understand.

"You know what I think?" he asked.

She didn't answer.

"I think you're desperate. I think you're reaching out to Calvert because it's driving you crazy that we can't have a baby. As if being his family again will make up for the family we can't have. Karin, I don't want that jerk in our lives. Who knows what trick he's leading you into. Has he asked you for money?"

"No," she said. "Well, sort of . . . but he paid me back. What happened is, I—"

"Karin— This is crazy. Can't you see that? This is *Calvert* we're talking about."

She stood up, furious. For the first time in weeks she'd felt the first glimmers of peace, like she could see the world a little clearer and it wasn't all bad. "I don't understand why you can't support me in this."

He sighed. "I'm sorry. I just feel like I have no idea who you are these days. You keep springing things on me. You're completely unpredictable. And I don't know what to do with that."

She was quiet. She could see where he was coming from. She had been putting him through a lot. "I think I've surprised myself too."

He said nothing for a long time. At last he turned back toward the eggs, and she could see that the set of his shoulders had loosened. "Well, I'm glad you went to see him if that's what you needed to do."

"Thank you," she said, and she tentatively slipped back into the kitchen chair. She didn't know why, but she had the odd sense that there was something he wasn't telling her, something he knew but couldn't say. She supposed she was being hypervigilant again. Paranoid. She tried to let the feeling go. She had no use for that kind of thinking anymore. And she supposed there was no sense in going into the details of her situation with Calvert either, especially since Gene obviously didn't want to hear. She wanted to focus on the positive from now on.

"Is it too late to place an order for a scrambled egg?" she asked.

"I thought you said you weren't hungry."

"I think maybe I am," she said.

October 9

Lana sat in the dark of the passenger seat of Eli's car, pinching extra fabric on the fingertips of her gloves with studious concentration. In the two weeks that had passed since she'd kissed him, she'd been stymied about what she would say to him when he returned from his latest trip. When she was a little girl in Calvert's house, Karin had taught her never to open the door to any room she was alone in, not even an inch. Because once the lock was slid back and the door cracked open, security was breached. Some part of her felt like that now with Eli, that curiosity had compelled her to open the door just enough to peck through, and now he would never allow her to shut it completely again.

"Where exactly are we going?" she asked.

He looked over at her in the darkness and his glasses caught the gold glint of a streetlight passing overhead. "Almost there."

She laughed—a nervous laugh for no reason, then went back to playing with her gloves. Wherever they were going, she knew what kind of conversation they were going to have when they got there. She wouldn't be able to deny that she was physically attracted to him, but she could stress that they were friends or they were nothing. As lovers, they had no future together. Their lives were headed in two different directions. But as friends, they might get by.

Then, if that didn't work, she would admit that she depended on *him* to enforce the boundaries of their friendship as much as she depended on herself. She would point to his sense of duty and honor and beg him not to ask more of her than she could give.

She looked out the passenger-side window. The night was sharply cold and the sky was clear and teeming with stars. He turned onto a small deserted driveway past the athletic fields. She began to suspect the worst.

"This is probably illegal," she said.

"Probably." He pulled into a clearing that wasn't quite a parking lot, then cut the engine. "Come on."

She didn't move.

"You want to talk? Let's talk. But I want to be outside walking when we do."

He got out of the car, not giving her much choice but to follow. She called on her deepest wells of courage and unbuckled her seat belt. Outside the car's warm cabin, the air was freezing, burning her cheeks. She had to jog to catch up with him; he covered the ground in long strides.

Around them, the trees had turned gold and red. Lana couldn't see them, but she could smell them—the bright sweetness of leaves fermenting on the branch. The grass under her sneakers crushed, brittle as breaking glass.

"Eli, this is stupid. What is this going to prove?"

He stopped, then took a few steps back and reached for her hand. This close, he smelled like chestnuts and tree bark. There was a knot in his brow, so when he spoke she expected him to sound angry. Instead his voice was soft.

"Patience," he said. His hand wrapped firmly around hers with a kind of entitlement she'd never expected, and he held it as they walked on. She didn't look at him when they stopped walking at last. She knew the width of his shoulders compared to hers, the slight lift of her chin needed to meet his eyes. She knew the space between their feet was mere inches, and that he was looking at her, reading her better than anyone else ever had.

"You know where we are," he said.

"Yes, I know."

She looked around—looked anywhere but at his face. The scenery had changed ever so slightly in the last decade. There was a building on the hill to the north that hadn't been there ten years ago. There was a path now where the wheels of many golf carts had worn the grass down to thin brown treads. The season was different as well; she and Eli had been out here in the early summer for finals week. A time for testing. Now the leaves were frozen on the branches, dulled by darkness but made to glow otherworldly by frost and moonlight.

"Eli . . ." She met his eyes carefully, her heart beating hard. She could see his pupils, fathomless as black holes. The feel of him, even all those decades ago, was still with her—the tough rise of his thigh behind his knee, the weight of his hips bearing down. "Come on," she said, keeping her voice light, almost teasing. "Take me back."

"Not yet. I've put off having this conversation with you for way too long."

"If we could just go somewhere else . . ."

"I want you to tell me a story. From the beginning. I want you to tell me the story of what happened. Right on this spot."

She thought, *This can't be happening.* She looked down at the grass beneath her feet as if it might have answers. Her heart beat hotly in her throat. How could she say the words aloud, words that she couldn't so much as whisper to herself? "This is silly. Come on, Eli. You're such a joker sometimes. Let's go get—"

"Lana." His voice had a cold, solid edge. "*Tell* me."

"Please. Don't do this."

"Fine. If you can't tell me, then I'll tell you." He put a hand on her rib cage, where her coat had fallen away from her body. "This is where we saw the fireball. Lana . . . this is where we made love."

She felt his words as if they were more than sound, almost as if he'd come into her body once again, a second time. And yet they were standing a foot apart, each in coats and gloves, and it had been years since that moment had passed.

"Don't be upset," he said.

"I'm not."

"It's just a memory. Right? No reason to be afraid of thinking about it." He leaned closer. She was so sensitive to his touch—she always had been—that she thought she could feel the unique pressure of each one of his fingers on her skin. "I've thought about it over the years. Even when I told myself it meant nothing, I thought about it. Did you?"

She couldn't answer. She caught a faint trace of mint on his breath.

"And I still think about it. About how your hair wrapped around my hand. About the way the light from the sunrise fell across your hip bones. Lana, I've thought about it a thousand times. Every time I see you. And I know you do too."

She held still, frozen in place.

"Will you tell me I'm wrong?" he asked.

"I can't," she said.

She sensed his relief, his whole body going slack. But only a moment later, he was looking at her with new focus and intention. "Why wouldn't you let me come to you like that again?"

"Would you believe me if I told you it wasn't good?"

He laughed. "Lana, you *came* against my hand."

Her face went hot. "I was afraid I'd lose you. I'm still afraid."

"Why?"

"Because we were such good friends. And we wanted different things from life back then. I wanted to travel the world and you wanted to stay here and settle down. But instead, look how it turned out. You're always traveling and I never have. Life gets so complicated and mixed up. . . . I just thought that as long as we stayed friends, I could have my life and you could have yours—and we'd always have each other. And do you know what else?"

"What?"

"I was right."

He blinked, and she knew he saw the logic of friendship, the safety of it. What she'd done, she'd done for both of them. He should thank her, in a way.

But instead, he only moved closer, lifted his hand from her body to her neck, and pushed his fingers into her hair until her head tipped slightly back. "Are you sure you were right?" he asked.

She turned her face away, embarrassed by what he knew: that he only needed to kiss her and her whole body would rock. She needed another tactic. She stepped away. "Eli. Please. If you've ever loved me, you'll let this go. You've got to."

She saw the hard confidence in his face waver. "Why?"

"Because if we sleep together, it could change things. Please . . . if you respect our friendship, if you respect what we've had together for these last ten years, then you won't try to change it."

"I'm not changing anything. How I've felt about you has never changed. And never will. I'm just not hiding it anymore."

"But you have to!" she said, panic rising.

"I don't see why."

She grabbed a handful of his jacket, frustrated that she could not get through. "Listen to me. We're friends. We *work* as friends. Please don't change the rules on me. Not now. Not when I've never needed you more."

"But don't you see how good it will be? Can you tell me you haven't imagined it?"

"I'm not talking about sex."

"Neither am I."

She took a deep breath. Why could he not see the safety, the logic, of backing away from the moment and not looking back? "I can't lie to you anymore. I want you. Deep down, I've wanted you for a long time. But I *can't* lose you. You and Karin are all I have. Do you understand? I can't imagine my life without you in it."

"I feel the same way."

"Right. And if we . . . if we do this, we risk losing everything."

"Or gaining everything," he said.

She let him go. "But what about our lifestyles? Our dreams? We're risking them too here. Don't you see?"

His voice was steady and calm. "We'll work it out. We always work things out."

Tears came to her eyes now. The logic of why she'd suffered for so long, why she'd spent so many years denying how she felt, why she'd settled for inferior men to come to her bed—all of the reasons were getting muddled up and slippery. Years of logic and rationale were vanishing, and what reasons she did throw at him he threw right back. Walls were crumbling, boundaries breaking down. She felt as if he was leaving her already, that he was already slipping out of her hands.

She wiped at the tears on her face, determined to try one more time. "I don't want to look back someday and wonder if sleeping with you was worth losing you."

"Oh, Lana." He touched her face, his caress gentle. "Is *not* sleeping with me worth losing me?"

Her breath caught. "What are you saying?"

He sighed. "I can't do this anymore." He stood so close the white of his breath met her face. "I can't stand one more minute of my life thinking that any day now some other man will scoop you up and have the life with you that I want. I want to wake up with you in the morning. I want to find your favorite place to be kissed. Whether we sleep together or not, we can never go back to being just friends."

She wrapped her arms around herself. She wanted the

same things he wanted. But desire wasn't the problem. The problem was everything else between them that desire put at stake. "I'm asking you to forget this. I'm *begging* you. Don't do this to me right now."

"And I'm telling you I can't forget. I need to know what we are," he said, the words caught between clenched teeth.

"But why do we have to name it?"

"Because. I'm in love with you. I've always been in love with you. And I'm done living a lie."

He kissed her.

She tried to reason with herself, tried to say, *But this is Eli.* She should not, in theory, go boneless at the touch of her best friend. But his mouth was a warm bloom against the cold night, gentle but persistent, and each way her mind turned to withdraw from the heat and press of his lips, it was as if he was there waiting to block her retreat, to palm the fire within and make a space for it to glow hotter. *This is Eli,* she told herself. *This is Eli.* And yet, the words that were meant to protect her from her own desire morphed and turned against her. For years, she'd been filling her life with substitutes, one after another, to fill the ache in her heart for the man she could not allow herself to have. Her body knew: This was Eli—the real thing. This was him, kissing her, at last, kissing, and as the admonitions of her mind grew smaller she wrapped her arms around his neck and—*oh, glorious*—kissed him back. Her Eli, at last.

She heard the low sound in his throat—so male and satisfied—and his arms wrapped around her waist and pulled her body against his. Her palms burned to touch him skin to skin. She was a teenager again, so hot she was melting, all liquid and instinct and need. Her lips followed his when he pulled back, and she thought, *I'll have him right here. Again.* If she was going to lose him, she would at least lose him with one last set of blazing memories to warm her when he was gone. She pulled on his jacket despite the freezing cold.

But he broke the connection. His breath went up in plumes. "No. Not here. And not like this."

She forced her breathing to even out, her heart to slow. "You're right." She gathered her thoughts, seeing just how close to going over the edge she'd been. "You're right. Sex won't give us any answers."

The corner of his lip tipped up. "Maybe not. But the questions will be fun." He ran his thumb over her lower lip. "I don't want you to think we're making love on a whim again. When it happens I want you to be there for it. Before, during, and after. *Years* after. It has to be a decision you make, something you won't be able to deny later on. God help me, Lana. I couldn't go through that again."

She stepped away from him, got her bearings. As she looked down—to make some distance between them if only for a moment—the curve of her belly was there, round as the curve of the overhead sky. It came as a surprise to remember reality. She put a hand on the crest of the half-sphere, felt the warmth coming from her own skin.

She looked up at him, the question on her lips far too complicated to speak.

"I know," he said.

And then both his hands were on her body, the swell

of the baby within her. And her heart couldn't take it. Tears welled up in her eyes.

"I love you," he said. "Everything that you are and everything that is you. Do you understand?"

She placed her hands on top of his, marveling. And then she knew the truth: She loved him—she was in love with him—and had been for quite some time.

"Let me take you home," he said gently.

"All right," she said.

Lana was quiet in the car on the way home, her face turned toward the window. Eli wished he knew what she was thinking. Row houses breezed by with their cheerfully lit porches decorated with pumpkins and bales of hay, and Eli silently willed her to reach over and take his hand, to assure him he'd done the right thing. But she didn't.

He pulled up to the curb at her apartment and cut the engine. He watched her take off her seat belt, moving it around the bump of her belly; he clicked his off as well.

"Eli . . . ," she said, his name spoken so softly it was mere air passing over her lips. When he looked at her, the shine of her eyes lit by streetlamps, the gleam of her inner, lower lip, he should have felt some tenderness toward her—the urge to protect her at all costs, even if it meant protecting her from *him*. But that's not what he felt. Desire, dark and ravenous, thickened in his blood.

"Can I kiss you again?" He touched her cheekbone, so soft, and her fingers curled around his.

She was silent.

"If you want me to, you'll have to say it. Tell me."

He saw hesitation flash across her face, but then she

leaned forward and kissed him. His heart was lifted high. How long had he waited for this, for her? Everything that he'd been looking for was here. Heat, passion, desire. He didn't want to rush her—he needed to hold back. And yet there was nothing more in the world he wanted at that moment than to drag her against him and push his hands inside her clothes.

She pulled away. Her eyes were glittery as the ocean under a full moon. "Are you going to . . . to come inside?"

He had to close his eyes a moment to take in the full impact of her words. For a moment he couldn't answer. He leaned back in his seat, slid his hand away from her body. Before them the street was empty and quiet. A breeze had picked up, and the moving branches made tangled shadows dance wildly on the asphalt. He willed his heart to slow, his breathing to even out. "No," he said. "No, I'm not."

She seemed surprised, but he wouldn't let it get to him. When they made love again, he didn't want it to be because *he* wanted to, like it was his decision and not hers. His body would hate him tonight. But he had to turn her down.

Finally, she reached for the door handle. How many times had they gone home together, led one another through each other's front doors, made themselves at home? The next time Eli went into her house, it would be different. It wouldn't be to watch a movie or share a bowl of pasta. It would be to take her to bed.

Cool air came in through the car door when she opened it. He waited for her to say good night. But she didn't. She only looked at him for a moment, her face unreadable. It wasn't until she was safely inside that he pulled away.

October 12

On her day off Karin sat on the couch with her foot propped up on the coffee table so she could blow on her toenail polish. It had been years since she'd painted her nails. And even though no one would see them since it was October, it pleased her that the small nubs of her toenails were the glossy purple of eggplant.

"Karin?"

Gene called her from the next room. She couldn't see him, but she knew just where he was, slumped over an array of bills on the kitchen table. How many times had she told him that if he had something to say to her, he should walk over to her and say it, instead of shouting through the wall? Or worse, waiting for her to be the one to get up? She shook her head, laughing to herself. Her husband had never been trainable.

She'd started to compose her answer—she was going to tell him that her toenails were too wet for walking—when suddenly he stood in the doorway, a piece of paper dangling from his hand.

"Care to explain *this*?" His voice barely hid his fury. He didn't hand her the paper, but winged it in her general direction, so it sliced the air before veering to land on the couch.

She reached far to get it. It was her credit card statement, and Gene had marked the third line down with a yellow highlighter. Calvert's motel.

"This was what I was talking about when I told you—"

"Stop." He held up his hand. "I don't want to hear it." He paced the room, and when he got to the other side, he kicked an end table so hard that it fell, knocking over their lamp.

She stood, no longer caring about her wet nails. "Gene—what on earth?"

"What an *idiot* I am. They told me somebody saw you with him at some hot-dog place. But you know what I thought? It must have been someone else. Couldn't have been *my* wife. Not *mine*."

"Gene—"

"And you don't even have the brains to pay in cash?"

"No! Gene, you don't understand. I—"

"Or are you going to tell me you were doing it for us? That you were just trying to get pregnant by some kind of twisted plan B?"

Karin cried out. That was the last straw. She picked up a pillow from the couch and hurled it at him with one hand. He caught it hard against his chest. For a second, it shut him up.

"How dare you insinuate that I'm *cheating* on you. Gene—I would never cheat on you. I swore it when we got married and it's still true now."

His eyes were wide and his breath was ragged. He spiked the pillow on the floor. "How stupid do you think I am? Karin—a bunch of the guys told me you've been hanging around with Andy Gervais. That you went on a date! And here I am holding the bill for a motel room that you paid for with *our* credit card! How exactly did you plan to explain that?"

Karin closed her eyes and fought to stay calm. Never in her life had she seen her husband so furious. But the fact that he was mad was the least of her worries. The big problem—the real problem—was that the man who was supposed to trust her perfectly and to the end of time, the man she'd sworn herself to, was telling her that he had no faith in her. It was a blow to her ego and her heart.

She put down the credit card bill and took a few slow steps toward him. When she looked up, she held his gaze with everything she had in her. "When I swore to be loyal and faithful to you, I meant it. If you really and truly think that I could—that I would ever—give myself to a man other than my husband, then this whole marriage has been nothing but a sham."

For a moment he held firm, the fury still thrashing in his eyes. But then she saw the slow, terrible crumbling of his anger, his strong frame wilting, and sheer sadness and regret in his eyes. "Karin . . ."

She didn't say anything. Her heart went out to him. This wasn't about cheating. The accusation was just a symptom of bigger things on his mind. She took him in her arms, felt the weight of his body as he leaned his shoulders against her, curling around her in a hug. His breath came more quickly once again, rage giving way to silent trembling.

"I'm sorry. I'm so sorry. I thought I was losing you," he said.

"Shh," she said. "I know."

"You must hate me."

"I don't hate you."

"You must think I'm an idiot."

"You're my idiot," she said.

He pulled away slightly and looked into her eyes. "Everyone told me you were seeing him. And you've been acting so strange. I had no other explanation."

Karin stepped away, ran a hand through her hair. "Actually, I *was* seeing him. But it's not what you think. He was helping me. And I didn't know how I could tell you without making you mad."

He sat down on the couch and she settled beside him. "What's going on?"

Karin pulled a pillow onto her lap and told him the story—about wanting to get Calvert out of town, about asking Andy for help. And she explained that the money she'd previously admitted to loaning to Calvert was in the form of a motel room. When she was done Gene shook his head.

"I don't understand this. You tell me everything."

"I'm sorry. I was trying to do the right thing for me and for Lana; I wanted him gone. And I didn't tell you about talking to Andy because I worried that you'd think I was overreacting and you'd tell me not to do it. In hindsight, I realize you would have been right."

He sighed, and when he spoke a new tenderness had crept into his voice. He took her hand. "Let's go away together. I don't care where. Let's just go."

"Now?" she asked, laughing.

"Yes. Right now."

"I can't," she said.

"Why not?"

"I . . . I have to be here for Lana."

"What does she have to do with this?"

"I can't just leave my sister when she's pregnant."

"It's *Lana's* pregnancy. Not yours. Lana can handle it on her own. She doesn't need you."

Karin's skin prickled. "But . . . she's my sister. And she does need me. You just don't understand."

"I understand that you're looking out for her. But you've got to give her some room. And besides, what's more important? Lana's pregnancy or our marriage? Because that's what's on the line."

Karin squeezed his fingers. "I swore I'd love you forever on the day we married. And you know I'll never go back on my word."

"Then come away with me. Please, Karin. I'm worried about us."

For a few moments, she thought about it. But how could she leave now? She wanted to be there for her sister; Lana had never needed her support more. "I love you. I want us to work this out."

"So do I. That's why I'm asking you to go away with me."

Karin nodded. "I'm not saying no."

"But you're not saying yes either."

"I'm just saying that I need a little more time. I have to think."

Gene stood. "Do that. And do it quickly." She watched him walk to the doorway and pause. "I can't save this marriage alone," he said. Then he left.

She leaned back against the sofa and closed her eyes. Gene was right. Something was wrong and going more wrong by the day. And yet she loved him as much now as on the day she said *I do*. And she knew—certain as the sunrise—that he loved her too. But something was off, a gear slowly falling out of alignment. She could pinpoint the night it all started, the exciting and life-changing night they decided yes, they were ready for a child.

I can't save this marriage alone . . . Karin closed her eyes. One of them had to save their relationship, but Karin was the one who could do it. Not Gene. There was only one way.

October 13

Mrs. Montaigne was the first customer of the day at the Wildflower Barn, smiling her big droopy smile and shuffling her way inside.

"Morning, Mrs. M.," Lana said.

"*Bonjour*, dear," Mrs. Montaigne said. She walked with all the physical dignity of a duchess gliding into a ball, but her skirt was stuck in her stockings on one side. "I just dropped by to pick up a book about carving pumpkins for my granddaughter."

Lana pointed her in the right direction, but Mrs. Montaigne didn't head toward the books. Instead she walked right up to Lana and put her hands on her belly with the same kind of ease with which she might have picked up merchandise off a shelf.

"Soccer ball," Mrs. Montaigne muttered. "A girl."

Lana laughed, and she felt like they were sharing an inside joke—all three of them.

"You're over halfway through," Mrs. Montaigne said. "Are you starting to get excited? Have you pointed the finger at the father yet?"

"It was an immaculate conception," Lana said, taking

Mrs. Montaigne's arm to hurry her walk toward the jack-o'-lantern books.

"You mean . . . ?" Mrs. Montaigne pointed toward the ceiling, her eyebrows raised. "Well, at least you know you'll get good child support."

"Funny," said Lana.

Four days had passed since she last saw Eli, since he'd kissed her. Every night, he called her to wish her good night. This was not unusual. Sometimes they would go for weeks where they would talk to each other every day. Other times they wouldn't see each other for months, and then Eli would return from a trip and everything would pick up exactly where it had left off.

But over the last four days, she'd felt different, amazingly close to him. She found herself waiting for his call in the evenings. And she fantasized about when and where he would kiss her again. What had happened the other night still resonated between them, more intense because of how difficult it was not to mention. More intense because she wasn't able to see him. She suspected it was all part of his plan.

Last night, she'd gone to a labor class, and she'd purposely not invited him to go with her. The group watched a video of multiple women giving birth—the looks on their faces pained but not panicked, while their husbands rubbed their wives' feet or spooned beside them on a hospital bed. Afterward the instructor wanted them to pair off, to discuss their visions of what the birth would be like. She said the relationship between mother and partner was never as important as it was the day of the baby's birth. She said emotional support was as vital to a laboring mother as the machine that monitored her and her baby's beating hearts. While the other couples spoke softly, holding hands and cooing at each other, Lana sat alone, filling out the worksheet by herself.

It had made her face an important fact: She didn't know what to expect from Eli, or where their relationship was going. And what's more, she didn't know what he expected of the fact that she was having a baby. Where did he imagine her child fit into whatever future they had? Her own desires had not changed—she still wanted to travel, to explore. And yet, when she looked into Eli's eyes she saw that his idea of the rest of his life was much different. He saw white-picket fences, children playing in the yard—a nice little family. But what was a dream-life to him was merely *settling* to her.

It was time to tell Karin flat out that she could have the baby. She couldn't have a family and have her dreams. Admittedly, she'd been putting the moment off. Once she made the offer of adoption to Karin, she would never be able to take it back. But she was well along in her pregnancy now and she needed to settle the adoption question once and for all; if she promised the baby to Karin, maybe it would end her growing attachment. She could stop thinking of the child as hers. And Eli could too.

Mrs. Montaigne left the Barn just as Karin was walking in. Her sister was wearing jeans and a long-sleeved thermal under a Wildflower Barn T-shirt. She made small talk with Mrs. Montaigne while holding the door.

"Did she buy anything?" Karin asked once she was gone. She plopped her stuff down on the counter and tucked her purse underneath.

"A book." Lana looked down at the inventory list that

she was supposed to be working on. Karin stared at her a moment longer than usual.

"You okay?"

Lana shrugged.

"I'm taking that as sister-speak for *No, I'm not*. How was the class?"

Lana tried to muster up some enthusiasm. "Fine. I should have had a partner."

Karin's voice rose. "They said they would accommodate single mothers! I knew you should have let me go with you. I'll call them right now."

"No, no! They did accommodate me. It just . . . felt weird."

Karin nodded. "Is Meggie here?"

"She's in the back assembling the gift baskets."

"Let's have her watch the register for a bit. We need to take a walk."

Lana nodded, her nerves fluttering. Whenever Karin pulled her aside, she had something to say. That could be good or bad. They paged Meggie to come to the register and then headed into the skeletal remains of the gardens outside. Just below the skyline, the far edge of the trees had turned fiery orange and red, so that Lana thought their true colors came out not on sunny days but on days like this, when the sky was overcast and gray. In the distance, a gaggle of Canada geese passed in a near-perfect V, flying south to warmer climes. She could hear their faint forlorn honking, but they flew so high that the beat of all those enormous wings seemed silent as wind.

"I don't know the best way to bring this up," Karin said. "I've been trying to think of what I can do to help."

"You already do so much," Lana assured her.

"But that's not what I mean. I want to help you. And the baby. And me too. But I don't want to offend you."

"Just spit it out."

Karin played with the cuff of her jacket. "I'm afraid you'll be mad. I hope you won't. I'm just trying to help. And of course, you can say no."

"What is it?"

"Are you still considering giving the baby up for adoption?"

"Yes." Lana held her breath.

Karin took her hand; it was chilly from the crisp fall air. "Do you want to ask me?"

Lana looked at her sister—her generous, fierce sister, who, under different circumstances, would be the soldier who dragged her comrades from the battlefield despite her own wounds.

"Do I want to ask you what?" Lana hedged, still unsure that she could go through with it.

"Do you want to ask me and Gene to adopt your baby?"

Lana looked down at their joined hands. And though she sealed her lips together, begging herself to stay quiet, she began to cry.

"Oh, Lana." Karin put an arm around her, pulled her closer. The fabric of her windbreaker wheezed when she moved. "You don't have to say it if you don't want to. You can just nod your head . . ."

Lana leaned against her sister, felt herself growing short of breath. As much as she wanted to, she could not live her life in two places at once. She had to choose: Eli and his vision of a quiet, settled family? Or her lifelong dream?

Giving the baby to Karin was the best possible outcome for everyone. Or, if it wasn't the best, it was the most realistic. And that was the best she could hope for right now.

"You would do that?" Lana managed. "I didn't think you wanted to adopt. I thought you and Gene were set against it."

"This is *your* baby we're talking about," Karin said, squeezing her closer. "So it's different. The baby would still be part of your family—as close as you are to me. But Gene and I, we could give it a good life, as its two parents. We could give it everything it needs."

Lana should have felt joy, freedom—this was the solution she'd wanted but had been too scared to ask for. "Does Gene . . . ?"

"He knows that we . . . we need this."

Lana imagined Gene giving a bouquet of flowers to her daughter after a school play, the pride in his eyes to be called *Dad*. There was no doubt that Gene would love the baby as his own. She looked up at the sky, to the birds that were leaving the hemisphere. They disappeared over the tree line and the air became quiet and still again.

Lana moved away from her sister's arm, pulling herself up straight. She took a deep breath and wiped the tears from her face. "After the baby's born I'm going to take a trip," she said, deciding, in that instant, to go away. "I'll be gone for a while. A year, at least."

"Oh, Lana." Karin too began to cry. "You're doing the right thing. You'll see. It's for the best."

Lana nodded. In the sky, one lone goose overhead caught her eye. It was honking furiously, the sound as biting as an oboe's song as it flew fast across the clouds. Lana wiggled her toes, the solid cold of the earth making her feet chilly, and then she took Karin's arm and walked with her back inside.

October 14

Eli sat at the wheel of his car, Lana at his side as he drove. Around them, the sun was going down and turning the lush mountains into tapestries of gold, green, and red. The highway took them toward Stowe, weaving and curving among the mountains, dipping into valleys and skimming the shoulders of high peaks and emerald green farms.

"It's beautiful," Lana said.

They drove in silence, awestruck by the play of thick autumn light and colorful foliage that rivaled the springtime meadows at the Wildflower Barn. There wasn't a billboard in sight, only occasional bald rock faces tinged pink by the evening. Even the pine trees, so tall and stark on the steeply sloping mountainsides, seemed to be faintly glowing.

Eli didn't dare speak until the show was over and they'd turned onto Route 100. "Is this okay? Dinner, I mean?"

"It's wonderful," Lana said. But she sounded a little distracted.

"What are you thinking about?"

When she spoke her words were as flat as if they had

been prerecorded at some earlier time. "I told Karin she could adopt the baby."

He bit down on the word that almost left his mouth: *No.* For a moment he panicked—the idea that Lana would give away the baby shocked him. He hadn't for a second thought she was serious about adoption. Sure, he'd heard her bring it up. But he felt like she was just experimenting with the idea more than she was committed to it. He hadn't liked the thought of her giving up the child, but he didn't want to put too much pressure on her either, so he'd kept his opinions to himself.

"It's the only thing I can do," she said, her tone flat once again.

"No, it's not."

"Then what do you suggest?"

"There are . . . choices."

"I can't keep it."

"Why not?"

"Please, Eli. We both know I can't."

"Why?"

"There's a thousand reasons," she said.

"Tell me one."

"Eli, you know me. I don't want to settle down. I want to live. I want to see the world. I have plans."

"But is that all of it?"

"What do you mean?"

Eli held back the sigh of frustration that gathered in his lungs. "Do you think maybe the reason is that you think you wouldn't be a good mother?"

Lana was quiet for a long time, so long that he wished he'd kept his theory to himself.

"It's not because I think I won't be a good mom," she said at last. "It's because I *know* I won't."

He thought back to all the times he'd seen his best friend leaning over a table of growing seedlings, examining leaves between her fingers with loving appreciation. Or about the times she'd stopped in a field of wildflowers to run her palms gingerly over the purple and pink tops of the dame's rocket and phlox, so lovely she might have been a vision of spring itself. Sure, she was forgetful and unpredictable. And sure, she had dreams of traveling. But even the most temperamental and delicate of flowers bloomed under her patient guidance, and he had no doubt that a child would do the same.

"Are you sure about that? Or are you just afraid?" he asked.

"I'm afraid of everything. I'm afraid I'm not going to get what I want from life—that I've ruined everything. I'm afraid of keeping the baby because in my heart I might always resent it for ruining my plans—and no child deserves that blame. But I'm afraid of giving it away too because . . . I don't know why. But now that I have, it's a decision I can't take back."

Eli squeezed her hand. Somewhere the sun was still above the horizon line, but here among the Green Mountains the dusk came earlier, and already the shadows were settling in for the night. He wished he knew the words to say to her that could make sense of a nonsensical world. "You don't have to do this alone. I'm with you. Do you understand what that means? I'm never going to leave you, Lana. I'll be here every step of the way."

She looked at him. Her eyes had turned pearlescent from the light and unfallen tears. "What do *you* think?"

"I think that deep down in your heart, you already love that baby."

"Yes. I do."

"If you love it, why not keep it?"

"Love isn't enough."

Eli brought her hand to his lips and kissed the back of it. "You'll be a wonderful mother. If you love that baby, it's yours."

"Don't you understand?" she asked softly. "I can't have it both ways. I can't have the life I want *and* be a good mother. It's because I love the baby that I have to let it go."

Lana paused on the sidewalk, looking up at the building before them with its white porch and pediment, its colonial redbrick walls, and its pretty black shutters. The inn was a relic of another time, brightly lit windows shining warmly against the night. If a horse-drawn carriage went jingling down the street right this moment, Lana wouldn't be entirely surprised. "*This* is where we're eating?"

"Is it okay?"

"Oh, yes," she said, and she took his arm as they walked inside.

She trembled nervously as he helped her take off her coat and handed it to the woman at the coat check. All at once questions about the baby and about the future were dwarfed by the huge and overwhelming question that stretched so tautly between them, here and now. As she walked before him, following the hostess into the beautiful dining room, she could feel Eli's gaze on her, as if her every step and breath mattered. She'd worn a gray wool skirt and black sweater that draped low around her shoulders, and she could feel the back of her neck burning where it was exposed. She was glad when they finally sat down.

The room was dim, dark wood paneling everywhere. The decor was elegant and yet unpretentious. The chandeliers were little more than tin lanterns, beautiful holes punched in them like nighttime stars. A single taper shimmered between them on the table in a glass hurricane lamp, and the cloth napkins were starched but soft. Lana had never been taken to a more perfect restaurant on a date—just the right blend of comfort and romance.

"This is amazing," she said.

"It's just the beginning," he replied.

The waiter came to their table and began to pour her a glass of wine without asking. She laughed and held up her hand. "Oh, I'm sorry. I can't drink."

The waiter glanced at Eli, then back at Lana. "This is a very special vintage," he said. And when he turned the bottle around she saw that it was sparkling cider, no doubt made in Vermont.

She smiled at Eli. "You thought of everything," she said.

They looked over their menus, chatting lightly, and placed their orders. For a moment, silence stretched out between them, filled by the sounds of clicking plates and other people's conversations. Eli excused himself for a moment and she sat at the table, looking around. The dining room was filled with couples sitting in Windsor chairs. They held hands across the tables, playing with each other's fingers, or they sat close to each other talking in low voices or not talking at all.

For a moment when Eli returned, she worried they wouldn't have anything to talk about. But sure enough, the conversation flowed easily, the food arrived, and the next thing she knew, very few people were left in the dining hall—and then there was just the two of them, their cooling cups of coffee, and the candle between them melting down.

She looked at the man across from her, the man she thought she knew but perhaps never truly had. In the light from the lanterns overhead his short hair gleamed almost golden, pieces going this way and that. His face was cleanly shaven and his gaze was warm. She felt as if the years were disappearing, as if she'd spent all this time trying not to know him, and she now found herself peeling away the layers she'd put between them to find something beautiful but genuine underneath. They were the same two people they'd always been, but there was a new underlying richness and density threading through their conversations, harmonic tones added to a familiar melody line.

She looked into the fizzy bubbles of her cider. "I have to tell you something."

His smile flickered. "Why do I have the feeling it isn't good?"

She smiled a little. "It's not bad. It's just something I've never told you before. Something I feel like I should say."

He nodded, waiting.

"That day after the fireball," she began. "The day you came to my dorm room and saw me with Chip . . ."

"So that was his name."

"Yes. I want to tell you . . . nothing happened with him that day."

He watched her carefully, leaning toward her with his elbows on the table, his face not registering any change of emotion. "I know what I saw."

She shook her head. "Chip wasn't interested in me, and I wasn't interested in him either. I . . . I don't know how to say this."

"Just come out with it."

"I meant for you to find us like that."

He sat back hard against his chair and was quiet for a long time. When he spoke, his voice was quiet. "You mean it wasn't real?"

She shook her head. "No. And I'm sorry."

"But . . . why?"

"Because I knew I wouldn't be able to control myself with you, not after what happened. Because I thought if I could make you stop . . . being attracted to me, we might have a chance as friends."

The waiter came to their table, and he'd started to say something when he seemed to notice how intensely Eli was concentrating. He excused himself right away.

Eli laughed a little under his breath. "You really thought *that* would make me stop wanting you?"

She nodded. "I thought if I could make your feelings go away, mine would go away too."

"Did they?" His face was half in shadows, and his voice was low and dark. She knew, with a clarity that both frightened and emboldened her, that it was useless to keep up the pretense of friendship anymore. She was already in too deep to go back. There was nothing to do but look forward. She wanted to be with him again, whatever the risk or cost. Even if it lasted only a moment, she wanted everything, everything without restrictions, just once.

"I thought they did," she said. "I was wrong."

He stood and walked toward her side of the table. He held out his hand to help her stand. "Come with me."

"Where are we going?"

He shook his head. "Just come on."

She glanced back at their table as Eli led them into the main foyer and up a beautifully carpeted stairwell. He held her hand tight, as if worried she might try to pull away. When he took a silver key from his pocket she wasn't surprised.

He didn't brush his fingers against her face and he didn't reach for her hand. The fresh, inviting smell of his cologne drew her in, enveloping her. Her heart pounded painfully hard in her chest.

"Stay with me," he said.

"I will."

He kissed her. Inside, the room was beautiful. Flames were dancing in the fireplace on the other side of the room, bathing the buttercream walls in red-amber light. The bed was covered in a patchwork quilt, a simple canopy suspended by four dark wood posts. A single red rose lay across one white pillow, and her heart danced with nerves like the flames that heated the air around them. She hadn't remembered feeling this nervous the last time she'd made love with him. But now there was so much more at stake.

"Come here," he said.

She gave herself entirely to the sensations of kissing him, the greedy press of his mouth. The thrill of attraction between them burned as hot as it ever had. When she was young, passion had engulfed her suddenly and completely, without warning. But this new attraction she felt was a slow, mysterious simmer—the dark smoke of a banked fire, the curl of a serpent constricting inch by inch.

Her clothes fell from her body silent as moonlight. He held her hand for balance while she stepped out of her dress, and she slid open the tiny buttons of his shirt—an image she'd envisioned a hundred times, so much more beautiful in real life. Laughing, she tugged his white undershirt out of his waistband and over his head, and she ran her hands over the smooth expanse of his chest and arms. He stayed like that for a minute, letting her fingers slide over his skin, his smile patient and amused. But when she met with the barrier of his belt, his easy grin contorted with a desire so fierce it looked like pain. He caught her hand and brought her with him to the bed.

For long minutes he watched her, barely touching, his breathing so even and steady she knew he was fighting to keep it that way. The firelight danced across his chest and painted shadows into the little valleys of muscle and bone. She felt no self-consciousness of her pregnant body under his gaze; instead, she was fascinated—held utterly rapt—by *his* fascination. He seemed to know the moment she could stand no more. And then his weight was carefully on her, heavy and warm, and she was so excruciatingly sensitive she imagined she could feel every stitch of the quilt scratching against her naked back. She was looking into his eyes when at last he raised himself up slightly on his knees, then pressed inside her. The whole world seemed suddenly magic, as if flowers bloomed in the sky and stars sprouted from the earth. She wrapped her arms around him, her fingers sliding against his hot skin, and gave herself completely at last.

Later they lay with the covers twisted around their ankles, the moonlight streaming through the slats in the window. Cars passed on the street outside, their tires whispering with the occasional clacking of a woman's high heels. The smooth sheets on her bare legs, the cool air on her hot skin, the way Eli traced lazy circles on her shoulder blade—there was no other word for this but *bliss.*

Never in her life had she felt so sensitized, so perfectly attuned to another person. For years she'd understood passion to be something bright and fleeting. A blaze that couldn't last. But that had been only a superficial layer of passion, a fire that burned the surface but left the deeper levels chilled. What she'd felt tonight was fundamental, resonant—an inferno that had started on the inside and worked its way out. She'd never known anything like it before.

She kissed his chest and when she pressed her nose to him it was like she remembered—she would always associate the smell with a clear night sky.

"Just once more," he said. "Say it just once more."

She kissed his earlobe, whispered into it: *Eli.* His sigh was full of contentment. His hand settled on the curve of her breast.

A moment later he jumped out of bed, so quick she barely had time to sit up before he'd already crossed the bedroom and gone to the window. He flicked open the window lock and lifted the pane in one smooth motion. She hurried to his side, careful to stay out of the sightlines of the street below. "What are you doing? Have you lost your mind?"

Freezing mountain air rushed into the warm room. He put a hand out the window and wiggled his fingers, palm up, as if testing for rain. "I'm checking to see if the sky is falling."

She stared. He was out of his mind.

"Nope." He pulled his hand back in. "And no four horsemen either. I think it's safe to say that life as we know it didn't end because we made love."

She rolled her eyes and laughed. "Get away from the window, you nuthead."

He shut it, then came straight toward her. His hands were firm on her rib cage and the flex of his arms pulled her in. After all the times she could remember standing before him fully clothed, the sudden shock of his warm naked skin made her hungry for him again.

He kissed her, laugher dying in the back of his throat. His hand curved around her ass, seeking the heat between her thighs. The pressure of his fingers made it impossible to open her eyes.

This moment was temporary insanity. She felt like Pandora, unable to resist opening the box that she knew would mean destruction. But what sweet destruction it was.

He was looking into her eyes when he came into her. She had one last thought before reason left completely. He was right. They would never be friends again.

November

Asters: Among the hardiest and last flowers of the year, the word *aster* comes from the Greek word for "star." Hence, if the stars aren't in your favor, you might be suffering a dis*aster* (a "bad star"). Though many flowers close at night to stay protected from cold and dew, asters remain wide open to the stars they were named for.

November 2

Karin had expected that the woman at the adoption agency would have raised an eyebrow at Lana's decision to give custody of her child to her sister, but apparently these kinds of things were routine. It was amazing how much paperwork was necessary—not to mention how much money Karin and Gene going to have to spend. She'd yet to tell her husband about what she'd begun because she knew she would need to tell him in just such a way that he wouldn't shoot down the idea again the moment he heard it. She was sure this was the most logical and good purpose of her life. In one stroke, she could help her sister, her marriage, and herself.

Now on the ride home, Lana was quiet. A few snowflakes swept over the hood of the car and up the windshield as they drove. The fields outside the city had been winterized, low grasses stretching for acres and acres in gentle dips and swells. Lana clutched the top of her seat belt as if her life depended on it.

"You're not having second thoughts, are you?" Karin asked, nervous.

The car filled with the sound of the radio.

"No. I slept with Eli."

At first she wasn't sure she'd heard right. "What? When?"

"The other night."

"But . . . why?"

Lana looked out the window. "I wanted to. It was . . . beautiful. Amazing. It was like we walked right up to the edge and jumped over—and it was more than I . . . more than I could have imagined—like being awake and dreaming at the same time. Do you think I'm out of my mind?"

Karin kept her eyes focused on the car in front of her, not wanting to react too strongly. "But you've tried this before with him, haven't you? In college? I thought you said it didn't work."

"It didn't. And I worry that it won't work this time either. We won't be able to pretend it didn't happen, like we did before."

Karin glanced at her sister in her peripheral vision. There was a worry in Lana's voice that gave her the chills. She'd always hoped that Lana would find for herself the kind of love that she had with Gene. Years ago she'd pulled for the idea of Lana and Eli getting married and settling down. Eli wanted to have a family someday, and Karin hoped that she and her sister would raise their children side by side in Vermont. But then, as time passed and there seemed to be no romance between them, she'd given up. It felt odd to be faced with those questions once again. "But you've been friends with Eli forever."

"Right. That's why I'm worried. What if we over-stepped?"

Karin said nothing for a long moment. She didn't blame her sister for not wanting to give her heart away. Until Karin had met Gene, she'd barely dated at all. But then when he came along, she knew she'd found the one, and so she'd thrown herself body and soul into loving him.

But Lana was more reserved, more cautious. It always seemed that her sister gave everything she had to her short-lived relationships—all her care and kindness. Just like she'd done with all those endless boarders at Calvert's house. And yet, she'd never given her heart. They'd been living in Vermont for years, but part of Lana still lived in that boardinghouse of ages ago.

"So what are you going to do? Are you going to run away? Tell him to leave you alone?"

"I don't know. What will I do if I lose him, Karin?"

Karin reached over and patted her sister's knee. "Just don't do anything stupid and you'll be fine. You and Eli have been through a lot together. I think you should just relax and see how it plays out."

"And just wait for him to dump me? Or disappear?"

Karin went on. "You'll have to communicate with him. Tell him everything. Even if you don't want to. He deserves that."

Lana nodded. The landscape rolled by, the trees turned

a soft gray-brown on the distant hills. Karin could feel her sister's nervousness, a palpable force in the minivan. She cracked her window an inch.

"And how is *your* communication going? Are you and Gene going to keep trying for your own?" Lana asked, her tone sounding so casual that Karin knew it was anything but.

"I think we're taking a breather."

"Have you told him that I said yes?"

"I tried to. A couple times now. But every time I say the word *adoption*, he cuts me off or changes the subject."

Lana appeared unfazed. "Let me know when you tell him. I can be there, if you want."

"Thank you." Karin put on her blinker and turned into the Barn. She wasn't entirely sure it would be a good idea to have Lana beside her when she broke the news. She didn't want Gene to feel uncomfortable or attacked. But who could say what was what anymore? If Lana and Eli were sleeping together, who knew what was possible?

She put the minivan in park and took off her seat belt to climb out, but Lana stopped her with a hand on her arm. "I'm glad you and Gene are going to adopt the baby. It deserves good parents. And there's no one better than you."

Karin didn't smile. She heard the tinge of sadness in her sister's voice and she wondered what it meant. "I hope you don't mind if I say this. I know you feel sort of out of control all the time. Trying to figure out what and who you want in life. But sometimes I think that you still look at the future through the past, and it warps things. If you could see it for what it really is, you'd be surprised."

"Maybe."

"What I'm saying is, I think you should talk to Calvert."

"Just because you made peace with him doesn't mean I have to."

"If you're nervous about the future, you have to figure out why by looking at the past," Karin said. The day that Calvert had arrived in town, Karin had believed she'd needed to fight to keep her sister from reconciling with him. Lana was always the nice one. Lana was more forgiving toward Calvert than Karin had been. But now Karin wondered if all Lana's projected goodwill toward their father hadn't been just for show. Amazingly, somewhere along the line they'd traded places. Karin was the one making peace while Lana was still all bottled up, pretending she didn't care. "Eli loves you. And you love him. There's no reason in the world it shouldn't work."

"But history repeats itself. Isn't that what they say?"

"Last time you ruined it on purpose. It's different now."

Lana looked down. "I hope so."

Karin pushed her car door open all the way. "Just stop worrying so much and enjoy it. It's the beginning of something. Not the end."

"Maybe you're right," Lana said. And yet as they climbed out of the minivan, Karin wasn't sure she'd convinced her.

That night Lana lay in Eli's arms, pressed to the smooth warmth of his skin. His hand played absently in her tousled hair. Not a moment after they'd arrived at his house, all of the pessimism she'd felt earlier in the day was shed like the clothes he'd slid from her body. She was unable to get enough of him. She felt an uneasy sense of immediacy, that she needed to make the most out of every moment and every second, that she needed to memorize the sound of his breathing and the smell of his skin. She clung to every word he said, as if they might slip away from her if she didn't listen carefully enough.

"Tell me something," he said. "Something you've never told me before."

She laughed and arranged herself to lay on her side, her head propped on one hand. "Something I've never told you before . . . *hmm*. There isn't really a lot . . . I can't think of anything!"

He scooted away so he could see her better, rolling onto his side to face her. A light was on in the hallway outside the door, and it cast soft yellow shadows over their faces and flesh. "Tell me when you lost your virginity."

"Haven't we already talked about that? I mean, I know when you lost yours."

"That's old news. The exchange student, with the corsage, in the science lab. How come I don't already know about you?"

"I don't know. I think it was pretty normal."

"Tell me."

"But why do you want to know?"

"I've always wondered. But I didn't feel like I could ask until now."

Lana fluffed up her pillow under her head. "Well, his name was John. I was sixteen and he was . . . I don't know. Early twenties? He came to the boardinghouse every few months. I don't remember much about him—

nothing concrete. It's more like a feeling of remembering what he was like. He was a musician. A rebel. Aloof. I used to lay white daisy petals along the headboard of my bed for each day I didn't see him, and I'd watch them curl up one at a time. Silly, right?"

"Everything's silly when you're sixteen. So what happened?"

"The usual," she said, laughing. "He used to show up every few months and I just thought he was the most wonderful thing that ever happened on the whole earth. He had these sunglasses like John Lennon, and I thought I was in love. I had this vision of him showing up one day and asking me to leave with him. I had this idea we'd be vagabonds living in his car and getting by on his music. It made sense to sleep with him."

"Karin let you get away with it?"

"I told her I was going to watch a movie at a friend's house. But afterward, from the way she looked at me, I think she knew."

Eli stroked her hair in long, smooth sweeps, but said nothing.

"Anyway," she said. "We obviously didn't run away together. One day, he said, 'See you next time.' And then I never saw him again."

"You must have been crushed."

"Brutally. But now I wonder what I saw in him in the first place."

"An exit sign."

"Something like that."

He drew her closer, his hand at the small of her back, pressing their bodies as close as was possible. Lana sighed, content. They lay in silence for a long time.

"I'm not going to leave," Eli said, his voice thick with sleepiness. "At least, I won't leave without coming back."

She thought of the way she'd been tethered to the boardinghouse all those years, watching the men come and go. She pressed her forehead flat against his chest. "I know."

"I don't like traveling all the time," he went on. "I plan to spend more time here, now."

"But will you miss it?"

"Well, no. I'll still have to do some traveling. But I never meant to travel quite so much. It just . . . happened. I guess I just never had a strong enough reason to stay."

Lana was quiet, emotions mixed. She heard what Eli was telling her—that he wanted to settle down. She was touched by his vision of having a future with her. If they made a life together, it would be a good life, full of love. But birds-of-paradise were winking orange in her mind.

She rubbed her cheek against Eli's chest and kissed him lightly. The streetlight imbued the room with a soft luster; the lights of the alarm clock glowed gently red. She stroked his arm in the silence and listened to the sound of his breathing as it slowly deepened and evened out. She felt so peaceful and blessed, to be able to lay like this with him, to feel with her body the moment he fell asleep.

"I love you," she said. She knew he couldn't hear her, but she wanted to say the words out loud. "I'm in love with you. No matter what happens, that's true."

She felt him stir. For a moment she held her breath, worried he'd heard her and yet wishing he had at the same time. She thought she was in the clear until a moment later, when she heard him whisper, soft as falling snow, "Then why not marry me?"

She didn't move, didn't speak. He lifted slightly onto his arm, to look at her in the moonlight.

"Do you . . . do you mean that?" she said, breathless.

He didn't reply. He stood and walked naked to the other side of the room. The top drawer of his dresser squeaked as he opened it, and when he returned to sit down on the bed he was holding a ring. No box, no velvet. Just a ring, lustrous in the moonlight between his index finger and thumb.

"It was my grandmother's," he said, turning it so it caught the light. "I've been holding on to it for a long time."

The ring was beautiful, classic yellow gold and an unpretentious diamond. She didn't reach for it, but she could imagine the feel of it on her finger; it would be snug and warm.

He let his hand fall, the ring along with it, and he leaned forward to kiss her shoulder. "You don't have to tell me yes or no."

"You mean, *ever*?"

"For as long as you love me, the invitation stands."

She watched as he put the ring back where he'd found it. On some level, she felt the fundamental and quiet rightness of what he proposed. She was connected to him. Her life was bound up with his so tightly that she would always love him, regardless of whether they would succeed as a couple in the end.

But how long would he wait for her if she went away? And if they were both coming and going, what kind of marriage would that be? Maybe the question would have been easier if he'd proposed *after* the baby was born. *After* she'd lived out her dreams for a while. If the timing was better, the word *yes* might have slipped effortlessly off her tongue.

"I'm sorry," she said, getting out of bed, the air cool on her naked skin. "This is just . . . it's a lot for me. Everything at once. A couple months ago, if you'd asked me what my future looked like, I wouldn't have said *this*. I never saw myself having a baby. Or getting married. Or . . . sleeping with you."

He was quiet as he came to stand beside her, the ring back in his dresser.

She tried hard to explain. "I have some things to work out in my own head before I can say yes."

When he looked at her, his gaze was firm, something hard yet beseeching in his stare. "Just promise me that if you have to end this, you won't do it badly. I don't think my heart can take another jolt like last time."

"I promise I'll never do anything like that again."

She didn't miss the narrowing of his eyes, the slight flicker that said he didn't entirely believe her. She smoothed back his hair, feelings of tenderness welling up inside her. She stood on her tiptoes and pressed a long, firm kiss on his forehead. The urge to comfort him was strong. "Do you want me to go home for tonight?"

He grabbed her wrist. "Do you want to go?"

"No."

"Then stay." He pulled lightly, until she was close to him again. His mouth was soft. "Stay."

She gave in, felt the need behind his kiss and answered it, fed it with a desire of her own. The down comforter crinkled softly between them as he pulled her to the bed, and he tugged hard to get it out of the way, seeking access, asking with his hands.

Once again, the future and the past became momentarily meaningless. All she knew right now was that she was *his*—that she always had been and always would be. He'd asked for her promise that she would not end it badly. She didn't know how to tell him the truth: Marriage or not, being with Eli so completely after so long was the best thing that had ever happened to her. She was not ready to give up her dreams of traveling, of leaving, for a while. But what he'd started, she would never end.

November 22

When the November wind blew in from the north, down through the Champlain Valley, the old boards of the Wildflower Barn hissed and moaned as if in pain. The sky was low and dark; sprinkles of snow were whipping through the bare tree branches and diving fast toward the brittle ground. Lana was alone at the computer. And though the store was technically open—they stocked some indoor plants from their small greenhouse and also carried gift items—the bell on the door was silent. Most of the ordering done at this time of year came through the company Web site. Flowers were always blooming somewhere.

Lana opened the next e-mail in the queue—her eyes were bleary and she ached from head to toe with fatigue. She knew she shouldn't have been staying up so late, but the rewards of spending a hot midnight in Eli's arms were far greater than the sleep she'd sacrificed for it.

Almost a month had passed since the night he'd brought her to the field behind the college, and with each day, Lana felt as if she was healing. She was happier than she used to be. The joy she felt being Eli's friend could not compare to the joy she felt being in his arms and bed. She'd believed it was impossible to take a perfect relationship and make it more perfect, to take two people who were so exceptionally close and bring them closer. She was learning, happily, that she'd been wrong.

She forced herself to focus on the e-mail before her. A customer was complaining that he'd been charged $23 for a high-end lawn rake that he purchased online, while his neighbor had paid only $16 for the rake in the store. She arched her back, then rubbed hard at the muscles above her hip bones. Massage was futile. Her backache felt deeper than her bones.

She hadn't gotten very far across the room to check on the price of the rake when the doorbell rang and Calvert was in the Barn, wearing his same old work boots, jeans, and a big black coat. She was getting a little tired of him sneaking up on her like this.

"What are you doing here?" she asked, walking gingerly toward him, step over careful step until the pain in her back subsided.

"I came to say bye."

She tilted her head. "Well then. Good-bye."

"But I want to talk to you first."

She frowned. "Forget it. Just go."

He looked at her for a long minute, the faded-denim blue of his eyes as sad as a winter day. He'd opened the

Barn door but stopped shy of leaving. "Please just let me say this one thing. Then I'll go."

She laughed. Pain shot through her, deep and low. She grabbed for her stomach uselessly, and she felt her belly harden under her hand. This wasn't a backache. She put her free hand on the shelf beside her for balance, breathing out to let go of the cramping. The force of the pain made her angry enough to lash out. "All these years later and *now* you can't wait anymore?"

"I think I should have handled things differently," he said. "I wasn't good to you girls. I know that now. And it bothers me. I won't be able to go on with my life until I set things right."

She couldn't speak. A hot sting slid through her abdomen, a knife slicing a crescent into her lower half. She tried to tell him, to say *help*. But her breath came in short, fast pants. She bent forward, cradling the ache.

In the distance she heard the sound of her father speaking, the most words he'd ever said to her at one time in her life. And yet his voice was only a blur in her ears. The muscles in her abdomen twisted and gripped; she could feel something moving, shifting. Karin had told her about Braxton-Hicks contractions—those painful practical jokers that sent first-time parents running for their overnight bags. But this didn't feel like what she imagined contractions would be. She doubled over, her arms wrapped tight around her belly, and her whole body cried out with pain and with something else, with *loss*.

Please, *God*, her heart prayed, pleaded.

She didn't hear Calvert coming toward her, calling her name.

• • •

Eli followed the receptionist's directions through the hospital turn-by-turn until at last he found Lana's room. By the time he reached her bedside, his heart was beating so loud he thought it might leap from his chest. Lana lay in a narrow white bed, her face turned away from the door. Karin stood fast when she saw him rush in, and he started to ask her what was happening, but she lifted a finger to her lips, her eyebrows raised exaggeratedly high. He recognized some of his own panic in her eyes.

"Come here," she whispered.

He followed her into the hallway, wishing Lana was awake, wishing he could take her hand and hear her voice and know she was okay. But for now, he would be happy just to have the facts. "What happened?"

"She went into premature labor," Karin said softly. "They stopped the contractions with saline and terbutaline, so she's in the clear for now. But there's no telling when they'll start again."

"Will the baby be okay?"

"I don't know," Karin said, pain in her voice. The skin around her eyes had faded to a dull blue-gray, and her hair was a mess, falling in kinked strands around her face. "The doctor said its heartbeat is strong—it's healthy so far. But it's too young to be born. They gave Lana some kind of steroid to speed up its lung development and prevent brain hemorrhaging, just in case it decides that it has to be born sooner rather than later. But we're praying it doesn't come to that."

Eli ran a hand through his hair. The moment felt surreal. Steroids and brain hemorrhages. He couldn't even imagine what Lana must be going through. He peered around Karin's shoulder to see her, so still and quiet, her pale hair pulled away from her face and falling against the paler pillows.

His heart ached to think that she'd almost lost the baby, and he realized just how attached to the child he'd become. Karin squeezed his arm. She too had something to lose. Probably, Karin already thought of the child as her own—as if *Lana* wasn't the woman in danger of losing a child. The idea didn't sit well with him, and he gently drew away his arm.

"She's okay right now," Karin said. "You should have seen her. She was a trouper. Really brave and strong."

"What will they do for her?"

"The doctor said bed rest."

"That's it?"

"There's really nothing more they can do. They could set her up with a really expensive system to monitor her day and night. But the doctor said it probably wouldn't change anything anyway. And you know how Lana feels about electronics."

"But *bed rest*? That just seems so nineteenth-century. They must have something better than that."

Karin smoothed back her hair. "Actually the doctor said bed rest wouldn't necessarily help either. She said there's no real proof that it works. But she said it's better to be safe than sorry."

Eli had to step away from her a moment, away from the conversation. Frustration made his blood boil. He felt helpless, angry, and too late. "So what the hell is going to keep her from having the baby?"

"I don't know," Karin said. "Rest. Taking care of herself. The baby will come when it wants to, but they want her to get to at least the thirty-five-week mark. Then, all we can do is give it a fighting chance."

"Hello." A woman in scrubs and a white coat stopped near them in the hallway and held out her hand to Eli. Her dark hair was pulled back stark and tight around her face. Eli hadn't even noticed her walking down the hall. "I'm Doctor Christianson. You must be . . ."

"Eli Ward." He shook her hand, knowing that she'd assumed he was the baby's father. "Karin was just getting me up to speed."

"Very good. I was only just passing by, but I wanted to stop and introduce myself."

Eli had to force himself to let go of her hand. "How long will you need to keep her here?"

She peered into the room. "We'll have to see how well she responds to the medicines, but it will probably be at least a couple of days. She's a fighter; I can tell. She's going to hold on to that baby for all she's worth."

Eli couldn't help but glance at Karin. She didn't look back.

"If you'll excuse me, I'm in kind of a rush. But I'll be back again very soon." Dr. Christianson began to walk down the hall, then paused and turned halfway around. "It's always seemed to me that the patients who have families, friends—people to hold their hands along the way—do the best. You all are very lucky to have each other. I include Lana's baby in that too."

Eli saw Karin rub at her eyes. Wordlessly, he put an arm around her and they sat down. All they could do now was wait.

• • •

Karin walked the long, sterile corridors of the hospital, hallways leading to hallways, doors opening to more doors. There was something nightmarish about all the tile and marble and low ceilings of white. Pictures of local heroes and finger paintings hung here and there on the walls, one no different from the other. It was late now, and the building was quiet, her steps echoing faintly. She knew the rooms around her were full of people, but as she passed through the gleaming marble corridors she felt entirely alone.

She found him in the cafeteria, a room of empty, industrial-blue tables and stainless-steel countertops. Her instincts had told her that Calvert wouldn't have left the hospital, that he was out of sight but still nearby, and she'd been right to trust herself. He sat leaning back in a chair with his knees sprawled open and his head tipped back to watch a muted TV.

"Why didn't you leave?" she asked, sitting down opposite him.

If she'd surprised him he didn't show it. He nodded toward the window. "I can see your minivan from here. I figured I'd know it, when you and Lana go."

Karin looked out the window, where a light dusting of snow came alive in the streetlights and turned the parking lot a gentle white. She had no sense of time or weather in the hospital; each second had ticked by the same as the last. The doctor had said the baby had a good chance, but Karin knew she wasn't out of the clear yet. She couldn't bear to be so close to having a child only to see the chance elude her once again.

"Are they gonna live?" Calvert asked. His eyes were glazed-over and puffy; worry lines bracketed his mouth.

"They'll both be fine," she assured him.

"Did someone tell the baby's father what happened?"

Karin laughed. "The baby's father doesn't believe the baby is his. He doesn't want anything to do with Lana anymore."

Calvert frowned. "A child should have a father."

"Well, I guess that's one thing we agree on," Karin said. She stood and pushed her chair in. "Listen, you don't have to stick around here. You can go, okay? I'll call over to the motel to let you know what happens."

"All right," he said.

She crossed her arms. "You know, I can't fix what happened between you and Lana. That's your business. But I don't think you should quit trying."

He nodded. "I appreciate you saying that."

"Go home and get some sleep."

"Sure thing," he said.

She turned to walk back out of the big, empty hall, and when she paused in the doorway to glance at him over her shoulder, she saw that he'd stretched his legs straight out before him and crossed his ankles. She knew he wouldn't be going anywhere at all.

Lana stared at the hospital ceiling, green-and-beige curtains surrounding her on all sides. The woman in the next bed over was snoring softly, but her television was blaring full blast. At the foot of her bed, Eli slept fitfully in a cheaply cushioned chair, his head craned at what looked to be a painful angle. From time to time, she could hear the squeak of a cart being wheeled down the long hall.

When she was a kid, she used to have an elementary

school teacher who would reclaim the class's attention by dropping a big flat book on the floor. The sound of it slamming onto the tile commanded their attention and changed the whole energy of the room. Lana felt as if the universe had done the same thing to her now. She hadn't been listening. Now she was.

She'd almost lost the baby today. She still might lose it. She lay stone-still, afraid to move, afraid to do anything but breathe. The possibility of a future without this child . . .

The truth was so powerful it was paralyzing. All bets were off. In the midst of wild pain, everything in her had focused on the one and only task of keeping her baby from being born no matter what it took. And it astonished her, the way her body had reacted even before her brain knew what was happening. The love that exploded inside her was so fierce it was nothing shy of possessive, and her basest instinct was maternal, protective, and stronger than she could have known. For months she'd doubted her own ability to be a parent. And yet now she knew the truth: No one could have the kind of feelings she'd had today—so primary and fundamental—and *not* be a good parent. Her love was too powerful, too strong, to allow that to happen. She was not like her father after all.

She remembered what the woman in the Barn had told her: *Dreams are tricky things.* She'd always wanted an adventure, to test her limits and see what she could see. But now, with a kind of clarity that felt like revelation, she knew she would sacrifice anything for the love of this child. She'd never been so certain of anything in her whole life. She would raise her baby as *her* baby. And she would love it. Always. If it lived.

November 24

Eli woke for no reason in the middle of the night. He was in Lana's bedroom, and even though he'd slept in her bed a number of times now, the wonder of opening his eyes to see her face, her contours shadowed and softly lit by the alarm clock lights, still made him feel choked with gratitude. Tonight was the first night she'd returned from the hospital, with strict instructions to take it very slow. He would have thought she'd sleep like the dead. But instead the sound of her breathing told him that she was awake.

"You okay?" he asked. He reached out a hand to her, felt the heat of her skin beneath the soft fleece of her pajamas.

"Fine so far."

"You can't sleep?"

"No," she said.

He moved toward her and stroked her hair. She snuggled deeper into her pillow and closer to him. He pressed his nose to her hair and smelled her shampoo, tea tree oil and mint. When she spoke, her words were muffled by cotton and he had to strain to hear them. "I don't want to give up this child. I want to keep it. For my own."

He sighed, struck by an overwhelming feeling of relief. He kissed her forehead gently. "That's wonderful. Lana, I'm so glad."

"But how am I going to tell her?"

"It's going to be hard."

"I'm a terrible person."

"You were confused. But I think you're starting to know what you want now." Lana was silent, and he fought back the urge to ask about what else she might have made a decision about, whether he would be welcomed as part of her family too. "You're going to be a good mother. And that child will live in a good, loving house. I know it, Lana. Because I know you."

"Thank you," she said.

He waited, holding his breath. Now was the part when she should agree to marry him. It made perfect sense, anyone could see that. He counted the seconds. He'd told himself he wouldn't bring up the subject of marriage again; the offer he'd made her had no expiration date, and so he had an obligation to be patient. And yet, even though he hadn't spoken about offering her his grandmother's ring, he could feel the subject stretching between them, unspoken and tense.

"I'm really tired," she said.

He waited a moment, then loosened his arms and let her go. The inches between them felt wide as a desert, and he wondered if she was already pulling away. Maybe something about accepting the baby made her less likely to accept him—as if she wanted to protect herself and her child from hurt by not letting the baby have any kind of father at all.

He wondered: If she couldn't shake him off gently, would she humiliate him again? Was she already planning how to send him on his way?

He pushed the thoughts from his mind. Their love for each other had always been strong, but their romance was still fragile and new. There was risk if he trusted her and risk if he didn't. He wanted the promise that she wouldn't break his heart again. He hoped she would give it soon.

November 25

Karin opened the door to Lana's house with her key and shouldered her way into the kitchen, glad that the Wildflower Barn's reduced winter hours allowed her a little extra time to care for her sister.

She put down her bags on the countertop and shouted hello. "I brought groceries."

She threw her keys on the kitchen table and dug around in her bags. She'd bought all the fixings for a small Thanksgiving dinner for tomorrow. She searched until she found a pint of ice cream and a couple of tabloid magazines that Lana had asked for. Since becoming bedridden Lana had apparently become addicted to celebrity gossip. Karin thought it was funny—this unexpected angle of her sister's personality—but she didn't judge.

"Hello?" She found Lana propped up on her pillows, staring at the shadow of her own hand against the wall. She looked stronger, more robust, than when Karin had last seen her in the hospital just a few days ago.

"Look," Lana said. "It's a duck."

Karin laughed and put the magazines among the other books on the messy shelf. She sat down on the edge of the bed. "I brought reinforcements."

Lana dropped her hand and turned to face her sister. There was an odd look in her eyes, a restlessness that had given way to resignation. She was going stir-crazy, by Karin's guess.

"Oh, Kari. So much has happened."

She laughed. "Angelina and Brad are adopting again?"

"No. Really. Important things. There's so much to tell you. I don't even know where to start."

"What's going on?" Karin handed her sister the ice cream and a spoon she'd grabbed from the kitchen, then she stood to tidy up the glasses and magazines and books on Lana's nightstand. She was glad she could be useful as she plucked a rumpled sweatshirt off Lana's bedside lamp and tossed it toward the hamper.

"No. Don't do that. Sit." Lana put down the ice cream and patted the side of the bed. "We have to talk."

Goose bumps ran up Karin's arms. "Talk?" She sat down slowly on the bedside chair, hoping she didn't know where the conversation was headed. Something about the tone of her sister's voice . . .

"Karin. Something's changed."

Karin sat with her spine straight, not looking at Lana's face and not allowing herself to jump to any conclusions she couldn't stand. She squeezed her fingers together hard, hoping and knowing it was useless to hope.

"I don't know how to say this," Lana said, her eyes awash with sadness. "But I can't give the baby up. My feelings have . . . they've changed."

Karin couldn't think of a word to say. Her mind felt as weightless as a cloud.

"I know it's terrible timing," Lana rushed on. "And I'm sorry. I'm so so sorry. But Karin, I lay here, and I swear I can close my eyes and get so deep inside myself that I can feel the baby's heart beating. I *have* to keep it. I can't stand the idea of letting it grow up while I just watch."

Slowly the truth, so monstrous and terrible, began to sink in. Lana wanted to take away her child. When Karin spoke, she could barely squeeze the words out through her clenched teeth. "No."

Lana frowned. "I'm sorry?"

"No, you *can't*," Karin said, her voice tight. Panic gathered speed inside her like the first tight currents of a maelstrom. "You're not thinking. What kind of mother would you be if you don't want your child one moment and want it the next? If you have all these big stupid dreams of living in Costa Rica of all places?"

Lana averted her eyes. "I can try."

"Sure. Of course you can try. Knitting is something you tried. Horseback riding is something you tried. Gossip magazines are something you're trying right now. But motherhood? It's not another hobby that you can pick up and then stop if you get bored. Be reasonable, for the baby's sake."

"I can't believe you have so little faith in me," she said softly.

Karin leaned forward in her chair, her hand pressing Lana's bedcovers. "It's not that I don't have faith in you. I think you're an amazing person. You live your life in . . . in this way that I never could. And I wish I could be more like you. But we're talking about a baby here, Lanie. We have to do the right thing."

"That's exactly what I'm trying to do," she said.

Karin sat on the edge of her chair, her back straight, her face turned away. Her hands were clasped tightly in her lap. "What are you going to do when that baby is two years old and all of a sudden you don't want it anymore? All of a sudden you want to drop everything and leave town."

"I'll want it," Lana said. "I'm not like Calvert. I trust myself now."

"But you're being irrational!" Karin said, her voice a touch too high.

"Why are you fighting me on this? Do you even realize what you're doing?"

"I'm trying to talk sense into you."

"You're trying to talk me out of keeping my own baby! You're trying to make me doubt myself because *you* want a baby so bad. Do you understand what that is, Karin?"

Karin's stomach cramped, and the word *manipulation* raced through her mind.

When Lana spoke again, her voice had softened. Tears were shining in her eyes. "I know you mean well. And I'm so sorry I wasn't strong enough or honest enough to understand this before. But if I give this child to you, I'll resent you for the rest of my life. There will be so much bad blood between us, I don't think we'll be able to come out the other side and still be as close as we are. I love you and the baby too much to lose you both."

Karin choked back the sound that almost left her throat, part sob and part laugh. "How can you do this to me?" she asked, humiliated by the quaver in her voice.

"I didn't want to hurt you." A tear slid down Lana's face, catching in the crevice beside her nose.

"You can NOT do this!" She slammed her fist on the bed, inches from Lana's hip. "Lana, you told me that baby is mine. *Mine*. I rearranged my house, my marriage, my whole life for that baby. You can't just play games with people like this."

"I'm sorry, but Karin, don't you think you might have pressured me a little over these last few weeks?"

"I didn't pressure you. Giving me the baby was the right thing to do!"

"I thought it was. I really did. But I was wrong."

Karin's arms fell to her sides. Numbness came over her, and she didn't try to stop it. She could think of no way to end the conversation on a winning note; it was as if it had already been scripted and Karin had no say in the words.

She couldn't bear the sight of her sister for another moment. She walked out of Lana's bedroom, past the grocery bags of Thankgiving foods that now wouldn't be used, and she didn't look back.

Lana heard her sister leave—heard her minivan start and speed away. She leaned her head back against the wall, trying to get her crying under control. Since she was a little girl, Karin had been her whole world—her sister, her mother, her friend. Once when they were children, they'd drawn matching "tattoos" of flowers on each other's arms, promising that even though the ink would fade, the tattoo would always be there—invisible—making them unified and the same. They'd needed that kind of solidarity with each other in Calvert's house. Lana still needed it now.

But this time . . . this time might truly have been the last straw. She had no idea how she was going to make this up to her sister. She'd made countless sacrifices for Karin over the years—staying in Vermont among them— but for all her efforts to keep her sister happy and to remain by her side, it seemed wrong that it should end like this.

She wiped the tears from her face and tried to calm

down, willing the panic to subside. This was the first time Lana could remember that she'd ever had the focus, strength, and desire to do something important that went against her sister's wishes. But instead of feeling proud for the first glimmer of real independence and self-assertion, she felt terrible. She'd finally done something startlingly good and right in her life—and it felt utterly and completely wrong.

They needed forgiveness between them. Compassion. Lana would do whatever it took to earn her sister's respect and understanding again—not that she entirely deserved it. She put her hands over the baby inside her and hoped she'd done the right thing.

"Gene." Karin found him sitting in the kitchen, eating a sandwich and reading the paper. She slammed the door behind her. The little radio on the kitchen counter was blaring commercials, the announcer's voice grating and loud. "Something's happened."

He dropped the paper, got to his feet, and crossed the room to stand before her. He was still wearing his work clothes, and he'd not yet taken off his dress shoes. She hated to ruin a perfectly peaceful moment after a long day, but here she stood, her eyes bloodshot and swollen with tears.

"What is it? Oh, honey . . . is it . . . are you . . . ?"

"No. I'm not pregnant. It's Lana . . . she—she—"

"What?"

"She said we can't have the baby!" she blurted, wrapping her arms around her husband's middle and burying her face in his chest.

He didn't move. "Wait. Slow down. I don't understand."

Karin rubbed her face on his shirt, the buttons scratching at her cheeks. "She told me we could have it. And then she took it back. I was *this* close. I was so so close. And now I've lost everything! All because of her."

He took her by the shoulders and pulled back enough to look into her eyes. "Did you *ask* her if we could have her baby?"

She stuttered, fumbling to explain.

"Did you, Karin? Did you ask her? Yes or no?"

She wrenched away from him. "I wanted to save our marriage."

Gene's face went as blank as if she'd just slapped him; his hands dropped to his sides and he took a few steps away from her. "Who are you anymore?"

"What do you mean?"

"I know you want a baby. But how bad? Enough to tear your family apart? Enough to manipulate your sister into giving you her child? Enough to ruin your marriage?"

Karin stuck out her chin. "What do you mean, 'ruin my marriage'?"

He was quiet.

"Gene, you have to do something. You have to help me. I don't know what to do."

She waited for him to speak, to tell her how they were going to fix this terrible mess. Instead he just said, "Oh, Karin. I don't think I can do this anymore."

"What are you talking about?"

"I'm . . . I'm leaving."

She wasn't sure she'd heard right. "What do you mean, leaving?"

"I'm leaving you."

She put her hands on her stomach; it churned under her palms. "You can't go now. Didn't you listen to me? Lana isn't giving us the baby after all."

"She was never giving us the baby."

She turned and hit the wall with the fat part of her fist. "You're *blaming* me? My heart is breaking in two and you're blaming me? You're supposed to help me, not make it worse!"

He took a few steps toward her, his strides slow but long. To her shock he leaned down and gave her the most tender, most tranquil kiss she'd felt in a long time. Some of the anger inside her dissolved and gave way to deep, heavy grief.

"I'm sorry," he said. Then he reached for the suitcase leaning beside the back door, the suitcase that she realized was already packed. How many times had she noticed it sitting there, and yet she hadn't acknowledged what it meant until now? It had been a hint. One of the many hints she should have been paying attention to. One of the many hints she hadn't let herself see.

"Wait! You can't go. I *need* you here."

The smile he gave her was full of pity and remorse.

She gripped the sleeve of his shirt. "I'll go with you. Just give me five minutes to pack."

"It's too late for that now."

She put a hand to her forehead and gathered her thoughts. "Okay. You're right. You know what? You're right. We'll just go. Come on. We can buy anything I need along the way."

She tried to push past him, out the back door, but he

stopped her with a hand on her arm. When he spoke his voice was quiet. "I said no."

She looked into his face, the brick wall of his eyes. The energy drained out of her. "Gene . . ."

He only shook his head.

Her bottom lip began to tremble. "Please don't leave me alone. Honey? Please?"

His face softened, those features she fell in love with years ago still the same, but full of a kind of sorrow she'd never seen before.

"I'm sorry for everything. Just please . . ." She put her hands on his chest. "Just please stay with me."

For a moment she saw the light in his eyes, a faint echo of the light that flickered so strongly there when they'd stood together before the altar and said, "I do." But no sooner had the light rose up than it went away again, leaving nothing but a cold, fathomless chill.

"I have to do this," he said. "And you have to let me. It's the right thing."

Her hands fell away from him. In her mind she saw a vision of herself, of what she must look like at this moment to him. All this time she'd believed she was trying to do the right thing. But the truth was, she'd done everything wrong. She'd treated him badly—she'd been thinking only of herself, of what *she* wanted, while his needs received only a passing glance. And she'd treated Lana horribly—her own sister. She'd been manipulative and selfish and above all, she'd been a liar; she'd lied to everyone. To herself.

"Where will you go?" she asked.

"My brother's got a spare bedroom."

"But that's two hours away. How will you go to work?"

"I'll find a way."

She fought the tears that threatened to fall. Obviously this wasn't some rash decision. He had it all planned out. "Is this permanent?"

"I hope not. I just need some time to think. And so do you."

She nodded and gripped her hands together to keep them from shaking. "Don't do this. I love you."

He looked at her for a long moment. She held her breath.

"I love you too," he said. Then he left.

November 29

Lana sat at the kitchen table, using tweezers to carefully arrange a purple and yellow Johnny-jump-up in the perfect position over a circle of pressed Queen Anne's lace. She'd always liked to save some flowers so she could frame them in the winter and have a little springtime beauty even when the ground froze. But this year she'd gone through most of her flower stash in half the usual time. She took a sip of her hot chocolate and sighed, wishing Karin was here with her to pass the time, wondering how long it would be until they talked again.

The doorbell rang and she stood slowly and carefully, her mind attuned to every ache and pain in detail that was more excruciating than any pain itself. She wasn't expecting Eli until later, when he planned to make them dinner. She walked slowly through the house, thinking that maybe Charlotte had dropped by—but Charlotte wasn't quite so trigger-happy with the doorbell as her current visitor was.

"I'm coming already!" The ringing was insistent, Westminster chimes vibrating through her last intact nerve. She flung open the door. "Yes?"

Ron was smiling sheepishly, holding a few stems of supermarket roses. She could see their singular, signature red even from a few feet away. In the past she'd grabbed up his store-bought flowers and put them to her face as if the smell hadn't been genetically bred out of them and replaced with perfume. Now, she only stared at them and wondered what she'd been thinking. Wildflowers were what she loved. *Wildflowers.* And Eli too.

"Are you feeling okay?" he asked.

"Yes, thank you. What do you want?"

"Can I come in?"

She weighed her options. The air coming in through the door was chilly and biting. It had snowed last night—not a lot—but enough to suggest that a white winter was in store. A flurry of snowflakes sparkled and sliced the air, whipping in the cold wind.

"Please?" His eyebrows were creased, pleading.

She wobbled a little on her feet. She was weak and wouldn't be able to have a conversation with him standing in the doorway. She had to sit down. "I really shouldn't have visitors."

"I won't stay long."

She sighed and stepped aside, feeling more than a little vulnerable when she compared her flimsy white nightdress to his big bomber jacket and boots. The baby elbowed her, wiggling as if anxious, and she found herself putting a hand to the spot and soothing the child in her mind. As Ron passed by he held out the roses. "No, thank you," she said.

She sat down gingerly on the couch, one hand cradling the underside of her belly, the other motioning for Ron to take the armchair a few feet away. He didn't. He plopped right down beside her, close but not touching. The roses lay awkwardly across his lap.

"You don't look very good. How are you feeling?"

"I almost lost the baby."

"But . . . I thought that's what you would have wanted."

"You thought wrong," she said.

He looked at her closely. She didn't know him well enough to be certain of the expression on his face, but she thought it was regret. "Listen. I want to apologize. I said some really terrible things to you in the Wildflower Barn that day."

She remembered the anger, the vehemence in his eyes. He'd stopped just shy of calling her a liar and denying that the child was his. He'd rejected her and the baby. "You made me feel terrible," she admitted. "Like it was my fault. Mine alone."

He nodded, somber. "I thought it was your fault. I mean, that's what it felt like. But that was then. I'd take it all back if you'd let me, now."

"Just tell me what you want."

He flinched at her tone. "I don't want it to be like this. So awkward between us. We can start over, you know."

"We can't start over."

"But I'm that baby's father. Aren't I?"

"Of course you are." Her throat went tight as if he'd

wrapped his fingers around it and squeezed. The words *custody battle* raced through her mind. "What are you saying?"

"I want to be in the child's life. Maybe you don't want me back right now. I can understand why. But I hope we might be able to make peace. I wigged out before. But I'm ready now—to do what I have to do."

She shifted in her seat, already weary from the conversation's physical and emotional demands. "This seems like it's coming out of nowhere. You were really mad that day in the Barn. It wasn't just fear. You were furious."

"I *was* furious," he admitted. "You trapped me. You might as well have backed me into a corner and put a gun to my head."

Lana nodded, her throat dry.

"I have no way of convincing you, but I've been wrestling with this every day." He leaned toward her, his expression pleading. "Lana, hear me out. I haven't been sleeping at night, thinking about this. It wouldn't be right if I never know my son and he never knows me. I just wouldn't be able to look myself in the eye ever again."

She began to tremble. He was right, of course. In her heart she wanted her child to know its father. For her baby's sake, she hoped Ron would care. "So what are you asking me? What do you want?"

"There's only one solution I can think of," Ron said, opening the flap of his coat and reaching into an inner pocket. "Lana . . ." He slid off the couch, the roses falling to his side, all his weight balanced on one knee. "I've been thinking about this a long time. Whether you say yes or not is your choice. But if you want that child to have a real father—a guy who will love it and do the best he can—I want to be there. For the baby and for you."

Lana sat still, speechless. She thought of her own mother, of the moment that Calvert had proposed and Ellen said yes. Had that turning point in their lives been a beautiful moment, one that made them both giddy and thrilled for the future? Or was it more like this, a complicated mix of relief, pleasure, and—she had to admit—resignation too?

She put a hand over her heart. "Oh, Ron. I knew you were a good person."

His gaze darted away. "Does this mean you'll say yes?"

"Is that really what you want?"

"Of course." He shifted as if it hurt him to stay down on one knee. "But, I mean, I sorta thought you wouldn't want to . . ."

She took the ring from his hand, looking at it for a long moment. It was a showy ring, with a large diamond in the center and braided ropes of white gold. It was nothing like the ring Eli had shown her, the one he promised to slip on her finger the moment she said the word. That ring was a little tarnished, spartan, and entirely lovely—an authentic way of saying *love*.

She closed the box in her hand, more certain now than ever before. She wasn't sure what kind of life she could make with Eli—she hadn't told him yes before because it had felt too soon, and because she could handle only one major life change at a time. But now, she knew that when the right time came, she would tell him yes with everything good and joyful within her. She didn't know where her dreams of traveling fit in, nor did she know what kind of life she would make for herself with him, but she knew with perfect clarity that she never wanted to make a life without him. She loved him more than she could stand.

She looked up at Ron, who appeared a bit stricken. She hadn't realized she'd been smiling. He must have thought she was going to say yes. "Ron, I do want you to be in our baby's life. But I don't think that having a false marriage would be good for any of us. I like you and I know you like me, but it's not love."

He nodded solemnly, distance in his eyes. She knew what it had cost him to come here and ask for her hand. She understood what he was prepared to sacrifice. His proposal wasn't one of love; it was a commitment to do right by their child, to put himself second. In some ways, the proposal took more guts than if he'd thought her the woman of his dreams.

"Oh, Ron." She smiled gently and leaned to wrap her arms around him. He hugged her back. "Thank you," she said, resting her cheek on his shoulder. "I'm so happy you want to be a part of the baby's life. And mine too." She let him go after a moment and then placed the ring back in his hand.

His sigh held a hint of relief. "And what about the baby?"

She tried to keep the concern off her face. Until now, she'd thought of herself as her baby's sole parent. She made all the decisions—just her. Now Ron was asking to be a part of the baby's life. And by extension, her own. How much control was she obligated to give him? How much would he want? She cleared her throat and spoke as calmly as she could. "Do you . . . are you going to want full custody?"

"Not if you don't want me to have it. I mean, I figured we'd kinda share or something like that. Like maybe I could see him every other weekend?"

"It might be a her."

"Maybe."

She smiled, relieved. The hard part of the conversation was over now; she could see it in the subtle relaxation of his face. She stood, gesturing for him to do the same. "Come on."

"Where are we going?"

"Don't you want to see the pictures from the ultrasound?"

"Yeah," he said. His voice sounded oddly young and shy. "I'll look at pictures. But just so you know, I don't want to be, like, in the delivery room when the baby's born. If that's okay. The whole thing sorta freaks me out."

"You and me both," she said. She laughed and squeezed his hand as they walked into the next room.

Eli juggled his grocery bags and attempted to pull his wool mitten off with his mouth so that he could unlock Lana's front door. But instead of finding it locked, he felt the key slip in and turn too easily. And in the same instant that adrenaline hit his brain, he heard her voice in the living room, and he saw the shape of her through the white curtain of the window.

She wasn't alone.

The image was like a punch to the gut: Ron down on one knee. And Lana, smiling at him—beaming, really—and gazing down at the ring in her hand.

Eli's body remembered before his brain did, as if his

reaction had been stored up in his muscles all this time. He felt as if it was happening again, the moment of pushing open the door of her dorm room all those years ago. The last decade of mustering up friendly smiles each time she introduced him to another date. The hope of offering her his grandmother's ring, and the knowledge that he might as well have held it out to empty air. Each day of his relationship with her, he'd faced down the specter of how easily he could lose her. How suddenly she might pull away from him. And that moment had come.

He watched as Lana looked at the man beside her, then embraced him. Eli backed away and almost tumbled down the concrete stairs. He hugged the grocery bags to his chest, his heart beating hard.

She didn't want to marry him—the man who was not the father of her child. The message was loud and clear.

There was no point in waiting around. And he wasn't going to walk into the same losing battle twice. As he headed back to his car, he let his anger become a hard, icy chill, his heart falling in temperature like the cooling, freezing air. He'd prepared for this. Expected it. He would not waste a moment replaying the scene in his mind, trying to decipher what he'd seen or not seen. If he doubted himself, uncertainty would only make the pain worse.

The wind picked up, blowing hard against his whole body, a chill slicing through his jeans. But he didn't duck his head or hunch his shoulders. He just stood up straighter, narrowed his tearing eyes, and pushed on.

December

> **Common mullein:** A rodlike roadside weed that can grow to five feet, this wild plant has gone by many names but was called *candelaria* by the Romans. The clusters of flowers were dried, soaked in fat, then lit on fire, giving light during the darkest time of year.

December 3

Eli stood alone in Moe's cramped living room, the weight of Moe's cordless phone pressing his hand. He stared hard at the number pad, its keys that were sticky with what he hoped was soda or beer. His thumb brushed over the number 1, but he did not press down.

For days, he'd disciplined himself. *Don't call her, don't call her.* He'd gone round and round with himself about the logic of staying silent. He'd pummeled his feelings to a pulp, shaking off self-pity and holding tight to anger and betrayal. He stayed busy, went out with Moe to drink and flirt madly with women, and at night he never got in bed or closed his eyes until he was utterly spent with exhaustion—to keep his mind from wandering in those dangerous moments before he fell asleep.

Yesterday, he'd offered to help out at the amateur astronomical society in Vermont. The Geminids meteor shower was only ten days away, and he'd said he'd be happy to drive out to their mini-convention and give a talk. It was late notice, but since it was being run by an old colleague, they'd readily agreed to have him. He liked the idea of getting away and being distracted. The convention was just far enough that he would need to get a hotel room, but not so far that he couldn't rush back home if called.

He sighed. There was no dignity in his behavior, in his longing. The spot in his heart that ached for Lana was like the dark, dense center of a black hole, so heavy it warped the fabric of his whole being, tugging not only at his loneliness, but at his sense of humor, his interests, his basic human needs. The world, so vibrant and shining two weeks ago, had gone dull.

Part of him wanted to speak to her, to find out the details of what he'd seen—or what he hadn't seen—that afternoon. But that was the emotional part of his brain—the untrustworthy and sniveling part of himself that he couldn't stand. The rational part of his brain knew that what he saw or what he merely *thought* he saw had the same effect. The instant Lana reached for that unmistakable little box, two things became clear.

First: She hadn't rejected Ron immediately. Her body language, her posture, the look on her face—nothing he saw suggested that she was uncomfortable or appalled. That worried him. Even if Ron's proposal had ultimately been turned down—he had no way of knowing if it was or wasn't—Lana's reaction wasn't the blatant and outright refusal he'd hoped it would be.

Second: There was the crushing realization that no

matter what, Ron would always share something with Lana that Eli did not. It hurt to think of it—that another man had fathered a child with the woman he loved. When he'd been pursuing Lana, his focus had been single-minded and driven—nothing could distract him from his goal. And so he hadn't given a second thought to Ron. But now it was clear Ron wanted some kind of future with Lana and her baby. And where did Eli fit into that? Was he totally pathetic to hope that he even fit in at all—he, who had nothing to do with the tightly bound circle of Lana, her baby, and Ron?

He bounced the weight of the phone in his hand, thinking. He'd let himself start believing that his future with Lana was one of stability—a quiet family life. He'd even begun to start thinking of her child as *his*, welcoming it with the same warmth and care that he would have if it had been his baby in her womb. But at the end of the day, facts were facts. The baby was Ron's, not his. He remembered the way Lana had looked on her birthday, the way Ron had come out of her bedroom with his open shirt—buttons *she* had opened. It killed him to think of it, then and now. Lana had *liked* Ron. Liked him enough to sleep with him. And if Lana wanted to consider marrying the man who had fathered her child . . . who was Eli to confuse things or stand in her way?

He had to give Lana some space—to give them both some space—so they both could be sure she would pick the man she wanted—not just because of a whim or an instinct, but a decision that was once and for all.

"Just call already."

He turned around, surprised to see Moe standing there in his pressed khakis and button-down shirt. His apartment was a mess, but his clothes were always movie-star neat.

"You've been staring at the phone for five minutes. Just dial."

Eli shook his head, glad to have been caught because it meant that the argument about whether to call Lana or not had been settled—at least temporarily. This was precisely the reason he was crashing at Moe's instead of sitting around and stewing in his own apartment. At least at Moe's, he wasn't surrounded by memories at every turn and he could get away from his own unhappiness from time to time. "Nah. Can't."

"Why not?"

"What would I say?"

"I would imagine that after everything you've been through, there would be a lot to say."

Eli sighed hard. He thought back over the last few weeks, images arriving in colors so vivid and stark it hurt to remember. Lana's eyelids lowered when he slid off the straps of her bra. The swell of her belly, naked and softly lit in his room. He loved her so much, a bigger love than he'd even thought himself capable of. And yet because of how much he loved her, he needed to give her room and step aside.

"Well," Moe said, lifting his black leather jacket from the coatrack and slipping it on, "I've got some errands to run, and then I have a date, so it looks like you've got the place to yourself."

"Great," Eli said, no hint of enthusiasm in his voice.

"Throw a party. Invite over some women. See if that girl you used to date . . . what's her name . . . ?"

"Kelly."

"See if Kelly wants to come over. Tell her you need some rebound therapy."

"That's the last thing I need."

Moe adjusted his coat on his shoulders, lifting it by the collar and letting it fall. "All I'm saying is, don't sit around and mope. We've gone over this a hundred times. I don't think she was setting you up to walk in on her and the mountain biker."

"It doesn't matter whether she was setting me up or not."

"How do you figure?"

"The phone hasn't exactly been ringing off the hook because she wants to talk."

"You don't know what she's thinking," Moe said.

Eli shrugged. "I don't really know what I'm thinking either."

"Up to you. But I think you should call."

"Have fun," Eli said, but Moe had already half closed the door behind him and probably didn't hear the words. And then Eli was alone.

Slowly he put the phone back in its cradle, wondering where Lana was, what she was doing now. Lana would have the baby shortly. He'd wanted to be there for the birth. They'd planned for it. He'd looked forward to the baby's birth day, not only because he'd wanted to be part of it, but because he'd been thrilled that Lana had wanted him to be part of it. But now that Ron was back . . . it made more sense to have the child's father in the delivery room. Not him.

His dreams for a future with her—for a family with her—had been so close, almost *promised*. He hadn't directly spoken aloud of the life he wanted to anyone, so afraid that saying the words would somehow stop his heart's dream from coming true. And yet silence had brought him nothing. Just him, the telephone, and his endless, humorless grief.

December 4

Lana lay in her bed, staring. Her alarm clock had started buzzing ten minutes ago, but she didn't turn it off. She just listened to it droning, demanding. The sound or the silence of it made little difference. Time crept like long winter shadows across the floor, the hours unchanging except for the slant of the sun.

Outside, the first serious freeze of the year had come on hard and fast. The streets had fallen eerily quiet, so silent that she felt as if she lived in a different place, somewhere chilled and far from civilization. It was hard to believe that the frozen, dark town she lived in now was the same town that celebrated spring with bloodroot and columbine. Everything and everyone had tucked in for the long winter. Charlotte was her only communication with the outside world. She stopped in to bring casseroles, bread, milk, toothpaste, DVDs, and magazines. But otherwise, Lana was alone.

There had been no specific moment when she realized that Eli was gone. The first few messages she'd left on his answering machine had been innocent—naive—enough. She supposed there must have been a good explanation for his not showing up to fix their dinner and not calling to explain. But then, the unease that had been niggling in the back of her mind had gained strength and pushed to the forefront overnight. She awoke with a knot in her stomach and misery saturating her whole body. She'd lost him. She knew.

And now she lay in bed, feeling as if her bones themselves had turned to heavy lead and trapped her against her mattress. She turned over in bed, bringing the baby with her. It protested, kicking her once before settling down. She knew it could sense her heartbreak, her longing. Her bed was empty without Eli in it. Her heart was too.

She hadn't realized how much her life's desires had changed until now. She'd begun to look forward to her life with Eli and her child. She saw the three of them happy, thriving, living their lives. But it was more than just the desire of a dream. She *counted* on that future. She needed it. And now there was a chance that it was gone.

On her nightstand was a letter Eli had written her, just a frayed-edge bit of notebook paper with very few words. He told her what had happened. That he'd seen her with Ron. And even though he didn't stick around to see if she really had accepted Ron's proposal, what he'd seen gave him pause. The tone of the letter was straightforward enough, but she could feel Eli's heartbreak underneath. Seeing Ron propose to her was upsetting, but it had triggered deeper, more powerful fears.

She could read between the lines: He didn't know if he could trust her. She wondered again and again if there was some way to prove herself to him. She envisioned herself calling him up, demanding he come to her house since she couldn't go out, and then setting him straight. But the shock of discovering that he didn't trust her now that she so thoroughly trusted herself . . . it hurt.

She could have written back to him, said *Of course I don't want Ron. I want you.* But his doubt was so enormous, such a force to be reckoned with, that she felt it would do little good to bother him with something as trifling as fact. The weakness in their relationship was huge. She hadn't seen it coming. His doubts were not the small and wondering and inconsequential kind; they called into question who she was—who he *thought* she was—and that was terrifying.

She felt the baby wiggle a little inside her. Her belly felt different now, a pressure so low and strong it was almost as if she needed to be constantly holding the child in place with her muscles. For days after she'd returned from the hospital, Eli had been at her side, unmindful of her messy hair, her swollen feet and hands, the circles of fatigue beneath her eyes. They'd talked about the day she would give birth; they planned for it and strategized their maneuvers with the precision of generals. It felt like more than just preparing for a baby; it felt like they were laying the groundwork for a future together. But now Eli was saying they both needed time to think. He'd told her to call him for anything—he said he was going away, not far. But merely knowing that she could dial him up in an emergency didn't mean nearly as much as if she could call him for no reason at all. His offer of help felt like a consolation prize.

In a few weeks, the child would be safe to deliver. In the scheme of her life, three weeks would be a drop in the proverbial bucket. But for now loneliness contorted the minutes into interminable hours. The sunlight shifted imperceptibly, inch by incremental inch, and the city turned up its collar and clenched its jaw against the bone-deep winter freeze. Lana lay alone in her bed, and she rubbed her belly and told her child stories of better seasons to come. In Greek mythology, spring came when Persephone was allowed to leave the underworld and visit her mother; their joy at reuniting brought the flowers back to barren land. It had always made sense to Lana that to tell the story of spring would be to tell the story of mothers and daughters, of reunion. She kissed the tips of her fingers and pressed them to her belly, swearing that everything would be better if they could only make it to spring.

December 7

Karin knocked on her sister's door, the first time she'd done so in years. Then, because she knew Lana wasn't supposed to get up to answer, she turned her key in the lock. Inside, the kitchen was messy, quiet, and dim. The lacy curtains of Lana's little windows were open, bathing the room in white winter light that was both luminous and cold. She moved toward Lana's room with the odd sense that the house had been abandoned for a long time.

She found Lana propped up in bed. She wasn't sleeping, but when she turned her head, her gaze lacked the clear-eyed alertness that said she was fully awake. Her hair was weighed down from days of not showering, and her skin was tired and dull. There was a television in the room, but it wasn't on. Karin trembled. Her sister, so flushed and vigorous after she'd returned from the hospital, was now wasting away.

"I know, I look terrible," Lana said. "You don't have to tell me."

"You look . . ." Karin's eyes grew watery. Lana was the best sight she'd seen in days. "I've missed you."

Lana nodded. Her voice was hollow and flat. "I'm glad you're here."

"How are you feeling?"

"I've been better."

Karin surveyed the room—clothes in bundles on the floor, a stack of filthy dishes, glasses that bore rings from liquid that had evaporated days ago. "What's going on here? Why didn't Eli clean this up for you?"

Lana raised her eyes back to the ceiling, and Karin got the sense that she'd been lying like that for some time. She paused long enough for Karin to look around, to realize there were no traces of Eli anywhere—the books, clothes, and other odds and ends Karin would have expected to see were conspicuously absent. She looked at Lana with a pang of concern.

When Lana finally spoke, her voice was lifeless and tired. "He's gone."

Gently, Karin sat on the edge of Lana's bed, feeling the strength of it buckle beneath her. She remembered the concern on Eli's face in the hospital, his frustration that he could not do more. Something didn't add up. "What happened?"

"He left me," Lana said. "I'll fill you in on the details later. When I can stand to. For now, let's just leave it there."

Karin sighed. "I would have come sooner if I knew. Who's been taking care of you?"

"Charlotte stops in. When she can."

Karin nodded. "And you didn't want to call me for help because you thought I was mad."

The sparkle of hope in Lana's eyes was more than Karin could stand. "You're not mad at me?"

"No. And also . . . I'm alone now too."

"I don't understand."

"Gene's gone away for a while. We're taking a break."

Lana's glassed-over eyes became a touch more focused. "Oh, Kari. I'm sorry."

"No. Don't be. He did the right thing." She paused, feeling for the first time in two weeks that she was about to do something unequivocally and totally right. She'd been thinking long and hard about who she was, what she'd done, and what she wanted from the future. It was time for her to start down a new path. And she wanted her sister beside her when she did. "I've been a mess. And I've done a lot of things wrong. To him. And to you too."

"You don't have to—"

"I want to. Please. Just let me get this off my chest." Karin took Lana's hand. "I got so focused on starting a family that I lost sight of the family I already have. I *did* pressure you to give me the baby. I couldn't see how desperate I was. How wrapped up in myself. You took the brunt of it, I'm afraid. You and Gene. So I owe you an apology. I'm sorry. I can't change what I did. But I'm sorry for it. I really am."

Lana's eyes were wet. "We both know I'm the one who should be apologizing to you."

"You need to do what's right for you and your baby. And for what it's worth, Lanie, I do think you're going to be a great mom. Wacky, but a really great mom."

Lana smiled and reached toward Karin to hug her. Karin felt the warmth of her sister's arms and she laid her head on Lana's shoulder. The tenderness she felt for her sister was warm and very welcome. Loving her sister—or Gene, or anyone—was so easy. Love, in its purest form, came so naturally, without complication. She felt the strength and solidity of it rooted firmly within her, and she knew her love for her family could never be compromised. Relationships were always a push and pull, a swinging forward and backward, changes propelled by dreams, circumstances, and time. And yet, Karin felt there was a sameness underlying all of it. Love as bedrock. And it made all the swinging back and forth seem, on the surface, kind of silly at times.

"Thank you for understanding," Lana said.

"I'm just sorry it took so long." Karin pulled away, feeling better than she had in weeks. She still had a ways to go before she really understood, but she was getting closer to something. She just didn't know what. She looked around the room and began to lay out a plan to clean up the mess around them.

December 14

Lana was sitting on the edge of her bed when she heard Calvert's voice as Karin let him into the living room—his too-loud, overly polite remarks—and she could picture him looking around, taking in her mismatched decorating as he stepped inside. She looked herself in the eye in her bedroom mirror, feeling and seeing a reflection of his nervousness in herself but certain of what she had to do.

Over the last week, she and Karin had spent a lot of time cooped up together. And they'd been talking a lot about their childhood—dredging up all those memories, good and bad. Until now, Lana hadn't wanted to revisit those old moments that she'd worked so hard to forget. But somehow, the conversations didn't feel like volunteering for a series of self-inflicted wounds. Instead she was growing closer to her sister, opening up to her as an equal, healing and getting control.

Yesterday, in the midst of a discussion about the way Calvert had treated his boarders, Karin had convinced Lana that she needed to talk to their father. When Lana had collapsed in the Wildflower Barn, Calvert had called the ambulance for her and stayed with her, talking softly and telling her it would be okay. He'd grabbed a sweatshirt from a display and put it under her head, and he'd found a blanket embroidered with cosmos to help stave off shock. At the very least, she owed him the courtesy of saying thanks.

Now, she walked slowly out of the bedroom, excruciatingly attuned to the pressure between her legs. She could feel that the baby was pressing downward now, its little heels tap-dancing on her diaphragm. She had a strong sense that she was carrying the baby inside her the same way that she might carry it in her arms; even the lightest bundle could become exhausting after too long. Being pregnant was no longer one of her body's functions, but had become its first and most basic function. The baby was impatient to be born and she soothed it, daily, saying, *Just a little more time.*

Calvert's eyes grew wide with worry when she turned the corner that led to the living room. Among the brightly colored tapestries and spangled saris that decorated the room, he looked completely out of place. He was dressed more nicely than she'd seen in a while. What hair he had left was slicked flat against the sides of his head; she could see the teeth marks from the comb he'd used to brush it back.

"Here she is," Karin said, and Lana could tell that she too was a little nervous. "I guess I'll just leave you two alone."

Lana sat down in the armchair on the opposite side of the room as Karin left. She had actually gotten dressed today, and her maternity jeans and blue sweater felt constricting and itchy on her skin. "Hi, Calvert."

"Lana." He shifted in his chair, uncomfortable. "How you feeling?"

"I'm hanging in there," she said.

"You like being . . . you know?"

She managed a smile. "I like it very much. I'd like to *stay* pregnant for at least a couple more weeks. For the baby's sake." She leaned back in her chair to accommodate her belly and clasped her hands. She liked that her father really did seem interested in her pregnancy—that he'd thought to ask if she *liked* how she felt. It was a nice consolation from a man who hadn't seemed to care much what she liked or didn't like ages ago.

"I brought this for you," he said, reaching into the bag beside him and pulling out a small present. "Karin told me that with everything going on, you weren't able to get together a baby shower. I hope you like it."

She took the small gift. It was wrapped in a muted

yellow paper, smiling ducks looking back at her. "You didn't need to do this . . ."

"Yeah, well . . . I did," he said.

She slid her thumb under a bit of masking tape and slowly opened the present. Inside was a kit to grow a child's garden. It was too old for a newborn. But Calvert most likely saw the child-friendly colors and baby-sized gardening tools, and it had inspired him.

"I know how you feel about flowers . . . ," he said.

Tears came to her eyes, and she blinked them back, remembering too vividly the moment when he'd given her a bit of jewelweed and shown her what flowers were for the first time. Could he know how much that moment still meant to her? She set the garden kit down gently on her lap. "Why did you have me?" she asked.

"What?"

"I understand why you had Karin—because it was an accident. But why *me*? Why didn't you stop at one?"

He took in a deep breath, then sighed. "Well, see, Karin wasn't totally an accident."

"Okay . . . ?"

He fidgeted in his seat, and he seemed to struggle for something to look at, something other than Lana's face. "Your mom and I . . . we were young. Dumb. We sorta kicked around the idea of getting married and having kids. And so we stopped being totally careful all the time."

Lana couldn't quite believe what she was hearing. "So Karin was intentional?"

"I wouldn't put it that way," he replied. "Neither one of us actually thought Ellen'd get pregnant. We just liked the danger of it. I imagine Ellen got to telling people it was an accident on account of the divorce. But at the time it felt like we were daring the gods or something. And when Ellen did conceive, I remember feeling . . . good. But scared too."

Lana bit the inside of her lip, not sure how to respond. She couldn't picture the man sitting before her now being joyfully reckless, tempting fate. He'd always seemed so insensitive, so resigned to whatever fate dealt him. At least, that was how he'd been when they moved in with him. He'd always tolerated them, but nothing more. "Well, even if Karin wasn't exactly an accident, why did you have *me*?"

Calvert grimaced, deep wrinkles pulling around his mouth. "It was your mother's idea mostly. And I'm afraid she didn't get a fair shake. She told me she wanted another baby, and what was I supposed to do?"

"You didn't want another baby?"

"No. But I went along."

"You could have told her no."

"I thought maybe if we had another one, I'd be happy."

Lana couldn't ignore the pang of sympathy she felt for him. "Were you happy?"

"I suppose not," he said, thoughtful and a little sad. "I wasn't cut out for a family. For kids. But you don't always know these things when you're young. And I made a mistake."

Lana turned the little garden kit over in her hands, the bright tulips and daffodils blurring as she spun it around. Her father looked at parenting a different way than she did. His reasons for having a child extended beyond the simple desire to be a parent. He'd wanted Karin and Lana to fix a problem—for Karin to be the thrill that kept a young romance going. And for Lana to be the glue to keep a failing marriage from falling apart.

But Lana wanted her baby only for its own sake. She wanted to search out the joy in life with her son or daughter by her side—to share that enjoyment. And maybe, if she did things right, to go someday from being called *Mother* to being called *Friend*. She wasn't giving up on her dreams of traveling—not by a long shot. But she hoped someday to have her child beside her when she saw the world. The baby had become an important and intrinsic part of the fabric of the future, bonding with her dreams the same way it had bonded with her body as the months passed.

Calvert slid his palms along his thighs as if they were sweaty. His gaze stayed focused on his hands. His words seemed measured and deliberate when at last he spoke. "You and Karin turned out real well. No thanks to me. I mean, I ignored you girls. I know I did. I thought it was unfair the way life turned out, and I took it out on you."

Lana was quiet, astonished by the simple way he admitted to doing wrong. It took courage, she knew, to be able to apologize so candidly. She respected him for that.

He looked up, his ice-blue eyes fathomless, when she looked on. "I'm not asking for you to all of a sudden forget everything. But I'd sleep a whole lot better at night if you'd tell me you forgive me. If you can."

She nodded and managed to smile. Forgiveness rolled up out of her soul, easy as breathing. She realized she'd been waiting for this moment a long time. "I'm over it," she said, to keep the moment light. "All of it. Water under the bridge."

"Thanks," he said.

She patted her belly, not quite realizing she'd done it. "So what will you do now?"

He shrugged. "Well, I might stick around 'til the baby's born. If it's okay with you."

"Where are you staying?"

"Karin called the cops off me a while back. So I'm in the Madison again. And I'm working too. Got a job at an office building. Custodial stuff."

Lana swallowed. "So, you're going to stay around here?"

"For a while. But I thought maybe I'd like to learn to drive a truck. I think I'd do good on the open road."

Lana smiled. "Well, for now, I'm glad you're here. I want the baby to meet you."

He looked down. "Thank you," he said.

December 21

The inside of the exam room at the obstetrician's office was oddly soundless given how busy the waiting room had been. Karin had joined her sister for her thirty-four-week appointment, and now Lana sat on the exam table, white paper crinkling beneath her flimsy gown. Under the harsh ceiling lights, Karin could set a watch by Lana's visible breathing, her belly rising and falling in arduous waves.

"How close am I?" Lana asked the nurse. "Can you tell?"

The nurse, who had a pretty heart-shaped face, smiled. "Well, it's hard to say. You're two centimeters dilated and about 40 percent effaced. You still have a ways to go."

"My back is hurting on and off," Lana said. "I'm worried it's contractions."

"It might be. If they're around ten minutes apart, then you'll want to head over to the hospital to get checked out. But otherwise, you'll just have to sit tight."

"Are you sure?" Lana asked.

The nurse laughed—a little pity in her eyes—and she patted Lana's shoulder. "First-time moms always rush off to the hospital at the first sign of labor. It's pretty common. But you have time. You have *lots* of time. Believe me. I was in labor for thirteen hours with my first. Just be sure that when your water breaks, you get to the hospital. Okay?"

"All right," Lana said. "I guess I'm just a little nervous."

"All new moms are. Just relax."

"Is there anything else we should know?" Karin asked. "Anything she shouldn't do?"

"She's got about six more days of bedrest. Then, as long as it's sensible, she can do anything she wants." She turned to look at Lana directly, a twinkle in her eye. "You can even go back to having sex."

Lana gave a weak grin. "Probably not going to happen."

Karin would have laughed, except that she knew just how Lana was feeling deep down. She'd talked to her husband only a handful of times since he left. Though she stood next to the phone every night, her hand gripping the receiver, she fought hard against the urge to call. He'd said he needed space, and she vowed to give it. When she did allow herself to talk to him, she always hung up the phone feeling farther away from him than before.

After Lana had dressed, she left the exam room as quickly as she could, leaving Karin there with only the nurse at the sink. She looked around at the posters of reproductive systems and pictures of childbirth stages and all the other incomprehensible medical illustrations that made her think of Ripley's "Believe It or Not." Karin's gaze lingered on a poster of fetal development, the way a child grows from an imperceptible speck rendered in miniaturist's detail to a full-term work of art.

She'd thought this would have been *her* moment. That she would have been here for her own baby by now.

"Do you need something?" the nurse asked, her thin eyebrows politely raised.

Karin paused, strangely paralyzed by the question.

All this time, she'd believed her sole purpose in life was to be a mother. She'd become obsessed—she could see that now. But her identity was bigger than that. Gene's absence had forced a realization: Her role in the world mattered deeply to the people around her, even if she didn't have a child of her own.

She didn't need to have a son or daughter to be complete. She wanted a family, certainly. She always would. But she would never again endanger the family she had now for the family she merely wished for. She *wanted* children. She *needed* her husband. Now it was just a matter of showing him, somehow, what she'd learned.

The nurse's smile was a little put-off. "I said, do you need something else?"

The answer came from someplace quiet and peaceful within her.

"No," she said. "No, I don't."

• • •

December 24

Eli stood on the porch looking out over the countryside, a light dusting of snow glowing faintly on the ground against the night. He could still hear the sounds of happy laughter inside the house behind him. Some old friends he'd become reacquainted with at the meteorite convention had invited him to dinner, and he'd been pleased to go. But about halfway through—among the cheerful adults drinking spiced wine, children crawling on all fours under the dining room table, and plates upon plates of festive cakes and pies—he'd become aware that his heart was giving a low, resonating cry. He'd had to escape for a moment. And so he'd excused himself.

On the porch, the air was painfully cold, smelling of snow and wood smoke, but he welcomed its bite. He pushed his hands deep into his jeans pockets, and when he sighed his breath was thick as white smoke. Above, the sky seemed higher and more endless than usual, stars punctuating the unthinkable black distance of space. Summer had warm air and friendly haze, but winter . . . winter had *this*: the clarity of vision that comes with hard, merciless cold.

He heard the sound of a woman laughing, and he thought of *her*. Always *her*. She hadn't called or e-mailed, as he'd hoped she might. Nothing indicated that she was at all interested in seeing or talking to him.

"Hey, man!" Clem, his friend from graduate school, smacked him cheerfully on the back as he came outside onto the porch. In the silence of the night, his boots made hollow thumps on the wooden slats. "Whatcha doing? It's freezing out here!"

Eli turned to him and smiled. "Just needed some air."

Clem hooked one hand around a thin beam on the porch, absentmindedly testing the strength of it with his weight. He wore a thick hunter's vest over his dress shirt, not much protection against the cold, but he seemed in no hurry to go back inside. "Sorry about the pumpkin."

"It's okay," Eli said, looking down at the smear of orange on his shirt.

"My Melly's a wild one. She's gonna be trouble down the line."

Eli laughed. Clem's youngest daughter had an impish look to her, straight dark hair and dancing green eyes. She was energetic, to say the least, and Eli liked her—even if she'd managed to stain his shirt with pie.

Clem cleared his throat. "I'd have thought you'd want to head back to Burlington by now, being that it's so close to Christmas."

Eli was quiet, not sure how much he wanted to say. He bumped the bottom of the porch with the toe of his boot. He was so frustrated with the story of his life at the moment, he wasn't that interested in hearing it spoken aloud. "You know how it is. I just had to get away for a while."

"Why's that?"

He paused, thoughtful. "I don't know. To test if my life will still be the same when I get back."

"I hear you there," Clem said.

Eli glanced at him. He used to be very close to Clem. They'd fallen out of touch when Clem had moved out here, far west of Burlington, to raise his family. But Eli saw no reason not to at least tell Clem the gist of what had happened to him over the past couple of months.

He did the best he could with the story, smoothing it out as he went, all the little ups and downs giving way to one larger, more streamlined arc. To keep from sounding too emotional as he spoke, he pretended the story belonged to someone other than him.

When he was done, Clem shook his head a little, a disbelieving smile on his face. "So let me get this straight. You have no idea if she's gonna marry the guy or not?" Clem laughed out loud and clapped Eli on the back. "Man, you got it bad."

"Tell me about it," he said. And oddly enough, he found himself laughing too. It felt good, he realized, to see how asinine the situation looked through Clem's eyes.

"You met my wife in there," Clem said, more statement than question.

"Yeah, she's great."

"Did you know she was sick when I met her? She had Lyme disease real bad. And man, you should have seen me. Within two weeks, nobody knew more about Lyme disease than me. She and I worked together for months, finding ways to beat it, or at least make it bearable. Then, one day led to another, and she started feeling better. And next thing I knew, we were split up."

Eli looked at Clem closely, his slight stubble and thick eyebrows. He and his wife seemed so happy, always touching each other on the shoulder or hand. Always connected. It was hard to imagine them apart. "Well, you obviously worked it out," Eli said.

"Yeah, after I quit being an idiot."

"I'm not following you."

"I freaked out. It was like, *Well, now that you're not sick, what do you need me for?* You know what I mean?"

Eli was quiet, realization slowing dawning. They stood in silence for a long minute. A light sprinkling of snow began to fall, flakes sparkling red, green, and yellow in the lights strung along the edge of the porch.

Clem breathed out, white rising up clear and strong. "Well," he said at last. "You coming back in?"

"In a minute," Eli said.

"Take your time," Clem said. "The eggnog supply is going strong."

Eli took a deep breath, filling his lungs with the cold air that was as heavy and refreshing as ice water. Snowflakes glittered in the dark and faded as they reached the ground, and inside, another round of laughter rose above the light music of flutes and guitars. He wanted this for himself—family, friends, laughter, love.

It had scared him, he realized, to think that Lana didn't need him. He liked when she'd needed him, when he had something to offer that no one else had. When Ron was gone and she was alone, he felt certain of his role—to support her, to be there for her, to be everything she needed. But once Ron showed up, and he was suddenly faced with the prospect of no longer being necessary to her . . . it had scared him half out of his mind.

In the clear sky above, a falling star streaked downward, a blaze of white, and his heart made a wish long before his mind could even articulate the words of it. It seemed like a good sign.

Tomorrow, he would go back. He wanted to be with

her on Christmas. Maybe Lana no longer needed him—maybe she never truly had—but he could only hope that she *wanted* him half as much as he wanted and needed her. If she did, the future—whatever it was—was theirs.

December 25

Karin and Lana took baby steps, shuffling along slippery asphalt in the parking lot. Early in the morning, they'd driven west forty minutes to Montpelier—a trip they made every Christmas morning. They'd loaded Karin's van with poinsettia, and then spent a few hours serving cinnamon buns and coffee to those in need. Karin had suggested they stay home because a storm had been predicted for the afternoon. But Lana had rejected the idea, saying they were needed since not too many people were willing to donate their time on the biggest holiday of the year.

Unfortunately, the snow had arrived sooner than predicted. They'd found that the sky had clouded over and a thin layer of ice had formed on every surface, gleaming crystalline and bright. The mountains were blurred by bad weather and the roads were tranquil and untraveled—eerie—as if even sound had been silenced by the ice.

"Maybe we should just stay here," Lana said, disappointment and weariness in her words.

Karin looked out at the snow-covered roads. "I think it will be okay. The ground is icy, but the roads are still fine. And the minivan is good in the snow."

As they crossed the parking lot, Lana stretched out her hand to steady herself and Karin reached for her arm. She could think of nothing worse than if her pregnant, bubble-bellied sister were to fall. Though they'd parked less than three hours ago, ice had formed a hard, clear shell around and on the windows and doors. It wasn't a glass-smooth type of ice, but instead a craterous and cloudy white that might have been the hard skin of some mythical dragon.

Karin pounded on the door handle and leaned all her weight on it to slide the panel open. She helped Lana climb inside, then started the car and headed back out into the cold to chip off what ice she could.

When the last window of the van was scraped off and Karin's arms burned from exertion, she banged her boots on the side step and climbed in. Lana was shivering in the backseat, her arms wrapped tightly around her body. She could sense Lana's sadness, her loneliness. She'd hoped the situation with Eli would have been resolved by now. And under different circumstances, she would have marched herself over to Eli's house and given him an earful. But she'd learned her lesson about getting too involved in her sister's life. Karin supported her, but Lana's choices were her own.

She heard Lana give a little squeak, the kind of sound she might make if she'd got a paper cut. Karin turned around in her seat. "You okay?"

Lana didn't speak for a long moment. She shut her eyes tight, gripping the top of her seat belt so hard that her knuckles went white. Karin felt a little twinge of worry, but in just a moment, Lana let out a big, ragged breath and then she seemed fine. "I'm okay."

"Are you sure? Because if something's wrong . . ."

"*Nothing's* wrong. I'm fine. I just don't understand why we're not driving already."

Karin turned back around in her seat, feeling thoroughly put in her place. Lana had been irritable all morning, snippy and at times even mean. It wasn't like her at all. But if Lana said she was fine, Karin had no choice but to take her at her word.

She put the engine in reverse to back out of the spot and felt the tires slip a little beneath them. She was sure the roads were better than the parking lot—really not bad at all. And Lana's was less than an hour away.

She glanced in the rearview to see Lana looking out the window, a scowl on her face as if she was furious. She could only imagine what her sister was going through. Each day that Lana didn't have the baby was a triumph, one more day that the baby could use to gather its strength for its break into the world. Lana never complained and never seemed to get overly emotional or worried. She'd told Karin she needed to focus on the positive, to keep her thoughts in a good place if she wanted to carry the baby to term. Karin agreed with her, but in the privacy of her mind, she couldn't help but feel that optimism would have been easier if Eli were around. She glanced in the mirror again.

"Do you want to stop for lunch?" she asked.

"I just want to go home," Lana said. Karin knew enough to let the subject drop. Until her sister had the baby, Lana was in charge. She put the van in four-wheel drive and slowly maneuvered the vehicle toward the exit. As she reached the main road, she saw that the plows had done a good job dealing with the ice. She settled back into her seat and sprayed the windshield with deicing fluid. The storm had turned the trees to glittering white, making kinked branches into smooth lines, rounding out corners and glossing over jagged edges. She had the sense that the worst was behind them now.

Half an hour later, Lana leaned her head back against the seat behind her, trying not to breathe too loudly or alert her sister that anything was wrong. Her stomach had been bothering her all morning while she'd been getting ready to go, and if it weren't for being pregnant, she would have taken some kind of medicine to sooth her bowels and calm her guts down. Instead she'd ended up running to the bathroom three times before they'd left the house, and she'd considered staying home. But eventually, the urge to go to the bathroom had subsided, even though the pain remained.

All day long, the cramps had become worse and worse. And now the ride home was taking much longer than normal. The highways had been fine, but now that they were skimming along the smaller back roads that would eventually lead to Lana's house, the minivan slowed to a crawl. Beyond the windows the countryside passed by, a patchwork of cleared fields and dense copses of old trees. Occasionally, chunks of ice fell from the branches overhead, shattering in hundreds of pieces against the roof and sailing wildly behind them.

"Almost there," Karin said. "You hanging in?"

Lana started to say yes, but a great wave of pain came over her, taking the breath from her lungs. Everything in her body protested against it. She curled her shoulders forward, trying to find a way to make it stop, but each way she turned the pain was there, confronting and consuming. She gripped the edge of the seat, trying not scare Karin. But her brain was racing and her heart was beating as hard as if she'd just run a marathon. She writhed in her seat, trying to slow down, to cool off, to make the wrenching pain abate.

For the last few weeks, she'd been concentrating unceasingly, willing her body not to give birth. She'd heard the nurse's warning that she shouldn't overreact, and she'd heeded it, ignoring twinges and spasms that seemed so immediately dangerous but had no more bearing than things that go bump in the night. She repeated her promise like a mantra: *I am not going to go into labor; I am not going to go into labor; I am not going to . . .*

A swell of pain squeezed her like a belt pulled too tight. This was not Braxton-Hicks. It was not stomach cramps. It was labor. And it was happening fast.

Lana took another deep, hard breath, bracing herself. She'd been trying not to make any noise, to keep Karin from worrying that something was wrong. But all that was going out the window and the urge to scream, to gasp and cry, was coming on strong now, as if making noise might somehow keep the pain at bay.

"*Karin*," she managed between breaths. She tugged on her seat belt, wanting it off. She loosened it as if she could loosen the ache within her. Suddenly, she felt her bladder let go, and she cried out, mortified. No, it wasn't her bladder. Her water had just broken. She squeezed every muscle within her, but the rush of fluid kept coming and coming, nonstop, more than she thought possible. How could there be so *much*? Karin's backseat would be ruined. She was in trouble. The baby was in trouble. She needed help. "Karin. *Please*. Stop."

"Hold on." Karin was leaning forward in the driver's seat, both hands wrapped tight around the wheel. Her concentration was intense. "The roads are . . . not really that great back here. I'm sorry. They were fine on the highway. But don't worry. I'll get us home."

"Not. Home." Lana braced herself for another contraction, pushing down hard on the floor with her heels. Nothing in the books had prepared her for how quickly the intervals between contractions shrank, and nothing could have warned her against the pain. In a matter of minutes, the cramping had taken on a life of its own, a furious monster raging within. *No*, she thought. *No, I'm not ready yet. Please, not yet.* She fought hard against the cramps, against the urges of her body, but there was no stopping them. When she spoke again, she was crying. What would make the misery go away? "Karin. Please— God, Karin—*please* pull over."

"What? Pull over?" Karin craned her face around nearly backward, so her cheek pressed the collar of her coat and her thick red scarf. "What's wrong? Are you oka—"

There was a loud, almost deafening bang on the roof of the van. And then the whole world slowed to a crawl. Between the moment of the bang and the moment a million little shards of ice went tinkling around the windows, Karin lost control. Lana watched her hands grip the wheel, she felt the tires lock beneath them, but still they were moving, sliding, slipping smoothly and inevitably off the road.

"Hold on!" Karin shouted.

Lana grabbed the armrest, holding on for her life. The noise was terrible, branches like millions of fingers screeching along the windows and doors. She felt the pressure of the seat belt tightening around her hips, then the jerk of a sudden halt. And when the minivan finally came to a stop they were resting at a dizzying angle, the hood braced roughly by the rocks and shrubs at the bottom of a ditch. The engine was still going and heat continued to blare from the vents, but the van was stuck. Between the ice and the angle, there was no way they would be able to back out to the road.

"Are you okay?" Karin yanked at her seat belt and climbed into the backseat.

"I'm not hurt," Lana said, breathing hard. The seat belt was digging into her skin. She fumbled with it to get it off, her fingers made worthless by panic and fear. She couldn't let herself come apart. She couldn't. She swore to herself they would be okay. "Are you?"

"No. Tell me what's wrong."

Lana meant to speak gently, to break the news with cool aplomb. But the words came rushing out. She worked at the waistline of her jeans. "I'm in labor."

"It just started now?"

"No. Hours ago."

"Why didn't you tell me?"

"I didn't *know*." The pressure of the wide elastic of her maternity jeans was too much, and she was cold and drenched from her crotch to her shins. She didn't care enough to tell Karin to look away: She just did her best to tug her pants down her hips, not watching for the panic and shock that she knew she'd find in Karin's eyes.

"Oh, my . . . Lana, are you sure? Because it might just be—"

Lana paused to glare, breathing hard. "Karin!" She was irrationally angry, furious. She wanted to break something. To put her fist through glass. To scream. But she forced herself to be rational. She knew she didn't have long before the pain came back again. She had to use this window to get things done. "My *water* just broke."

Karin blinked. She moved toward Lana's feet to help tug her jeans off over her heels, and Lana started to work on getting off her jacket. She was sweating hot, boiling, and she could feel the first embers of her next contraction firing up inside, like the tremors of some advancing army. There was a battle ahead. She tried to talk herself down from the panic. But she was scared out of her mind. She wasn't prepared for labor. She wasn't prepared to have her baby in a car. And she was afraid of what would happen to the child if she did. "We have to do something. We have to get back!"

"Okay. No problem. There's no problem here. I'll just call an ambulance. We have time."

Lana shook her head, clenching her teeth. "We might not have time."

"How far apart?" Karin asked.

"I don't know exactly. Five minutes?"

"What!"

For a second Lana caught herself laughing—on the brink of hysteria and fear. The look on her sister's face was so exaggerated, so replete with surprise, it was almost funny. But the contraction that had been gathering speed like a tsunami rose up from her core and crested with new ferocity, the pressure making her feel like she might split apart.

"I *lied*. Oh, God, I *lied*," she said, shifting and twisting her body against the pain, trying to find a way to make it stop. She couldn't seem to keep herself from shouting.

"*LESS* than five minutes now. Oh, God, Karin. Please. Help me!"

"I can handle this, I can handle this," Karin was saying, digging around in her purse.

Lana clenched her teeth. Time slowed. The contraction seemed to last forever, and when it withdrew, she prayed the pain would stop. Prayed hard that somehow it might just go away, wait a little while, until they could get help. Burning, stretching, cramping—she felt as if her body were turning itself inside out. Every nerve inside her fired pain. It scared her. She was supposed to be like the women in the films, quiet and focused and calm. But this hurt so bad. There had to be something wrong. "Karin. Please help."

"What's wrong?"

"I don't know," Lana said. "It hurts. Oh, *God*, it hurts."

Karin smoothed Lana's hair from her eyes. "Lana. Honey. Look at me. It's supposed to hurt. It's going to hurt like hell."

Lana gripped Karin's hand and squeezed. "I'm scared."

Karin nodded. "Me too."

Through the haze of pain and panic, Lana could see that her sister had turned so pale her color nearly rivaled that of the icy landscape around them. "What is it?" Lana asked, trying not to hyperventilate. "What are you not telling me?"

Karin's mouth pressed into a thin, grave line. "My charger. I left it at my house when I moved in with you."

"So what does that mean?"

Karin held up the dull face of the phone for Lana to see. "It means we're on our own."

Eli drove the long roads back to Burlington, the ground getting slipperier by the moment. He drove slow, concentrating. He passed an empty car on the side of the road, abandoned by its driver, and he took his foot off the gas pedal just a fraction of an inch.

Patience, he told himself. His windows were fogging up. He switched the heat in his car to high, but it did little good. It had been a long time since his old car had any serious heat. He turned up the radio, hummed a little, and tried to make himself relax. He was feeling anxious, but it was more than just the driving that had got to him. It was the hope and expectation of knowing that he would see Lana soon—for better or worse. And yet, beneath that, beneath the anxiousness, he couldn't shake the strange, impractical feeling that something was wrong.

When at last he got to Lana's, he saw Calvert sitting in an old pickup truck, the engine running and the windows fogging at the edges on the inside. Immediately, he went on high alert. Eli parked quickly beside him, then braced himself against the cold and ice to knock on Calvert's window. "What are you doing here?"

Calvert rolled down the glass. "They went to volunteer or something. Should have been back by now," he said, lifting the brim of his baseball cap so he could better see Eli's face.

"What are you talking about?"

Calvert huffed, frustrated. "They *went* to *Montpelier*. Should've been back an hour ago."

"The roads are bad," Eli said.

"I already factored that in." Calvert shook his head. "Karin said to meet her here. I called her cell phone four times, but it goes right to voice mail."

Eli ran his hand over his face, less and less confident by the moment. All morning, he'd had the niggling feeling that something just wasn't right. But he'd doubted himself—he'd thought it was just nerves. "I don't have a good feeling."

"Truth be told, neither do I. I'm wondering if they're at the hospital."

Eli nodded. The same thought had occurred to him as well. "Did you call over there?"

"No cell phone," Calvert said.

Eli shook his head. Like father, like daughter. "Why am I not surprised?"

"Look, you want to ride over with me?"

Eli paused, looking over the rusted and falling-down truck. "Where'd you get the wheels?"

"On loan from a guy at work."

Eli nodded. He didn't have time for follow-ups and didn't really care. "No offense, but I can't imagine Lana would be happy to see you if she is at the hospital having the baby."

Calvert frowned. "Lana and me are square."

Eli crossed his arms, ducking his head down into the collar of his coat to keep the ice off his glasses. There was something in Calvert's eyes that made Eli know he wasn't lying. He didn't like the man, but that didn't matter at the moment. He had to find Lana. And Calvert was his only ally.

"I'll take my car," Eli said.

"No offense. But the truck's better in the snow than your Bug."

Eli glanced toward his small green car, little more than an ice-coated lump of emerald on the street. "Fine," he said. "Let's just hurry."

"Get in," Calvert said.

Along the desolate roadside, Karin pulled the frozen air deep into her lungs, wincing against the chill, and then she watched her breath going up in white streaks toward the heavy sky. She scanned the long road in both directions. Not a car in sight. They were in the middle of wide and sweeping farmland, and though Karin had driven the road often enough to know that there were houses nearby, the closest one was a half mile away. There was no time for walking that far through the ice.

She put her hands on her hips and quickly surveyed the area, racking her brain to see if she could think of one last thing that might help alert a passing driver that their minivan—not visible in the craggy and shrub-tangled trough—had gone off the road. She'd attached an orange emergency flag to a tree branch and stood it up between two rocks. She'd taken everything in the minivan that she didn't anticipate needing and she'd strewn it along the roadside, hoping it would pique someone's curiosity. Because of the mess she'd made, she was sure some attentive and alert person would investigate. But until then, they had to sit tight.

Slowly and carefully, she climbed her way through the gleaming and frozen underbrush into the craggy ditch. She heaved her weight against the sliding door to open it, then thrust her body as quickly as she could inside the van. The door slammed shut with the finality of a falling blade.

When she looked at her sister, fear gripped her gut. Lana looked terrible. Her eyes were wild, panicky. Her mouth was pursed into an open "O" as she pushed air—machinelike—in and out of her lungs. The floor of Karin's minivan was ruined, blood and fluid soaking the carpet. Lana was shifting and arching her back and moving her legs around, and Karin had to hold back tears to see it. She had to be strong. For both of them. She said a prayer, pleading that Lana and the baby would come through, that someone would find them, that somehow it would all be okay.

"How are you?" Karin asked.

Lana looked at her, her breathing fast, her forehead shiny with sweat. She'd braced her legs against the passenger seat and the driver's, the van so slanted that the angle of her body was more reclining than lying down. Tears were streaming down her face. "Karin . . ."

Karin didn't press her to talk. Though Lana was in hideous pain, the labor seemed to be progressing as it should—except that it all was happening so fast. Karin wrapped her arms around her sister, Lana squeezing her so tight it hurt. She whimpered like some small, dying animal, and Karin brushed her hair back away from her face.

"Was there anyone up there?" Lana managed, her voice full of vulnerability and hope. Karin got the feeling that the words were incredibly hard to muster—not just the sounds, but the focus to say them.

"No one yet. But someone will find us. I'm sure of it. Someone will see."

Lana pushed the flat of her palm hard against Karin's shoulder, pushing her away. "Oh, God . . . *Not again.* Not—I can't do this anym—"

Her sentence dropped off halfway through, and Karin could see from her face the force of the contraction that gripped her. Lana had wrapped one of the seat belts around her palm, holding on as if her life depended on it. Karin trembled. How could she deliver a baby? What if there was a complication? If Lana started bleeding? If the baby wouldn't breathe?

With her free hand, Lana reached for her sister and gripped her fingers so hard it burned. She cried out through the pain. What if the baby was born backward? What if the cord got in the way?

Stop it, Karin, she told herself. *Stop.* She couldn't allow herself to think the worst. She had to stay positive.

Gently, she pulled free of Lana's hand. She moved carefully between Lana's legs, and to her shock and horror, the baby was crowning—just the faintest patch of skin and a slight sheen of blonde, baby-fine hair. She swallowed hard, hoping not to let her fear show.

She would have to deliver the baby. Now. There was no choice. It was coming, ready or not. There was no telling what was going on in Lana's body—if something had gone wrong. But at least the baby was facing the right way, so Karin said a prayer of thanks for that.

She watched until the tension in Lana's body momentarily waned, Lana's muscles going loose as an overstretched rubber band. Her breathing was loud and deep. "You're almost done, Lanie. Sweetheart, give me your hand."

Lana reached for her sister's fingers, no doubt meaning to hold on for dear life. But instead, Karin guided Lana's fingers to touch the baby's head.

"Oh, God!" Lana's gaze slammed against Karin's. "What will we do?"

Karin kept her voice calm. "It's okay. I promise. It's all going to be fine."

She gave Lana's foot a squeeze through her sock, then moved quickly to the glove compartment, where she kept her extra antibacterial gel. She took off her cotton gloves and smeared it all along her forearms. She pulled on the sterile latex gloves in the emergency kit that Lana had bought for her last Christmas. She thought now that the gift must have been providence. It dazzled her, sometimes, how the world worked. While she'd been planning for her own baby, she'd probably seen more video footage of births than a first-year med school student. She was no expert. But as long as nothing went wrong, by God's grace she would know what to do.

"Another one!" Lana shouted, holding tight with both hands to the strap of the seat belt over her head. Her forehead was beaded with sweat. "I have to push. *Please*. I'm *pushing*!"

"You're doing great." Karin moved back into place, scared and yet mesmerized at the same time. She could see how efficiently Lana's body worked, the way her muscles moved the baby along the birth canal with perfect certainty, the way the fullness of her belly shifted slightly as each contraction bore down. Lana was red-faced and sweaty, her face more panicked by the moment. A blood vessel in her eye had burst and turned the white pupil a bright, fiery red. Karin could tell the moment the contraction waned, her own body relaxing with her sister's.

Lana pushed her hair out of her face. "Are you . . . okay?" she asked between breaths.

"Me? Yes. Why?"

Her arm shot over her head, searching for the seat belt that had somehow become her lifeline. "Because I'm ready to have this baby now."

At the hospital, the receptionist—who wore reading glasses studded with a million tiny beads—had stopped being friendly toward them. "I told you, Mr. Biel. Your daughter isn't here. Asking me the same question in three different ways is not going to change my answer."

Calvert frowned and Eli stepped away from the high counter, pulling off his hat and angrily scratching his head. The emergency room was a mess, the snow bringing all sorts of people to the hospital for all sorts of reasons. Frustrated, Eli slunk away from the receptionist's desk, toward the waiting area. "I don't like this."

"Me neither," Calvert said.

Eli sat down hard on one of the chairs in the waiting area, planning his next move. He couldn't just sit here and wait. He had to take action. Somehow, he had to find Lana. And then he had to tell her that he loved her, that he'd been an idiot, that he wanted her back, if she'd have him. "Here's what we're going to do," he said. "I'm going to take your friend's truck and start looking for Karin's minivan. You're going to stay here in case they show."

"You want to take the truck?"

Eli nodded. "I know the roads better. Where did you say they were coming from?"

"Montpelier."

"And where were they going after?"

"Lana's."

Eli pushed his glasses higher up on his face, thinking of which road Karin would have taken to get from Montpelier to her house. He decided his best shot was to backtrack, to start at her house and then head in the direction of their seminar. Unless they decided to change their course, he knew the roads they would most likely take. He held his hand out to take Calvert's keys. "Good. That gives me at least some idea of where to look. I can guess which roads they'd take." He went to the nurse's station to borrow a pen and paper, and when he returned he'd written his cell phone number down. "Call me the second you hear anything."

"You're a good man. And you'll be a good father to that baby. I can tell."

Eli nodded once, then walked through the automatic doors of the hospital and flipped his collar up to block the wind.

"I think . . . oh, God . . . this is it." Lana drew her knees wider and pulled them in a V toward her chest. Her eyes were bright with terror.

"It's okay, it's okay," Karin said quickly. "Lana. You *have* to calm down. Take a deep breath with me. Take a deep breath." Karin took a deep, full breath, Lana's eyes locked on hers.

Then, Karin stopped breathing. Time pressed to a halt. The heaters blared, the falling ice scratched at the hood of the van, and instantly, all the worry, all the fear that she would botch things up, left her mind. Karin felt her own knowledge of what to do as if it had been sitting there and waiting centuries for her. Technology had changed, but this, this process—so elemental and innate—never had. "Only push if there's a contraction."

"There is!" Lana pressed hard and strong. A blue vein swelled in her forehead; her lips were drawn back wide and tight. When the baby's head emerged, Karin's instincts took over. She supported the head, cleaned out its mouth and nose as best she could with her fingers, then checked to make sure the cord wasn't wrapped around the baby's neck.

Lana was saying *Kare, Kare, Kare*, her voice wild with panic. Karin kept her voice calm and soothing when she spoke. "It's okay, Lanie. Listen to me. The baby's head is out. You're doing a great job. Just stay calm. Everything is going to be just fine."

"I'm too tired," Lana muttered. "I can't do any more."

"Yes, you can," Karin said. "Just one more push. That's all we need."

"Oh, G-o-o-o-o-o-d!"

Lana didn't have to tell her another contraction had come on. Lana's face went red as mercury, her features contorted in anguish, and Karin shifted her focus back to the baby. A moment later, she guided the first shoulder out, then the second, and with a gush of blood and fluid, a child was in her hands.

A baby. A perfect, vigorous child, its little blue arms flailing and its head moving back and forth in surprise. She quickly picked up her coat and held its slippery body carefully with the cloth. She kept it level with Lana's abdomen, with its feet slightly above its head as she'd read a thousand times. She did her best to clean out the rest of its nose and mouth and she'd just started to panic that she'd done something wrong when suddenly, the baby made the smallest, sweetest sound she'd ever heard, a cry so fragile it was almost a mewing. Ice broke off a treetop and hit the roof of the car. She stared in wonder, transfixed.

"A girl," she said softly. "It's a girl."

She looked up at Lana, whose face had gone slack with the sudden shock of no longer having to push. "Is she okay?"

"I think so . . ." Karin had to make a decision about whether or not to cut the cord. It was better to let the doctors do it, she knew. But how long would that be? She waited a moment for the cord to stop pulsing, then she wrapped a strip of gauze around it and tied it off with one of her shoelaces as tightly as she could. With a deep breath, she cut the cord with sterile scissors from her emergency kit and then searched her brain frantically for what to do next. She knew she had to keep the baby warm and that Lana needed to nurse her right away. The silvery shine of the heat blanket in her emergency kit caught her eye, and she wrapped the baby in it for warmth. Not the most comfortable texture against a newborn's skin, but it would do the job.

Suddenly, as she was readjusting her weight so she could rise and give the baby to her sister, she realized the emergency was most likely over. They'd all survived. The branches tapped against the windows, the sleet melted gently in the heat from the defrosters, and the baby, so small and sweet, was pinkening and squirming mightily in her hands.

"A girl?" Lana said, her voice striking Karin as oddly fragile, given the enormous strength she'd been capable of just moments ago.

"Yes. Your daughter," Karin said.

With all the joy in her heart, she placed the baby in her sister's arms.

Lana lay quietly in the backseat of the minivan, listening to the tinkling of the ice—a sound that only intensified the otherworldly silence. Karin had gone outside to stand on the roadside and flag down anyone who might help. And now Lana was alone with her baby, her daughter, for the first time.

She was vaguely aware of her own soreness, the trauma her body had been through, but the pain that had threatened to rip her in two just minutes ago was now no more relevant than a song playing gently in her mind. She shivered slightly even though the van was warm, and she guessed her trembling was more from the labor than from the cold. Her baby was now pressed to her skin for warmth and swaddled in a heat blanket and in Karin's thick coat. In the back of her mind, Lana worried that she was okay. She knew that at thirty-five weeks there was a very real chance that the baby's lungs weren't strong enough and that its sucking reflex had yet to kick in. And yet the baby had nursed weakly for a few minutes, then closed her swollen eyes and lapsed into a deep, intense sleep, her breathing light but even. Lana would feel much better once the doctors could examine them both. But for the moment, the pain was tolerable and her daughter seemed absolutely . . . flawless. No cloud forests or wild orchids could ever compare with this.

She was so glad Karin had been here with her. But she only wished Eli were here too. Eli, Ron, and Calvert. This miracle belonged to them—to all of them—as well. She brushed her lips against the baby's forehead and whispered, "You're going to have more family than you know what to do with."

The door to the minivan slid open and though the baby didn't open her eyes, her face wrinkled at the sound.

"I found help," Karin said.

And when Lana looked up, Eli was there, his hand braced against the doorframe and his coat falling open as he climbed inside.

"Are you . . ." His words trailed off as he saw the bundle in her lap. She knew what he was seeing—all the blood, the relative gore of childbirth in Karin's car. She'd delivered the placenta not long ago, and Karin had thrown an old rag over it and moved it out of Lana's way. Still, Eli must have thought someone had died.

"We're fine," she assured him. Her eyes began to tear. She hadn't realized how badly she'd needed him to be here. She couldn't take her eyes off him. Seeing him made her know everything was going to be okay.

"Eli." Karin's voice broke her concentration. "Can I take your cell phone?"

Lana came back to reality. "Is the ambulance . . . ?"

"It's coming," Eli said.

Karin reached out and took Eli's cell. "I just . . . I talked to Gene to say Merry Christmas this morning, but I just need to tell him about the baby. If you need me, I'll be up by the road. I want to make sure the ambulance doesn't drive past us." She looked at Lana for a long moment, a warm smile brightening her face. "Lana, you were amazing."

"I'm glad you were here," Lana said.

A moment later, Karin was outside, the door sliding closed behind her. And Lana and Eli were alone. His brown knit hat was pulled down to his eyebrows and his glasses were flecked with melted ice. The way he was looking at her, Lana thought he'd never seen her before. She knew he was holding his breath.

"Please, come here," she whispered.

He leaned closer, unable to look away from the baby. "Oh . . . Lana."

She felt tears come to her eyes, to have Eli and her baby both beside her. It seemed so very right, the journey coming to an end. "It's a girl," she said.

"It's a miracle," he said.

"Maybe that's her name," Lana said. "Winter Miracle Biel."

Then Eli was laughing—crying too—and he leaned forward and pressed a strong, relieved kiss to her lips. She closed her eyes for a moment to savor it. When she opened them, he was running the back of his index finger over the baby's cheek, and her nose wrinkled a little at his touch. "I was so worried," he said, his voice full of yearning and relief. "I wanted to do something to help. But I didn't know if I could find you. I didn't know how to help."

"It's okay," Lana said, sensing the panic in his voice.

He picked up her hand and rubbed her ring finger with his thumb. "You didn't get . . . engaged."

"No," she said. "How could I marry him when I want you?"

He shook his head. "I've been such an idiot."

"*Shhh*. We'll talk about this later." She touched his cheek, quieting him. "Do you still love me?"

He nodded, his gaze not leaving hers.

"Then we can get through anything," she said.

Epilogue

Five Years Later . . .

—————————— *April* ——————————

The fields behind the Wildflower Barn were not yet in full bloom, but thin traces of color were showing on every branch and shrub, giving the landscape an air of softness though nothing in particular presented a flower of its own. The afternoon was chilly, and Lana stood outside to keep an eye on Winter, who was walking back and forth along the edge of the meadow—one hand swinging and the other holding the phone to her ear as she talked to Ron. Like her mother, there was no keeping her inside.

Lana held a photo of bright pink bougainvillea, the color of its petals blaring louder than pealing bells. She sighed wistfully, remembering. She didn't hear her husband arrive at her side.

"That again?" Eli asked gently.

She laughed, a little embarrassed to have been caught. She put the photograph down on the little picnic table at her side, among a handful of other pictures from her travels that she was considering framing. "I can't stop thinking about it. The hiking, the kayaking, the rope walk . . . I had such a wonderful time."

"We'll have to take Winter on our next trip."

"I think if it was legal for her to buy a plane ticket, she'd beat us there."

He put an arm around her shoulders. They watched Winter walking back and forth among the sprigs pushing up out of the ground, her long blonde hair trailing all the way down her back. Eli pressed a kiss to Lana's temple, and she caught the smell of his skin. She leaned into him, sighing and content.

Three years ago, Eli had proposed the idea of legally adopting Winter as his daughter, and Ron had agreed. Ron loved Winter, in his way. But Eli was her father, the man she called *Dad*. They shared a close bond, so close that Lana had a hard time deciding which of them looked up to the other more. Eli answered Winter's endless questions with a patience that was equally endless. He talked to her like she was part scientist and part princess. Lana warned him not to spoil her, but in truth, it warmed her heart.

She turned when she heard voices coming from the barn behind her, Gene and Karin walking toward them side by side. They were both dressed for work, in jeans, sneakers, and light coats. Michael, the newest hire, walked slowly behind them. He wore the regulation Wildflower Barn polo shirt and jeans, but he still had the air of a young man who wasn't quite comfortable in his own clothes. His sandy blond hair had been cut brutally short at his last foster home, and there was a tattoo of a fish on his neck. He'd been talking recently about having it removed.

"We're heading over to Calvert's," Karin called as she got closer.

Lana laughed and looked at Michael. "How'd *you* get roped into this?"

"Roped?" Gene clasped the boy's shoulder. "He volunteered. It's not every day a teenage guy gets to clean out an old man's basement with his family."

"Okay," Lana said. "We'll be over later with sandwiches. Call if you think of anything you need in the meantime."

Gene wrapped an arm around Karin, and Karin smiled. "See you soon."

Lana watched in silence as they walked away, then turned back around to make sure Winter hadn't wandered. She rested her head on Eli's shoulder as Winter talked animatedly at the edge of the lawn. "That Michael's a good kid," Lana said.

"He makes Karin happy."

"And Karin makes him happy too. I think she and Gene finally found their purpose, opening up their house as a foster home to older children. It does everyone good."

Lana glanced down. And at her feet, a single irascible dandelion was pushing up through the grass, the first of the army of dandelions that would soon descend on the fields around the Barn. Already, one single flower had gone to seed—much earlier than the others—and without thinking, Lana plucked it and stood to blow the seeds into the yard.

"What are you doing?" Winter's voice startled her. The look in her eyes was totally transparent; she'd seen the tempting white blow ball in Lana's hand and she wanted it for her own. "Can I have it?" she asked, bouncing on her tiptoes with excitement.

Lana held up the little white puff, considering. So many generations had flirted with the idea that flowers could tell the future or divine the truth. Dandelions could predict how many children you would have. Buttercups held under a chin could predict if a person liked butter. If you could catch a bit of milkweed floss in the air, your wish would come true.

But it was all so silly—to think that flowers could possibly predict an unpredictable future. Lana twirled the white puffball in her hand. Five years ago, she never would have imagined this moment as a future she could be happy with. And yet she *was* happy. If wildflowers like this one predicted anything, it was only that happiness was entirely graspable, but at the same time out of her hands.

Lana looked down at her daughter. She gave her sternest frown. "Are you going to blow all these seeds over my newly tilled field?"

"Yes," Winter said.

Eli laughed. "The woman knows her mind."

"That she does." Lana shared a secret smile with her husband and handed the little round ball to her daughter. "By all means, Winter. Enjoy."

Notes and Acknowledgments

Big huge thanks: To my editor Michele Bidelspach. To my agent, Kim Lionetti of Bookends. To those who contributed by sharing your particular expertise and generosity: Erin Berberian, Diana and Chris Borie of the Vermont Wildflower Farm, Lisa Karakaya, Kriste Matrisch, Mike Meeker, Dr. Cynthia D. Morgan, Tiana Santasiere, Tia, and Laura Venner. Thanks also to Garth Baxter, David, Erica, Lee Hyat of Author Sound Relations, Keri Rand, Mom, Deborah Wiseman, Writer's Relief, and all of you who have so generously helped me with this oddball dream of being a writer—especially those readers who so kindly tell friends and family about my books. And finally, thanks to Matt Shauger: love, there just aren't enough words.

Jack Sanders's book *The Secrets of Wildflowers* is an absolute treasure that I relied on and enjoyed immeasurably. As for descriptions of Vermont, I've taken a fair amount of artistic license, but I think the most obvious and egregious example is that the Dragonboat Festival is actually in August, not July. Sorry! There's no reasoning with muses sometimes.

Dear Reader,

When I was younger, my family and I used to go to my grandparents' cabin in the hills of Pennsylvania, where we'd go on long hikes, climb trees, build forts, sing around campfires (yes, we really did that!), make homemade ice cream, and then drop into our beds—already asleep before our heads hit the pillows.

It's probably no surprise that the setting for my first book, SIMPLE WISHES, takes place in just such a cabin. After making a terrible mistake in New York City, my heroine, Adele, must return to the cottage she inherited from her estranged mother. But it's not exactly a pleasure trove to her, at first. Memories of a difficult childhood haunt her at every turn.

It's only through the love and friendship of her new neighbors that she has a chance at making a good life for herself. Her neighbor Beatrice, an elderly grandmother, challenges her to think differently about her mother and her past. And Jay, the sexy carpenter who lives next door, teaches her to stop fighting so hard. Love is there for all of us, when we're open to it.

It's a deep, emotional read that—I'm extremely pleased to say—got a favorable reception from critics and readers alike (you can only imagine how relieved I was, since it was my first book!).

I hope you'll join Adele on her journey into the deepest secrets of the heart in SIMPLE WISHES. For more information, visit me on my Web site: www.lisadalebooks.com.

Happy reading!

Lisa Dale

THE DISH

Where authors give you the inside scoop!

From the desk of Lisa Dale

Dear Reader,

Do you believe in love at first sight? I do. The moment I set foot in Burlington, Vermont, two summers ago, I knew I was wildly, head-over-heels, never-to-recover in love with Vermont.

It was a no-brainer to set IT HAPPENED ONE NIGHT (on sale now) on the beautiful shores of Lake Champlain. Lana Biel longs to leave her family's Vermont wildflower farm so she can travel and see the world. And her sister Karin wants nothing more than to put down roots and conceive the child she and her husband just can't seem to have. When a lighthearted fling with a mountain biker leaves Lana expecting, she finds herself tumbling headlong into motherhood while her sister Karin can only look on.

For help, Lana turns to Eli Ward, a professional meteorite hunter and her best friend for the last ten years. But Eli's keeping secrets that could turn their friendship on its head. As the Vermont seasons change and the flowers in the wildflower meadows begin to fade, Lana must make some meaningful decisions about her family, her friendships, her love life, and her dreams.

Many of my girlfriends are new moms—and what a lifestyle change motherhood brings! At some point I think all women must wrestle with the question, *Can* we have it all? The kids, the job, the freedom, *and* the man of our dreams? Lana lives for her future and pins all her hopes on traveling the world. But what happens when fate has other plans?

I hope you'll read about Lana, Karin, and Eli's journey as they discover the courage within. Please check out my website at www.LisaDaleBooks.com. I love to hear from readers and hope you'll be in touch.

Happy reading!

Lisa Dale

♥ ♥ ♥ ♥ ♥ ♥ ♥ ♥ ♥ ♥ ♥ ♥ ♥ ♥ ♥ ♥

From the desk of Caridad Piñeiro

Dear Reader,

I have a confession to make—I'm a science geek.

I've always been fascinated with how things work, and so it was no surprise that I decided to major in science when I went to Villanova. It was probably more of a surprise that I did a switch after college to pursue a career in law and then decided to return to my first love—writing.

What wasn't a surprise with my writing is that over the years my love of science and how things work has always managed to make it into my various novels. Whether they were paranormals, romance, or suspense, the science geek in me always found a way to research and try something new in each novel.

Of course, this is more true for SINS OF THE FLESH (on sale now) than for any of my other novels. With SINS OF THE FLESH (and the rest of the upcoming books in the SINS series), I let the science nerd out of the closet and delved into some of my favorite subjects in college—genetics, immunology, and biology. I also got to use some of the interesting developments that have been going on over the years since I graduated.

Interesting things like the GFPs (green fluorescent proteins) that make Caterina glow—the ones whose creators were acknowledged with the 2008 Nobel Prize in chemistry. Did you know that scientists have developed cats that glow in the dark? GFPs let them trace and mark where genes are going!

There are lots of other factual instances in SINS OF THE FLESH based on new developments in gene therapy as well as my own musings on where splicing human and nonhuman genes may take us in the future.

Tossed in with all that science are some of the things that I love most when I write—a determined heroine who is not afraid to fight her own battles and a hero who is strong enough to embrace the love of family and a special woman.

Mix all those parts together and I hope you will find yourself hooked on the world I've created for the SINS series!

Wishing you all the best and much edge-of-seat reading,

*Want to know more about romances at
Grand Central Publishing and Forever?
Get the scoop online!*

GRAND CENTRAL PUBLISHING'S ROMANCE HOME PAGE

Visit us at www.hachettebookgroup.com/romance
for all the latest news, reviews, and chapter excerpts!

NEW AND UPCOMING TITLES

Each month we feature our new titles
and reader favorites.

CONTESTS AND GIVEAWAYS

We give away galleys, autographed copies,
and all kinds of fun stuff.

AUTHOR INFO

You'll find bios, articles, and links to personal
Web sites for all your favorite authors—and
so much more!

THE BUZZ

Sign up for our monthly romance newsletter,
and be the first to read all about it!